# PARK AVENUE

## ALSO BY
## RENÉE AHDIEH

*The Beautiful*
*The Damned*
*The Righteous*
*The Ruined*

*Flame in the Mist*
*Smoke in the Sun*

*The Wrath & the Dawn*
*The Rose & the Dagger*

# PARK AVENUE

*A Novel*

Renée Ahdieh

FLATIRON BOOKS
NEW YORK

This is a work of fiction. All the names, characters, organizations, places, and events portrayed in this work are either products of the author's imagination or used fictitiously.


For information, address Flatiron Books, 120 Broadway, New York, NY 10271. EU Representative: Macmillan Publishers Ireland Ltd., 1st Floor, The Liffey Trust Centre, 117–126 Sheriff Street Upper, Dublin 1, D01 YC43.

www.flatironbooks.com

Designed by Devan Norman

The Library of Congress has cataloged the hardcover edition as follows:

Names: Ahdieh, Renée, author.
Title: Park avenue : a novel / Renée Ahdieh.
Description: New York : Flatiron Books, 2025.
Identifiers: LCCN 2024034370 | ISBN 9781250897954 (hardcover) | ISBN 9781250897961 (ebook)
Subjects: LCGFT: Legal fiction (Literature). | Novels.
Classification: LCC PS3601.H35 P37 2025 | DDC 813/.6—dc23/eng/20240726
LC record available at https://lccn.loc.gov/2024034370

ISBN 978-1-250-89797-8 (trade paperback)



First Flatiron Books Paperback Edition: 2026

10 9 8 7 6 5 4 3 2 1

*For anyone who left home hoping for a better life in a new land*

*For the children of immigrants,*
*who spend their lives straddling two worlds*

*For Victor, Cyrus, and Noura, always*

# PARK AVENUE

*If you're going to tell a lie, make it a good one.*

My mother used to say this all the time. She claimed we were given a handful of good lies in life, and we should take care not to waste them. Once we wasted our lies, no one would believe us, even when we needed them to.

Even when our lies were the truth.

# THE MOST BEAUTIFUL BAG IN THE WORLD

In order to understand Jia Song, it is necessary to begin at the beginning.

Not in a tedious, *David Copperfield* kind of way. After all, Jia remembered nothing of when she was born. Who did, save for the sort of Dickensian male worthy of his namesake?

The beginning for Jia Song could have been any number of formative moments in the life of a child from an immigrant family. It could have been the time in fifth grade when she was chased at recess by three boys tugging the corners of their eyes and yelling "Ching chong ching," their cackles ringing through the schoolyard like racist hyenas . . . right until Jia spun on her heel and hawked Korean hot sauce in their eyes with the precision of a spitting cobra. They cried like babies, and Jia was suspended from school for her role in the Gochujang Caper, as she liked to call it. She was in a Nancy Drew phase.

Her mother had been embarrassed, her father amused. *Chal hae-suh,* he'd said under his breath as he'd squeezed her shoulder. *Good job.* Then he'd offered her a single, emphatic nod. Like she'd handled her shit and he didn't have to worry about her anymore. Her mother had whirled on him, Korean words flying from her lips. A litany on the importance of decorum and good character and setting a proper example and on and on and on.

Not that Jia's punishment mattered. There would never be a minute of any day when it was not worth it just to recall the memory of their swollen faces, snot dribbling down their chins as one of them wailed for his mommy.

But no, that occasion wasn't the beginning.

Nor was it the night Jia's grandfather died of a heart attack when she was thirteen. She had been the first to know he'd left this world for the next. Why? Because Harabugi's ghost had come to tell her—in a calm, rational manner—that it was up to her now to make sense of this mess.

In retrospect, Jia supposed that night was as good as any to call a beginning.

Still, that was not quite it.

The beginning for Jia Song was a January in the early aughts, the day Alexandra Niarchos came into the Song family's Lower East Side bodega carrying an Hermès Birkin bag.

At the time, Lexi Niarchos ruled over Manhattan's social scene, her bladed cheeks and glossy lips framed by that season's most coveted style of bedhead. The young socialite's white teeth and huge Oliver Peoples sunglasses gleamed from the pages of the gossip columns and fashion magazines fifteen-year-old Jia devoured.

But Jia was unprepared for the impression this chance meeting with Lexi Niarchos would leave on her. That lone interaction of no more than three minutes would alter the course of her life.

It was freezing that January morning. Cold in a city kind of way. Bracing and metallic, the chill rumbling around iron bars and whistling through steel grates. It was still dark outside, smoke and radiator exhaust unfurling against the sky. Jia had decided to go with her mother to work so that she could study for her biology exam later that day. When the brass bell chimed above the door to their bodega, Jia barely glanced up from where she sat beside the cash register, her textbook resting on her lap. From the tiny stockroom, the faint strains of her mother's endless argument with Medicare over Halmunni's insulin harmonized with the Korean drama playing on their ancient tube television behind Jia to form a twisted symphony. A fucked-up soundtrack for their exceptionally ordinary life.

A strange scent wound through Jia's nostrils. The scent of oiled leather. Something expensive and *extra*ordinary, like polished hunting boots at Balmoral Castle. It mingled with the faint perfume of rose petals and melting sugar. Jia looked up just as Lexi Niarchos plunked down a large tan bag on the cracked Formica countertop. Lexi's French-tipped fingernails gleamed as she twisted open her glass bottle of green tea with a loud *pop*.

Jia couldn't speak. Couldn't muster a blink.

It wasn't the canary yellow diamond on Lexi Niarchos's ring finger, which meant her latest Greek shipping heir beau had *finally* bitten the bullet after an interminable eleven months. Nor was it Lexi's theatrical fur coat, dangling from one shoulder as she stood before Jia with a blasé expression, as if this were not the most ridiculous thing to happen to Jia in her entire life.

In fact, it wasn't even that Lexi Niarchos had deigned to grace the Song family's bodega on her way to Teterboro or wherever the fuck she was going at 6:30 a.m. on a Tuesday in full makeup and a floor-length chinchilla coat. It wasn't this celebrity that managed to suck the air out of the tiny space and narrow everything around Jia to a single, solitary focus, like a missile homing beacon.

Signal locked. Loaded. Ready to fire.

It was the Most Beautiful Bag in the World.

Jia had never seen anything like it. Smooth caramel. Immaculate white stitching with gold embellishments. Encased in a halo of gilded light. Embossed by the Midas touch itself.

*Hermès.*

One side of Lexi's glossy lips kicked up. She dropped a stack of bridal magazines in front of Jia and raised her eyebrows. "Don't forget the tea, hon," she said, wagging the bottle between her fingers before taking an unhurried sip.

In slow-moving horror, Jia watched the condensation from the bottle drip toward the Most Beautiful Bag in the World. It landed on the tan leather, darkening the caramel as if it were blood seeping from an open wound.

Jia screamed.

Lexi startled, then laughed, the sound filled with air and ease. "Holy shit, you scared me." Her canary diamond flashed around the bodega, prisms bouncing off the plastic-wrapped cigarettes and carefully arranged packs of gum. "Don't worry, it's Barenia leather. It's okay if it gets wet. In fact, they say Birkins only get better with age. Then they really begin to tell their own story." Another round of airy laughter flitted through the bodega, like its own inside joke. "Isn't that great?"

It sounded like total bullshit. Under normal circumstances, Jia would have gathered every detail of this encounter to share with her best friends, Nidhi and Elisa, to be analyzed and dissected like a tarot reading, so that they might laugh and mock Lexi Niarchos into the wee hours of the morning over their customary bowl of ramyun and dumplings.

But that damn bag. It possessed some kind of dark magic, like Snow White's apple or Sleeping Beauty's spindle. And just like those foolish princesses, Jia felt herself lured into a glittering spiderweb.

As Jia rang up Lexi's purchases, she could not take her eyes off the Birkin. The smell of Barenia leather intoxicated her, beckoning her closer with the promise of a story yet to be told. Any story.

Her story, perhaps.

Long after Lexi Niarchos glided out of the bodega into the early dawn light, Jia sat immobile on her stool.

For years, she'd admired people with nice things. Envied them. Mocked them, even. Once or twice, she'd considered saving up money to buy herself or her mother something expensive. Last year, she'd found a tester bottle of Chanel Chance at an outlet mall in New Jersey and had bought it for her mother, who'd promptly declared the scent too overpowering. So Jia took it and saved it for special occasions. Whenever she wore it, she felt herself standing a little taller, as if that single spray of perfume were a kind of armor or an invisible shield.

She laughed to herself. Then she stared at the words of her biology textbook until they swam.

Why not her? Why should only the Lexi Niarchoses of the world know what it felt like to glide through life with beautiful things and invisible shields?

With bags that told their own stories.

Jia remembered her father the day of the Gochujang Caper. His single, emphatic nod. Like she had handled her shit. Her harabugi's glistening eyes as his ghost had prophesied that it was up to her now to make sense of this mess.

The story of that Hermès bag—and all it meant—promised a future where Jia Song took care of everything and no one would need to worry about her. A future beyond the walls of this bodega.

A future kissed by the Midas touch.

# CAVEAT EMPTOR

Now for a brief interlude.

This author—who, alas, is not as charming as Jia Song and wishes to remain anonymous because of unresolved legal proceedings—asks for your indulgence while we step forward some twenty-odd years. Take a deep breath. In through the nose, out through the mouth. Settle in for the journey.

At your leisure, please select your favorite piece of classical music. Let its melody fill your mind and ease your body into a deeper sense of relaxation. Perhaps the song you've chosen is the lovely "Berceuse and Finale" from Stravinsky's *L'oiseau de feu*. Or Debussy's "Clair de lune," the piano chords soft and luminous, like snow falling against a night sky. For those inclined to the melancholic, the adagietto from Mahler's Symphony No. 5 might be more in keeping with your sensibilities.

And if your medicine of choice is chaos? This author is not one to offer judgment.

Rage against that machine.

—

There is an art to buying a Birkin.

In all seriousness. Take a bite of the apple. Touch the spindle.

It's a whole new world.

Purchasing a brand-new Birkin is not as simple as clicking a "Buy" button or walking into any Hermès boutique and flourishing a black Amex like a magic wand.

Those in the know understand that it can take years of networking and thousands of dollars before any Birkin—much less a specific type of leather and color combination—is offered to even the most well-heeled buyer.

Ludicrous, non? After all, the customer is always right, and money talks. Alas, not in a world where purses appreciate at a greater rate than gold. Yes, it's true. With an average annual return of more than 14 percent over the last thirty years, a well-kept Birkin is a better investment than actual gold. Indeed, a serious argument can even be made that Birkins perform better than the stock market. Impossible, you say?

Should we step into the ring and trade factual blows, mon ami?

Another day, perhaps. Another dollar.

First and foremost, a potential purchaser must choose a physical store. This might seem preposterous, but nothing about buying an upward-of-five-figures handbag should come as a surprise. The store's location is of immense importance. Certain boutiques receive prime selections befitting their clientele and allure. Dubai, for instance. Until humans wise up or Mother Nature decides to chew us up and spit us out, oil money will forever be en vogue. Seoul, Tokyo, Beijing, and Singapore, of course. Asian wealth epitomizes the ideal mix of old and new. Elegant with a dash of outrageous. Paris, sans question, for Paris is never a question. Madison Avenue, naturally. These are places where money not only talks but sings with unmistakable gusto.

Alas, popular locations such as these can be double-edged swords. The best sales associates—SAs, as they are known in common parlance—have handfuls of top-tier, cutthroat clients. Husbands and wives and assistants to wealthy power brokers and celebrities, itching for their next Himalaya Niloticus crocodile fix.

It's simple economics. By keeping the tightest of reins on their supply, Hermès controls global demand like a gifted dominatrix. A small allotment of so-called quota bags is offered to stores and then filtered to the salivating masses. Many Birkin collectors swear that boutiques in less-frequented locales are the perfect place to score a coveted quota bag, such as a Birkin or a Kelly. Others claim the best way to gain access is through a well-established relationship with an SA.

And the secondary market? That would necessitate a chapter all its own.

Suffice it to say: caveat emptor on all counts.

Buyer, beware.

# FIREBREATHER

"Are you sure it's a Birkin 30 in Barenia Faubourg? You know I'm not interested in another—" Before she could finish her sentence, Jia Song's wet snow boots slid across the slick granite floor of the skyscraper housing Whitman Volker, one of Manhattan's most prestigious law firms. The metal art installation flashed into view above her, a thousand scalelike discs soughing on silk strings like whispered threats. *Hic sunt dracones.*

*Here be dragons.*

"Fuck." Jia braced herself for the humiliation of a fall. First thing at work. On a Friday.

Just in time, the tip of her umbrella struck the floor, catching her on a precipice. The second she managed to steady herself and regain her composure, her phone slipped from her grasp, clattering to the granite in staccato bursts of sound. Jia squeezed her eyes shut, her thoughts pounding in her skull. The champagne. Richard. Everything about last night.

Regret was a stale cracker on her tongue. Salty. Dry. Unsatisfying.

"Jia?" the muffled voice of her SA, Anka, cried out in the distance. "Are you all right?"

Cold wind gusted at Jia's back, the revolving doors behind her hissing.

"Jia Song." This time the voice was louder. Just over her shoulder.

She spun around, recognition flushing her skin. "Mr. Volker?"

Benjamin Volker. The biggest, baddest fire-breather of them all.

What was her firm's managing partner doing at work so early on a Friday?

Benjamin Volker's weathered features crinkled at the edges. Ten years ago, he would have been a silver fox. Now he'd aged into that perfect blend of powerful and wise. Gandalf in a three-piece suit. Zegna. Always

Zegna. "Here before seven," he said. "Good to see that making partner hasn't gotten to your head yet."

"*Junior* partner." It wouldn't hurt for Ben Volker to know Jia was hungry for more.

"With your work ethic, I have no doubt you'll make senior partner one day." His polished brogues resumed their strides across the gleaming granite. Unlike Jia—who'd been a public-transit peasant since moving to Brooklyn seven years ago—he'd been dropped off outside the revolving doors by a chauffeured Maybach. Jia wondered if Ben had ever worn boots to trudge through the grimy snow while carrying his good shoes to work.

She doubted it.

"Hope you have a great day, Mr. Volker," she called after him, grimacing as the words escaped her mouth. Trite. Insipid. Worst of all, forgettable.

Ben paused, then turned back toward her. "Pardon the"—he *almost* smirked—"impolitic question, but your family is Korean, correct? Candace thought they might be Japanese, but I'm fairly certain you're Korean."

"Yes." Jia kept her quip in check. "We're—I'm—Korean American." She wouldn't waste another chance to impress him. Besides, she'd learned the hard way that lighthearted jokes about microaggressions didn't land well on the overlords.

"Do you speak Korean?"

"Er . . . yes. But I'm more comfortable in English. I can understand everything that's said to me in Korean and can converse well enough to get by, but from a business standpoint, I"—Jia wanted to fold in on herself, as if she were a note being tucked into an envelope—"prefer English." Such a shit time for honesty.

Ben Volker nodded once, his head canting to the left like it was hinging on a decision. A bubble of eagerness gathered in Jia's throat. She swallowed it, hating how much being a middle child had screwed her for life. A people pleaser, they called it. The human equivalent of a goddamned labradoodle.

"I believe I have a client for you." Ben nodded again, his decision made. "It would be a favor to me, as this is a referral from a personal friend."

The bubble threatened to burst in Jia's throat. "Of course."

"Clear your desk and report directly to me. Pass your current caseload on to a few first years." He paused a moment in thought. "Tell Kim to help you dole out the work."

She mirrored his crisp nod. Keep it simple. Like one of the guys.

"Good. Come to the conference room beside my office at nine. I'll be along soon after."

"Yes, Mr. Volker."

"Ben," he corrected. "In the meantime, I want you to read everything you can on the family of Chilsoo 'Seven' Park. They live in Lenox Hill on Park Avenue, and they own a cosmetics company called Mirae."

"I will." Jia refrained from offering him a firm handshake. "Thank you, Ben."

Without another word, Benjamin Volker continued toward the elevator bank, leaving Jia frozen in his wake.

A personal favor to the firm's managing partner. A chance to further distinguish herself from the pack of hungry wolves at her firm. To become the kind of awe-inspiring attorney Jia had always dreamed of being. A vested senior partner, sharing in the profits. Whitman Volker's next Emily Bhatia, the youngest senior partner in the firm's sixty-year history, with the highest billables for the last four years running. Emily Bhatia, who'd never given Jia more than a passing glance, despite Jia's countless attempts to garner her attention.

Never mind the celebratory champagne hangover and the visceral memory of Richard's pale backside as he snored in Jia's bed this morning. A lesson she still refused to learn.

Regret was the last thing on her mind now.

Her first official day as a junior partner at Whitman Volker, Jia Song was shedding the lizard skin of her former life—one of M&A drudgery and black holes of legal minutiae—to become something bigger and badder.

A fire-breather in her own right.

She glanced up at the ceiling's flashing scales once more, refraining from raising her right fist to the sky in triumph.

*Hic sunt dracones.*

"Jia Song!" a muffled voice shouted with exasperation from beside her foot.

"Jesus!" Jia stooped for her long-forgotten phone. "Anka, I'm so sorry. Now, about that Birkin. Are you sure it's a Barenia Faubourg with gold hardware? And what size is it, again?" She resumed her walk toward the elevator bank. "I can be there tomorrow."

---

Mirae. The Korean word for future.

Jia liked it. It sounded hopeful. A tad optimistic, with just the right dash of ego.

As far as stories went, the tale of Mirae epitomized the sort of American Dream that resonated in the ears of immigrants around the world.

But Jia knew there was a sinister underbelly to many American Dreams. She'd been there in the nineties when the only lenders who would give her parents reasonable lines of credit for their bodega had been ones who looked like them. She'd stood firm when a roofing company had accosted her mother for payment, trying to blame Umma's "bad English" for their poor bookkeeping. In 1998, her father's cousin in Queens had been beaten by her ex-husband. The police had done nothing, despite numerous recorded incidents of abuse. In one of the reports teenage Jia had read in secret at night, she'd seen an offhand comment about it being "difficult to understand the victim." As if it were a challenge to interpret the meaning behind a black eye, a fractured nose, and a broken jaw. Her father's cousin and kids had slept on the floor of the Songs' apartment for two months until the rest of the community found a place for them.

Jia had witnessed firsthand the struggles her family had experienced with their business. The constant worries about making payroll and the endless supply chain issues and broken refrigeration units with thousand-dollar parts and indecipherable inspection notices and harebrained schemes to sell Spam kimbap and Halmunni's kalbi sauce under the table in an attempt to become New York's Next Big Thing.

Three months ago, a white man had come into their bodega in the middle of the afternoon carrying nothing but a bat. Without warning, he'd started trashing the shelves and shouting racial epithets at Jia's father and their part-time employee, Yung Hee. Her father had defended them with a box cutter until the Syrian florist across the way could call for the police. The man was carted away in handcuffs and sentenced to a year in a mental rehabilitation facility. His attorney claimed he'd suffered a psychotic break after Yung Hee had ended their relationship.

He was released from the facility two months later.

The Syrian florist, Amna, had *tsk*ed when she heard. "The more things change, the more they don't," she'd said to Jia.

Jia wondered what the underbelly of Mirae's fairy tale looked like.

On the silvery surface, Mirae's story began in the early eighties as Mirae Dry Cleaning with just two employees, Chilsoo and Jeeyun Park, the son of a fishmonger and the daughter of a haenyeo, one of South Korea's famed diving women. Seven and Jenny, as they were known to their American friends, had immigrated to Flushing, Queens, and started with a single dry cleaner, which had become two and then five, all within a handful of years. In the midst of building an empire, they managed to have three children: first twin girls and then a boy. All three were now in their thirties, like Jia and her brothers.

Seven had a head for business, while Jenny proved excellent at managing the day-to-day affairs. Together they parlayed their success into nail salons in Queens, followed by hair salons and spas in Manhattan. In the midnineties, they created a company that began selling Korean beauty products by mail, the first of its kind, complete with proper catalogs catering to Western consumers. No more of the indecipherable English translations that had made teenage Jia cringe. Jenny made sure to hire workers fluent in both Korean and English, which opened their fledgling online business to the world of global commerce. When the Hallyu wave crested, Jenny and Seven were poised at the exact right place and time, their website brimming with the best in Korean beauty.

Conservative estimates now valued Mirae at almost a billion dollars.

Mirae. The future. One of power and promise, even for Korean immigrants who'd arrived on the shores of America unable to speak a word of English, with only four hundred dollars to their names.

The question of what the future might hold was something that had consumed Jia from the age of thirteen, the year her grandfather had put her in charge of their family's destiny. An honor, of course, but also a lofty responsibility for a young girl with Jonathan Taylor Thomas posters and Baby-Sitters Club paperbacks strewn across her bedroom floor.

It wasn't that Jia had some sixth sense–ish ability to speak to the dead. This was a very specific, onetime occurrence. Her grandfather's ghost had sought her out, probably because he and Jia had always shared a special connection, like their passion for late-night Oreos with crunchy peanut butter or the way they both shuddered at the sound of someone eating a banana. As if their souls had been aligned from the beginning.

It happened on a blustery fall night. Jia woke from a deep sleep with a start. Bare tree branches scratched at her window, hail plinking against the roof. Lightning cut across the purple sky, followed by a crackle of thunder.

It was then that she saw him sitting there, at the foot of her bed.

"Harabugi?" she said. "What are you doing?" Jia should have been frightened. After all, he was a ghost, and ghosts were supposed to be scary. But she wasn't afraid. Maybe it was because Harabugi didn't look different. Perhaps a little paler. A little . . . less of himself. In any case, she realized, before he uttered a single word, that he wasn't alive anymore.

Another flicker of lightning sliced through the darkness, a boom of thunder nipping at its heels. The ghost of her harabugi smiled, the crook of his lips sad. "From now on, you must take care of our family." His accented voice wound through Jia's ears, reminding her of the songs he liked to sing on their karaoke machine. Their favorites. Kim Gun-mo ballads, his eyes squeezed shut, his features twisted in blissful agony.

"What?" Jia said. "Why?"

"Because you will be the one. Not your brothers. Not your cousins. You."

"What?" She scrubbed her nose with the heel of one hand and blinked the dregs of sleep from her eyes.

"I'm trusting you." Harabugi smiled again. "It will be up to you now to make sense of this mess. Take care of your brothers. Make sure your halmunni has her medicine. Bring your umma flowers on her birthday, and don't let your appa lend his friends too much money. I know you will make me proud. Song Jihae, you are destined for true greatness." And then he'd vanished in a final burst of lightning.

Jia kicked off her covers and flicked on the lamp.

"Harabugi?" she called out, her heart in her stomach. Jia sat there for a full fifteen minutes, waiting for him to return, as if she were in denial. It wasn't until she heard movement below—the creaking of wooden floorboards and the whining of cabinet doors opening and closing—that she went downstairs.

In the kitchen, Jia stopped short. Her mother was sitting at the darkened breakfast bar, holding a mug of tea while silent tears glazed her cheeks.

"Umma?" Jia whispered the question, though she already knew the answer.

"Your harabugi," her mother said softly. "He—"

"I know," Jia said in Korean. "Ah-ra, Umma. I know."

That night, her harabugi, the wisest person in the world, had told her she was destined for true greatness while entrusting her with the fate of their family. But it wasn't until two years later—the morning that Lexi Niarchos wandered into the Song family's bodega—that Jia truly accepted the responsibility and made the decision to bring great things into her life and the lives of those she loved.

In order to make her destiny a reality, she needed a high-paying job. The sort of career that would make her harabugi proud. Working hard to graduate at the top of her class was the first step. Refusing to fall in love with the first toad who said "Kiss me" was the next. College at NYU and law school at Columbia were logical decisions. The debt was not, which was why she chose the best firm that recruited her during her summer internships. Whenever the stress caught up to Jia, she would think about the wonderful things she would be able to do and buy with the money she would make as a powerful attorney. The prestige and security she would have if she refused to blink and gave every day her all.

At night, she dreamed about walking down Madison Avenue in a white cashmere coat with a jaunty hat, oversize sunglasses, and a caramel-colored Birkin. About one day sauntering into a small shop and changing another girl's life with a measure of much-needed audacity.

But in the harsh light of day, Jia refused to be starry-eyed. After all, learning of her destiny as her family's savior had come at the cost of losing her harabugi.

Even now, at the age of thirty-four, she never stopped being vigilant, never failed to question the good fortune that came her way, wondering, waiting. Because in life, there was always a balance that would come due.

Jia's therapist told her that she needed to pause. Reflect. Seek gratitude.

Simple enough, right?

Jia glanced out the narrow window in the corner of her new office at Whitman Volker. Her window was no wider than the length of a size-thirteen tennis shoe. An oily film clung to its surface, as if a hundred hand-prints had pressed on the outside, begging to be let in.

At least it was something. A window. An office. Junior partner in less than seven years!

"A shoebox with a cutout," Jia murmured. Like one of the dioramas of her favorite books she'd made in elementary school. One hell of a metaphor.

*Gratitude and empathy are the keys to lasting happiness.* She heard the words pronounced in her therapist Gail's sonorous voice. The sort of voice cultivated to convey trust, for four hundred bucks an hour. A small price to pay for lasting happiness.

*The best way to deal with your anxiety is to have a system in place to stop the spiral before it begins. Consciously shift your perspective to one of gratitude, Jia. Harboring suspicion makes you seem suspicious. Choose to give everyone—including yourself—the benefit of the doubt.*

"But what if none of us deserves it?" Jia muttered as she glanced down at her bare feet, sandwiched between her snow boots and the pair of good shoes she'd stuffed in her bag while Richard snored in the early morning darkness.

"Fuck!" She shouted the single syllable, then shrank into herself, her eyes locked on the door.

Sure enough, a knock sounded a second later.

"Yes?" Jia cleared her throat and lifted her chin.

"Is everything all right, Jia?" Nate Willoughby pushed open the door without waiting for a response. Of course it was Never Late Nate. Jia had nicknames for all the first years she worked with, except for the few she didn't hate. It was her way of making them seem less like shark-toothed guppies in need of a culling.

Never Late Nate's favorite icebreaker was to tell people he'd been born ten weeks early on a yacht, which made him a gunner with sea legs. Never mind the fact that his mother almost died, a fact Jia learned much later, listening as Nate chuckled while sharing the tale. Men who chuckled were the worst. The nicest thing she could say about Nate Willoughby was that he wore a tan well. At least once a week, Jia daydreamed of tying him down so that she could admire his physique while drowning him in a bucket, just to test out his sea legs theory.

She could hear Gail now. Could see her patient, veneered smile. *Jia, it's not always a good idea to entertain such violent thoughts, even in jest. Instead, why don't we—*

"Everything's fine, Nate." Jia grinned, folding her hands beneath her chin.

"I just thought I heard—"

"Find out if any of the other first years wear size seven-and-a-half shoes, please."

Nate drew back, his eyes wide. "Like, the . . . female first years?"

Fucking Yalies. Jia sharpened her smile. "No. I've decided to wear men's shoes from this day forth."

A frown pulled at his face. Her sarcasm failed to land well on any kind of overlord, especially future ones like Never Late Nate.

"Be a pal and ask around, would you?" Jia said. "Nothing higher than three inches and *no* red bottoms. I'm not a clown."

"Sure thing." His stare pierced into hers. A second too late, Jia realized the reason when his gaze dropped to the floor and back up again.

Jia tucked her feet out of sight and hated herself for it. Nate made mistakes, too. Just last week, she'd had to fix the Shatner commas in one of his briefs.

"Did you step in something?" he pressed.

"Yes," Jia lied. "Dog shit." That was better than him knowing she'd brought shoes from two different pairs.

"I thought I smelled something."

A familiar anger flared in Jia's chest, hot and fast. "Just find me some shoes, Ken."

"Nate," he corrected, his tanned brow creasing.

"Uh-huh." She grinned and let her eyes squint like a stereotype, for good measure.

His expression quizzical, Nate took hold of the door handle. "Congrats on making junior partner, Jia. You deserve it."

"I know."

"Holler if you need anything else. I'll be right outside."

Ready and waiting to kill her if it meant getting a leg up. "Will do," she said through gritted teeth. Then she clicked open the next article on her computer, which was an *Architectural Digest* spread on Sora Park-Vandeveld's home in the current building du jour on Billionaires' Row.

The perfectly styled photos revealed a slender Korean woman about Jia's age dressed in Prada and Zimmermann, her long black hair shining like onyx in the sun. Two small children clambered at her feet, their faces artfully hidden from view. The Park-Vandeveld manse sported white walls and light oak floors, with accents of black metal and jade silk. Subdued and elegant, save for splashy art and the occasional item of whimsy meant to "bring character to every corner and highlight cherished memories."

A further internet search told Jia that Sora had attended Harvard for undergrad and Johns Hopkins for medical school, where she'd graduated summa cum laude and had embarked on a career as a pediatrician. In residency at Cedars-Sinai, she met Dr. Charles Alexander Vandeveld III, future dermatologist to Manhattan's über-rich and scion of one of its wealthiest families. His grandmother was a DuPont, and his father could trace his roots back to the Astors. Sora and Alex had married five years ago in a star-studded gala at his family's summer home in East Hampton and had two children since.

Sora's younger twin sister, Suzy, lived in an immense loft in SoHo. A graduate of the Rhode Island School of Design, Suzy had begun her career as a mixed-media painter and sculptor with all the eyes of the art world upon her. Though she had yet to hold a full show of her own, she hobnobbed with the city's elite and was often spotted on the edges of paparazzi photos at a club or gallery opening, her elbows linked with actors and other LA-to-Brooklyn transplants.

In contrast to the twins, Jia could find very little information on the youngest member of the Park family. His English name, Jia discovered, was rather unfortunate: Mark. Mark Park. As such, he used his Korean name, Minsoo, in professional settings. A Stanford graduate, Minsoo Park worked at a hedge fund on Wall Street known for its extreme discretion and its small, select clientele. He lived in a co-op in Tribeca and enjoyed playing golf and driving Italian supercars.

In short, the Park family was rich. Very rich.

Jia inhaled through her nose. "I don't know what they want from me," she sang under her breath. "It's like the more money we come across, the more problems we see." Her attention snagged on the clock. Less than half an hour to refresh her hair and makeup before she was due at the conference room on the opposite side of the floor.

But first she needed to find Nate. If this family was anything like their online personas suggested, Jia would rather eat glass than meet them wearing mismatched shoes.

Trepidation settled in her stomach, mixed with a tinge of excitement. Like that last bite of a Cheongyang chili pepper, seeds and all. The bite you know is going to be too hot but eat anyway, just to relish the burn.

Jia hadn't decided what this mirae would bring her. But she was prepared to take the bad along with the good.

"The Parks of Park Avenue," she said with a smirk. "Do your worst."

# GIJIBAE

Ben Volker was already seated in the conference room when Jia arrived ten minutes before nine o'clock. Without saying a word, he managed to take her off guard, yet again.

She'd expected to deal with the ego of a man accustomed to being in charge. After all, Ben was a named partner, and Jia was his junior, in more respects than one. He represented billion-dollar deals and did the kind of pro bono work Jia dreamed of taking on later in her career, when she vacationed in the Hamptons and owned a restored Porsche from the early nineties. Like James Bond, but Korean American. And a lady, of course. Her gun of choice would be the law, not a Walther PPK. And when Jia Song took aim for justice, she would not miss.

Ben frowned, as if he could see her ridiculous fantasy playing out before him like a poorly scripted movie trailer.

Jia straightened. She was here in a support capacity. Nothing more, especially when they were client-facing. Ben Volker was in charge.

Except . . . it didn't appear like he was.

Ben had chosen to sit against the wall in a small chair meant for transcribers and secretaries, rather than at the head of the immense conference table running the length of the glass-walled chamber reserved for the firm's top clients.

The ones they meant to impress.

This table had been among the many reasons Jia had chosen to intern at Whitman Volker the summer after her second year at Columbia Law. It was a custom piece, known throughout the furniture world as a river table. Two pieces of live-edge oak framed a channel of rich black resin finished by a layer of epoxy so perfect, Jia could see her reflection in it. A Dutch master had crafted it to the specific dimensions of the room, using wood from a hundred-year-old tree he'd chopped down himself. It was intimidating and elegant. Something that spoke for itself. Exactly what Jia aspired to be.

She stared at Ben sitting in the corner, his legs crossed, the face of his Patek Philippe watch gleaming. Jia waited for him to speak.

He raised his eyebrows.

"I . . . read everything I could find on the Park family." She clutched her folder and pushed her feet deeper into the toe bed of her borrowed size-eight heels. A hair too big, but a vast improvement over the mismatched alternative.

"Good. You're running point on this."

"I am?"

Ben nodded. "I possess very little information on this situation. As I said, this is a referral from a friend. The Park family business is with CHM. This appears to be a personal matter."

"I see." Jia refrained from making a face. This meant there was trouble in the family. One member of the family might be suing another, which was why the law firm handling their business could not represent whoever Ben and Jia were about to meet.

"I will be learning about the situation at the same time as you," Ben said. He checked his watch again. "I believe we will be dealing primarily with the kids."

"Mark is thirty-one. Sora and Suzy are thirty-four." Jia was thirty-four. Did Ben think she was a kid?

"I know," Ben said.

Guess that answered her question. Was sweat pooling on her upper lip? It would only be a matter of time before she began perspiring through her taupe silk shirt and charcoal blazer. "Perhaps we—"

"It's no secret that the firm has been seeking opportunities to work with major players in the beauty industry for quite some time. Globally, it's worth over half a trillion dollars. The Park family's current case appears to be personal, but this could be a chance to get their company's business in the future." Ben locked eyes with her, his gaze piercing. "This requires the kind of undivided attention I'm unable to offer clients as managing director, but I expect you to devote yourself entirely to their needs and report to me at every turn. I want to stay fully abreast of everything, and all major decisions should be run through me first."

Jia threw back her shoulders while he spoke, as if he were a military commander issuing orders to his subordinate. "Of course."

"I'm aware this is not a small ask. But I believe you're up to it, Jia." He recrossed an ankle over a knee. "And if you're successful in getting the Park family to move their business to us, I will recommend you for senior partner next year."

Jia's pulse trilled in her veins. The ambient noises around her faded to a dull roar. Senior partner only a year after making junior partner? Had that ever happened at Whitman Volker?

"That would make you the youngest senior partner in the firm's history." One side of Ben's mouth kicked up.

Younger than Emily Bhatia.

Jia nodded slowly, taking time to process her swirling thoughts. Becoming a vested senior partner was not a given for any lawyer. If she made this happen, she could reach that goal by the age of thirty-five, with all the trappings and money and influence that came along with the title. Everything she'd spent her entire life working toward would be possible. Security for herself and her family. Honoring her grandfather's last request. A self-made multimillionaire before she turned forty.

But only if she could win over the Park family and their billion-dollar business.

A wave of anxiety built in Jia's stomach, cresting at the base of her throat. *Breathe*, she admonished herself. *Think of the worst thing that can happen. Have a plan to deal with it moving forward. Always forward.* She waited for the pounding of her heart to subside.

A well-dressed young man rounded the corner, just beyond the glass wall parallel to the river table. He was accompanied by Ben's secretary, Candace, who opened the gleaming door to the conference room.

"Would you care for something to drink, Mr. Park?" Candace asked as soon as they crossed the threshold. "We have bottled water—still and sparkling—as well as any kind of coffee or tea or soda you would like."

"I'll have a bottled water, please. Still," Minsoo Park said with a tight smile. He moved with smooth, precise steps toward Ben and Jia, his navy pinstriped suit perfectly pressed. Almost old-fashioned. The starched white collar on his otherwise robin's-egg blue shirt reminded Jia a bit of Gordon Gekko. A hint of lavender silk suspenders and a solid gold tie clip peeked out from beneath his double-breasted jacket. His two-toned Rolex was tasteful rather than outlandish, and she could bet he had the same pair of Ferragamo shoes in every color imaginable.

Ben stepped aside to make room for Jia, allowing her to take the lead . . . which, really?

Jia almost laughed. Instead, it came out as a nervous snort.

Humor was, as always, the best medicine. It never failed to brighten the darkness.

"Good morning, Mr. Park." Jia reached a hand toward him, trying her best to appear unruffled. "My name is Jia Song."

His otherwise even brow furrowed. He shook her hand, and Jia caught a whiff of his cologne. The soothing musk of vetiver. "It's nice to meet you, Ms. Song, but I was under the impression we were speaking with one of the named partners."

"I'm Benjamin Volker," Ben said, gliding forward. "Jia is one of our finest junior partners. We'll be working together on this."

Minsoo Park shook Ben's hand slowly. He looked from Ben's smiling face to Jia's. Then back to Ben. When he glanced at Jia again, they shared an understanding.

Minsoo knew why Jia was here. And he didn't like it.

Which meant Jia would have to work even harder to earn his trust. It was something she loved and hated about her people. They wanted to work with their own kind. But they wanted their own kind to deserve it.

Minsoo Park thought Jia was only here because she was Korean, not because she was competent. Jia had to make a choice. She could either let her anxiety take control or use it to stoke her anger. It was an old remedy, one Gail would not advise. But it had proven useful to Jia on more than one occasion.

It was easy for her to choose anger. Letting anger take the reins felt empowering. The Korean part of her wanted to rage at him. Demand that he start calling her noona and defer to her as his elder. Who did this jashik think he was? The American part of her hunkered down for a barroom brawl.

Jia's jaw set. "Please have a seat." As soon as the words left her mouth, she realized her voice had changed. It no longer sounded accommodating or eager to please. There was a sharpness now, as if it had accepted Minsoo's wordless challenge.

*Pistols at dawn, motherfucker,* it said.

Maybe the youngest Park sibling wouldn't like her. But he would respect her.

If Minsoo noticed Jia's reaction, he didn't show it. "My sisters should be along shortly." He sat in a swivel chair on the opposite side of the table. "I spoke to Sora twenty minutes ago, and she was on the way."

He did not mention Suzy, Jia noted.

Ben sat across from Minsoo, and Jia selected the chair beside her boss. "Should we wait until they both arrive to begin?" she said, refusing to operate from a place of deference. Ben wanted her to take the lead, and Minsoo Park didn't like that she was here at all. Jia was determined to carve out space for herself, even if she had to do it with a dull knife.

Minsoo nodded. "We should at least wait for Sora. She and I are on the same page, more or less. Suzy—well, I'm not sure Suzy will be much help. She's not exactly reliable. My father refers to her as Punxsutawney Phil."

Ben chuckled. Minsoo chuckled in return, but it felt rehearsed. As if he'd stolen the line because he'd been told to. Like, *use that, it's a good one.* Nevertheless, their laughter grated on Jia. One day, she was determined to write a think piece on The Chuckling of Men in Meetings.

Minsoo inhaled, his mouth puckering like he'd taken a bite out of a lemon. "I wanted to mention something before my sisters arrived that is . . . pertinent, as it may complicate matters moving forward."

Jia nodded. "Please go ahead."

"Suzy and Sora have not spoken in over two years," Minsoo said.

Jia did not react. "I see." She had many follow-up questions, but from Minsoo's body language, Jia gathered he would not be forthcoming. Minsoo

Park—like many Koreans Jia knew—would rather swallow rusty nails than air his family's dirty laundry in public. He was sharing this limited amount of information because he knew, without a doubt, that what was about to unfold would be unpleasant. It was necessary for Ben and Jia to be prepared.

"If they are"—Minsoo took his time choosing his next words, like Halmunni selecting a piece of fruit—"impolite to each other, that is the reason why." The lemon sucking continued. "Sora will try her best. Suzy will do her worst. Understand, they are . . . both in the wrong. I will not get involved unless I am forced to." He leaned forward, his ankle crossing over one knee, showing navy silk socks and old-fashioned garters to match his lavender suspenders. "It goes without saying that this is all privileged information."

"It goes without saying," Ben echoed. The entire time Minsoo spoke, Whitman Volker's managing partner had mirrored their newest client's movements in an effort to put him at ease. Law firms made their living off fraught situations like this. Family drama never failed to set the cash registers ringing. And family drama among centimillionaires? It was better than striking an oil geyser in Texas. The more bullshit WhitVo's first years had to sift through, the more billable hours the firm could collect.

The Park family could easily become one of the firm's largest accounts. If this was an estate battle between the siblings, it could turn into a full-on fistfight. The only thing that gave Jia pause was this: she did not recall reading about either Seven's or Jenny's impending demise.

What, then, were the Park siblings fighting about? Why had the twins been at odds for years?

She glanced back at Minsoo and found him staring at nothing, his features caught between sadness and resignation.

For the first time since meeting him, Jia felt a drop of sympathy. For all his aloofness, Minsoo Park wanted to protect his sisters in the quiet way she'd longed for her older brother, James, to look out for her and their younger brother, Jason. Too bad James Song had been more interested in riced-out Hondas and gaming.

Then again, Minsoo was Sora and Suzy's younger brother. Maybe it had nothing to do with age or birth order. Maybe it was just the luck of the draw.

Jia, Ben, and Minsoo waited in silence for a few more minutes, checking messages on their respective phones until the glass door to the conference room swung open with a depressurizing sound, like the hatch on a space station. When Jia glanced toward the entrance, the welcoming smile on her face faltered.

The woman standing beyond the threshold was staring at Jia from straight down her nose, her expression a perfect portrait of judgment. As if Jia were a pulae. A bug meant to be squished to a pulp beneath her polished heel.

Sora Park-Vandeveld. The Grand Gijibae herself.

Her long blue-black hair was parted down the middle, the ends curled halfway down her back. Her YSL sunglasses were cat-eyed, her diamond studs flawless. The bell sleeves on her white button-down shirt peeked out from underneath the cuffs of her oversize mohair coat. Her tailored pencil skirt and midcalf black boots were coordinated in matching lengths. The handle of a noir Hermès Kelly 28 with palladium hardware was tucked into the crook of her left elbow.

She was flawless. Lithe. A fixed presence in the front row at Fashion Week. The kind of fancy *Korean* Korean girl who'd disdained Jia at Columbia.

Of course Sora preferred a Kelly over a Birkin. She was just the type of gijibae to do that. Jia knew Sora Park-Vandeveld's kind of Korean girl quite well. She could bet Sora spoke the highest form of jondaemal with the same ease that Jia used to cuss out bad drivers on the BQE.

Jondaemal was the sort of Korean high speech that made Jia feel most like a fish out of water around other Koreans. To her, it drew invisible lines where there had been none. In wealthier families, children often addressed their parents and grandparents using jondaemal. A generation or so ago, it was unheard of to use anything less within "proper" circles. In modern Korean business settings, it was often a requirement.

Jia had used banmal—casual Korean—with all the members of her family, even her grandparents, since she was a child. It was why she hesitated to speak Korean outside her home.

The few times she'd spoken jondaemal around *Korean* Koreans, she'd felt their judgment. Felt her blood warm and her skin flush when she'd uttered the wrong ending to a phrase or misused a greeting or failed to perform some ridiculous rule of etiquette, like Julia Roberts with the escargot spoon in *Pretty Woman*.

Sora Park-Vandeveld hated Jia on sight, before they'd shared a single exchange. No amount of pleasantries would help now. It burned Jia's biscuits to see this kind of scenario play out. How the patriarchy insisted on setting powerful women against each other, as if one woman couldn't rise to the top without stepping on a few of her own kind to get there. Jia wanted to deny this fact. Make mincemeat out of it. Why did Sora Park-Vandeveld have to hate her? They could help each other. Maybe even be fast friends. They were both Korean. Both the children of self-made immigrants. Sure, Sora was incandescently wealthy and married to an Astor or whatever. Did that mean she couldn't fraternize with the child of bodega owners from Queens?

Jia met Sora's ice-cold glare and swore she could see rime crystallizing around the edges of her YSLs.

On another day, Jia might have withered. But she refused to let this gijibae get the better of her. If Sora wanted to hate her without any good reason, Jia was happy to return the sentiment. She stood and made her way toward Sora, her strides determined. As she walked, she felt her borrowed shoes slide from her sweaty skin. "I'm Jia Song." She extended her hand in welcome.

And tripped in front of Sora Park-Vandeveld, her body sprawling like a supplicant at the gijibae's feet.

"Jia." Ben Volker leaped into action, stooping beside Jia, hammering the final nail on her coffin of humiliation.

"Minsoo-ya," Sora said softly, addressing her younger brother in angelic tones while she removed her sunglasses and crossed her arms. "Eegae mohyah?" She stared down at Jia as if Jia were the pulae-est of pulae.

*Minsoo, dear. What the hell is this?*

# RED RUM

Jia wanted to unhinge her jaw and swallow herself whole. Even during puberty, she hadn't been this clumsy. In fact, she'd played volleyball in high school and danced well at school functions, and on normal mornings she managed to walk in straight lines without tripping at the first sign of distress.

Today was for day drinking. It was official.

With Ben's help, Jia stood and straightened her hair and clothing. Her wounded pride was a matter to be dealt with alone. Later. With a fourth of Michter's and a cilice belt.

Refusing to be deterred, Jia smiled again at Sora and held out her hand once more. "I promise that will be the only mistake I make, *Suzy*," she joked.

It was petty. So petty. But Jia felt a stab of satisfaction nonetheless.

"Hmm," Sora said.

Minsoo Park exhaled with the weariness of a much older man. "Ms. Song is working with Benjamin Volker on our case," he said to his sister.

"I see." Sora took Jia's hand and shook it like a soiled dishrag. "It's nice to meet you, Ms. Song." Her smile was serene, her eyes the color of teakwood.

"Please have a seat, Mrs. Park-Vandeveld." Jia plastered a grin on her face. "Would you care for something to drink?"

"A Perrier with lemon, please," Sora replied. "No ice."

Candace stepped forward, her ruddy cheeks darkening, her blond curls trembling. "I'll grab one right away." She mouthed an apology to Jia, who waved it off. What Jia really wanted to do was pantomime slicing her own throat, but no one would appreciate her dark sense of humor. Not here, at least.

Her therapist, Gail, would have a field day.

Sora sat beside her brother and made no move to shed her mohair coat. She folded her sunglasses and set them down. Both Park siblings moved with the same sort of deliberation. The simplest motion had a practiced air to it, as if they meant to pose even in rest.

"Mr. Volker?" Sora's attention slid to Ben, her head shifting like a hawk's.

"It's a pleasure to meet you, Ms. Park-Vandeveld. Your father-in-law speaks so highly of you." Ben rose to shake her hand.

The Parks' connection to Whitman Volker was through the Vandeveld family. The ones with relatives who were DuPonts and Astors. They were likely trying to protect the wealth Sora was meant to inherit.

The hint of a smile toyed with Sora's lips. "Chip is such a dear."

Jia knew Sora was referring to Charles Alexander Vandeveld II. There was something odd about calling a man who collected Klimt paintings "Chip," as if he were a buddy you met at the corner bar every Thursday night.

"He says you've been playing squash at the club together for the last fifteen years," Sora continued. There was a hint of an accent in the way she spoke. Nothing meaningful or specific. Just a rounding of tones and a lengthening of vowels, like the way Madonna spoke while she was married to Guy Ritchie.

Ben said, "Only when Chip lets me win."

Sora laughed, and it reminded Jia of the bells chiming at Mass during transubstantiation, when the bread and wine changed into the actual body and blood of Jesus Christ.

Jia leaned back in her chair to study Sora from a distance. She wasn't sure if she wanted to slow-clap or scream. The pole up this chick's backside had to be shoved straight through to her head. The urge to laugh took hold of Jia. She wanted to tilt her head to the sky and crow. To release a ribald, robust guffaw into the modern chandelier hanging above the conference table. She bet if she laughed loud enough, she could make the rectangular crystals tremble as if she were a giant stomping around the room yelling "fee-fi-fo-fum."

"Well, fuck me sideways." The door to the conference room *thunk*ed shut. The young woman standing beyond the threshold blew her balayaged bangs off her forehead. "And I tried so hard to get here early." She plodded toward the side of the table where her brother and sister sat. Stopped. Smirked. Reconsidered. And then took the seat beside Jia.

"I'm Suzy." She shoved her right hand in Jia's face. "Who are you?"

"Jia Song." She shook Suzy Park's hand, impressed by both her grip and the six Cartier LOVE bangles clinking together on her wrist, which seemed incongruous with the rest of Suzy's ensemble. She wore a flowing Réalisation Par maxi dress with a flowery print over a thin black turtleneck and at least five different gold necklaces of varying lengths. A large green puffer coat, emerald Doc Marten boots, and a vintage Balenciaga tote completed the outfit. Artsy and expensive, albeit a bit young.

"Hmm," Suzy said in an unnerving echo of her twin. "You're Korean, aren't you?"

"Yes," Jia replied with a smile that failed to reach her eyes. "I am."

"Did you go to Harvard Law?" Suzy pressed, focusing on Jia with an intent expression.

"No. Columbia."

Suzy snorted. "Were your parents proud of you?"

"Yes."

"Even though you didn't go to Harvard?"

Jia's fake grin widened. "Were your parents proud of you even though you didn't go to Harvard?"

"Nope." Suzy cackled. "My mom loves me, but she was never proud. And my dad can go suck a big fat—"

"I think we should probably get started," Minsoo interrupted in a quiet but firm voice.

Suzy laughed. "Ah, Marky." A sigh flew from her lips. "I missed you."

"Ms. Song," Sora began, zeroing in on Jia. "Mr. Volker." She turned to Ben. Jia had to admit she was impressed by Sora's dedicated efforts to ignore her twin. "We don't want to waste too much of your time. My father-in-law recommended your firm because of your discretion and because of your history in dealing with delicate financial matters."

Jia nodded. "Please go ahead, Mrs. Park-Vandeveld."

"I can assure you, we will handle this matter with the highest levels of both prudence and professionalism," Ben added.

Sora picked up her sunglasses and tapped one of the earpieces on the smooth surface of the river table, the noise rhythmic. "We find ourselves in a rather . . . uncomfortable situation."

Suzy snickered. She inclined in her swivel chair and tossed her wavy hair over one shoulder, fluffing it with her hands as if she were already bored by the entire affair.

Though Sora did not acknowledge Suzy's presence, her cheeks hollowed. "My mother has been battling breast cancer for three years now. She underwent a double mastectomy and reconstructive surgery last year, but unfortunately the cancer has continued to spread." She inhaled through her nose. "Her current prognosis is . . . distressing, to say the least. The doctors said they would be surprised if she makes it past this summer."

A thick silence settled on the space. Suzy's expression sobered. Minsoo looked away. "I'm sorry to hear that." Jia's reply was gentle. "Cancer is a terrible thing for any family to endure."

Sora blinked at Jia, the tapping of her sunglasses ceasing for a moment.

"Thank you," Minsoo said. "It hasn't been easy for us. Our mother has always been the center of our family."

"Whatever." Suzy's voice dripped with acid. "Since she got sick, you avoid her like the plague. When was the last time you actually stayed at Umma's house for more than an hour?"

Minsoo grimaced. "Please, Chagan-noona," he said to Suzy. "Chaebal, putak handa." Even the way he pleaded with her was careful. The consummate diplomat. Then Minsoo turned back to Sora, who continued to ignore her sister's presence, though Jia noticed a wash of color rising in Sora's cheeks and signs of tension banding across her brow. It took Jia a moment to realize why, and once she did, it became a struggle to conceal her reaction. Her awful, unforgivable glee.

Sora Park-Vandeveld was embarrassed. Whatever she was about to share was deeply shameful. A source of unending humiliation. Jia knew it was wrong. But she found herself leaning forward, her fingers gripping her Montblanc pen with the eagerness of an ambulance chaser.

"About two months ago, my father filed for a divorce from my mother," Sora said, the words curdling in the air the second they left her mouth.

"Fucking asshole," Suzy whispered, her open palm striking the river table. "Couldn't even wait until she was dead."

"He already left her a year ago," Sora continued. "They'd been separated for a while before that, though they lived in the same house. It wasn't a huge surprise that he filed for a divorce. We . . . haven't been on great terms with him since he left our mother."

"I'm sure you can understand why," Minsoo added, giving Sora's forearm a reassuring pat.

That did it. Minsoo was officially Jia's favorite Park sibling.

"Of course." Jia nodded.

"But in the last couple of weeks"—Sora took a breath—"we've received truly disturbing information." Her features hardened. "My parents didn't have a prenup, as they were married before they amassed their wealth. They built Mirae together, and my mother always trusted my father with the financial side of things. She never knew exactly how much money they had, but she knew they had a lot of it. After years of struggling to make ends meet, she had money to buy whatever she wanted whenever she wanted. She never asked questions. Three years ago, *Forbes* estimated their company was worth nearly a billion dollars." Sora paused. "So when my father brought financial documents to my mother's divorce attorney, we were all shocked. He claimed they were worth around twenty-five million."

Jia's eyebrows shot up, her pen halting above her notepad. Frowning, Ben rested his elbows along the edge of the table.

Sora's small hands—their lone adornment a massive, cushion-cut heirloom diamond with a ridiculous name—balled into fists. "Ludicrous," she whispered. "Twenty-five million? My parents own a yacht that is worth twice that. They have a house in the Cayman Islands, an apartment in Le Marais, a condo in Kangnam, an olive tree estate in Crete, and, of course, the Park Avenue residence. Their real estate portfolio alone must be worth in excess of a hundred million dollars." She eased back in her chair. "My father is *lying*. My brother and I believe he is trying to conceal the majority of our wealth from us."

"May I ask why he would go to such lengths to lie about the money?" Jia posed the question in what she hoped was a neutral tone.

For an instant, no one answered. Minsoo shifted in his chair, waiting for Sora to make her decision.

"You may ask," Sora replied. "But your guess is as good as ours."

Interesting. Sora Park-Vandeveld had just told her first bald-faced lie, which meant the truth was something she did not wish to admit, at least not in front of her attorneys. Given how cagey both Sora and Minsoo were, it would take considerable effort on Jia's part to uncover the truth. Or maybe she could just plan a drunk lunch with Suzy.

"I quietly looked at the paperwork my father presented to my mother's divorce lawyer," Minsoo said. "I'm sure you understand why I could not ask the forensic accountant at my company to have a peek. At least, not without drawing the kind of attention we do not want, especially at such a delicate moment. This kind of inner turmoil wreaks havoc on publicly traded companies like Mirae. Anyway, my conclusion after studying the financial documents is the same as Sora's. Our father has hidden the majority of our family's fortune, and he's done it well. The paper trail is a quagmire. It will take a herculean effort to weed through everything."

"Especially," Sora interjected, her expression grim, "since our mother doesn't wish to challenge my father's pittance of a settlement. He offered her fifteen million and the Park Avenue property to walk away."

Silence hung in the air for a beat.

"May I ask why your mother won't challenge it?" Ben steepled his hands before him.

"She's fought so hard already," Jia answered without thinking. "The money has never been what mattered to her. And the shame of this entire situation is . . . soul deep."

The silence widened. All three Park siblings considered Jia, their faces careful.

"Yes." Minsoo blinked. "Precisely."

Jia eased back into her chair, her mind a thoughtful whirl. "If I may go a step further, I suppose the three of you wish to challenge the settlement on your mother's behalf, as it directly affects your inheritance." She paused. "This is an indelicate question, but . . . is your father pursuing a relationship with someone else?"

Discomfort rippled through the room, and Jia worried she'd overstepped.

Suzy smirked at her. "Maybe you're not just an affirmative action hire after all, Columbia. Also, I should probably let you know—since my brother and sister don't really visit my mother—that I'm pretty sure the staff is helping our father fuck us over." She rested her chin on her stacked palms, her head tilted conspiratorially. "Like, I swear I saw one of the maids at Park Avenue tuck mail into her skirt pocket before my mother's house manager, Darius, could go through it. You should definitely talk to him, Columbia. Earn those billable hours. Darius is a good egg."

Minsoo winced. "I'm sorry, Ms. Song. I hope you're not terribly offended. We know you must be more than capable, especially at a firm like Whitman Volker."

"Oh, what bullshit," Suzy said. "Tell me you didn't think the same thing. Of course they pulled their Korean lawyer into this. Like, oh, this will make everything perfect! They can talk about kimchi and BTS and bulgogi. We'll make sure they bond while we bill them a thousand bucks an hour."

Jia watched Sora bare her teeth as she finally glanced toward her twin, the first and only time she'd deigned to acknowledge Suzy's presence. "Takchuh," she murmured.

"Whoa." Suzy dragged out the word, her arms flailing as she looked to the four corners of the conference room. "Did you just talk to *me*?" Her mouth hung open with theatrical emphasis. "Like, I don't even care that you told me to shut the fuck up. Did you just *speak to me*, Unyee?"

Sora crossed her arms and stared straight through her sister. Jia swore she could hear Sora's brain counting to ten. Swore she could see the way Sora nursed her anger as if it were an affliction. There was probably a Gail in her head, too.

Suzy's grin turned malicious. "Did they tell you why my sister hasn't spoken to me in years?"

"Noona," Minsoo said. "Don't. Please."

She ignored her brother. "I'll tell you why."

Minsoo exhaled in a rush of air. "Suzy, this is not—" Sora placed a hand on his arm. In silence—with nothing but a look—she told him not to intervene. To let things play out.

Jia's heartbeat quickened. Biting her lower lip, she wordlessly begged Suzy not to take her twin's bait, though she longed to hear everything the most dramatic Park sibling had to say.

Suzy almost vibrated with anticipation. As if she knew her sister was daring her. Knew it and didn't care. They were playing chicken, and Suzy would be damned before she swerved first.

"I was skinnier two years ago," she began with an impish smile as she gestured toward her ample chest. "My sister and I were the same size, believe it or not. A two. Perfect for social media and couture samples. Like, I basically lived off jelly beans and vodka sodas." She rolled her eyes. "Anyway, I'd always worshipped Sora. My mother used to dress us alike, and Sora hated it, but I loved looking like her. Even tried to copy her style a few times before I realized I don't like underwear that makes me feel like a sausage in a casing. In fact," she said with a wink at Ben, "I don't care for underwear at all."

Now she was being ridiculous. Merely trying to get a rise out of them. Armed with a tactful pivot, Jia opened her mouth, but Suzy cut her off.

"Okay, okay, I won't talk about underwear anymore. Mee-an," she apologized, holding up both her hands in scornful surrender.

"Noona," Minsoo tried again. "Please."

But Suzy ignored him a second time. "A little more than two years ago, Sora and I were invited to a Halloween party at Ali Shaffir's penthouse. We decided it would be fun to dress the same and style our hair so that no one could tell us apart. I mean, white people already have a hard time with Asians. It was going to be a hoot. We dressed like the twins from *The Shining*, like the whole pale blue dress and the knee-high stockings with the patent leather Mary Janes. Manolo Blahnik, of course. The whole kit was . . ." She mimed a chef's kiss.

Jia glanced at Sora, who continued staring straight through her sister, her arms crossed, her face devoid of emotion.

"Here's where things get interesting," Suzy said. "Right before we get to the party, I try to convince both Sora and Alex to do molly with me. They were so much fun before they had kids. Well, Sora was fun. Alex is . . . well, Alex. Like, he will drink you under the table, but he's the squarest of squares. The kind who will try swinging in his fifties, if you know what I mean."

"Koomahn," Minsoo begged her to stop. He turned toward Sora, his expression pleading. "Noona, please just—"

"No," Sora said, her voice soft. "Let her finish."

Jia tried to smile. "Maybe we can return to discussing more of what you would like Whitman Volker to—"

"I said"—Sora glared at Jia—"let her finish."

Anxiety made Jia want to wither under Sora's thousand-yard stare. Anger made her want to sit taller. To insist that they at least try the brakes on the runaway train.

"You heard Lady Vandeveld," Suzy teased. "Don't worry. I'm almost finished." She grinned at Jia and Ben, who shifted in his chair with obvious discomfort. "Sora and Alex wouldn't take any molly. But I definitely took some about five minutes before we arrived at Ali's building. Man, I don't remember a lot of that party. But I do know I was having a crazy amount of fun. I danced. I drank." She took a deep breath. "I met someone."

A bead of perspiration slipped between Jia's breasts, pooling in the bottom of her sensible cotton bra. In fifteen minutes, it would be impossible to hide the sweat.

Suzy tossed her hair and grinned, but Jia noticed an edge to it. An unmistakable glimmer of pain. All the f-bombs and underwear talk couldn't mask the truth of it. "He was flirty and fun," she said. "Dressed like Batman. He even did the whole gruff voice thing. We role-played a bit, and then we wound up in Maxine Shaffir's infamous closet. Yeah, you know.

The one with a hundred pairs of Jimmy Choos and all those emerald-green Chanel bags."

Even before Suzy shared the next part of the story, Jia knew what had happened. She cleared her throat. "Suzy, why don't we—"

"We'd been going at it—you know, fucking like coked-out rabbits—for maybe five minutes when the door to Maxine's closet opened, like a scene out of *Downton Abbey* or some shit. Six women, including my sister, were standing with Maxine, watching me get railed by the masked Caped Crusader . . . I mean, by none other than Dr. Charles Alexander Vandeveld the third." There was no sparkle in Suzy's gaze now, nor did she seem to take any pleasure in relaying these details. A single tear slid down her cheek. "You know the worst part? In that awful moment, Sora pretended everything was fine. For the sake of saving face, she played along. Then after the party, she forgave Alex. He said he thought I was her all along, and she fucking believed him. But when I told her I had no idea Batman was Alex—that I'd forgotten entirely, especially because he didn't put on his mask until we arrived at the party—she attacked me. Can you believe it? She forgave her cheating, drunk husband without blinking an eye, but she turned her back on me, like the hypocritical, coldhearted bitch she is."

Minsoo closed his eyes and sighed.

Suzy winked. "Don't worry, though. Sora may have given me a black eye, but I definitely took a hunk of that angelic hair with me. And now I know exactly how Alex likes to have his—"

A single lemon wedge—along with the contents of an entire glass of Perrier—struck Suzy Park's face with superhuman speed. Jia hadn't even noticed Sora Park-Vandeveld stand, much less take aim. The splash back from the seltzer hit the right side of Jia's blazer, droplets soaking into her silk collar and one of her borrowed shoes.

Sora put on her sunglasses. "You fucking whore," she said to Suzy.

Before anyone could say a word, Sora Park-Vandeveld glided from the room.

# ALEA IACTA EST

Now would be a prudent time to reflect on these revelations.

This author is aware of the thoughts that must race through a reader's mind at this point in the tale. Rest assured, they are the same thoughts this author once shared.

Namely: How could Suzy Park not have known what she was doing in Maxine Shaffir's closet? And if she had recognized Batman was her sister's husband, how could she have dared to play the victim?

Upon further contemplation, it is appalling to realize how quickly blame was placed on Suzy. One hopes a fair share of responsibility was doled out to Dr. Charles Alexander Vandeveld III in due time. But, this author regrets to admit, the first and freshest pall of disdain was for Sora's sister. Her twin. The other half of their whole.

The sting of this betrayal resonates to the core, for it is not of the everyday variety. Naturally, inquiring minds would like to know the truth. After all, it is much easier to steep in hatred when armed with the incontrovertible.

The truth, however, is an interesting animal in its own right. This author would ask, once again, for a measure of patience. All will be revealed soon. But it does bear repeating: this is a story of lies. Not just the lies we tell one another but the lies we tell ourselves.

And no, this author is not Suzy, the most pitiable of the three Park siblings.

For that, this author is grateful.

# ROSÉ TTEOKBOKKI

The evolution of Korean cuisine was a topic that frequently brought Jia and her mother to a head. Mihyun Song was a purist. To her, Korean food was best left untouched and unspoiled by the influence of other (specifically American) traditions.

"Hamburgers and spaghetti are not culture," Jia's umma would say, curling her upper lip like a cartoon character. "Spaghetti is Italian. Hamburg is a city in Germany. Americans can't even make their own food without stealing from someone else."

"Don't lie, Umma," Jia would tease. "Appa told me how much you craved McDonald's when you were pregnant with us."

"It's because you broke me. You and your brothers broke your umma. You should say you're sorry . . . and buy me a new car. It's the least you can do."

"Why? You're fixed now. Back to hating everything that isn't Korean."

Inevitably, a piece of fruit or a harmless cooking utensil would fly in Jia's direction.

"One day," Umma would threaten, "your mouth won't be able to cash those checks." Then she would pause. "And don't correct your mom. You know what I mean."

Jia smiled to herself as she surveyed the collection of ingredients assembled on the pale quartz countertop of her Williamsburg apartment. Tonight she was preparing a meal that would cause her umma endless grief.

Rosé tteokbokki. A hybrid of Korean street food and the richest kind of Italian pasta. Chewy cylindrical rice cakes simmered in a thick sauce of Korean red pepper paste, cream, and shallots, then topped with sausage and steamed broccoli and finished with slices of Kraft American cheese. It had recently become Jia's favorite comfort food, and she was ready to share its glory with the two women who had been her best friends since childhood, when they all lived in the same run-down apartment complex in Queens.

"Cream?" Nidhi lifted the cardboard container and sent Jia a quizzical glance, her straight dark bangs falling to one side of her face. "In tteokbokki?" She stressed the wrong syllable, speaking the word with an inflection reminiscent of Hindi. Her mispronunciation, as always, comforted Jia, just like it did when Elisa insisted on saying "ahnyonghasaeyo" and bowing every time she greeted Umma, in what could only be classified as a stylish butchery of the Korean language.

Jia suspected the rush of comfort flowing through her veins had everything to do with the deep love she felt for her dearest friends. She could never mock them for their mistakes, especially considering her own insecurities. Who was Jia to criticize? Elisa spoke Spanish, English, and French fluently, and Nidhi switched back and forth between Hindi and Marathi with ease. Even if someone were to offer Jia a ticket of winning lottery numbers, she still couldn't roll her *r*'s when she ordered tostones rellenos, any more than she could tell you what kind of sorcery went into the making of a dosa as large as a side table.

"Don't look so suspicious," Jia said to Nidhi as she grabbed a large metal bowl from under her sink and dumped the bag of frozen rice cakes into it. "When have I ever led you astray?" She covered the rice cakes with water to help them thaw.

Elisa scrunched her gamine features. "All the time," she replied, her sweet voice incongruous with her murderous stare. "Remember when you made us eat those fire noodles? That chicken thing?"

"Buldak. The buldak ramyun." Nidhi groaned and then shuddered.

"Pour one out for my culo," Elisa said. "It was on fire for a week."

"You just need to get used to spicy things," Jia insisted as she began chopping up a shallot.

"I'm Indian." Nidhi arched a brow. "I can do spicy. Those noodles are an offering to a dark god."

Elisa pursed her lips. "Coño, Jia, we've been friends for twenty years. How much more of this shit—literal shit—do we need to take?"

Jia cut into a head of broccoli to arrange some florets for steaming. "Look, the whole reason I'm making this dish is so I can apologize for the fire noodles. Cream mixed with the gochujang makes the dish less spicy. It's the perfect combination of Korean and Italian food. I promise you'll love it."

Using a spoonful of soup soy sauce, she seasoned the mixture of cream and gochujang simmering in a pot on the stove. Elisa peered over her shoulder, her glass of rosé tilting perilously above the gas range. She sniffed. "It does smell good."

"Wait until I add the American cheese," Jia said. "It's wrong how right it tastes. I'm going to throw in some Parmesan, too."

Nidhi snickered from her perch at the small bar. "Have you made this for your mom? I'm always fascinated that the same person who adores Spam with Umma's level of passion can possess such a hatred for Kraft Singles."

"You should have heard her." Jia poured the soaked and strained rice cakes into the bubbling sauce. "It was performance art. 'Everything is ruined,'" she imitated in her mother's lightly accented English. "'Your generation ruins everything. First it was all the sugar in the naengmyon and now it's chemical cheese in our tteokbokki.'"

Elisa stuck a spoon in the sauce to steal a taste. "Mmm." She bobbed her head of short Audrey Hepburn hair from side to side. "Koreans are amazing. Whoever came up with this is brilliant. A spicy, creamy, savory sauce over rice cakes and sausage? Heaven."

"A drunk person came up with the idea," Nidhi said. "It looks like the kind of drunk food you both love."

Jia smirked. "Grab a bowl and some kimchi. As soon as I throw in the broccoli, it's game on."

"And then will you *finally* let us weigh in on this Parks of Park Avenue drama?" Elisa said. "I have been waiting all day!"

Jia reached for her own glass of rosé. "After that clown car of a morning, let me have a drink." She took a sip. "Okay. Lay it on me, the way only a gossipmonger like you can."

"I can't believe you had to google them." Elisa rolled her eyes. "You're the worst Korean. Not only are the Parks one of the richest Korean families in Manhattan, they are basically royalty. Sora is on the short list for the next Met Gala, and Suzy escorted the cast of that Oscar-winning movie all over the city last fall."

"Even I knew that one." Nidhi sipped her tonic and lime.

"I mean, I knew they were important," Jia said. "I buy stuff on Mirae's website all the time. As soon as I saw the logo, I made the connection. I just never bothered to learn about the family who owned it." She topped the rosé tteokbokki with the steamed broccoli and waited for the rice cakes and sausage to finish cooking. "Plus"—she shrugged—"I try not to pay too much attention to Korean society here. It's like the wealth Olympics, a bunch of poncy Seoulites trying to outdo each other over Macallan 18 and A5 Wagyu from Kagoshima Prefecture or whatever."

Elisa waved off her protests. "That's wealth no matter where you go. And don't lie. Anyone who treats Hermès like a religion is absolutely invested in the wealth Olympics. You're a pendeja if you say otherwise." She laughed. "The worst kind of hypocrite."

Jia felt a spike of irritation. When they were children, Elisa's brutal honesty had caused disagreements with Jia on more than one occasion. They had even gone a whole three months without talking the summer following eighth grade. It was Nidhi's tearful plea that brought them together four days before their freshman year of high school.

Once again, Jia's mind drifted to Suzy and Sora. How it must have felt to be called a hypocrite and a bitch by your own twin. Elisa would probably delight in Suzy Park's company, at least for a time. There was something similar in the way they both commanded a room. But Elisa would soon realize—just as Jia had—that it would be difficult to maintain a friendship with the younger Park twin. Elisa would never tolerate the hint of cruelty that lurked behind Suzy's smile. It wouldn't matter to her that there was a deep well of pain at its heart. Elisa would see, just as Jia did, that Suzy knew she was being cruel. Knew it and didn't care, as long as someone was sharing in her pain.

Elisa Perez was direct, but she was never, ever cruel. She'd known cruelty, and to her it was an unforgivable offense.

"Maybe I did know more about the Parks of Park Avenue than I cared to admit," Jia confessed, her back to her friends while she prepared three bowls of tteokbokki. "But I wasn't sure about any of the rumors, especially since I heard it seventh-hand from some cousin's friend's sister or whatever." She grated fresh Parmesan on top of each serving and took care to wipe the edges of the bowls with a damp paper towel. Ever since Jia was a child, she'd held a firm belief in the full sensory experience of a good meal.

When Jia turned around—a trio of bowls balanced in her hands—she stopped short. In the center of the table was a small cake. Her favorite one from Milk Bar.

Elisa lit the single candle positioned amid the colorful sprinkles.

Heat flooded Jia's cheeks. "I told you not to. You know I hate making a big deal out of stuff like this."

"No one cares what you think." Elisa winked.

Nidhi pulled out the chair closest to the cake. "Besides, how could we just ignore you making partner?" She shooed Jia into the seat and then helped pass around the food.

Jia groaned. "You know my parents messed me up about stuff like this."

"All our parents messed us up in some way or another," Nidhi said.

"My parents threw a dance party every time I lost a tooth, and I'm still a mess." Elisa sat down at the small table running parallel to the breakfast bar and blew on a steaming bite of tteokbokki. "You made partner, dude. We're celebrating it. End of story."

"*Junior* partner," Jia corrected, then blew out the candle.

Elisa paused, her chopsticks a hairsbreadth from her mouth. "What the fuck?" She leaned back in her chair, outraged. "*Junior* partner? That's it. Give me back the cake. I refuse to celebrate such mediocrity."

Jia rolled her eyes. "Fine. Fine. I'll stop."

"In all seriousness though, it's time you got over this, Jia," Nidhi interjected. "You can't argue with us every time we want to celebrate you. It's getting old."

"Old habits die hard." Jia stuffed a piping-hot rice cake into her mouth.

"Plus," Elisa said midchew, "I am so over any woman trying to minimize herself or her achievements. It reeks of the patriarchy." She waved around her chopsticks. "Who proclaimed that in order for us to succeed we literally need to take up less space? I'll tell you who: *men*. Fuck that. I won't buy into it, and neither should you. I'm going to take up all the space. It's my life's mission." Elisa stabbed a rice cake and bit into it with gusto. "This is damn good, by the way. You're forgiven for burning my culo with fire noodles."

Jia had read somewhere that every person was basically an amalgamation of the five people they spent the most time with. If that was true, Jia at least had that part of her life handled . . . more or less.

The part about knowing herself and being comfortable in her own skin?

On that score, there was still a fair amount of work to be done.

Jia chose to change the subject. "By the way, have you heard anything through the grapevine about Seven or Jenny Park?" She tried to pose the question to Elisa as nonchalantly as possible.

"Why do you ask?" Elisa's nostrils flared. "Start by telling me everything you know."

"You're a bloodhound," Jia said.

"Claro." Elisa held up both hands on either side of her head. "It's why I'm good at my job."

Jia swallowed another bite before replying. "You know I can't give you any specifics. It's all privileged information." She sent Elisa a pointed look. "Furthermore, I *especially* can't give a gossip columnist any details."

"Furthermore?" Elisa teased. "No one uses that word outside of legal briefs. And don't worry; I'll pry the truth out of you somehow."

"You know she's never going to leave you alone about this," Nidhi said. "It's almost like you want her to make you spill the beans. Like you're begging her to. Stop this, or you'll regret it." She pushed back from the breakfast bar, making her way to the electric kettle on the kitchen countertop.

Nidhi Maheshwari had served as the trio's personal Jiminy Cricket for the better part of twenty-five years. The only child of a hardworking single father, Nidhi's tolerance for bullshit was as high as it was wide. She was patience personified, as evinced by the countless times she'd waited in line for hours to purchase the newest drop of limited editions coveted by sneakerheads the world over. Unlike Elisa, Nidhi would make sure Jia was done with her excuses before dressing her down in under twenty syllables. No curse words. No embellishments. Just truth.

"I told you about the Park family because it's information a doorman or anyone loitering in the lobby might know." Jia stared Elisa down from across the table. "Don't press me on this, E. But I could use any information you could provide."

"No quid pro quo, eh?" Elisa crossed her arms and crooked a brow.

Jia sipped her wine. "Nope."

"But you'll feed me whenever I ask."

After a moment of teasing consideration, Jia nodded.

Elisa *hmph*ed. "For at least three months."

Nidhi rummaged through Jia's cabinets. "Since when did you start trying to make deals? I thought strong-arming was your method of choice."

"I don't know," Elisa replied with a grin. "Dealmaking always seems to work for you, so I'm giving it a try."

"But I'm not nearly so transparent. Never start by asking for something you really want. Always be willing to lose the first negotiation, so that when you win what you truly desire, it seems only fair," Nidhi intoned with ease, her years of experience as a New York City real estate agent coming to the fore. "Jia, where are your cardamom pods? They're not in the spice drawer."

"I think . . . I might have left them beside the tea filters." Jia turned back toward Elisa. "Well? Did you hear anything interesting about Seven or Jenny?"

"I know that Jenny Park hasn't been seen in public for at least a year or so. The rumor mill saw her leaving a plastic surgery clinic around then, heavily bandaged. Maybe she had a botched surgery? Are they suing the doctor? Is she horribly disfigured?" She leaned back, her expression filled with dismay. "Coño, did she *die*? Is it a negligent homicide kind of thing?"

Jia shook her head. These rumors made sense given the fact that Jenny Park had undergone reconstructive surgery following her double mastectomy. "She's not dead. Chill out."

"Why is it important for you to know what's going on with Jenny Park?" Nidhi asked.

“Right now, it’s important for me to have as much information as possible about all of them,” Jia said.

“Then you should speak to her privately,” Elisa said.

Jia tilted her head thoughtfully. “I have to admit, I’ve already been thinking about doing just that. If she’s open to it.”

“What’s with that look?” Nidhi asked. “Like you’re not telling us something scandalous, despite the fact that you desperately want to.”

“I can’t hide anything from you, Nids.” Jia sighed. “It’s why I knew I could never be a trial attorney.”

Nidhi stood to stir the small pot of tea leaves and spices boiling on the stove, the scent of cloves and cardamom and cinnamon suffusing the air. “You’re also a terrible liar, which presents you with an even bigger challenge. After all, *lawyer* and *liar* are the samc word. Just spelled differently.”

“I’m not a bad liar,” Jia said. “I just don’t like to lie unless it’s absolutely necessary.”

“And what constitutes necessary?” Nidhi asked.

Jia exhaled. “That’s the million-dollar question, isn’t it?”

“Billion-dollar, in the case of the Park family,” Elisa added.

“I guess I . . .” Jia hesitated, wondering how to avoid divulging any privileged information. “I’m worried Jenny Park won’t want to speak candidly with me, especially considering how reclusive she’s been the last few months. And I’m pretty sure I need to talk to her.” Another hard truth. If Jenny Park wasn’t willing to cooperate, the entire venture could prove to be a waste of WhitVo’s time and resources.

“Will her kids help? If so, take one of them with you,” Nidhi suggested. “I would assume she’d be willing to listen to her kids, if not to you.”

Jia nodded. “It’s not a bad idea.” If she asked Suzy for help, it would be a chance to glean more information from both Suzy and Jenny Park, in one fell swoop.

Nidhi began slowly stirring milk and honey into the tea. The smell of hot chai wafted to the ceiling, causing both Elisa and Jia to take deep breaths at the same time.

“Chai would be perfect with tteokbokki,” Jia mused. “Let’s all quit our jobs and start a restaurant.”

Nidhi hummed in agreement as she poured them each a cup. "Is there a time when chai isn't perfect though?"

"*That* is the billion-dollar question." Elisa laughed. "God, that smells good."

"Speaking of smells," Nidhi began in an innocent tone. "Was that Davidoff Cool Water I smelled in your bathroom, J? I thought you agreed to quit that annoying habit."

"Average Dick?" Elisa gasped like an actor from a black-and-white film. "You banged Average Dick again? J'accuse!"

Jia groaned. "Richard doesn't wear Davidoff Cool Water. Don't be an asshole."

"Only if you stop being an idiot." Nidhi sipped her tea. "You'll never try dating again if you keep turning to Richard whenever you get an itch you can't scratch."

"He's not even a good fuck buddy," Elisa said as she stirred her chai with renewed vigor. "Can you at least find someone fun?"

"Let's talk about something else." Jia groaned again. "We have more important things to discuss than guys, and I'm not in the mood to dissect—for the eleventy-billionth time—why my one and only meaningful relationship messed me up for life."

"Zain was an aberration," Elisa said.

Nidhi nodded. "An alien species."

"From the distant planet known as Peril," Elisa finished.

"I do love you both." Jia took another sip of tea.

"Ditto," they chimed in unison.

# GOLD ON GOLD

Jia's phone blared to life at 7:08 the next morning, squawking with unforgivable glee for so early on a Saturday.

"Anka?" Jia croaked through bleary half sleep.

"Jia?" Nervousness tinged the Hermès SA's voice. "Did I wake you?"

"Yeah." Jia cleared her throat. "But it's all right. What's going on?"

"I'm so sorry to call this early, but I wanted to catch you before you made plans for the day."

Jia rubbed her eyes. "Sure."

"I have . . . not-so-great news." Anka's Polish accent became more pronounced, which was a sure indication of discomfort. Like the time Jia's cousins from Seoul wandered into Anka's boutique on a whim, only to become irate once they were told they could not, in fact, purchase a quota bag on the spot.

Jia sat up. Today was the day she was supposed to pick up her Birkin. The bag she'd been dreaming about since she was fourteen. The symbol she'd hinged her life upon. "What happened?" she deadpanned. "Is it the wrong size?"

"No." Anka leaned into the word, letting it resonate. "But I must start by apologizing. The information I received about this shipment was incorrect." Jia could sense Anka's hand-wringing, even through the phone. "It was my mistake to call you before confirming anything, I was just so excited. You've been working with me for so many years. I thought I had finally found your bag."

Jia took a deep breath. "It's okay, Anka. Just tell me what happened. Is it not gold on gold? Is the hardware palladium?"

"It's gold on gold. It's just not Barenia Faubourg leather. It's Togo."

Silence filled Jia's end of the phone for a moment. "I knew it was too good to be true," she murmured. "I fucking knew it. What are the chances that I would make junior partner and get my dream bag all within twenty-four hours?"

"I know it's not the right leather." Anka began picking up the pace of the conversation. "But everything else is exactly what you wanted. The size, the hardware, and the color. It's simply stunning. Would you like to come in and at least take a look?"

"No," Jia answered without hesitation. "If it's not Barenia leather, I'm not interested."

"Maybe we could—"

"Nothing smells like Barenia, Anka. You and I both know it."

Anka sighed. "I know. I'm sorry. Truly."

Air flew from Jia's lips in a rush. "I shouldn't be so disappointed. It's just a bag, in the grand scheme of things."

"This isn't just a bag. It's a *Birkin*."

"Oh, I know. Believe me." Jia's laughter was dark.

"I won't stop trying to make it happen for you, Jia," Anka replied, her tone fervent. "You're always at the top of my list. Before the end of the year, we will get your Birkin. Please don't lose faith."

"Don't worry," Jia said. "I won't buy secondhand. I want the champagne. I want the private unboxing under the amber lights. And then I want to watch my Birkin get wrapped up with all the trimmings so I can dance down Madison with it like Gene Kelly in *Singin' in the Rain*."

Anka laughed. "I'll bring the champagne."

"You make it happen for me, and *I'll* bring the champagne. Roederer, because Clicquot is so last season."

The SA's laughter continued. "Then I'll bring the almond croissants. I know how much you love them."

"Deal," Jia said.

"Thank you for being so understanding about this."

"Don't worry. I'll be mad at you tomorrow, when I've had a chance to let it sink in."

Anka laughed again. "I'll be in touch. Have a great weekend."

"You too." Jia waited until the call ended to flop back onto her pillow and stare up at the ceiling. The face of her disappointment was flat and white. Expansive as a snowstorm.

Every opportunity came with a cost. If the cost of working with the Park family meant Jia had to wait longer for her Birkin, then so be it. Later was not the same as never.

Her phone buzzed.

Umma: *Are you coming for dinner tomorrow?*

Jia paused before replying. *It depends on work.*

Three dots blinked and faded, blinked and faded. A sure sign Jia's mom was trying to work out the best way to guilt her only daughter into making an appearance.

*Zain called me last night*, Umma wrote.

Jia sat up. *Why?*

More dots.

*I called him on his birthday. So he called to wish me a happy birthday, too. Isn't that nice?*

One of Jia's eyes twitched. *Your birthday was two weeks ago.*

*He is a nice boy. Maybe you can invite him to come to dinner one night. He said he missed eating at my house.*

Jia closed her eyes. This was so like Zain. Even though they were well and truly done, he couldn't help but remind her of what she'd lost. He'd always been slyly cruel like that; Jia had just realized it too late.

There were so many things she wanted to say to her mother. So many cutting retorts and angry whataboutisms. But it never seemed like Umma heard her in these moments. Any moment when Jia mentioned her feelings, really. So she held her tongue, just as she had with her parents from a very early age. She swallowed. It was getting harder and harder to check her emotions. The sharp pain that stabbed through her body whenever someone mentioned the failure of her first and only significant relationship. Mostly she couldn't shake the feeling that her mother wasn't on her side when it came to Zain. That Umma believed Jia was the reason things hadn't worked out between them.

She remembered one of the last fights she'd had with him, just before they'd ended things for real six months ago. With the cutting precision of a litigator, he'd mocked Jia's Hermès obsession. Called her tacky and materialistic. As if he weren't the one wearing bespoke four-thousand-dollar suits to work and tithing to the church of Rolex. But Zain had never understood Jia. He'd never tried to put himself in the shoes of anyone he considered beneath him.

And he did consider Jia beneath him, despite his statements to the contrary.

Jia first realized this truth the afternoon she overheard Zain rebuke families of limited means who were brazen enough to own a big-screen TV and a satellite dish. He ridiculed them to his law school friends, saying perhaps it was better for "people like that" to save up for their children's college fund rather than have three hundred channels of Cinemax.

His cruelty had struck Jia like an arrow. In the past, she'd enjoyed Zain's pithy observations. His debonair charm managed to cloud her mind in the best of ways. It was like living in a golden haze. When they were together, Jia didn't worry as much. He would wrap her small hand in his large one, and her anxiety wouldn't be so loud. She didn't have to take charge all the time. Zain seemed to know what to say and do in any situation.

But numbness spread across Jia's limbs as she overheard Zain talk about "people like that." All she could think about were the moments in her childhood when her parents would carve out free time from their work at the bodega. Those Sunday nights when her family watched a Korean show together via satellite, huddled up on their couch in front of their secondhand TV, an immense relic of the tube era, complete with a wooden box.

Umma would cut fruit. Appa would drink a cold beer. Sometimes Jia would fight with Jason and James over Pocky sticks or rice candy or which one of them had the larger share of shrimp chips. Other nights, they would chew on ohjinguh in companionable silence and share laughter at the maudlin jokes from a world away.

These were some of Jia's most precious childhood memories. The Song family hadn't had luxuries. Her parents hadn't been able to save in any significant way for their college tuitions.

But to Jia, those memories were priceless.

She'd known then how Zain really felt about her. About where she came from. And who she was.

Later, when they were alone, Jia had told Zain that everyone—no matter their means—deserved something to be excited about. Something to share with their friends and families at the end of a long day. Zain could mock people who didn't possess these little luxuries because large TVs had been a way of life for him. His family's wealth was something he'd been born into.

"People like that," Jia had said, her words barbed, "are all too quick to pass judgment on everyone but themselves."

It had been the beginning of the end for them. That end had sent Jia into an emotional tailspin she was still recovering from.

Jia's phone buzzed again.

Umma: *I'll see you tomorrow.*

With a sigh, Jia wrote: *Okay. Let me know if I can bring anything.*

If Zain knew that Jia was about to begin working on a billion-dollar account that would make her career, he would be as bitter as a dandelion leaf. The competitive side of him would rankle at the very idea.

The thought warmed Jia's veins. Made her grin at the snow-white expanse above her. If she played her cards right, the Park family would set her up for life. The sky would be the limit for her dreams. Gilded armor around every member of the Song family.

Gold on gold forever.

# PEOPLE IN TWO-STORY PENTHOUSES

The doorman wore white gloves. And a hat. On a Sunday afternoon.

Jia had never encountered a doorman with white gloves and a hat.

After spending most of Friday preparing for this meeting with Jenny Park, she'd thought she was ready. But the second she crossed the marble threshold of the Park family's Park Avenue co-op building two days later, Jia knew for certain that she was walking into a different world. It wasn't like Alice falling down a rabbit hole. It was more like stepping through a looking glass. On one side, everything seemed familiar. On the other, it appeared distorted. Unreal.

The floor of the lobby was patterned in alternating tiles of black and white marble, positioned at a diagonal to further distort reality. The air was perfumed by sandalwood and sweet incense. Floral arrangements towered above Jia, their waxen fronds drooping over polished mahogany tables. Hanging from the center of the alcoved ceiling was an art deco chandelier constructed of mirrored crystals arranged like an upside-down wedding cake.

"Good afternoon, Ms. Park," the doorman said as he ushered Suzy through the lobby, which was larger than most Manhattan apartments. He turned to Jia with an expectant gaze. His smile, though pleasant, was edged. As if he knew Jia was nothing more than an interloper, despite her smart suit and beige Gucci pumps.

"Hiya, Anthony." Suzy grinned at the doorman. "How are Gemma and the twins?"

"They just had their sixth birthday party yesterday. Pink everything,"

Anthony replied with a warm smile. "And they really appreciated the gifts. Gemma is making sure they send out their thank-you cards, so expect them soon."

"No thank-yous are necessary." Suzy ignored his protests. "I wanted a pink bicycle when I was their age. It feels good to gift people the things I never had."

Her comment—as well as her generosity—took Jia aback. Forced her to look at Suzy Park with fresh eyes. Jia had almost forgotten that the Park family wasn't always so fabulously wealthy. There was a time in the not-so-distant past when they couldn't buy everything their hearts desired. Seven and Jenny Park had come to New York with very little, just like Jia's parents. Perhaps Jia should stop thinking Suzy Park lived on the other side.

Maybe they were both still trying to see through the same looking glass.

"Did the driver get my packages from the personal shopper at Bergdorf?" Suzy asked Anthony.

Jia stopped her eyes from rolling into the back of her head. In fewer than fifteen words, Suzy Park had managed to erase every trace of her goodwill.

Anthony nodded. "I left them with Darius. Please don't forget to register your guest so that we can avoid any unpleasantness." He gestured toward a young woman seated behind an expansive, leathered granite countertop in the back of the lobby. To her right sat a burgundy book with a golden pen perched on its lined pages.

"Of course, of course." As soon as they were out of Anthony's earshot, Suzy glanced at Jia. "Follow my lead, Columbia." She grinned at the woman behind the counter. "Hiya, Francine. I know I'm supposed to register all my guests, but the girl behind me is . . . hmm . . . how can I put this delicately?" She paused to drum her fingers along the ledge. "We're sleeping together, and I don't really want that information to become anyone else's business, so can we put her down under a pseudonym?" She batted her eyes. "I'd really appreciate it. Didn't you tell me you were a huge fan of David Chang? I bet we can send over a special order from Momofuku this week."

Suzy Park's brazenness shouldn't have shocked Jia. Nevertheless, she stood with her mouth agape for three seconds before snapping her lips shut and nodding at Francine as if everything Suzy had said was the gospel truth.

Francine peered up at Suzy from beneath her mascaraed eyelashes. "You know your father doesn't like it when you do this, Ms. Park. He insisted that I check all the IDs of any penthouse guests and keep an accurate record of their comings and goings."

"Yeah, but my father doesn't live here anymore, now does he?" Suzy rested both her elbows atop the leathered granite. "Momofuku has some excellent noodles, by the way. There are a few off-the-menu items I'm sure David's kitchen would be happy to prepare for you. To die for, I tell you." She slapped her palm against the stone for emphasis.

Francine's voice dropped to a whisper. "I like his spicy noodles the best."

"Me too." Suzy's eyes sparkled. "This is Mabel Maplethorpe, my special friend." She pointed at Jia with her thumb.

"Maplethorpe, with an *e*?" Francine began scribbling on the burgundy pad as she noted the time.

"You're a doll, Francine. I'll be in touch about the noodles." Then Suzy breezed toward the bank of elevators around the corner as if she owned the entire building.

Jia followed in silence. Once the silver doors slid closed, Suzy inserted a key card in a designated slot and pressed the button labeled PH.

"Mabel Maplethorpe?" Jia said.

"I had to choose something that sounded Waspy and boring . . . though I guess it does kind of have a porn star ring to it." Suzy laughed softly. "Regardless, I'd rather shit in my hands than have my father know we've spoken to a lawyer. As soon as he saw your name, his goons would google you, some phone calls would be made, and life would get real." She paused. "I mean, even realer than it is now with the cancer, the lying, and the thievery."

"I understand," Jia said. "I guess I should thank you for not forcing me to lie directly."

"Isn't that like second nature for a lawyer?"

"I'm not a fan of misrepresenting what I do or who I am."

"Straitlaced, huh? Give me a few weeks. We'll change all that. I bet the worst thing you did in college was weed."

In a conversation rife with improprieties, discussing the use of illicit substances with a client seemed especially inappropriate. But Jia knew it was important to earn Suzy's trust. "I may have tried shrooms, too," she admitted. "My roommate might have put them on a pizza while we watched *The Wizard of Oz.*"

"Did you maybe listen to Pink Floyd at the same time?"

"Possibly."

"What happened?"

"It's possible that I puked in my crush's hamper."

Suzy guffawed as the elevator slid to a stop. "I knew I liked you."

The doors purred open, and cool air blew across Jia's face. She tried hard not to react like a kid at Disneyland. The foyer of the Park family's penthouse was two stories high. A crystal-encrusted chandelier the size of a Volkswagen Beetle hung above a round table of smooth concrete and wrought iron. White orchids bloomed from a jade vase, giving off an intoxicating fragrance. A mixture of musk and honey.

Money. Everything smelled like money.

What kind of people had a two-story penthouse in the heart of Manhattan?

The Park family did.

Suzy noticed Jia staring up at the crystal chandelier. "It's vintage Schonbek, from the turn of the century. We flew it in from Prague on the company jet. It was hanging in a castle outside the city for over a hundred years."

"It looks like something from the Beast's castle," Jia murmured.

"As in *Beauty and the Beast?*"

Jia nodded. "Like it could come to life at any second."

"You know," Suzy mused as she glanced around the foyer, "this *is* kind of like the Beast's castle. Seven is Beast, and my mom is Beauty. Or she was." She blew her curtain bangs out of her face. "I don't know. It all kind of went to hell the day Umma cut her hair short and stopped dyeing it because of the chemo." She eyed Jia sidelong. "You know how it is. Korean ladies are ageless for decades, then overnight they become nine-hundred-year-old crones with bubbling cauldrons."

Laughter burst from Jia's mouth. It was too easy to enjoy Suzy Park's company. "Nice. Please pass 'Go' and collect two hundred dollars."

Suzy raised a shoulder, her brown eyes sparkling. "You're my girlfriend for the day. Keep complimenting me, and I'll make a pass at more than 'Go,' Columbia."

A flush crept up Jia's neck. One of the most sacrosanct rules of the legal profession was that a lawyer never—under any circumstances—slept with their client. "Just so we're clear, you know that's not going to happen, right?"

"Calm down. Your La Perlas are safe. You're not my type, and I haven't been with a girl in years. Honestly, you'd have no luck with any of us. Sora is straighter than a ruler, and pussies make Marky tremble in his Italian loafers."

Jia's eyes widened. "I didn't realize he was gay."

"Oh, yeah. It's not really a secret. He's been with the same guy since his sophomore year at Stanford. We don't make a big deal out of it because of our father. He keeps denying that gay is a thing." She shook her head disdainfully. "Keeps trying to set Marky up on dates with the daughters of rich Korean fuckwads."

A string tugged at Jia's heart. Life had not been easy for her favorite Park sibling, of that there could be no doubt. It had taken years for Jia's Catholic parents to see through their own prejudices. They'd had countless arguments around the dinner table, a rare instance when Jia, Jason, and James presented a united front. She could imagine how her parents would have reacted if any of them came out.

The pressure a chaebol family like the Parks placed on their only son must be immense.

"I'm sorry to hear that," Jia said. "It must be difficult for your brother."

"Yeah, it's like a shitty K-drama. Except no one is coming to bribe us with an envelope of money. More like the opposite."

"Actually, I like those kinds of dramas."

"Me too. It's a good break from reality."

Jia caught herself before snickering. She wondered if Suzy Park had any inkling of reality, or if the notion had slipped through her fingers the day she added the third twelve-thousand-dollar Cartier LOVE bracelet to her stack.

Suzy continued, "So, do you want a tour, or should we just go straight to—" Something caught her attention over Jia's right shoulder, and her face spread into a wide smile. "Darius!"

Jia turned as a man in his thirties strolled into the foyer. When he returned Suzy's smile, Jia gripped the handle of her bag. Suzy had mentioned her mother's house manager at their Friday morning meeting. But the person standing before them now was not at all what Jia had pictured.

"It's good to see you, Suzy," Darius said. Suzy threw her arms around him and planted a kiss on both his cheeks. "I'm sorry it took me a while to greet you," he continued in a warm baritone that reminded Jia of sipping whiskey by a fire. "Jenny wanted to have lunch in her sitting room, so I was making sure Celeste had everything they needed." He pivoted Jia's way. "Hi. I'm Darius Rohani, the Park family's house manager." He held out his hand.

Why was Jenny Park's butler not a reedy British man with pasty skin and a sonorous drone? Why was he young, handsome, and dressed in charcoal slacks and a navy T-shirt? Even worse, he reminded Jia of Zain. The same dark eyes, tanned skin, and black hair. The same easy swagger. This wasn't fair.

Jia straightened her shoulders and focused on Darius Rohani's forehead. "My name is Jia Song." She shook his hand, her voice curt. "It's nice to meet you."

Darius's thick brows furrowed, his long eyelashes casting shadows across his cheeks. When he reached to take their coats, the muscles in his forearm flexed, and his cologne drifted over her.

He smelled good. Too good.

"Why do you always smell like a trap, Darius?" Suzy teased as if she'd yanked the thought straight from Jia's head. "What are you wearing?"

"I'm not falling for that, Suzy," he replied without missing a beat. "I've told you before; it's workplace harassment."

"Ew." Suzy wrinkled her nose. "I already said I won't sleep with you. Stop asking."

Darius exhaled, the sound steeped in patience. "I apologize, Ms. Song. Suzy enjoys watching people squirm. She'll stop soon."

A whistle burst from Suzy's lips. "Handled. Look at that. We really don't pay you enough."

"No," Darius agreed. "You don't." He grinned again, and Jia wanted to gnash her teeth. No. Fate would not get the better of her. Not today. Not ever.

No man was going to cloud Jia's mind again.

Besides, there was no way Darius Rohani was single. In fact, he was probably married with three kids. And he worked for Jia's clients, which made him off-limits in all the ways that mattered.

"Would you like a tour of the home, Ms. Song?" Darius asked.

"No," Jia said through a tight smile. "I think we should meet with Mrs. Park now."

"Damn," Suzy said. "You sound pissed."

"I'm not." Jia dropped her shoulders and relaxed her neck. "I'm just ready to get to work."

Suzy shot her a dubious look. "Well, you're shit out of luck, then. Umma knows you're Korean, so she insisted on feeding you. It's her way of showing off. And you can't refuse." She snorted. "But you know that already."

Jia sighed in agreement. "Telling a Korean mother you won't eat her food is like going to war without a weapon."

Darius laughed. Jia forced the knots in her chest to unwind. If she didn't stop behaving like a brat, it was possible Jenny Park would notice, and Jia would rather—as Suzy so eloquently stated—shit in her own hands than have the Park matriarch see her as anything less than a consummate professional.

Darius Rohani hadn't done anything wrong. This was Jia's problem.

She would handle it.

"Do we have any geotjuri left from Friday?" Suzy asked Darius while kicking off her Louboutin boots.

With infinite patience, Darius placed Suzy's shoes inside the nearby coat closet. Jia followed, her Gucci pumps in hand. "I think so," he replied.

"Great." Suzy glided from the foyer. "My mother swears her recipe for geotjuri came to her in a dream," she said to Jia. "It's the best. I want to learn how to make it, but she refuses to teach me or give me the recipe."

"Honestly, she probably doesn't even have it written down," Jia said.

Suzy nodded. "A pinch of this, a taste of that. You know the drill."

"The worst," Jia finished. "The only conclusion I've made is that my mom enjoys seeing me fail in the kitchen. She's touched in the head like that."

Darius's low laughter echoed through the corridor as they walked toward the center of the penthouse. "Do you like to cook?"

"I do," Jia said, meeting his eyes full-on, for the first time. "Unless my mother is in the kitchen with me. Then it's like I'm twelve years old again, ruining the rice for the fourth time."

He nodded in commiseration. "I once set my kitchen on fire trying to make rice."

"It's a great story," Suzy said. "But I treasure any story where Darius fails at something." She glared at him. "Are you going to make that saffron chicken with the pistachios for me again, or am I going to have to threaten you?"

Darius ushered them through the main room, another modest affair with two pristine sofas shaped like pillowy clouds, matching porcelain vases from the Silla dynasty, a lacquered ebony coffee table, and floor-to-ceiling damask drapes extending the full height of the two-story penthouse. "I'll make tachin for your birthday," he said to Suzy.

"That's three months from now!"

When Darius reached for the crystal doorknob to a room off the main living space, his forearm brushed Jia's elbow, the friction causing a small shock.

She gasped in surprise. "I'm sorry—"

He jumped back. "My apologies—"

They locked eyes.

Under no circumstances would Jia look away first.

Darius cleared his throat, his attention fixing on a piece of modern art behind Jia. Her pulse thrummed through her body, hummingbird wings pounding in her ears.

"Hmm." Suzy Park tapped her stockinged foot on the white maple floors, her expression knowing. "I think it's time we all acknowledged the big pink—"

"Suzy, please," Darius interrupted. His voice was stern, like that of an older brother. "Your mother is waiting."

Suzy's mouth hung open, caught between silence and speech. Then she smirked at Jia. "Sure. No problem, Darius the Great." She slithered through the open door, her laughter echoing like a Disney villain.

Jia closed her eyes. She felt exposed. She couldn't even choose anger anymore. Without it, she would be left with nothing but anxiety. That hungry monster she forever struggled to keep at bay. The more she fed it, the bigger it got. The louder it howled.

She opened her eyes. No. She would not feed the monster. Not today.

Darius was just another good-looking guy. Suzy was simply an amusing bully with a bank account. Jenny Park was a wealthy client with a problem to solve.

And Jia was an attorney with all the answers.

# A TESTAMENT OF TEETH

Aside from her constant fear of breaking a piece of priceless art, Jia found herself strangely at ease. She supposed it wasn't great how little effort it took to settle into a penthouse worth north of fifty million dollars. Lunch was an old-school Korean affair: soondubu jigae, a spicy stew of soft tofu crumbled over pork and finished with sliced zucchini and a barely set egg. Jenny Park's recipe for geotjuri was everything Suzy had promised. Fresh cabbage and carrots with just the right crunch of heat. Just the right bite of umami.

Jenny Park spoke fewer than five times over the course of lunch. After asking about Jia's family and education in elegantly accented English, the Park matriarch chose to sit back and listen. Twice, she smiled at Jia during her daughter's animated storytelling, her expression indulgent. During a lull in the conversation, Jia noticed Jenny glance beyond the small tower of books beside her toward the wall of windows overlooking a breathtaking view of the park. Then the older woman's attention caught on a ribbon of light stretching across the pale Kashan rug beneath their feet. She tilted her head of chin-length silver hair. A look of peace settled on her face.

If Jia had to guess, Jenny Park was a bit of a romantic.

As the meal began to wind down, Jia waited for an opportunity to shift the conversation. She needed to know, sooner rather than later, if Jenny Park would change her mind and support her children in challenging their father's divorce settlement.

The housekeeper, Celeste, cleared away the dishes from lunch, and the trio of women moved from the round table beside the balcony toward the middle of the room. With Darius's help, Jenny Park took a seat on an antique sofa of cream-colored silk, her cashmere sweater and trouser set blending into the background as if she'd chosen them for that exact reason.

She looked small amid the surfeit of tasseled pillows. Thin and frail, like a baby bird. Her skin was free of makeup, her eyes warm but tired. The veins in her hands were raised, her lips pale. Jia watched her in silence, wondering who Jenny Park had been in her heyday, before the ravages of breast cancer had leeched the life from her body. Undoubtedly, she'd been beautiful. She was beautiful still, but Jia sensed a dwindling strength, metered out with care. As if Jenny wished to keep it in reserve. As if she knew every breath was on borrowed time.

Just then, the sun struck the wall of windows to Jia's left with a brilliant wash of light. It caramelized everything around them, like they'd crossed into a kind of liminal space between heaven and earth. Not purgatory. But something softer. Sweeter.

Jia gazed around, seeing the room in a literal new light. Along the far wall was a long, low sabangtakja made of scented red pine, paulownia, and brass. The traditional Korean cabinet was lacquered a deep crimson, the smell reminding Jia of a cedar-lined closet.

On the wall above the sabangtakja was a collection of artwork Jia recognized. Her mother had a small print by this artist framed above the fireplace in their family room. It took Jia less than an instant to realize she was in the presence of a signed original.

She studied the work in the golden afternoon glow.

"You enjoy that painting." When Jenny Park spoke, her voice was crisp and clear. "Like me, you are drawn to the work of Hyewon." No-nonsense and to the point. It reminded Jia of her mother, but with a soothing resonance. As if the last word she spoke was the beginning of a song. "May I ask what draws you to a two-hundred-year-old court painting?"

Jia blinked. It was the first unusual question Jenny Park had asked her, and it struck her as a test. She inhaled, taking her time before responding. "I've seen Joseon-era art like this before, but the men always seemed to be the focus. Like the women were drawn for their pleasure alone. In this painting, the women are the focus. They are smiling and joyful, and the men are relegated to the background." She turned back to Jenny Park and raised her right shoulder. "But maybe I'm only seeing what I want to see."

"I see the same thing." She considered Jia, as if the setting sun had cast her in warmer tones as well.

Suzy guffawed. "No wonder Appa hated that painting. What a dick."

"Park Sujin," Jenny Park scolded. "He is your father."

"He can be my father and still be a dick," Suzy retorted.

"Don't act embarrassing, please." Jenny Park took the tea Celeste offered her with a grateful nod.

Suzy pursed her lips. "Look, Umma, you need to start telling it like it is, especially around Jia. She's our lawyer. She knows what Appa did. It's okay to be pissed about it and vent. Seven Park is a selfish, cheating asshole. There. I said it. I'll never understand why you keep protecting him."

The first sign of consternation marred Jenny Park's brow. "I am not protecting him."

"Well, then, stop protecting us! We aren't children anymore. It's okay for us to realize our parents aren't perfect. Healthy, even. My therapist says it's unburdening for everyone."

Jenny Park sighed. She looked at Jia again. "Sometimes it is hard to realize your children grew up with a different mentality. This is a very Western notion—the idea that we should be able to say whatever we want to free ourselves from our burdens."

Suzy wilted into the cushions on the silk couch and glowered at the box-beamed ceiling. "Here we go again. Umma, talking openly about difficult shit isn't about trying to free myself from a burden. We're making sure you're not screwed out of what you're rightfully owed. What Appa is doing is wrong. Period. Please understand that it's not 'Western'"—she made air quotes—"of us to want to fight back. To want justice."

With a grimace, Jenny sipped her tea. Jia noticed that her bottom teeth were at odds with the perfect porcelain veneers on top. The lower ones were a bit crooked. A tad discolored. Again, she was struck by how much Jenny Park reminded her of her mother. They were both around the same age. They'd both grown up in a postwar Korea with limited dental care. In recent years, Jia's umma had been plagued by issues with her teeth.

Last year, Jia had paid more than eight thousand dollars for two dental implants for her mother.

Their parents' teeth had become weathered testaments to their lives. For Jia's mother, her receding gums no longer held fast to their roots. For Suzy's mother, half her smile was engineered to be perfect, the other relegated to a shadowy past.

Jenny Park put down her small celadon teacup. "Sujin-ah, you should wait until your mom finishes speaking before you talk. Your impatience is something you need to work on."

Suzy's eyes fluttered shut for a beat. "God, this makes me so freaking tired. Jia, will you please say something?"

The Korean part of Jia wished to defer to her elder. Wished to grant Jenny Park leave to finish her lecture. But the American attorney in Jia knew Suzy had offered her a perfect opportunity to execute her sales pitch. "Mrs. Park," Jia began.

"Please call me Jenny."

Jia shifted uncomfortably in her seat. She wasn't used to addressing Korean women her mother's age by their given names. "Of course," she replied, her tone hesitant.

Jenny folded her hands on her lap. "Do you have a Korean name, Jia?"

Another test. Jia shuddered to think how the afternoon might have transpired if she weren't afforded the benefit of the doubt that came with their shared heritage. In fact, she suspected that another lawyer would never have been granted the opportunity to meet in private with the matriarch of the Park family.

"Song Jihae hago hamnyida." Jia bowed her head, introducing herself in formal Korean.

Jenny Park bowed in return and spoke to Jia in Korean for the first time. "It is a privilege to make your acquaintance," she said in the highest level of jondaemal, which immediately sent a frisson of anxiety through Jia's body. "I am not sure that you will change my mind on this matter, but I promised my daughter I would hear what you have to say," she finished in English.

Jia thought quickly. It was clear her planned pitch—to speak to Whitman

Volker's effectiveness at client advocacy, to cite her own success rates in negotiations, to tout the numerous large accounts and the various skilled personnel the firm kept on retainer, and on and on and on—was not going to work on a middle-aged Korean woman suffering from terminal breast cancer, who harbored an appreciation for feminist artwork from the Joseon dynasty.

Jia shifted tack. "When I was a child," she said, "my mother loved to tell everyone how stubborn I was. How I wouldn't stop arguing or fidgeting with a toy or a puzzle until it was perfect. How I talked back all the time. It used to embarrass me, and I remember being angry at her for it. I thought she was always criticizing me. But, actually, I think she told people because she was proud of me. Even if it meant I was a difficult child, there was some part of her that knew this trait would serve me well."

Jenny listened. Reached again for her cup of tea. "Stubbornness is not always a bad thing," she agreed. "As long as one has the time for it." Her expression darkened.

Jia nodded. "Time is without a doubt a luxury."

"I'm sure you can understand why I do not wish for my remaining time to be spent in anger, fighting over numbers and . . . *things*," Jenny said.

"Umma, you don't have to do it." Exasperation sharpened Suzy's tone. "Jia will do it for you. That's what we are trying to say. For the love of God, just *try*. It is gutting us that you won't even try. That you would let Appa do this to you and just—" Angry tears began to stream down her face.

"Already you are becoming emotional, and we haven't even begun," Jenny said to her daughter. "This is not good for any of us."

"I'm just telling you how I feel," Suzy cried. "How we all feel!"

"I understand," Jenny said. "There are many times I want to say how I feel, too." She gazed at Suzy with no small amount of sympathy. "I, too, feel deep anger and deep shame, Sujin-ah. I, too, want to yell at people and demand they hear what I have to say. But I need you to listen. Please. Take my advice."

"God, no more lectures." Suzy swiped at her cheeks. "Jia, help me."

Jenny looked at Jia. "I think this is something you should hear, too, Song Jihae."

Jia nodded. "Of course."

Jenny winced again and adjusted her position on the couch. "Here in America, you are taught that your body and soul are two different things. That one is a mere vessel for the other. In Buddhism, we believe that our bodies and hearts and minds are one single essence." She held up her index finger and paused to take a halting breath, the toll of the afternoon becoming more apparent with each passing minute. "If we take in joy, we become joy. If we consume anger, we become anger. If we sit with pain, it becomes indistinguishable from who we are in truth."

"Umma, *we get it*. You don't want us to become hateful." Suzy yanked at the sleeves of her oversize button-down shirt. "Let us at least try to find out what Appa did, and I swear I'll let it go. You always say you'd do anything for your kids. If that's true, then please let us try."

"What if we gave ourselves a time limit?" Jia asked, the idea forming as she spoke. Ben Volker would disapprove of her suggestion. As would any attorney trying to maximize their potential billable hours. Especially one trying to make senior partner next year. But if Jia failed to get a foot in the door, she wouldn't even have the chance to prove her mettle.

Jenny inhaled. But she did not object.

Suzy slid to the edge of her seat. "That's a great idea. Yeah. That way you would be reassured that this wouldn't get dragged out forever. I love that. Sora and Marky would love it, too." She backhanded Jia's knee. "Nice, Columbia. Putting a client's needs before the almighty dollar."

Jenny reached for her tea again. "You are sure your brother and sister are willing to work together with you and not argue?"

Suzy's eyes widened. "Absolutely. We are totally on the same page. This is literally the first thing we've agreed on in years, aside from our collective desire to punch Appa in the dick."

"You spoke with your unyee?" Jenny asked, her brows raised. "Sora talked to you?"

Suzy nodded so hard Jia worried her head would fall off. "Tell her." She grabbed Jia's wrist. "Tell her that we were all at the meeting, and that we want the same outcome. That we're working together to make sense of everything."

Suzy's wording reminded Jia of the night her grandfather died. When he'd said something similar about her place in her own family.

That Jia Song was destined to make sense of this mess.

Jia steeled her spine and faced Jenny Park. "What your daughter says is accurate. All three of your children are united when it comes to moving forward." Then . . . she told a lie. A small white one. Even so, it brought a bitter taste to her tongue. "Moreover, they *want* to work together. Not all family members in these situations are like-minded, and it's often to their own detriment. I believe Sora, Suzy, and Minsoo presenting a united front will ultimately produce a favorable outcome for us."

It was wrong to lie. Jia realized that. Especially to a woman who had mere months to live. But Jia knew what Jenny Park needed to hear. The words and thoughts she craved. The hope that her family would be better, not worse, for her decision to fight her soon-to-be ex-husband's duplicity.

Jenny Park glanced from Suzy to Jia. One minute passed. Suzy was ready to bounce out of her seat, so Jia placed a light touch on her elbow.

*Wait*, she wanted to say. *Just wait.*

"Han dahl," Jenny murmured. "No more than thirty days. That is all the time and energy I am willing to give."

The moment Suzy began to cheer, Jenny eyed her sidelong. "If I learn that you are arguing with your brother and sister, I will not support this any longer."

"Fuck yes," Suzy crowed, both her hands lifted to the ceiling.

"Park Sujin!" Jenny raised her voice for the first time, her eyes flashing. "You know how much Umma hates that word."

"Sorry, sorry." Suzy wriggled her fingers and stretched them in front of her like she was a pianist about to perform a piece by Chopin. Then she turned to Jia. "All right, so the first thing I think you should do is speak to Darius."

Jia resisted the urge to frown. "Why?"

"I told you, remember?" Suzy's words faded to a whisper, her eyes shifting from side to side. "Some of our help is in on it. I think my dad has paid them to keep tabs on us. Darius will be able to give us the inside scoop. And don't worry about trusting him. We literally trust him with our mother's life."

Jenny exhaled. It was as if the last bit of energy in her body was leaving her in a single breath. She leaned into the cushions on her right, her thin, cashmere-covered legs coming to rest beside her. Then she propped her head in her hand and closed her eyes.

"You know I'm right, Umma," Suzy continued in hushed tones. "Like, why did Orlagh leave all of a sudden after being our chef for over ten years? She loved you. I think Appa said something to her. Maybe even threatened her. And what about Svetlana?" She made a face. "Appa paid for her to relocate to the Caymans after I confronted her about what she was doing with the mail that day."

Jia began writing. "Do we know where Orlagh is now?"

"She returned to Edinburgh to take care of her daughter, who recently had her first baby," Jenny replied quietly.

"And is Svetlana still in your father's employ?" Jia asked.

Suzy's face twisted. "I'm not sure, honestly, I haven't been to the islands since last Christmas. But I wouldn't be surprised to hear that Svetlana is running that whole house. My father's whore, Ani, was living there rent-free until last month."

"May I ask where they are now?" Jia kept her voice even.

"Ani and my father are probably in our Paris apartment in Le Marais." Suzy shrugged. "But they'll need to come back to New York soon."

"Why?" When she didn't receive an immediate answer, Jia glanced up from her notes. Suzy's cheeks were red, her eyes imploring, which meant she had made a mistake.

That she had shared something . . . embarrassing.

What the hell could embarrass Suzy Park?

"I think this is a great start," Jia said quickly. Jenny Park had gone through more than enough for a single afternoon. "In the near future," Jia said to Suzy, "it would be great if you could put us in touch with any pertinent financial advisers. Our office will have a forensic accountant begin sorting through everything."

Jenny sighed. "Then you will want to speak with my husband's older sister in Kangnam. She has managed my finances for decades."

"Don't worry," Suzy interjected. "Como is one of my mother's dearest friends. She has no love for my father. But Como won't talk to you about this over the phone or email. With everything that's happened, we've all become a bit paranoid. You'll have to go to Korea." She brightened. "Just let me know when you want to go, and I'll make all the arrangements. Have you ever flown on a G6?"

"I can't say that I have," Jia said.

"I'll clear my schedule so I can go with you. But first, let's arrange a time for you to talk to Darius. Like, tomorrow, if possible."

Jia knew she should feel pleased by this turn of events. After all, she'd managed to convince Jenny Park to alter her course of inaction. But instead, she felt uneasy, as if she'd taken a step down an unlit path with no end in sight.

She chastened herself. It was only natural for her to feel unnerved. A mere thirty days to win over the Park family while uncovering years of financial subterfuge? But she'd always relished a challenge. And this was sure to be one for the ages.

Many things still did not make sense, and it was becoming clearer with each interaction that the Park family traded in dark secrets, even among themselves. Why would Seven Park and his paramour need to return to New York soon? What could have caused Suzy Park that sudden flush of embarrassment?

The wheels in Jia's mind began turning, the rhythm soothing. Familiar. This was another puzzle for her to solve. One with many moving pieces.

A handsome butler. A chef in Edinburgh. A turncoat in the Caymans. A whore in Paris. A sister-in-law in Seoul.

Nothing about the Park family was ordinary. But Jia suspected this journey through the extraordinary would not be meant for the pages of *Architectural Digest* or *Forbes.*

It would be a set of shining teeth, its sharpened fangs glittering in the shadows.

# ET TU, BRUTE?

A word to the wise: Private jets and exotic locales are well and good. But, lest we forget, this is not a simple story of beautiful excess. Nor is it a fairy tale with an obligatory happy ending.

Treachery is afoot.

And it lurks just outside the door, a hand on the crystal doorknob.

Always listening.

# THE CORNER OF FIFTY-EIGHTH AND FIFTH

## *T Minus 28 Days*

Jia had a love/hate relationship with Bergdorf Goodman.

She loved the history of it, the tale of an immigrant from Alsace partnering with a Jewish merchant on the cusp of the twentieth century. How one of its first locations would eventually become Rockefeller Center. The beaux arts style of its flagship store—constructed on the site of Cornelius Vanderbilt's former residence—never failed to captivate her. It wasn't merely beautiful. Its lines and angles and its iron balustrades and deep cornices hearkened to a different time. Its own peculiar kind of excess.

So why did Jia also hate it? She appreciated the finer things in life and understood that they often came with an inaccessible price tag and a fair amount of pretentiousness. Those were accepted facts. Her Hermès obsession proved they were far from deal-breakers. Why, then, did she never shop at Bergdorf's? Why did the very idea of it set her teeth on edge?

Maybe it was the ladies-who-lunch crowd, picking at their forty-dollar Gotham salads. Maybe it was the puffy-lipped sales associates with their disapproving frowns. Maybe it was the fact that she never felt at ease within its scented, amber-lit walls. As if the bas-relief panels themselves had judged her and found her wanting.

Or maybe Jia was just an asshole. The worst kind of hypocrite, as Elisa had joked.

Whatever the reason, Jia knew today wouldn't go well. She'd known it the second she received this text from Suzy Park:

*Meet Darius at 2pm today on the corner of 58th and 5th*

Of course they were meeting at Bergdorf's.

But, like, why? Couldn't they meet at a coffee shop? Or link up for a light lunch, in the most nonromantic setting she could find? A shawarma beside the Seventh Avenue station. A pretzel with mustard on the Lower East Side. An H&H bagel, even. She didn't care if it made her sound like a Zagat-waving tourist; their whitefish had stolen her heart the day it first graced her lips. Plus . . . there was no chance she would fantasize about doing anything romantic after eating smoked fish spread.

Not that she would ever think about Darius Rohani like that.

Jia tapped her foot against the sidewalk and tilted her head toward the sky. The edge of her Ray-Bans cut across her vision, splitting the world before her in two, half a hazy green patina, half a wash of caramel.

Her annoyance continued to spike.

Why couldn't they have met at her office? The fancy one with the river table and the glass walls?

As Jia had suspected, Suzy Park was going to be a massive PITA. But, for a thousand bucks an hour, Suzy got what she wanted. And Suzy wanted Jia to meet with Darius not a second later than now.

Now meant Bergdorf Goodman.

Jia continued waiting on the corner, her Moncler puffer jacket slung across her forearm and her ivory sweater clinging to her skin in a sticky, less-than-appealing way. Early spring in New York was a fickle fucker. Layers were a choice made from necessity.

Jia checked her watch, a Cartier Tank Française gifted by her family the day she graduated law school. Both her brothers had pointed out, on countless occasions, that their participation in said gift was not voluntary. Whenever her younger brother Jason's gaze snagged on the watch, he would cringe before complaining about how much ramen he had to eat so that he could contribute to it.

His complaints didn't dissuade Jia from wearing the watch in his presence. They only made her want to wear it more. Especially since it became clear early on that Jason considered the watch a down payment on free legal advice . . . for the rest of his life. Now, that jashik thought it was okay to send Jia anything he needed to sign, often giving her twenty minutes to weigh in. One time, he actually sent Jia his gym membership paperwork, certain that the second paragraph in section A, clause 3, had to be legally unenforceable.

Men.

2:06 p.m.

Darius Rohani was six minutes late.

Jia brightened at the thought. Maybe he wouldn't show up. Then she could delay this dreaded chat for another day. Spending a sunny spring afternoon with him at Bergdorf's was the last thing she wanted to do. In fact, she'd prefer working with Never Late Nate on the Anderson brief. Followed by a simple root canal. Then maybe she could—

"Hello there." Darius sauntered up from her left. A light gust of wind—worthy of a rom-com movie reel—tousled his wavy black hair and caused the hem of his button-down shirt to billow away from his body, revealing the taut lines of tanned muscle along his stomach.

"You're sex minutes late," Jia blurted.

Darius's thick eyebrows shot up. A grin toyed at the edges of his mouth, accentuating the angles of his perfect five-o'clock shadow. "You want to try that again?"

"Nope." Jia's ears went hot. "Why are you late?"

He shrugged. "Persian."

"Is that a thing?"

Amusement flared in his brown eyes, the color reminding Jia of her favorite chocolate chip walnut cookies at Levain. "When my cousin got married in Seattle," Darius said, "his bride was three hours late to the wedding. All the other guests were freaking out, and all the Persians were sitting around drinking tea and telling jokes." He smiled. "Trust me. Sex minutes late is nothing."

Jia smothered a grin. Curt and testy was her attitude du jour. At least she could make sure Darius didn't like her. Because he was entirely too likable for his own good. "I suppose it doesn't bother your employer that you're chronically tardy."

"I'm sure it does. I just make up for it in other ways. Like today."

She snorted, the sound caustic. "Yeah, having to meet their attorney to help prepare for a multimillion-dollar lawsuit definitely wasn't in the initial job description."

He raised his hands in surrender. "Look, I can tell I've pissed you off. Behbakhsheed. I'll try not to be late next time, but no promises. Can we start over?"

Jia huffed. Looked away. Then sighed. Why couldn't he just be a dick back to her? "Yeah. Okay."

"Great." He nodded with another grin. "Let's go. We have a fashion show to attend."

# L'AMOUR EST UN OISEAU REBELLE

*T Minus 28 Days*

A fashion show? Was Darius Rohani serious?

Because Jia Song wanted to be serious. She was supposed to be asking probing questions. Digging beneath the seething surface of the Park family. Trying to understand the whos, the whys, the wheres, the whats, and the hows. Moving heaven and earth to arm Whitman Volker with the tools to track down hundreds of millions of dollars in hidden bank accounts. All with the end goal of making Seven Park, quite literally, pay for what he'd done.

Instead, Jia sat on the edge of a wingback chair, trying to stop herself from running her hands along the blush silk fabric. She eyed Darius, lounging on a nearby chaise with unforgivable ease.

When his fingers casually brushed across the damask, Jia swallowed.

He had beautiful hands. Of course he did.

She'd always had a thing for guys with great hands.

Jia cleared her throat and looked around the room.

She thought she'd understood what was happening when she followed Darius into Bergdorf's fifteen minutes ago. Apparently the Park family's house manager also moonlighted as some sort of stylist. Everywhere they walked in the store, someone nodded at him or smiled hello.

The guy at the Frédéric Malle fragrance counter threw his arms wide at the sight of Darius, then pressed a kiss to each of his cheeks. A lady seated before a wall of gleaming Celine bags called out to him so that she could share pictures of her newest grandchild.

It was like watching statues come to life. Gone were the looks of perennial judgment. The arched brows that Jia had become so familiar with at shops like this. Especially from the elegantly coiffed sales associates, who she just *knew* were rolling their eyes at the very sight of her. *Another* Korean with too much money, too little taste, and an LV obsession.

In fact, Jia did own a Louis Vuitton wallet. That awful Murakami one.

But with Darius, she was welcomed as if she were one of them. And now she was sitting in a dimly lit waiting room—on a chair that had to be worth thousands of dollars—while pretending to sip Dom Pérignon. On a Tuesday. Just because.

Not even five minutes passed before a woman blew through the doorway like a summer storm. Her dark brown hair was pulled back from her face in a low bun at the nape of her neck. The only makeup she wore to accent her tanned skin was the perfect shade of red lipstick and sharp winged eyeliner. Her floral-printed silk blouse and understated slacks were freshly pressed, and her large gold jewelry managed to look tasteful rather than ostentatious. If Jia had to guess, she was probably no older than fifty. But every single one of those fifty years had been lived with panache. Like Sophia Loren in her heyday.

"Darius!" she chimed, with the slightest accent. Italian. Or perhaps Greek? "I am so happy you received my message about changing the time."

"It's been too long, Allegra," Darius said.

"I can't believe another season has passed already. Is Jenny doing well?"

"Busy spending time with the grandkids and learning calligraphy."

Interesting. He didn't even flinch when he lied. Jia quirked her lips to one side. Darius Rohani would make an excellent con artist. Charming and deceitful were a potent combination.

"Please send her my best," Allegra said. Then she glanced at Jia, her curiosity plain.

Darius turned to Jia. "Allegra, this is my friend Jia. She's here to weigh in on this season's offerings." He leaned in, dropping his voice. "As always, your privacy and discretion would be most appreciated."

"Ovviamente," Allegra said, her fingers rounding to form Os. "Lovely to meet you, Jia. You're a friend of the family?"

Jia bared her teeth in an overlarge smile. Then she nodded, unwilling to lie as openly as Darius. "Wonderful to meet you, too."

"Shall we?" Allegra said, gesturing for them to follow. "Darius, I set aside the same space as last time, so you won't be bothered in the slightest," she continued as they walked down a hallway that reminded Jia of the soothing labyrinth inside an expensive spa.

They entered a large beige room with an elegant jacquard sofa along one wall and a swath of floor-to-ceiling ivory velvet curtains running parallel to it. Rows of artfully positioned track lights were aimed at the center of the space as if it were a stage.

Darius and Jia sat beside each other on the jacquard sofa while Allegra offered Darius an iPad in a navy leather Goyard case.

She bent closer to him and spoke under her breath, as if they were scholars in a library at Oxford. "As usual, I've curated your custom page so that each ensemble is featured in the order it is shown, from head to toe, including the jewelry." She scrolled up and down the iPad screen with a manicured finger.

Darius nodded, following along with her. "Are all the available colors listed as well? I've noticed that Jenny seems drawn to warmer tones this season."

"Absolutely." Allegra pointed at a tab running along the side of the webpage. "Just make the selection you prefer. I will be happy to adjust the entire ensemble so that the finished effect will be perfetto."

"Thank you, Allegra. You're the best of the best. Jenny would trust no one else with her wardrobe." Darius smiled up at her with such sincerity that a flush rose in Allegra's cheeks.

"Save those smiles for your wife, you handsome devil," she clucked with an embarrassed laugh. Then Allegra took her leave in a flurry of floral perfume and D&G silk.

So. As Jia had suspected, Darius Rohani had a wife. No ring. But a wife.

Interesting. Such great news. Jia felt no twinge of disappointment in her stomach. Absolutely none.

The next second, the house lights dimmed as if they were at the theater, while the stage lights in the center of the room brightened. An aria from Georges Bizet's *Carmen* began to play at a low volume from speakers set into the walls and ceiling.

Then the ivory curtains parted, and a slender middle-aged Asian woman strolled into the room without preamble, clad in light oatmeal cashmere from head to toe. She glided down the unmarked runway with quiet confidence before pausing to adjust the strap on her caramel crossbody bag to make it wearable on one shoulder. The warm gold on the clasp and buckle of the purse matched the small gold flowers and pendant hanging around her neck.

Boucheron, if Jia had to guess. Though none of the branding on anything the model wore was visible, this simple everyday outfit had to be outrageously expensive. The billionaire's version of a sweat suit. From the cut of the cardigan to the subtle sheen of the white T-shirt beneath it, from the drape of the whisper-thin cashmere pants to the supple leather of her taupe loafers, everything screamed money.

"What is happening?" Jia muttered, her words barely audible.

Darius inclined his head in her direction. "Jenny doesn't like to go out to shop. I'm sure you can understand why, given her condition." He opened the iPad to peruse the selections of the first ensemble. "Since Jenny got sick, Allegra has coordinated a special viewing for us each season. Sometimes I call Jenny or send her pictures, but mostly I look at the clothes Allegra has chosen and make suggestions based on Jenny's current needs and wishes. Then Allegra orders everything in the right size and color combinations and coordinates the tailoring before having it all wrapped and sent discreetly to Park Avenue."

It was easy for Jia to remind herself that the world of the Park family was a world removed from her own. This private fashion show embodied a new level of entitlement. But part of her was beginning to understand the whys of this situation. Minsoo's warning about how important it was to make sure the public did not know of Jenny's illness resonated, especially now. Mirae was a publicly traded company. The wealthiest families in Manhattan social circles shopped at and ate at and frequented the same establishments. If one among them got wind that Jenny Park was ill, tongues would surely wag. Likely not in the Park family's favor.

Maybe the private fashion show *did* make a little bit of sense. Or maybe the expensive perfume of peonies and musk being pumped into the air had gone straight to Jia's head.

"You're wondering why a few pictures won't suffice?" His voice held a smile.

"I'm wondering . . . many things. I would bet a lunch at Via Carota that this model is the exact same size as Jenny Park."

Darius hummed in agreement. "Similar coloring and build as well. Just as Jenny requested."

In front of them, the model shrugged off the cardigan and draped it across her back, tying the arms in a loose knot around her neck.

"Casual," Jia murmured. "Totally normal." The model strolled back toward the curtain. Jia decided to take her first actual sip from the glass of Dom dangling from her fingertips. "When in Rome . . ." She offered a gumbeh to the empty space in front of her.

Darius laughed. "Nothing about this is normal. But the Park family is especially important here. When you spend this kind of money, accommodations are made. Not so long ago, this sort of private shopping with a personal fashion show was not that uncommon. I think it happened a fair amount in the middle of last century."

"Like in *Singin' in the Rain*," Jia said. "'Beautiful girl, you're a lovely picture,'" she sang softly.

"'Beautiful girl, you're a gorgeous mixer,'" Darius chimed in, his baritone pitch-perfect.

Jia crossed her arms in disbelief. No grown man should randomly be able to sing a line from a Gene Kelly movie that well.

He shrugged. "High school theater."

"My grandfather loved Gene Kelly musicals. *Singin' in the Rain* is my favorite. I used to watch it with him whenever I was home sick from school."

"Solid choice. It's mostly aged well, which can't be said for all movies from that era. Still hilarious."

"Right?" Jia grinned. "Jean Hagen's nasal accent? Dee-lit-teer-ee-us."

"And Moses? Those dance sequences are still a pinnacle of Hollywood cinema."

"Don't tell me you dance, too."

"Like a proud Middle Easterner. With a shoulder shake and a napkin spinning in the air."

It was Jia's turn to laugh. She couldn't help it. She liked him. Way too much for comfort.

Darius studied her a moment. Then looked away.

Jia rolled her eyes. "Were you going to tell me how much nicer I look when I'm laughing?"

"No," he countered. "I was going to say that was the first time I think I saw the real you."

Jia snorted. "You suck at one-liners. I'm beginning to understand why Suzy enjoys finding out you're bad at something."

When he smiled at her and her chest swelled, Jia realized she needed to do a much better job ignoring her inconvenient—and inappropriate—attraction to Darius Rohani.

Attempting to conceal the rising color in her cheeks, Jia leaned over to remove a white legal pad and her trusty Montblanc from her black Prada tote. Darius was nothing more than a source of information, one she could not afford to ignore. His position granted him unusual access to the Park family and their most intimate secrets, which meant he could prove invaluable to Whitman Volker, as long as Jia managed to establish two things: that Darius was indeed loyal to Jenny Park, and that he would tell Jia the truth. Neither of which she accepted as fact. Not yet, at least.

Because even though Suzy Park wanted Jia to treat Darius as a trusted ally, Jia had no reason of her own to do so. This was not just about hearing what Darius had to say. This was an interview to make sure he merited their trust.

"Suzy insisted that it was important for me to speak with you," Jia said the moment the bouclé-clad model began her return journey toward the ivory curtains. "I'm hoping you would be willing to share any information you feel is relevant, especially with a mind to uncovering why her father would try to conceal so much money from his family."

"Frankly, I'm more interested in how," Darius said. "Aren't you?"

Jia's eyes narrowed. "We have a forensic accounting team working on it."

He nodded. “And it’s important for you to establish motive. At least that’s what they say on *Law & Order.*”

“Right.” She pursed her lips and waited, unsure of whether he was being snide or funny.

He offered her a sheepish half smile. “Look, I thought we were making some headway a moment ago,” he said. “I’m sorry we had to meet like this. I know it’s less than ideal. But Suzy did mention it was important for us to speak freely. She preferred that it not happen at the house. Last week with Jenny couldn’t be avoided because she doesn’t go out in public.”

“And why do you think Suzy would prefer if these matters were not discussed in the house?”

Darius considered her. “Suzy is convinced her father has spies all over the building.”

She met his gaze without flinching. “What do you think?”

He waited a beat, clearly weighing his response. “If I’m honest, I don’t like any of this.”

Another deft avoidance of her question. “Can you be more specific?”

Darius sighed. “I never wanted to put Jenny through this ordeal. She doesn’t deserve the stress or the scrutiny, especially after all she’s had to overcome.”

The way his face softened told Jia there was much more to it. Either Darius was an Oscar-worthy actor, or he held great affection for Jenny Park. But why? It was obvious the Park siblings trusted Darius Rohani, but Jia wasn’t convinced as to why they trusted him. If their father was indeed paying the help to spy on his family, Darius would be a perfect mark.

Why wouldn’t he just take Seven Park’s money?

Darius continued studying her. “You’re wondering if you can trust me.”

“Wouldn’t you be wondering the same thing?”

“Without a doubt. But I really can’t convince you in an hour on a Tuesday afternoon that I’m worthy of your trust. Not if you’re any good at your job.”

“Maybe you should try anyway.”

“What might start to convince you?”

“Rigorous honesty. No more evasions.”

"All right." He adjusted himself on the chaise so that his body was parallel to hers. As if he had nothing to hide. "Ask away." His cologne wafted in her direction. Leather and oud, which was basically smoke mixed with sin.

"How did you come to be in the Park family's employ?" she asked in a clipped tone.

"I started working part-time for Jenny Park when I was in high school. Mostly Gristedes runs and picking up her dry cleaning. My father was her chauffeur."

Surprise flared through Jia. "Was?"

"He passed away last year." Darius didn't flinch when he said it, but his voice lowered.

"I'm sorry to hear that." Jia wasn't even willing to consider the idea of losing either of her parents. It was difficult enough when her harabugi died. As far as Jia was concerned, Umma and Appa would be alive to criticize her for decades, wrinkling and silvering well into their nineties.

"Before my father died, he asked me to promise that I would look out for Jenny." Darius paused. For the first time, a hint of discomfort crept into his face. "I'm going to go ahead and tell you something, because I suspect it will come up in whatever dossiers your firm is compiling."

"Dossiers?" Jia arched a brow. "Like I'm a down-on-my-luck detective in a film noir?"

He laughed. "You know what I mean. A firm like yours is bound to look into everyone in the Park family's employ, especially if there are suspicions that information is being sold to the highest bidder."

Jia nodded. "A safe assumption." In fact, she was due to receive their private investigator's initial reports this week.

"Anyway," Darius continued. "It's not like it was much of a secret, but my father was in love with Jenny."

Jia's pen halted above her legal pad. Did Jenny Park have an affair with Darius's father? Was that the real reason for Jenny and Seven's separation?

"I don't believe it was ever physical," he said, "and I'm not even certain it was reciprocated. Jenny wasn't the type of person to cheat. But my mother died in a car accident when I was fourteen. My father never remarried, and he was extremely protective of Jenny. They were quite close." He smiled, but it didn't touch his eyes. "Don't worry; I'm not some secret love child. Definitely one hundred percent the child of my Iranian parents."

"I mean, wouldn't that be an eleventh-hour revelation though? Another hat in the inheritance ring." Jia shouldn't be going along with his attempts at levity, but she felt suddenly protective of Darius. As if his open vulnerability had inured her to him.

Damn. This guy was good.

"Do you want me to do a DNA test?" Darius asked. Again, she couldn't tell if he was being sarcastic. It unsettled her how nimbly he shifted from being candid to inscrutable.

"Maybe," she said. "And how did you become the Park family's house manager?"

His expression turned thoughtful. "When we found out about Jenny's cancer, my dad asked for my help. I felt like I owed it to Jenny for everything she'd done for me. She paid for all my education: my student loans at Penn, my MBA at Fordham, the works. Before this, I had a job at a nonprofit, making sixty-five thousand a year, when she asked me to be the house manager and her personal assistant."

"So a salary raise, I'm guessing?" Jia tapped her pen against her white legal pad. Then startled when she realized she'd circled the word "wife?" three times.

"I don't know many house managers who make more than three hundred grand a year." He met her stare without blinking.

"You're insinuating that you can't be bought. But let's be honest, three hundred grand is nothing to people like the Parks. It would be a drop in the bucket to double it."

"You're not wrong. Anyone can be bought," Darius said. "I'm just saying it would take a lot. Besides that, my father made me promise to see this through and be there for Jenny . . . until the end." His face tensed. Then he relaxed and leaned into the chaise. "How did I do?"

Jia considered him. She understood why Jenny Park and her three children seemed to accept Darius as a trusted ally without question. In many ways, he came across as another member of the family. Though Jia knew it was foolish to trust anyone so easily, she found herself wanting to believe everything Darius had to say.

Which meant he was either earnest or a frighteningly good liar.

"I suppose you did fine . . . for now." Jia finished jotting down some bullet points with additional notes for follow-up.

The model spun slowly at the end of the runway, this time in Chanel evening wear, a quilted black Caviar clutch in one hand. Then she vanished behind the curtains once again to change into her next offering.

Darius regarded Jia, his gaze circumspect. "All this one-sided, rigorous honesty has made me curious. Do I get to ask you any questions about yourself?"

"No."

"Not even one? I mean, why should I trust *you*?"

"You shouldn't." Jia twisted her pen closed. "I'm a corporate attorney at a top-five firm. We're ruthless, and we like money. But I also work for Jenny Park and her children, so our fortunes seem to align for the moment."

He angled his head. "It's not just about the money for you though."

"No," she agreed. "I also enjoy winning."

"Which means you hate to lose."

"It's possible to enjoy winning and have no problem losing."

"Yes, it's possible. But not for you. Am I wrong?"

Jia squirmed. "Fine. You can ask me one question."

Darius crossed his arms. "Okay. Who is Jia Song?"

"What?"

"It's a simple question. Who are you?"

What an odd thing to ask. "I supposed I'm . . . a woman. A daughter. The child of Korean immigrants. A friend. A sister. A lawyer."

Darius nodded. "I like it."

"Why did you ask that particular question?"

"Because it seems like an easy one. And the way people answer it often sheds light onto their priorities."

"All right, who are you?"

"I'm Darius Rohani." He grinned. "I enjoy cooking, traveling, and all kinds of stories."

"Generic. Careful. Disturbingly easygoing."

"See?"

"Yeah, but you messed up." Jia leaned closer. "Because it's clear one of your priorities is a desire to hide."

"And you're probably too honest for your own good," he replied without missing a beat.

She shrugged. "Or maybe I'm just luring you in. Making it easier for you to trust me."

"It worked. I trust you."

"I'm thankful for that." She eased back into the sofa, curious to know more than Darius's history with the Park family. "You're a smart guy. Off the record, what is your take on all of this?"

She seemed to have caught him off guard. "Didn't I just give it to you?" he said.

"No. You told me that Suzy thinks their staff is colluding with her father to hide the family's wealth, which I already heard from Suzy herself. Why do you think her father would do that? Also, how did he manage it?"

"Off the record?" He recrossed his arms, his biceps shifting beneath his blue button-down.

Jia nodded.

"I think the Park family is worth a hell of a lot more than twenty-five million dollars, as Seven claims. I think he's probably hidden the bulk of their wealth in convoluted offshore accounts in several different countries."

"None of that is news. I'm not looking for a cached answer, Darius. I want your genuine take. Why do you think he's gone to so much trouble? Because he's not just screwing over his wife; he's screwing over his kids. Why would he feel justified in doing that?"

Darius chewed the inside of his cheek. It was obvious this was a much meatier question than he wanted to answer. He wanted to keep this interaction light. To remain charmingly unhelpful when it came to anything serious. Bergdorf's. A fashion show. Champagne and Bizet on a Tuesday. Darius Rohani had taken specific pains to skip over the surface of this meeting like a stone across a lake.

It made Jia hungry for why.

"Does he want to get back at his kids for not taking his side in the divorce?" she prompted. "Even when people deny it, that often happens in families. Parents want to punish their kids for choosing sides in a situation designed to do just that. How can any child, regardless of age, remain neutral while their family is being torn apart?"

Still Darius said nothing.

Jia continued, hoping she would be able to pick up on any kind of reaction from him. "It's just that, from everything I've read and heard about Seven Park, he strikes me as someone who cares a great deal about legacy and aspires to something bigger and better. He wants to be a chaebol: the head of a Korean dynastic conglomerate. And a chaebol wouldn't leave the company to someone outside the family."

Darius frowned, a look of genuine consternation spreading across his face. He muttered an unintelligible word. Then appeared to make some kind of decision. "Look, I'm not going to be the guy who lies to you and tells you I haven't chosen a side. Everything I say should be filtered through that lens. So it's not as if I've been neutral."

"But you also haven't really been helpful."

Darius slid down in his seat ever so slightly. "Okay. Fine. Off the record, Sora, Suzy, and Minsoo are leaving out very important details. I'm not sure why. But I suspect it's out of shame."

"You're talking about their father's new girlfriend?" Jia pressed. "Does he want to marry her?"

"That's part of it, sure. But not all of it."

"Then why the haste? Why can't he wait until his wife—"

Darius flinched. She stopped herself from saying the word. Because even though Jia intended to question him in a manner devoid of emotion, she couldn't quite bring herself to be that merciless. It was clear he wasn't ready to speak so bluntly about Jenny Park's impending death.

Jia sensed herself starting to ease up on Darius. The personal side of her wanted to avoid upsetting him, which meant the professional side needed to continue doing just that. She hardened herself and surged forward, her suspicions mounting. "Does Seven's girlfriend have anything to do with

Suzy's observations regarding the help? Why is there such urgency around finalizing what may likely be an unnecessary divorce? And why was one member of the family's staff allegedly promoted for stealing personal documents, while another was apparently let go without reason?"

"Orlagh quit," Darius said coldly. "She wasn't fired."

"Okay. Why do you think she quit?"

"I don't think Orlagh wanted to quit. In fact, I'm pretty sure Seven made her leave."

"Okay. But *what* makes you think that?"

"You're relentless." Darius's laughter was dark. "All right. Fuck it. If you want to continue this from a place of conjecture, I'm pretty sure Orlagh was the person who uncovered the reason why Seven is trying to hammer out a hatchet divorce agreement even though his wife was diagnosed with terminal cancer."

"Which is?"

He exhaled in a huff. "I'm not sure how, but I believe Orlagh is the one who discovered that Seven's girlfriend is pregnant. Three days after Minsoo, Suzy, and Sora found out, Orlagh left New York without even saying goodbye."

"Okay." Jia had suspected as much, especially after Suzy became unusually tight-lipped at their lunch with Jenny. "So—"

"You're exactly right about Seven wanting to be a chaebol. His girlfriend is pregnant with a boy."

"Seven already has a son."

Darius sent her a wry look. One underscored by obvious disgust.

Jia blinked again. "Oh. Gross."

"Yeah."

"Alas, not unexpected." Jia tucked her hair behind an ear. "I'm not sure how it is with your parents' generation of Persians, but my parents' generation of Koreans is happy to be supportive of anyone else whose kids come out, as long as it's not one of their own."

"I think my mom would have worked through it," Darius said. "My dad would have been . . . sad for me. And for himself. Not sure he would have become the sort of immigrant parent who defiantly told people, daring them to say something."

"Whereas our generation?" Jia shot Darius a knowing look.

"Marching with our kid in every Pride parade."

"Punching all the Nazis," Jia added.

"Proof that generational progress is necessary."

"But also painful."

Darius ruffled his hair. "Sometimes the pain is necessary, too."

Jia nodded. "Agreed."

"Seven is more the see-no-evil type," Darius said. "He's never been nasty to Minsoo, at least not directly. But he also hasn't accepted it. Keeps thinking Minsoo can change if he wants to. Like being gay is a switch that can be flipped."

"So gross," Jia said. "But I understand now. If Sora, Suzy, and Minsoo don't secure their birthright before this divorce is finalized, it could be in serious jeopardy, especially since none of them took their father's side in any of this."

"Exactly."

The model returned from behind the curtain, this time in a set of printed silk Olivia von Halle pajamas, a matching robe, and mink-lined slippers.

Jia thought for a moment, her words dropping to a whisper. "Do you know if Sora, Suzy, or Minsoo have designs on running Mirae one day? I didn't pick up on any 'heavy is the head that wears the crown' stuff when I first met them."

"You'll have to ask them."

An infuriating answer. If Jia were a betting woman, she would bet that Darius knew exactly which of the siblings aspired to be the next CEO.

"You know they're not going to tell me. They're going to make me work for it." Jia tapped the tip of her pen against her palm, her annoyance plain. "I had to learn this much from you, and you weren't exactly easy."

"Did you . . . want me to be easy?" Darius offered her a suggestive grin.

His words—and the slow way he said them—sent a frisson of heat through Jia's body. Before she could wrangle her thoughts, a very specific set of images was conjured in her mind. A silk chair. A scented room. His beautiful hands. The famous aria from *Carmen* blasting through the speakers.

*L'amour est un oiseau rebelle.* Love is a rebellious bird.

The model turned at the end of the runway, her silk robe billowing around her, catching flickers of cool light.

Jia felt Darius freeze across from her. She met his gaze. His eyes were wide. As aware of her as she was of him.

Her face went hot. She bit her lip.

Darius exhaled slowly. "Damn," he breathed.

He felt the same attraction. She knew it.

"Well, that was a stupid thing for an unavailable guy to say." Her voice was bitter.

Darius winced. "Yeah, so . . . I'm not unavailable."

"Allegra said you had a wife."

"I don't." He didn't look away. Why wouldn't he look away? "I was engaged. I'm not anymore. It's easier not to correct people."

"Well." Jia stopped herself from squirming the moment the model vanished behind the curtain again. "There's that."

Dammit. Dammit. Dammit.

"Listen," he said, "I know you can't—"

"Did Orlagh learn anything else of value?" she interrupted, her skin still tingling. "Or is it possible she was paid off before she could divulge anything more? Did Seven send her away as punishment?"

Darius didn't answer immediately. Jia held her breath and hoped he would play along, for both their sakes.

"I know you think I'm being difficult, but I truly don't know," he said, finally shifting his attention to his suede loafers. "From my perspective, Orlagh wasn't the type to run her mouth or accept a bribe. I suspect she found out about the baby and didn't want to tell Jenny, which was why she likely told Sora or Suzy. In fact, Jenny still doesn't know about the baby. It was enough when she learned about the cheating. That was an especially hard pill to swallow. The girlfriend is the same age as the twins."

"How did you find out about the baby if Jenny doesn't know?"

Another wry grin. "How do you think?"

It took Jia less than a second to answer. "Suzy." She really needed to take Suzy for drinks.

Darius nodded.

Jia took a moment to think. "You know, none of you are doing Jenny any favors by hiding this from her."

"I agree," Darius said. "But it's not my place to tell her."

"Why not? It's clear she trusts you. From what I've gathered, I bet she almost sees you as a member of her family."

"Maybe. But I'm not. And I won't interfere to that point, especially because telling Jenny about the baby would cause her pain."

"Do Jenny's kids coddle her like this?"

He laughed softly. "We all do. After Jenny's cancer diagnosis, I suppose everyone who loved her became protective of her. Orlagh and Jenny were close. Not like best friends. They didn't confide in each other when it came to deepest, darkest secrets. But almost like sisters. Jenny's like that. She treats everyone like she's their unyee."

Jia couldn't help but smile when he said that. "It's always good to have an elder sister. Just ask my younger brother."

Darius returned her smile. Then he bent forward and rested both his elbows on his knees, considering her again. "I'm impressed."

Her hackles raised. "Why? Did you not expect I would be able to do my job well?"

"It's not that at all. Most of the lawyers the Parks work with are all business. It's easy to keep them at arm's length. But you've managed to strike the perfect balance of formal and familiar." He looked at her with admiration. "As you can imagine, I didn't come here intending to share much. You're very good at what you do, Jia. I don't usually speak so freely to someone I barely know." He looked so charming that Jia wanted to spit.

Anger and attraction continued to war within her. If Jia were watching this scene unfold in a movie, she'd think she was being played. It was always the handsome ones. The ones who made you feel special. So warm and safe and different from all the rest.

Just like Zain.

Jia dropped her pen into her Prada tote and sat up. "I think that's enough for today."

Though his eyes cut for an instant, Darius nodded. "Off to Scotland, I presume?"

"Maybe," she demurred. "Thank you for your time." She stood and put out her hand for him to shake.

He got to his feet. Hesitated for a second. And then grasped her hand in his.

Another mistake.

Jia pulled away as if her fingers had been burned. Then she spun in place and walked directly into Allegra . . . and two plates of tiramisu. With mumbled apologies and a face as red as a baboon's ass, Jia fled the scene, chocolate powder staining her sweater and cold coffee dripping into her underwear.

# ACTUS LEGIS NEMINI FACIT INJURIAM

Ah, the delights of witnessing another person's misfortune.

Don't fret. It's entirely human to do so. It's why gossipmongers exist and why bad news always outweighs the good. I'm not speaking of true horrors. Only a monster would relish the sight of real suffering. I'm speaking of small embarrassments. Little shames. The Germans even have a word for it, as they so often do.

Schadenfreude.

Of course, all things are relative. One person's genuine horror may seem small and delightful to another.

Why else would anyone greedily consume news about a beautiful Hollywood starlet being cheated on by her godlike spouse? Better still if the cheating in question was with another stunning actress, her past as sordid and sinful as a stack of Page Six columns.

It's only their lives. Their loves. Their happiness. Money can simply buy them more.

That is what we do. Consume and consume and consume until there is nothing left but bones. Voracious little beasties with an appetite for disaster.

As I said before, don't fret. A veritable banquet is nigh.

Our lovely heroine was right to worry about betrayal.

# JANUS COINS AND BAD JOKES

## *T Minus 27 Days*

The knock at the door to Jia's office on Wednesday afternoon was hesitant.

"Come in?" It wasn't meant to sound like a question, but Jia felt compelled to match like with like.

"I'm so sorry." Ben Volker's secretary, Candace, peered through the crack in the doorway. "Kim is out to lunch."

Jia straightened. "No apologies necessary. Is there something I can help you with?"

Candace gnawed her lower lip. "Ben isn't here right now, but Suzy Park is in our waiting room."

Jia stood at once. "Did she have an appointment?"

Candace shook her head. "She insisted on speaking with you, even if she had to wait."

"Of course." Jia hurried into the hallway outside her office, Candace at her heels. The second they rounded the first corner, Jia stopped short.

An impeccably dressed Emily Bhatia was standing in the center of the bullpen, the area of open cubicles where all the junior associates worked. She spoke in hushed tones to Never Late Nate and another first year Jia had dubbed the Dormouse, on account of her sleepy-eyed stare.

The next second, Suzy Park flashed into view. A flustered Candace tried to usher their surprise guest back toward the waiting area, but Suzy sidestepped her with the ease of a line dancer in an Alabama honky-tonk.

"Jia!" An impish smile on her face, Suzy pivoted once more in a swirl of Mongolian fur, an immense metal-studded bag swinging from one elbow.

"So glad you're here." She angled her line of sight and pointed behind Jia. "Is that your office? Great!" She didn't wait for an answer.

Emily and Nate turned to watch the budding commotion, a frown and a smirk touching their respective lips.

A mortified Jia stepped aside to allow Suzy to pass. Then she realized Suzy's entire body was vibrating. Despite her efforts to appear in control and at ease, she clearly suffered from anxiety, just like Jia. It was obvious in the tense way Suzy moved. The liquid light in her eyes that shifted at any sound or motion. The hypervigilance of a caged animal.

Jia's first instinct had been to act firm and stern. She didn't want to set a precedent that she would allow Suzy to barge into her office whenever she pleased. But when she realized how nervous Suzy was, she stopped herself. Decided to let this play out, despite the audience in the bullpen.

"I probably should have called." Suzy paused just outside Jia's office. "But I figured you would be accommodating. You seem like the kind of proper Korean who wouldn't throw a fit, at least not in public."

Jia pursed her lips. "You're mostly correct."

Never Late Nate and the Dormouse watched with the eager interest of rubberneckers at a five-car pileup. The Dormouse coughed, the sound more like a squeak, and Jia eyed her disapprovingly. Though she couldn't blame her. Since it was around lunchtime, the office was mostly absent of its normal hustle and bustle. Why had Emily chosen today of all days to come to the bullpen? Why did it have to be her of all people bearing witness to the unusual behavior of Jia's newest client?

Jia took a steadying breath before closing her office door. Suzy sauntered behind the desk to sit in Jia's swivel chair.

"Suzy?" Jia offered her a patient smile, though her features remained tight. "Is there something I can—"

"Your office is really fucking small." Suzy looked around, taking in the narrow window and Jia's framed diplomas and the single picture of Jia with Nidhi and Elisa perched at the edge of her desk. "I thought you were important. Aren't you a partner?"

"Junior partner," Jia said softly. She'd noticed Ben Volker do this on more than one occasion. The more intense a situation became, the softer he would pitch his voice. Jia liked the danger of it. The suggestion of someone with absolute control. It forced people to listen. She crossed her arms. "The only file on my desk is yours. Your family's situation is of utmost importance to our firm, and I hate to lose at anything. Those facts alone should tell you all you need to know about me. Not the size of my office."

"So it's not about the size, huh? It's about the motion of the ocean." Suzy laughed at her own bad joke.

Jia's nostrils flared. "Suzy, what do—"

"Speaking of sex, Darius told me you talked yesterday."

Jia took another long breath before responding. "We did speak, yes."

"What did he tell you?"

Jia forced her stomach muscles to unclench and her knees to relax. Then she took one of the chairs positioned off to the side and situated it across from Suzy. She had to admit that Suzy's attempt to unseat her—quite literally—was effective. Sitting across from her own desk was deeply strange.

What Suzy was trying to do was obvious. Jia was well-versed in the tactic. Suzy wanted to be in control of Jia. In control of the situation. Which meant that Suzy felt anything but in control.

Jia needed to be patient with her. Something was clearly bothering Suzy. Bothering her enough to draw unwanted attention their way. Suzy arriving at the firm without an appointment and making a rather obvious scene was precisely the opposite of keeping the low profile Minsoo had explicitly requested.

Suzy folded her hands beneath her chin and propped her elbows along the edge of Jia's desk. "I'm waiting. What did Darius tell you?"

Jia shrugged. "He didn't really tell me much. Most of it was information I already knew."

"All right. What did he tell you that you didn't already know?"

"Suzy," Jia said. "What's wrong?"

Suzy leaned back in the swivel chair. Her shoulder-length curls looked particularly wild, as if they had been left to air-dry after twenty minutes in a sauna. A stark contrast to Sora's smooth and straight hair. Champagne-colored glitter had been pressed on her eyelids above strips of long false lashes. It could have looked cheap or dated or juvenile, but it had been done with skill. By the hand of an artist. Pains had been taken with Suzy's appearance.

Elisa used to say she was most dangerous when she had the best makeup. As if she'd painted on armor, daring anyone to cross her.

Suzy cocked her head to one side. "He told you about the baby."

"He told me about the baby." Jia paused. "But I'm curious why I had to find out about it from him."

"Because we aren't telling many people. We don't want my mom to find out. Not yet."

"Why?"

She fluffed her hair. "We just got Umma to agree to fight, after trying for months without any success. If she finds out our dad is having another baby, we're worried she'll just turtle back into her shell and give up once and for all."

"I see." Jia nodded. "But I'm your attorney. So I'm still not sure why I had to find out from Darius."

"That one is easy. I told him to tell you."

Interesting. "Why?"

"That way neither Sora nor Marky could be mad at me for making sure you found out, which, by the way, I agree that you should have been told from the beginning. I said as much, but it's not like either of them give a shit what I think."

"Okay." They weren't even touching at the surface of why Suzy was here. There had to be more. "Is there anything else you'd like to—"

"Did he tell you about the slut banging my father and trying to steal our money?" Suzy shuddered, then pretended to gag.

Jia frowned at the word. Even though she understood why Suzy referred to her father's lover that way, she'd always disliked hearing any woman call another woman a slut. It felt like they were perpetuating the patriarchy. After all, Seven Park wasn't exactly a saint. "No," she said. "He didn't tell me much, other than to say she was a good deal younger than your father."

"Did he tell you she's a month younger than me and Sora? When she was a teenager, she was a fucking Abercrombie model." Suzy laughed, the sound high-pitched and tight. "One of those half-dressed chicks who stood in the center of the mall, smelling like a vat of cheap perfume. Stupid peasant bitch."

Jia didn't have time for this pettiness. "Why are you here, Suzy? I'd like to help in whatever way I can."

Suzy's right knee bounced under the desk, causing her entire body to tremble. "Really I wanted to see if Darius had done what I asked him to do. I told you he was a good egg. You should just bone him. I know you want to."

Jia said nothing. Despite Suzy's defiant posture and wide-eyed glare, Jia was certain something had happened to make her feel deeply uncomfortable. Jia could either ignore her instincts and accept that Suzy was simply trying to get attention, or she could push the issue and force Suzy to say what had caused her to act out like this.

Jia had no small amount of experience with people like Suzy. In fact, it no longer surprised her how many people raised in circles of ultra-wealth behaved like this. As if they were rebellious teenagers trying to get a rise out of their parents. Teenagers had a bad reputation for a reason. Trying to draw out a reaction from someone by swearing like a sailor and doing or saying shocking things was annoying to deal with, at baseline. From a thirty-four-year-old woman who absolutely knew better?

Annoyed didn't begin to describe how Jia felt about it.

A smart attorney would defuse the situation. Would do whatever it took to make sure Suzy Park left the office without ruffling any feathers, including her own.

Jia blinked. And knowingly chose chaos. "Suzy, what did Minsoo do to piss you off?"

A momentary flash of surprise crossed Suzy's face. She recovered the next instant. "What are you talking about?" She straightened and pushed back into the chair, her hands spread along the length of the desk in a power pose. As if she was ready to fight.

Jia's suspicions were correct. Pay dirt. "It's the middle of the workday. Please help me help you. What did your brother do?"

"Besides be his normal Janice self?" Suzy's lips thinned into a line. "Nothing."

"What do you mean by 'Janice'?"

"It's what Sora and I always called any two-faced, backstabbing piece of shit who got in our way."

"Like a two-headed Janus coin."

"Right, Columbia." Suzy laughed. "With the whole betrayer element thrown in for good measure. Like Judas, too. And among the three of us? Marky is the biggest Janice of all."

"Okay. Do you want to talk about it?"

"No." She continued laughing as if she were deeply amused rather than deeply troubled. "But I did want to tell you to watch out. There are two things my brother excels at: anything to do with numbers and checking out when you most need him. My dad knows Marky is the weakest link, and he's already digging into him. I bet he starts making promises he never intends to keep. Ripping more holes into the fabric of our lives and taking a Louisville slugger to both headlights. Along with a bunch of other lyrics from silly country songs."

Jia listened intently. "Does your brother have designs on running the company one day?"

"He says no. But his eyes say yes." Suzy cackled.

Jia closed her eyes. She wouldn't let Suzy get under her skin. "So you're saying you think your brother might possibly be conspiring with your father, potentially to undermine our investigation. Therefore, you're worried we can't trust him, correct?"

"Columbia, you really aren't as dumb as your haircut would lead me to believe."

"Suzy, please. What makes you think this? What did your brother do?"

With an unctuous grin, Suzy said, "Last week, when we met with you, none of us had talked to Seven for over six months. But then my father texted me late last night to say he spoke with Marky that afternoon. He said it was a very good conversation. He said they were able to work through some of their issues and have a productive discussion moving forward. He called it 'healing.'" She pantomimed air quotes.

Jia took a moment to think. "Is it possible your father is lying?"

"Look, anything is possible. My father is practically pathological. But

Marky hasn't taken any of my phone calls all morning. And I called him five times. If it looks like a Janice, sounds like a Janice, and quacks like a Janice, it's probably a fucking Janice." Her knee resumed bouncing underneath the desk. "I would call Sora to talk about it, but . . . yeah. That wouldn't go well."

Jia refrained from closing her eyes again, though she desperately wanted a moment to count to ten. "Okay. Is there something you would like me to do?"

"You were there when we promised my mom we wouldn't fight. Well, now I'm ready to fight. So I need you to fix it before that happens." She looked at the ceiling. "I think I can stand it for maybe about a week or so before I light a match and burn my brother down. So . . . plenty of time." She made a shooing motion. "Get to it."

"Suzy, I'm not a therapist. Have you considered—"

"No therapy." She glowered at Jia. "Talk to Marky. Tell him to watch his back. Actually, that's not a good idea. Find out exactly what my father said to him. Remind him that we are supposed to be in this together. And that the first one to separate from the group in horror films is always the first one to die."

Jia sighed. "Where is Minsoo right now?"

"In Munich. For work. He'll be back in a few days, I think."

"I'll talk to him. No promises."

"Good job, Columbia. In the meantime, stop jerking around and get back to work. It's the middle of the day." Suzy grinned, spun around in Jia's chair, and then left in a breeze of stringy black fur and Santal 33.

Jia put her forehead on her desk and concentrated on breathing. Then she began to dream of becoming senior partner just one year from now. Of Whitman Volker's potential share in the Park family's fortune. A percentage of a billion dollars—even a small one—equated to millions and millions lining the coffers of her law firm's vault.

This case might make her lose her mind. The least it could do was make her career.

# OPIUM AND IDIOMS

## *T Minus 25 Days*

Jia had a confession.

Unlike most people she knew, she loved long plane rides.

In fact, the longer, the better. Her flights of choice were overnight hauls. The ones that departed around midnight, when most of the passengers were already soft and bleary-eyed before the plane took off.

Ever since Jia was a child, her favorite thing about going to visit her relatives in Korea—the part of the journey she looked forward to the most—was the fifteen-hour jaunt between JFK and Seoul. It was a perfect time, to her. Before leaving, she would plan how many mystery books to take. How many crosswords she wanted to solve. She would put on the headphones attached to her silver Sony Discman, organize her favorite Mariah Carey, Janet Jackson, and Backstreet Boys CDs, arrange everything in her carry-on backpack, and delight in the hours she would get to spend alone with her favorite things. Uninterrupted. Unbothered.

Jia would wait with bated breath until the captain turned off the overhead lights. Bide her time, watching for the moment when everyone around her would fall into a restless sleep somewhere over the ocean.

Then she would turn on her reading light and while away the hours.

Maybe it was because Jia had two annoying brothers and no door on her bedroom (a long story), but this quiet time to herself, when no one else was awake to pester her or ask her questions, was more precious than gold. These long plane rides were probably the reason Jia became an avowed night owl. During college, she would select classes later in the afternoon so that she could stay up into the wee hours studying. Law school and work had changed all that, but Jia not-so-secretly yearned for those moments in her past when the night felt like it was all hers.

Some people called her an introvert. Jia liked to think it was more than that. To her, it was about balance. She could relish a noisy day spent with her friends in the heart of Central Park, children squealing around her, tourists pointing in the distance, and salami, basil, and fresh mozzarella sandwiches from Little Italy making a mess on her hands. The balance was the long bath that followed. The ritual of steaming bubbles and ice-cold Pellegrino garnished with lemon and mint. The crack of a fresh spine on a new book club selection. That delicious solitude of having nothing and no one to answer to, save time itself.

Jia couldn't remember the last time she'd honored this beloved ritual, and she suspected she wouldn't get many chances in her near future, especially with clients as demanding as the Park family.

So when she chose her flight from JFK to Heathrow instead of directly into Scotland, she chose it because it was an overnight. Besides that, Nidhi told her the high-speed train from London to Edinburgh took around four hours and offered breathtaking views of the English countryside.

Naturally, Nidhi shared that fact the second before inviting herself along for the journey. After several years of being unable to travel, she was ready to "get out of Dodge." Plus, she hadn't seen her family in Hounslow in a long time. She figured it was a great opportunity to "kill two birds with one stone."

That was the moment Jia put a moratorium on idioms for the duration of the trip. After making sure to warn Nidhi not to intrude on her sacred flying space. Thankfully, Nidhi had disappeared behind the screen separating their business-class pods not long after the plane settled at cruising altitude.

Which left Jia to her thoughts . . . and hours' worth of reading material in preparation for the coming interaction with Orlagh Campbell, the Park family's private chef for the last ten years.

When Jia first informed Suzy of her intention to interview Orlagh at her home in Falkirk—a forty-minute car ride from Edinburgh—Suzy had offered her the use of the company's G6 jet. Jia had politely declined. She knew the pitfalls of those kinds of luxuries. It was like the proverbial sound of breaking glass, an illusion forever shattered. The first time she'd flown business class to their firm's West Coast offices five years ago, it was over for her. She could never go back. Especially for any flight longer than three hours. Gone were her fond remembrances of fifteen-hour journeys to Seoul smashed between a cold window and her snoring brother's hot breath.

Never again. A seat that folded down into a bed? Actual plates and real silver cutlery? Food that didn't look as if it had already been eaten and vomited back up?

Done, done, and done.

The realization that all it took was one trip to San Francisco for Jia to sneer down her nose at economy class made her feel like she'd sold her soul for a bag of beans. Like she was a mustache-twirling goon munching on ortolans for breakfast and slathering veal with foie gras for dessert.

When she'd confessed to feeling guilty about the whole thing—as if she'd caught some elitist bug and needed to be nursed back to sanity—Zain had teased her. Joked that he'd always known she was "one of those women" who couldn't go backward in lifestyle. Then he'd proceeded to lament because now that Jia had a taste of the finer things, it was all she would ever want. Of course, he also made sure to thank himself for pushing her to go on the trip. As if he'd been a positive influence. The reason for such a golden opportunity, rather than Jia enjoying the fruits of her own success.

At the time, she'd laughed along with him.

But Jia should have seen the signs. The subtle way he put her down while making it seem as though he were lifting her up. It was an art, really. She hated how still, to this day, many of the things Zain had said to her in passing would sting in her memory. How she would look back and wonder what kind of stupid, insecure girl would fall for such a callous, beautiful man.

In therapy, Gail would tell Jia to let the words flow. To let them rinse off her skin as if she were taking a shower. *Painful words always find a place to land*, Gail would say. *Be sure to send them down the drain before they dig their nails into you.*

She wondered what painful words haunted Jenny Park. What untold offenses fed Seven in his quest to cut off the mother of his children from everything they'd built together. What jabs and strikes poked holes in Suzy and Sora's relationship, putting any kind of resolution far out of reach.

It appeared everyone was haunted by the words they couldn't wash away.

After Jia was sure Nidhi had gone to sleep, she spent the next two hours of the plane ride to London reading. She began by going through the large file given to her earlier today by the private investigators her firm had on retainer. Jia knew it was probably easier for her to work off something digital, but she'd always preferred paper to screens. Nothing was better than the smell of paper. A book of any kind, old or new. It was like a curl of smoke from an opium den, beckoning her inside, telling her to get lost forever.

Not that Jia had ever been in an opium den. But the novel she'd been reading the night before Ben Volker introduced her to the Park family was all about San Francisco's Chinatown at the turn of the twentieth century. A time when opium and gangs ran the docks. This was why Jia loved stories so much. The right book could transport her to a different time and place. To a different world or mindset. The right story could transform her for a moment . . . or a lifetime.

Jia shook her head. She'd decided not to bring any leisure books on this trip for a reason.

With a decisive breath, she returned to the thick file on her lap. Within it were contents detailing the lives of all the staff members employed by the Park family, along with the preliminary findings from the forensic accountant. She'd made it halfway through pages containing the information on Seven and Jenny Park's current financial situation—the accounts that were common knowledge, of course—when the screen separating her from the business class pod beside her began to slide down.

"Oh, good," Nidhi said. "You're awake." She held up the immense guidebook in her hands.

Jia almost groaned. Nidhi had always been the trip planner in their trio of friends. The summer between sophomore and junior years of college, they'd spent three weeks riding the Eurail around western Europe. Late one night—after drinking more house wine at their hostel than anyone would advise—Elisa and Jia had ritualistically burned Nidhi's copy of *Let's Go Italy* in a pizza oven on the sketchy outskirts of Naples. Over ten years later, they still maintained that Nidhi must have lost it. A secret they would take to their graves.

"What's up?" Jia closed the file on her lap and glowered in the direction of the guidebook.

Nonplussed, Nidhi opened it to a marked page in the middle. "I know you said you didn't think you would have the time, but there's a new Indian restaurant in Covent Garden that I really want to try. Boasts the best biryani in town."

"Nids, I told you this isn't a vacation. I'm pressed for time as it is. I have less than twenty-five days to prove the impossible."

"Yes, but you still have to eat." Nidhi's dark eyes were round like an owl's, her features unmoved. "No one will report you for eating *well*. Room service is complete nonsense. How many chicken Caesar salads and club sandwiches can one human consume?"

"You forgot the fries. There is no such thing as too many fries." Jia opened her file again. "Ask your cousins to go with you."

"Do you know how many cousins I have in the greater London area? I can't afford it."

Jia arched a brow at Nidhi. "How many millions in sales did you do last quarter?"

"You know what I mean. I can't retire at fifty if I buy Michelin-starred meals for all three hundred of my cousins. Word will get out. People will start bringing plus-ones. Then it just disintegrates into bread throwing and mayhem." She shuddered. "I realize I'm becoming an unflattering stereotype, but my people are good with money for a reason. Nana used to say that cheap is only an insult if you don't have money."

A smile tugged at the corner of Jia's mouth. "You said you wanted to visit your family."

"That's different from taking them all out to eat. Besides, Manisha Auntie is a great cook."

Jia rolled her eyes. "Fine. Go hang out with them while I take the train to Edinburgh. Once I'm back, we can try the restaurant. But only if I never have to see that guidebook again."

Nidhi made a face. "So grouchy. Sorry I interrupted your private flying time."

"Forgiven." Jia turned back to her pages. From the corner of her eye, she noticed Nidhi continuing to study her, her expression contemplative, like the Jiminy Cricket she was.

"What is it?" Jia asked.

Nidhi leaned over to look at the pile of papers on Jia's lap. "What are you reading?"

Jia dropped her voice. "Files on the Park family. Why?"

"You're shorter than usual. And you've got lines on your face." Nidhi drew in the air with her index finger to illustrate. "They haven't gone away since we boarded. If anything, they've gotten worse. Are you okay?"

"Jesus, fine, I'll go to E's aesthetician. I get it. SPF isn't enough. It's time for me to stop screwing around like I'm twenty-five. I'll get Botox."

"No. This isn't about botulinum toxin." Nidhi frowned. "Don't deflect. This is not going to get easier. Stress only compounds when left to its own devices. What are you doing tonight to stop it from getting worse?"

Jia stared at the large screen in front of her and fought the urge to lash out at one of her dearest friends. If anything, that urge proved just how right Nidhi was. And even though Jia wanted to tell Nidhi not to worry, she knew Nidhi was looking out for her, in that way only someone who cared about her a great deal would. The kind of friend more than willing to share the burden, if it meant helping to lighten the load.

There were few things in life of which Jia was absolutely certain. And she was certain that the luckiest of stars had struck her the day she met Nidhi and Elisa.

"Look, I know you might hate me for this," Nidhi pressed. "Frankly, I don't care, because one of the great things about you is your ability to forgive people, but stress is something you've always internalized to your own detriment. You don't have to carry the weight of the world on your shoulders alone." She settled back in her seat so that she could position herself to face Jia head-on. "Instead of doing that, why don't we talk about it?" Nidhi glanced again at the file on Jia's lap. "Anything good?"

"Can't say yet." Jia sighed, long and low. "Or ever, actually."

"Any idea how someone could hide that much money? How would he even go about doing it?"

"When you have enough money, you can pay people to do just about anything."

Nidhi's nod was solemn. "Maybe he hid it for tax purposes, and now he's afraid to admit it because then he would have to pay all those back taxes?" Leave it to Nidhi to look for a way to give even the most villainous villain the benefit of the doubt. Her earnest optimism was often a balm to Jia's snide realism.

As for Elisa's amused pessimism? There wasn't much either of them could do about that.

"It's possible about the taxes. Unlikely. But possible." Jia angled toward Nidhi while struggling how to phrase what she wished to say.

What they usually did in these situations—though it toed the line of propriety—was speak in hypotheticals. *If* Nidhi had a well-known client looking for a new home that could accommodate a cedar-lined sex dungeon, or *if* Elisa uncovered news that a famous actress's trailer had been suspiciously swaying during downtime with her costar, or *if* Jia was forced to converse with a client who wished to speak solely on Zoom from his pitch-dark penthouse clad in nothing but underwear and suspenders . . .

It was all about the hypotheticals.

And even though Jia desperately wanted to speak to her friend about Seven Park's forthcoming bundle of joy, the real reason she wanted to confide in Nidhi about what happened at Bergdorf's was so she could ask her what to do about her silly schoolgirl crush on Darius. How endlessly frustrating it was that the first guy she felt drawn to after her gut punch of a breakup with Zain had to be in the employ of her newest, biggest client.

Of course, Darius felt the same attraction. Of course he did. That was just how this shit went. If Jia were actively looking for someone to date, all she'd come across would be a sea of scroll trolls: the guys on dating apps who desperately needed to pay a penance or some kind of toll before anyone would even consider swiping right. The ones grinning while holding a giant fish on a lure always seemed to have a particular affinity for Jia. Why? Just . . . why?

Literally and metaphorically gross.

Jia wondered what might happen if she were to change her profile pic to an image of herself shoe shopping at Saks, her smile enraptured, her eyes wild with ecstasy. That would definitely hook a man. She just knew it would. Plus it had the added benefit of being exactly as relevant as the godforsaken fish pic.

Darius would probably laugh if she told him. And dare her, without words, to try it.

Jia looked down at her lap, mildly disgusted with herself. Here she was, traveling across the Atlantic with her incredibly accomplished friend on the most important work trip of her life, and the only thing she truly wanted to talk about was a boy.

Would this ever end? Or would they just be seventy-year-old biddies on a fictional front porch, lamenting their lost loves?

Jia refused to be a walking, talking failure of a Bechdel test.

"So"—she leaned toward Nidhi with a conspiratorial look—"hypothetically . . ."

Nidhi nodded, making an X over her chest in a cross-your-heart, hope-to-die gesture. "Yes, yes."

"Hypothetically," Jia continued, "what would you say if I knew about a client who is about to go through a divorce because they may or may not have a mistress pregnant with a boy?"

Nidhi's brow furrowed. "Why does the gender matter? Hypothetically," she added.

"Because, hypothetically, this client may want to pass along his company to his son . . . and he may be disinclined to name any of his current children as his successor."

"Because?" Nidhi's eyes turned into slits.

"Because they are, hypothetically, not on his side in the divorce . . . and, though he hasn't said it aloud, he doesn't approve of his gay son's lifestyle."

"Ugh," Nidhi groaned. "Love the sinner, hate the sin nonsense?"

Jia nodded. "Hypothetically."

"Well," Nidhi said, "if we are, hypothetically, talking about someone who cheated on his wife, impregnated his mistress, and is now trying to disinherit his children, I think if I were representing the rest of his family, I would probably brandish a bagh nakh right before telling him to stick it where the sun doesn't shine." She blinked. "Does that count as an idiom? Am I going to have to a pay a fine for breaking your moratorium?"

"In this case, I'll allow it. Also I don't think that counts as an idiom."

"Blessings and virtue, blessings and virtue." Nidhi waved her hands. "Any headway on figuring out where the money went?"

Another sigh flew past Jia's lips. "Not really. We are just touching the surface. I'm hoping this trip will point me in the right direction. Otherwise, we might have to start getting nasty with depositions and subpoenas. Stuff the other side can use to stall." Her voice fell below a whisper. "And we don't have the luxury of time."

Nidhi's responding nod was grave. "This is . . . a lot of pressure to put on yourself. Especially with such a short deadline."

"My boss said the same thing. He was ticked off when I told him Jenny Park agreed to give us only one month, but it was the best I could do."

"Of course. You always give it your all, Jia. I just want to make sure you're taking care of yourself, too."

"Don't worry about me," Jia said, her annoyance spiking again. "I'm used to it. If I can't handle this kind of pressure, then I have no business being the youngest senior partner at my firm. Speaking of, I should probably get back to it."

Nidhi's features softened, as if she wanted to press further. But instead she nodded and raised the divider between them.

Jia stared down at the file in her lap. Let the letters and numbers swim before her eyes while she worked through her emotions. As Minsoo Park had detailed, the trail for the Park family's money was—on the surface—fairly simple. Seven and Jenny Park had several joint accounts, as well as two savings accounts, along with a few retirement accounts and a handful of brokerage accounts. The total sum of these accounts was around twenty-six million dollars. All Jenny Park's personal expenses were being pulled from one of their joint accounts. Once a month, seventy-five thousand dollars was deposited into that account. Expenses for the staff were deducted from another joint account. The only property currently in both their names was the Park Avenue residence. The other residences Sora had mentioned, as well as an impressive yacht moored off the coast of Crete and a custom Gulfstream jet, were held either in a trust or in the company's name.

At first glance, it appeared that Seven Park's assertion with respect to their family's assets was accurate. In fact, he might even come across as generous in his initial settlement offer. Fifteen million dollars and the largest, most expensive home in their portfolio could be considered more than fair.

But even if these bank statements offered the full picture, Seven stood to make many hundreds of millions more simply by hanging on to their company after his wife's passing. A fortune he could then decide to bestow as he saw fit, without anyone's input or interference.

All Jia could hope to uncover was some evidence—anything—that suggested that Seven was not offering a complete, accurate picture of the family's finances. It was a gamble to begin by questioning the chef who had abruptly left Jenny Park's employ.

But speaking with Orlagh Campbell was as good a place as any to start.

Jia switched around the files on her lap and opened another to reread its contents. To make sure she familiarized herself with as many details as possible. Her time as a lawyer had taught her that it wasn't enough to know the law inside and out. A good attorney—in any field of law—was also adept at reading people. At understanding their goals and preferred methods of communication. At being able to answer questions before they were asked and provide the kind of unblinking reassurance Gerard Butler conveyed in all his movies.

*I've got this. If any fucker gets in our way, I'll blow the dobber to smithereens.*

Now more than ever, Jia wished she had a Scottish accent.

Orlagh Campbell was fifty-six years old. Born and raised outside Edinburgh, she attended cooking school at Le Cordon Bleu, then promptly began to work in middle-of-the-mill kitchens in Manchester, followed by a stint in London. On a whim, Orlagh decided to travel to New York City with a colleague to attend a convention on specialized cookware.

A few introductions were made, and Orlagh was hired as the sous-chef at the restaurant of the moment on the Upper East Side. The grueling pace and long hours began to wear on her as she aged into her midforties. Opportunities to become an establishment's chef de cuisine—often offered to her male counterparts—were not offered to her. The dream of running her own kitchen appeared to be slipping from her grasp. Without that, it would be difficult for Orlagh to become the kind of chef who helmed a franchise or fielded offers to merchandise her wares or wrote a bestselling cookbook, all things she'd fantasized about making happen for herself and for her college-age daughter back in Scotland.

More introductions were made. Not long after that, Orlagh began to work as a private chef, catering to residents of Billionaires' Row. Soon she was referred to Jenny Park to cook for an event celebrating Minsoo's graduation from Stanford. She and Jenny worked together on the menu, Orlagh delighting at the chance to learn how to prepare Korean cuisine from someone who enjoyed cooking it. Jenny and Orlagh became fast friends. They traded recipes and left each other notes on a small whiteboard Jenny kept on top of her desk. Suggestions for a pinch more sugar or a new way to brine pork or an interesting addition to a recipe neither of them had considered before.

After several years of Orlagh catering all the family's special events, Jenny asked her to work for their family exclusively, full-time. Their friendship had only solidified further over the following decade. Orlagh had even attended several of Jenny Park's chemo treatments, sitting with her in the waiting room and eating Popsicles while they watched Korean dramas together.

Just as Darius had mentioned at Bergdorf's, it appeared that Jenny and Orlagh were more than just an employer and her employee. In fact, everyone around Jenny seemed to have been in her employ for years. Loyalty seemed to matter a great deal to her.

Jia wondered how deeply Seven's betrayal had cut.

If anything, this proved she needed to speak to Jenny again. That much was certain.

As Jia sifted through the contents of the larger, accordion-style folder containing all the smaller files, she came across the tab with Darius Hossein Rohani's name on it. Curious to see if the firm's investigators had collected any information outside what Darius had already offered her—and eager to learn if they'd managed to obtain any details about his failed engagement—Jia opened it.

The perfect diversion.

Her eyes scanned the words collected within the file, her pupils flashing quickly over the contents, watching for anything that stood out.

Information on his background zipped through her mind like ticker tape. How his family had fled Iran just before the fall of the shah. The death of his mother in a terrible automobile accident outside the city. A car traveling in the opposite direction had struck black ice on a chilly February evening before careening into Darius's mother's car. She was killed instantly.

Jia wondered what it must have been like to lose his mother at such a young age.

Her eyes continued roving over the file. How he graduated as the salutatorian of his public high school in Brooklyn. His years at Penn. Pictures of a younger, more disheveled version of him, grinning among his peers and cheering on the Knicks at the Garden, all undoubtedly purloined from social media. A single shot of Darius with his arm slung around the waist of a pretty, petite blond girl with an enviable rack, holding a Fordham diploma.

All of a sudden, Jia's face went hot. Her eyes widened with shock.

Followed by a spike of rage so sudden and severe that it sent her pulse thudding into her ears and her heart clambering into her throat.

He'd lied to her about his past. He'd deliberately concealed a part of himself that he—of all people—should have disclosed to her.

And it stung. Stung her far deeper than it should have, for the worst reason.

She read the lines again. She'd known it. Even while she smiled at Darius and allowed blurry fantasies to glimmer through her imagination, she'd known to expect this betrayal.

"That lying prick," she whispered.

*Sorry, Gail,* Jia thought to herself.

But these words weren't going to wash off her skin anytime soon.

# SCOTS WHA HAE

*T Minus 24 Days*

At least four times during the rest of their flight to London, Jia considered revealing to Nidhi what she'd learned about Darius Rohani's past. She'd been so close to confessing everything. The stupid crush and her strange suspicion that he would betray her, followed by the proof.

But Jia hadn't said anything.

Perhaps it was out of shame. Or maybe it was because she couldn't bear to hear her friend's wise rejoinders about not making assumptions and letting him have a chance to explain before jumping to conclusions. Regardless, Jia was in no mood to grant Darius clemency. Nor was she in the right headspace to listen to Jiminy Cricket wax poetic about giving this jackass the benefit of the doubt.

It was better to forget about it, for now at least. Tuck her fury away for future Jia to deal with. She didn't have time for this. She was here to work. Here to prove that she belonged in the room with the Benjamin Volkers and Emily Bhatias of the legal world.

No perfidious man with beautiful hands was going to distract her from that task.

Traveling to a new country was just the kind of diversion she needed. Jia had never been to Scotland before, though she'd often daydreamed about it, especially as a Harry Potter–obsessed child. Craggy castles of stained stone and misty windblown moors had taken residence in her mind. Made her believe in magic.

Now that she was an adult, those kinds of dreams eluded her. But as soon as she stepped outside the Waverley train station in Edinburgh, she became convinced the whole country was haunted. That magic, just maybe, did indeed still have a foothold in this world.

She couldn't articulate why. It was simply a feeling. Like déjà vu or a glitch in the matrix. Something about how the world around her appeared to have grayed, all while managing to look sharper and more vivid in the same instant. The way the starlight caught on a flicker of shadow. The sound of a keening wail buoyed on a gust of wind. Horse hooves clattering down cobblestones. It was like a glimpse of the past through a hidden portal. The modern and the ancient together as one.

That was what it was. Edinburgh felt like a living, breathing contradiction. As if a place could seem cold and uninviting at first glance, only to welcome you inside to warm yourself by the fire, a cheeky glint in its eye.

It was dusk, but the sky was almost black. An eerie mist hovered in the air, the pavement glistening at her feet. It was fiendishly chilly. Each breath shrouded Jia's face in smoke. She swore she heard the chittering of bats behind her. At least it sounded like it might be bats.

Jia had no idea what bats sounded like.

The driver—a tall older man named Hamish with a soft midsection and a set brow—tugged her small Rimowa suitcase at a crisp pace toward a waiting black Mercedes-AMG sedan. A moment later they were whisking off into the velvet darkness on their way to the Balmoral.

Jia had enjoyed traveling from an early age. But she'd come to find, as she grew older, that her imagination often set her up for disappointment. She blamed social media for a lot of it. All the curated pictures and endless hype fueled impossible expectations. No beach looked that pristine, its water glinting like a polished aquamarine. No city could possibly be that exciting, no vignette quite so perfect.

In the harsh light of day, the truth revealed itself, which was why it was better for Jia to have no expectations. No regrets and no expectations. This phrase had more or less become her motto when it came to any new experience.

But Edinburgh was proving to be an exception. When the city's raised center first came into view, Jia found herself marveling at the sight. The way the Royal Mile perched atop a sharp jutting of rock, as if the mountain had suddenly punched through the earth like a fist, looking every bit as old world and awe-inspiring as it did in pictures.

There really was a castle at its apex, complete with sooty-looking stones and rigid crenellations and snapping crests. Red lights glowed along its fortifying walls, bathing the ancient structure in a wash of rosy hues.

"Beautiful," she said. She noticed Hamish glance at her in the rearview mirror. She smiled in reply. No matter how often she used car services, Jia still didn't feel comfortable riding anywhere in total silence.

"Is that Castle Rock?" she asked Hamish. "Or is it better to call it Old Town?"

"Old Town rests on Castle Rock, miss," he replied without looking away from the road, the *r*'s rolling from his tongue with a lovely Scottish burr.

"Does the red color have some significance?"

"Aye. It's to do with the fact that the rock was formed millions of years ago from an exploding volcano."

"I didn't know that." Jia stared beyond the tinted glass, trying to get a closer look.

"'Tis why they chose this place to build a castle. The way the lava cooled formed all these spaces deep beneath the rock. Almost like caves or hollows. Thousands of people made homes within them for centuries. Can you imagine? Carving homes out of volcanic rock with nothing more than the simplest of tools." The pride in his voice reminded Jia of how her harabugi talked about his childhood along the southern coast of Korea. The tales about the fishermen wrangling their boats in a storm. How the wind would howl, and the waves would lash, but they would work together to make sure everyone returned safely, come hell or high water. One story in particular he told so often that Jia and her brothers would furtively mouth the words to one another while he spoke. Never in a mean way, always out of fondness, punctuated by secret smiles.

Jia nearly grinned at the memory, despite the twinge of missing her grandfather. "Have you lived in Edinburgh a long time?"

"Aye." Hamish said. "Was born here. Plan to die here, too."

Jia's favorite places to visit in the world were ones like this. Places where people wished to live their entire lives, as if the soil itself had seeped into their bones. "I bet you know all the great places to visit and the best restaurants in town."

"Aye. Would you care for some dinner recommendations?"

Jia opened her mouth to admit she didn't have time for dinner, but then a spark of rebellion fizzed through her. Maybe it was because she wanted to distract herself from her anger at Darius. Or maybe it was because she knew, deep down, that Nidhi was right about the tedium of room service club sandwiches.

Or maybe she simply appreciated how Hamish had reminded her of her grandfather.

"You know, I would love to try something truly Scottish." Jia leaned forward, trying her best to engage him from the back seat. "I bet people probably say this all the time, but I mean it. I don't want any frills. I'd like to know where people who've lived in Edinburgh their entire lives go to eat."

Hamish laughed, but it sounded polite. "You've read some things and want to try haggis and Cullen skink. You ken what's in them?"

Jia nodded. "My family is from Korea. I'm not about to be scared of offal. We like to cook ours in blood."

This time he laughed in earnest. "I'd like to try that. And you're sure you wouldn't want to keep to any of the finer places around your hotel?"

"Don't worry about me. I can find my way around, especially if it means eating a good meal. If there's one thing a Korean can do, it's eat and drink well wherever we go." Jia grinned. "I've always believed food is our love language. My mother doesn't know how to tell me she's proud of me or that something I've done or said is meaningful to her. All she knows how to do is feed me until I can't eat another bite. Right before telling me I'm getting fat."

He guffawed again. "You've convinced me. I have some places in the New Town and Grassmarket to recommend. 'Twill be easy for you to find your way back to the Balmoral from there."

"Wonderful. Thank you so much, Hamish."

He nodded, his features relaxed. Almost fond. "Then if it's all right with you, I'll return tomorrow morning at ten sharp for the drive to Falkirk."

"That's perfect."

"Will you be wanting to stop and see any sights there?"

Jia thought for a moment. She shouldn't. But that unsettled feeling that had struck her on the plane was dissipating in Hamish's presence. Perhaps a small detour on their way back to the hotel wouldn't be a bad idea. "I'm not sure I'll have the time. Is there much to see around Falkirk?"

"Aye. 'Tis one of my favorite cities. After Edinburgh."

"Really?" Jia searched her mind for any recollections she might have of Falkirk. Sadly, the best she could think of was a scene from a Mel Gibson movie. "Unfortunately, the only thing I know offhand about Falkirk is the battle that occurred there. The one William Wallace lost."

"Och, you'd best watch what you're saying about the Wallace, lass!"

Dismay flared on her face. "I'm so sorry—"

His laughter echoed through the car. "I'm only teasing. Shouldna still be angry about something that happened eight hundred years ago, but that's Scotland. Longer memories you won't find, especially when it comes to slights. And the English."

"*That* I can understand well, sir." Jia laughed.

"Truly you'll love the town. 'Tis a lovely place, with its own kind of magic. Not as gloomy as Edinburgh."

"Strangely I think I enjoy the gloom."

"I believe there's a Scotswoman in you, as well." He paused. "But do me a favor. It won't do for you to only recall Wallace's loss at Falkirk. What happened there paved the way for the Bruce's victory at Bannockburn. The darkest paths often lead to the brightest light. All we need is a bit of faith." He paused to clear his throat. "'*Who for Scotland's King and Law / Freedom's sword will strongly draw / Freeman stand or freeman fall / Let him follow me!*'" His words boomed through the darkened interior of the Mercedes sedan.

Jia applauded.

"In a past life, I was a stage actor."

"You still are. Your voice reminds me of Anthony Hopkins."

"Taught the rascal everything he knows." Hamish winked. "If you get the chance, read the rest of that poem. It's one of my favorites. Robert Burns's 'Scots Wha Hae.'"

Jia nodded. "I'll do that, Hamish. Gladly. And thank you again."

"Of course, miss."

"Jia," she corrected. "If we're sharing how we like our offal and performing poetry on the fly, you should call me Jia."

"Aye, Jia." His eyes twinkled.

Again her heart ached as if a string around it had been pulled tight. Harabugi's eyes had always twinkled when he looked at Jia. She'd sworn she could see a better version of herself in their reflection. Harabugi would have liked Hamish. Just as Jia knew he would have loved Scotland.

She squeezed her hands into fists. The work she was doing—the power and success almost within her reach—would guarantee that Jia could take her parents to all the places her grandfather had never been able to go.

Maybe money didn't solve all problems, but she could make damned certain it would never be an obstacle.

# BONA FIDE

It cannot have escaped our dear readers' notice that this author delights in words of all stripes, from origins both modern and ancient. It is likely because this author has been a voracious reader for most of their life. A student of many languages, so to speak. The language of love, of course. The language of loss, naturally, for it is love's lonely twin.

In loving languages, this author has also found a great passion for the way words are used to tell stories. How they manage to engender trust. Or how they can create a sense of ominousness with seemingly little effort. A change in cadence. A shift in rhythm. The shortening of sounds and the lengthening of silence.

How, from nowhere, a voice emerges.

These types of voices have fascinated this author for years. But why do certain voices engender trust, while others evoke suspicion? How simple is it to don the guise of one only to shed it for another with the ease of shrugging out of a coat?

It is, without a doubt, a great deal of fun to try on many different coats, is it not? We may discover that one does not suit, or another may offer a surprising change of pace, but at the end of the day, are we not inclined to pretend we are someone else—someone richer, more attractive, more interesting—every once in a while?

Lately this author has become fascinated by the way words from another language infiltrate popular dialogue until they are accepted as common parlance. Over the centuries, many Latin legal terms have managed to do this. Often they are used without the speaker truly knowing their meaning. *Bona fide*, *per se*, *alter ego*, *affidavit*, and *pro bono* come to mind.

But two stand out for both their meaning and significance.

*Bona fide*, which is routinely mispronounced. The second part of the phrase, *fide*, does not rhyme with *pride*, but rather has two syllables. *Bone-ah fee-day*. Many readers may understand this phrase to mean *genuine* or *true*, but, in fact, its meaning is more complicated than that. In legal circles, *bona fide* suggests something done in good faith, with good intentions, regardless of the outcome.

The second Latin legal term of note is *culpa*. Often the phrase *mea culpa* is spoken to suggest a person might be at fault. But there are several kinds of fault, as they pertain to the law. Three, to be exact:

Gross negligence.

Ordinary negligence.

And slight negligence.

Reader, please forgive this author for what may one day be perceived to be ordinary negligence. A case could be made for gross negligence, perhaps. It would depend on the storytelling skills of the attorney—the chosen voice—making the argument, as always.

But please believe this author when they say they were bona fide, from the beginning.

For the things within our control, mea culpa. For the things that are not?

Behold your chosen villain in whatever light you deem worthy. It would be well-earned.

# TRAUMA RESPONSE

## T Minus 23 Days

The knock came at the door to Jia's hotel room just as she was stepping into her Lanvin flats. Certain it had to be the cleaning service, she paused to rummage through the closet for an umbrella. Of course it would be raining in Falkirk, today of all days.

Orlagh Campbell still had not returned any of Jia's six phone calls, nor had she responded to the three voicemails or any of the four emails Jia had sent. Truth be told, Jia wasn't surprised that Orlagh was avoiding her. Returning the calls of an attorney representing a former employer could not be high on anyone's list of favorite things to do. It was why Jia had elected to make the trip to Scotland in person. Emails and messages were easy enough to ignore. Someone standing on your doorstep, waiting in the rain? Not so much.

The knocking resumed, this time more insistent.

"One minute," Jia said over her shoulder as she scanned the room a final time. Maybe there were umbrellas at the concierge desk.

The tiny, anxiety-laden voice that never failed to follow Jia wherever she went whispered in her ear: *What if Orlagh refuses to meet with you? How are you going to convince her to help?*

*What are you going to do, Jia Song?*

*Bang. Bang. Bang.*

Jia sucked in her cheeks. In two strides, she arrived at the door and yanked it open, a peevish look on her face.

"Hello." Minsoo Park smiled at her, his expression otherwise inscrutable.

Jia cleared her throat in astonishment. "Hi."

He glanced left and right. "Did I catch you at a bad time?"

"Uh." Jia's eyes went wide. She checked her watch. 9:51 a.m. "I'm actually on my way out the door."

Minsoo nodded. "Great. I'll come with you to Falkirk."

"How do you know where I'm going?" Jia blurted.

His smile was indulgent. Patiently patronizing. "Why would you be in Scotland if not to speak with Orlagh? Also I asked your secretary to put me in touch with the car service here."

Of course he did. Since this was all being billed to the Park family, Minsoo decided he was entitled to know Jia's comings and goings.

But why not just ask her directly?

Jia's last conversation with Suzy Park rang through her ears like a muted scream. Suzy had wanted her to speak to Minsoo as soon as he returned from his business trip in Germany because she suspected her brother might have made some kind of under-the-table deal with their father. Maybe he was here to cause trouble. Or report back to Seven on Jia's findings. She pulled the door closed behind her and frowned up at him. "There's no need for you to come with me."

Minsoo stepped aside to let her pass, nonplussed. "Don't worry. I'm just along for the ride. I won't get in your way."

Flustered, Jia straightened the collar of her trench coat. "Please don't take this the wrong way, but I think it might be better if I speak to Ms. Campbell alone."

Minsoo nodded. "That's fine. I can wait in the car while you interview her. But I'd like to talk to her myself once you're done."

To think, he was supposed to be Jia's favorite Park sibling. Her nose wrinkled again. She wanted to ask Minsoo why he hadn't called to tell her he would be coming. It wasn't a long flight from Munich to Edinburgh. But she didn't deserve to be ambushed by her own client.

In stilted silence, Jia and Minsoo made their way down the warmly lit hall toward the elevator. As they descended to the lobby, he appeared engrossed in messages on his phone. Unperturbed.

"Did I catch you off guard?" Minsoo asked without looking up.

"Yes." If he was going to be direct, he deserved nothing less from her.

He smirked, his eyes still trained on his screen. "Sorry I didn't call."

"No, you're not."

Minsoo met her gaze and shrugged. "You're right. I'm not."

"Why are you here?"

"Because I'm pretty sure Suzy freaked out and told you I was betraying my family."

Jia said nothing. The elevator door chimed open, and she marched into the grand lobby of the Balmoral with the youngest Park sibling at her side, his three-piece navy suit, burgundy tie, and double-breasted wool coat a perfect complement to the space.

"Am I wrong?" he pressed.

Jia pursed her lips and hitched her Prada tote higher on her shoulder.

"Didn't think so," Minsoo said. "It's smart of Suzy to act like a drama queen. No one sees her as a threat, even when they should."

Jia struggled to conceal her disbelief. The Parks were something else. In less than forty-eight hours, two of the siblings had sought her out to undermine each other. On two different continents, no less. Should she be expecting Sora to jump from behind a velvet curtain at any second?

"I'm not going to make the mistake of underestimating Suzy," Minsoo continued as he followed Jia through the arched entryway into a gray Scottish morning. "Not about this. It's too important."

Jia stopped short. "So you flew all the way here to convince me you're not in league with your father? Kind of begs the point."

Minsoo paused beside her but didn't reply, which raised Jia's hackles further.

"Interesting," she murmured.

He exhaled hard, his breath clouding his face for a moment. "Suzy thrives in situations like this, where every little thing seems like life or death. If you let her, she'll spend hours wailing about the way someone looked at her at lunch or how this person didn't punctuate a text message properly and therefore must despise her."

Gail would probably say Suzy's behavior was a trauma response. "Okay." Jia crossed her arms. "If you knew this about your sister, then why didn't you answer her texts?"

"I don't have the time or the inclination to humor her."

Jia doubted that. It was far more likely that Minsoo Park enjoyed pushing buttons every bit as much as his sister did. "But you have the time to fly to Scotland unannounced to look over my shoulder while I work?"

Minsoo lowered his phone and met her gaze full-on. "Look, I'm sorry. I'm not here to micromanage you. It's true I hold things close to the chest. My colleagues would say I enjoy strategizing, but I'm not cruel. This isn't a transaction to me. This is about my family."

"If you were me, wouldn't all this make you even more suspicious?"

"Not necessarily." Minsoo put his hands in the pockets of his rich brown coat. "I'm here to make sure no one bribed Orlagh or bullied her into silence. Frankly, I don't think she's going to talk to you, especially with the NDA my father would have made her sign." He took a step closer to Jia and dropped his voice, again the picture of sincerity. "If my father mistreated her, I want to make things right. You're welcome to stay and hear what I have to say, and I'll give you complete privacy when you're with Orlagh, but I don't think either of us can afford to waste a second of our *limited* time." With that, he made his way over to the black Mercedes-AMG, where Hamish stood waiting. Then Minsoo glanced over his shoulder, his eyebrows raised.

After a beat, Jia joined them. Minsoo was right. She didn't have time to waste. As much as she wanted to doubt him, Minsoo's behavior was consistent with the protective vibe Jia had noted in their first meeting. But she wasn't about to let her guard down. If he wanted to speak in person with Orlagh Campbell, that was his prerogative. Doing her job effectively was hers.

---

True to his word, the youngest Park sibling did not disturb Jia the entire fifty-minute drive to Falkirk. Instead, they both assumed the appearance of being engrossed in their respective work, he on his phone and she with her notes, worrying a copy of Orlagh Campbell's resignation letter between her fingers.

Part of Jia wanted to engage Minsoo in a real conversation. Every minute she spent around him, she felt as though she were observing the tip of an iceberg. Or maybe a duck gliding across a pond with seeming ease, all while its feet moved under the water in a ceaseless frenzy.

Minsoo took pains to appear in control. That was probably his trauma response.

Jia almost laughed. If she could get any of these three adult babies to be honest with her, she could probably get to the bottom of everything in a matter of days.

Hamish peered at Jia through the rearview mirror, a touch of sympathy in his expression. "We're nearly there, miss."

They were back to *miss*. It felt like Minsoo Park had conspired to ruin her entire day. "Thank you, Hamish." Jia smiled at him. Then she attempted to call the number her firm's private investigators had provided for Orlagh Campbell a seventh and final time.

Again, it went straight to voicemail.

No matter. If Jia had to stand in the rain and bang on the front door of a house on the outskirts of a town in northern Scotland, she would do it. Perhaps it was unconventional. Surely a PI could have done this. But, as Minsoo had said, Jia did not have a second to waste. Moreover, she didn't want any underlings involved in the exchange of information relevant to this case. She wanted to hear it from the horse's mouth.

Jesus, she sounded like Nidhi.

The Mercedes glided to a halt in front of a small two-story home that reminded Jia of a gingerbread house, its windows designed with crisscrossed mullions, its walls a mixture of wood and stucco, topped by a low roofline. All the curtains were pulled shut, though the grass was freshly cut, the flowers neatly tended.

She took a deep breath before glancing at Minsoo. He nodded once. Jia slid from the black Mercedes—her borrowed umbrella sheltering her from the misting rain—and walked up to the front door.

She felt alive and aware, her skin uncomfortably tight. The smell of iron and loam filled her lungs, the scent of newly fallen rain on tilled earth. A damp chill toyed with the ties of her trench coat, and the sound of waterdrops striking stone echoed in her ears.

She knocked on the door.

No one answered.

The tips of her fingers tingling, Jia waited a moment and knocked again.

The beige curtains covering the mullioned window rustled.

Jia knocked louder, her heart beating faster.

The lock clicked, and the door opened six inches. Half the face of a woman in her late twenties or early thirties appeared, shadows cloaking the room behind her. She considered Jia for a beat, her straight auburn hair hanging limp past her shoulders, her gray eyes brimming with suspicion.

"Hello." Jia smiled. "My name is Jia Song. I'm here to speak with Orlagh Campbell."

The woman blinked. Her eyes narrowed. "Why do you want to speak with my mother?"

Jia inhaled and smiled once more. She recalled from the investigator's file that Orlagh's only daughter's name was Fiona. Disclosing she knew that would only stir this woman's ire. She'd wait until Fiona introduced herself. "I was hoping to speak directly with Orlagh please, if you don't—"

"You're part of that family, aren't you?"

It was Jia's turn to blink. "Which family?" The quiet accusation in Fiona's voice made the hairs on the back of Jia's neck stand on end.

"The Park family." Deep lines etched around her mouth. "That rich Korean family."

"I'm not a member of the Park family." Jia stood taller and squared her shoulders. "But I do represent them." The misting rain began to fall harder, striking her borrowed umbrella with the quickening beat of a snare drum.

"In what capacity?" Fiona asked.

If Orlagh Campbell was half as tough as her daughter, this conversation would be challenging. Perhaps Minsoo had been right to come. But Orlagh was a friend of Jenny's. Jia wanted to trust that the family's longtime chef wouldn't betray her dying friend by conspiring with a philandering husband. "I'm a lawyer."

Fiona opened the door six inches wider and crossed her slender arms. "I was wondering when one of your kind would grace my doorstep." Somewhere in the darkness deep within the home, a baby began to wail.

"I can come back later if that will be more con—"

"No," Fiona said, her pale lips pressed into a line. "It won't be more convenient. I don't wish to see you ever again." She sighed and twisted the long ends of her auburn hair into a quick bun. "Wait here." With that, she closed the door.

A minute passed before Fiona returned, holding a manila envelope the size of a piece of paper. "Here," she said, shoving it through the six-inch gap.

Jia took a step back, frustration taking hold of her. Of all the things she'd been expecting, a gatekeeping daughter had not been one of them. "I was really hoping to speak with your mother. I know she and Jenny Park were—"

"You can't speak to my mother," Fiona replied. "My mother . . ." Her voice wavered, the words trailing into a whisper. "Is dead."

Jia's body went numb. "What? How? I mean, I—"

"Last week," Fiona said. Her eyes started to water. Then anger descended on her like a thundercloud. "Take this cursed thing and go. Never show your face here again. I'll deny it till the cows come a-lowing if anyone asks me where you got this."

"Please, if I could just—"

"Take it and go away." She swiped at streams of angry tears. "I'll never be able to prove it. None of us will. But that damned thing . . . my mother died for it, mark my words. 'Tis a family of murdering thieves."

Jia stumbled backward as Orlagh Campbell's daughter shoved the envelope into her chest and slammed the door shut.

Jia remained frozen on the front stoop, the manila envelope clasped in her hands. She wanted to open it, but Fiona's accusation roared in her ears.

A *family of murdering thieves.*

Minsoo Park was waiting in the car, undoubtedly watching everything that had transpired. Without turning around, Jia looked in the reflection of the windows in front of her. The falling rain obscured the inside of the black AMG from view. She had to hope that Minsoo couldn't see what Fiona had passed to her. Her fingers shaking, Jia pinched open the brass tabs. Three sheets of thick paper slid into her waiting fingers.

Without a second thought, Jia crammed the copy of Orlagh's resignation letter into the envelope, in case Minsoo asked her about its contents. Before she folded up the three pages and stuffed them into her trench coat, Jia glanced at the lines of numbers and letters in front of her. They swam through her brain like water rushing over rocks in a creek bed.

It was a bank statement.

From an account in the Cayman Islands. Dated five months ago.

With a balance of almost $167 million.

# THE TRUST LIES

## T Minus 22 Days

Jia spoke to the abstract drawing on the taupe wall behind Gail's head, as she always did. It comforted her to do that. The way its black lines and blank spaces looked like the head of a friendly dog or the front of an old-timey car or a sketch of a mother done by a whimsical child.

But in certain lights it turned sinister. Once, Jia swore it looked like a leering Count Orlok, the vampire's shoulders hunched as it licked its fangs and glared into her eyes.

Even then, the drawing comforted her. In this odd little Rorschach test, Jia knew she could see a reflection of her inner self. She trusted it, sometimes even more than she trusted her therapist of the last two years.

"What did your client say when he learned that this person had accused his family of committing a crime?" Gail asked in her trademark soothing voice.

"He didn't react. It was like he shut down the second he heard what had happened," Jia said to the drawing. "He didn't speak to me after that. He disappeared as soon as we returned to our hotel, and I haven't heard from him since." She recalled what Suzy had said about her brother being good at two things: money and checking out when you most needed him.

Jia wondered why.

Gail's head canted left, the light of the nearby Tiffany lamp flashing in her dark-framed glasses. "That must have been difficult for you." She tucked one side of her Anna Wintour bob behind an ear. "I'm sure you wanted to hear his reaction."

Jia chose her next words with care. "You know, I thought I wanted to. But every time I looked his way or attempted to engage him, he acted as if I wasn't there at all. Just continued working on his phone. It unnerved me. Almost like"—she hesitated—"like I was dealing with a sociopath or something. I mean, what kind of person doesn't react to being accused of a serious crime? By the end of the trip, I didn't want to know what he was thinking anymore."

Her mind flashed back to the memory. The second Jia had returned to the Balmoral, she'd reached out to Benjamin Volker and their firm's investigators. The official inquest into Orlagh Campbell's death had yet to be completed, but hospital records indicated that she had succumbed to a stroke. Her daughter had found her unresponsive on the floor of the bathroom, per the police in Falkirk. The reason the private investigators had failed to uncover Orlagh's death during their initial search was simple: nothing was officially on the record, given the fact that she'd perished only a few days ago.

It also seemed—the investigator admitted to Jia over the phone—as though everything around Orlagh's death was being intentionally obfuscated.

As if someone had something to hide.

Worry plagued Jia that night. The cool conversation she'd had with Ben hadn't helped. If the hospital records indicated that Orlagh had died of a stroke, then Fiona's accusations were baseless, he'd stated dismissively. Jia shouldn't worry about it. "The daughter," he'd said, was most likely speaking from a place of pain and loss. No one in the Park family could have killed her mother.

Right?

Jia's thoughts had circled in a constant loop. Maybe Fiona held the Park family responsible in a metaphorical way. Perhaps the stress of Orlagh's abrupt resignation, coupled with the fact that she'd purloined documents that did not belong to her when she left, had taken its toll. She could have been threatened or bullied into an uncomfortable silence, which further weighed on her.

Ben had warned Jia not to look for trouble. Jia understood his meaning well.

It wasn't her place to speculate or do the police's job. Nevertheless, she'd brought her worries to therapy. Careful not to disclose any specifics, of course.

Gail was exactly the kind of therapist Jia needed. When Jia had first started meeting with her, she would joke to Elisa and Nidhi about how her therapist had been a cat in a previous life. There was something feline about the way Gail carried herself. She didn't walk; she slinked. Her general air was one of detachment, like a cat licking its paw on a windowsill while the world burned below. It used to irk Jia. Now, as with the vampire drawing, it comforted her.

As an attorney, Jia couldn't divulge anything in the way of specifics when it came to her clients. Privilege prohibited her from speaking about them at all. She was blurring a line by opening the Park family's situation up for discussion, even in the most general terms.

But it wasn't every day that one of her clients was accused of murder. And the sight of the balance in the Cayman Islands bank account had been seared on the back of Jia's eyelids for the last twenty-four hours. Her next move needed to be made with care, which was why she'd decided to speak with Gail today, despite the jet lag and general exhaustion.

It was time to decide who to trust.

Sora, the Grand Gijibae? She'd made it clear how much she respected a pulae like Jia. Suzy, the Predictably Unpredictable Mess? Not the wisest choice, considering her penchant for paranoia. Minsoo, the Second Coming of Patrick Bateman? Nope. Not after the way he shut down and pretended as if nothing had happened. As if the daughter of their longtime chef hadn't accused his family of murder.

Last of all was Darius, the Lying Liar Who Lies. Jia's gaze hardened at the mere thought.

Gail continued watching Jia, her eyes steady. "You know, I've heard you mention several times that this is a family with a great deal of money."

Jia raised a shoulder. "Most of our firm's clients are quite wealthy."

"Yes," Gail agreed, "but I've noticed something particular in the way you speak about this family. It's different."

"How so?" Jia's pulse quickened.

"I feel like there's a lot of anger there. It's unusual."

Jia stopped her hands from turning into fists and proving Gail's point. "What kind of anger?"

"I'm not sure. But it's interesting to me because I've often suspected a deep well of anger resides in you. I wondered when it would make itself known."

Jia waited in uncomfortable silence, her hands rigid at her sides.

"The nature of your job does mean that you're often engaging with families and individuals who are quite wealthy, as you've already stated," Gail said. "But I wonder if your anger at this particular family stems from anger at yourself."

"I don't know why I would be angry at myself because of *them*."

"I think you believe money and success are incredibly important tools. And these people are taking them for granted." Another head tilt, this time in the opposite direction. "This calls into question the narrative you have in your mind about what it means to be successful. What it means to be able to provide for yourself and the ones you love. It's one of your fundamental tenets. You've done all this work to get someplace—to do *something*—and this family makes you realize that everything you've done still may not be enough to solve everyone's problems."

"I would never be in this kind of situation, for more reasons than one."

"Ah." Gail nodded. "There's judgment there. Resentment. *Anger*."

Jia swallowed. "If I'm angry, it's only because this family is making my job incredibly difficult."

"It's your job to handle difficult things. I'm not saying that to minimize your effort or the toll it takes on you. If what you did were easy, more people would be able to do it, right?"

"I suppose so." Jia sighed. "But I guess I'm wondering what the point is in all this. Wouldn't you be resentful, too?"

"I might be. I might also pity them." Gail shifted in her seat, folding one knee under the other.

"I suppose I feel both emotions."

Gail nodded. "Two extremes. It's difficult, I'm sure. But knowing this will help you make your decision about moving forward." She smiled slowly. Just like a cat. "What have I said before about trust?"

Jia refrained from rolling her eyes. It was a Gail Truism. One of *her* fundamental tenets. Something Jia had learned early in their sessions.

Gail said, "A lot of people believe that the opposite of anxiety is calm. Finding peace. I believe the opposite of anxiety is trust. Trust in a process, in an outcome, in a situation, or in a person. Ask yourself, 'Where are my anxieties in this situation? Where are my anxieties under my control?' Then you'll find where the trust lies."

"The trust lies," Jia murmured. "That's an interesting way of phrasing it."

A giggle flew from Gail's lips. Gail's giggle was the main reason Jia had chosen her from the four other therapists she'd interviewed. It was completely incongruous with everything else about her. It sounded girlish and silly and fun. Almost fake. Like the first time Jia ever heard Anderson Cooper laugh on TV.

It made Jia trust Gail. Probably because the sound of it had settled her anxieties about making the decision. Jia exhaled in a huff. Then aimed a begrudging smile in Gail's direction. "Thank you. I think I know what I need to do next."

Gail nodded and began taking notes. Just like that, she was back to licking her paw while the world burned.

# OLD KING COLE

## T Minus 22 Days

As soon as Jia left Gail's office, she texted Suzy Park, asking her to meet tonight, if possible.

Gail's point about her anxieties had been the deciding factor. When it came to the Park siblings, it was strange how quickly the tables had turned. Jia usually put more stock in first impressions. But the unsettling way that Minsoo had reacted in Scotland had lingered with Jia. He hadn't even asked what was inside the manila envelope.

How could he not even ask?

The only answer Jia could come up with was that he already knew. She'd thought Suzy might be paranoid when it came to her younger brother. Blowing things out of proportion as befitted her love of spectacle.

Now she wasn't so sure.

Jia waited for Suzy in the dark bar appointed in leather and richly stained wood at the St. Regis Hotel on Fifty-Fifth, staring at the mural on the wall behind her. The famous Maxfield Parrish mural of Old King Cole himself. Then she looked down at the leopard-print carpet and suppressed a smile.

The last time she'd come to the King Cole Bar was with Elisa and Nidhi, a little more than a year ago. They'd agreed to try the bar's famous Bloody Mary—allegedly invented in this exact spot—and decide whether it was worthy of the claim. Elisa and Jia would drink theirs with the requisite vodka, and Nidhi, who did not consume alcohol, would try one without.

After sipping their beverages and enjoying their bar bites for an hour or so, a slightly tipsy Elisa had decided to share the story behind the immense mural that provided the bar with its namesake.

"Did you know that John Jacob Astor himself commissioned that painting of Old King Cole sitting on his throne?" she asked, inclining her head toward it.

Jia's eyebrows shot up. "As in John Jacob Astor, the wealthiest passenger on the *Titanic*?"

"The very one." Elisa took another sip of her Bloody Mary and settled into her seat. "Legend has it that good old JJ had been trying to commission Maxfield Parrish to paint something for his Knickerbocker Hotel for quite some time. He offered Parrish an ungodly sum of money. Like almost a quarter of a million dollars in today's money. Finally Parrish agreed. The two hotheads fought about the mural like cats in heat, to the point where it was said that Parrish loathed the very sight of Astor. When he delivered the final product, he made sure to stick it to good old JJ in the best way possible." She paused to take another sip of her drink, delighting in the looks of annoyance shared between Jia and Nidhi.

"Finish the story, dammit," Jia said.

"Hang on, hang on. Tengo un fumete." Elisa squirmed around, reaching toward her hip to adjust something.

"A . . . what?" Nidhi looked up at the ceiling with a lost expression, trying to translate Elisa's Spanish into something she understood.

"Un fumete," Elisa repeated. Then she dropped her voice. "A wedgie."

"But, like, isn't *fumete* something to do with smoking?" Jia wondered aloud.

Elisa nodded, a sparkle in her eyes. "Yeah, like my asshole took a drag of my underwear." She placed an imaginary cigarette in her mouth and sucked in a quick breath. "Get it?"

"Oh my god." Jia put her head on the bar to stop herself from barking out a laugh.

Nidhi rolled her eyes, though she, too, was struggling not to laugh. "Finish the story, Perez."

"Okay, okay." Elisa rested her elbows on the table. "So while Parrish was working on the painting, he basically decided to troll his nemesis by painting John Jacob Astor as Old King Cole himself. And the reason all the courtiers around him look like they are trying to stop themselves from laughing is because . . . Old King Cole has just let one rip." She finished with a loud fart noise, her tongue jutting diagonally from between her lips.

At that, Jia spat out her last sip of Bloody Mary, her shoulders shaking with uncontrollable mirth. Nidhi covered her face with both hands, girlish giggles bursting from between her fingers. Elisa's delighted guffaw echoed into the high ceilings above them.

Frankly, Jia had been impressed they weren't kicked out.

"What's so funny?" Suzy said in a breathless voice as she swirled into her seat.

"You know," Jia said, "you really had to be there."

Suzy blew out a stream of air. "I hate when people say that. If it's funny, I want to hear it."

Jia bent toward Suzy. "I'll tell you after."

"After what?" She slid a sly glance in Jia's direction.

"Stop it, Suzy."

Crossing her arms, Suzy leaned back in her chair. "So boring. So what was so important that I had to meet you tonight, as soon as possible?"

Jia removed the bank statement from her purse and slipped it toward Suzy. "Don't react."

Suzy took the paper in both hands and stared down at it for a second. "Holy . . . shit." She looked up at Jia, her expression one of unbridled excitement. "Holy—"

"Stop," Jia said. "Just breathe."

Suzy nodded. "This is incredible. We got him. We got that fucker," she crowed softly.

"Now, just wait. There are no names associated with this bank account statement. Only numbers. We still need to tie everything to your dad. But this is a fantastic start."

"Can't Orlagh just tie this to my dad? How did she find it? Where?"

Jia chewed on the inside of her cheek, her nerves igniting. Pinpricks danced across her skin. Here was the real test.

Fiona had all but accused the Park family of murder. She had said they would never be able to prove it, but the look on her face had been one of unbridled anguish. Fiona believed it. In her bones, she thought the Park family was the cause of her mother's death.

Jia wanted to believe it was impossible. But people had killed over far less.

Regardless of the truth, this case had taken a darker turn over the course of the last two days. And Jia wasn't about to ignore her instincts. Everything she did moving forward needed to be done with judicious care. As if she were plotting out a chess game, planning her next five moves in advance.

Jia steeled herself and faced Suzy head-on, ready to deliver the bad news. "Orlagh can't tie this to your dad, unfortunately." She did not take her eyes off Suzy's face as she spoke. "Orlagh is dead."

The color leached from Suzy's skin. "Wh-what?"

"She died last week." Jia watched Suzy intently, searching for any signs of subterfuge or deception. Her reaction would be as telling as her brother's detachment had been.

Suzy swallowed hard, the knot at the base of her throat shifting, as if she were fighting the urge to vomit. "How?"

"The authorities don't have an official word on that yet." The less information Jia provided, the better.

"What the fuck." Suzy met Jia's gaze with a start. "Do you think my father could have done this?" Her voice was barely a sound.

Jia kept her expression neutral. Suzy had brought up her father's possible culpability in under a minute. Which meant the idea was not as far-fetched as Jia had hoped. She forced herself to relax. To present an air of assurance.

She was Gerard Butler, armed with a lethal stare and a metaphorical grenade launcher.

"I'm not sure what to think," Jia said. "But I do know I need to go to the Cayman Islands as soon as possible. Also, I want to reiterate how important it is for all of us to be careful with any relevant information we may find. I hate to succumb to paranoia—because it's likely Orlagh died of natural causes—but I've never believed in coincidences."

"Neither have I," Suzy said on a wobbly exhale. "When are you going to the Caymans?"

"I'd like to leave tomorrow."

Suzy bit her lower lip, lost in thought. Then she steadied herself. "No. Not the Caymans. This is too important. We need to show this to Como in person. Immediately. Ask her what it all means, and if she sees anything she can corroborate. Maybe something in my mom's finances?"

"Your aunt in Seoul? Why?" Jia said. "Don't get me wrong, I think we should talk to her eventually. Just not now. The fewer people who see this document, the better. It's our smoking gun. The next clue points to the Caymans, and I'd like to follow up on it first."

"No." It was clear Suzy would brook no further protests. "We are going to take this to Como tomorrow and see what she says."

"I don't think that's the right move, Suzy." Como was Seven Park's biological sister. And even though all the Park siblings seemed to trust that her loyalty was with their mother and not her brother, Jia felt ill at ease at the thought of bringing another person connected to Seven into the fold.

"I think it's exactly the right move," Suzy countered. "Como has managed my mother's money for decades. She would know what she was looking at. I'd send it to Minsoo, but that fucker still hasn't responded to my messages, like the Janice that he is." She crossed her arms. "Have you talked to him about any of this?"

"He knows Orlagh is dead, but I didn't share the bank statement with him," Jia said. It was the truth. And if Minsoo hadn't divulged to Suzy that he'd accompanied Jia to Falkirk, she wasn't about to. "Also, I haven't spoken with your sister yet."

Another firm nod. "Then it's you and me leaving for Seoul. Tomorrow night, on the company jet. I'll text you the details."

Jia weighed her options. She wanted to protest further. But she'd already acknowledged that she would need to speak with Suzy's aunt at some point. It went against her better judgment, but she could move the trip to the Caymans to later this week, as soon as they returned. And it didn't feel like Suzy was giving her a choice.

Choices. They were the bane of an anxious person's existence. Nevertheless, Jia had chosen to make her bed with Suzy Park. Now she needed to lie in it.

"Okay," Jia said with obvious reluctance. "But promise me we'll hold both the Seoul trip and the Caymans trip close to the vest. Be careful who you tell about where we're going and why. Also I'd prefer if you didn't even hint anything about the Caymans bank account until we share the information in person."

"Even with my mom?" Suzy asked.

Jia nodded. "If the staff around her can't be trusted, it's better to tell as few people as possible. You never know who could be listening. Then, when we share what we've learned, we can gauge their reactions. It's easier to catch people in a lie when you catch them off guard."

Suzy nodded, a knowing light in her gaze. "That's what you did with me tonight, isn't it?"

Jia didn't reply.

"Huh." Suzy recrossed her arms. "Tricky, tricky. I like your style, Jia Song." An impish smile curved up her face. "And I like it even better that you told me before you told Sora."

Jia sent her a sarcastic grin. If Jia had her way, she wouldn't have revealed the bank statement to anyone until it was necessary. But she needed access to corroborating information and to all the people involved. And the Park sibling most likely to grant her that access without asking too many questions or forcing her to jump through too many hoops was Suzy.

Suzy nodded. "You're right. We need to be careful. And we also need to have a reason why you're coming on this trip, just in case my dad asks questions."

When Jia saw the gleam in Suzy's eyes, she said, "Suzy, I'm not comfortable continuing to lie about—"

"Don't worry." A triumphant look spread across Suzy's face. Followed by a devious grin. "I have a plan. From now on, if anyone asks, you're Darius's girlfriend."

"What?" Jia barked. "Stop messing around."

"Shh," Suzy chastised. "You're the one always telling me to control myself in public. Come on. It makes sense. Darius has to come with me to Seoul because my mom will insist on it. She doesn't trust me to be good without someone watching my back. The last time I went, I almost got arrested outside a bar. So stupid. It was just a few prescription pills and like half a vial of hash oil." She flipped her hair. "Korean culture is so old-school. She hates when I embarrass her around her people." A thought appeared to dawn on her. "Also, after all this stuff about Orlagh's death, it's probably a good idea for you to stop traveling places alone on our behalf." She frowned. "Not that I really believe my father had someone killed. I guess I just . . . don't *not* believe it."

Jia's nostrils flared. "I fail to see how this means I should act like a rom-com character with a pretend boyfriend. Unless you just want to see me laid low." The second she uttered the words, she closed her eyes and braced herself for another bad joke.

"Ah, too easy, too easy," Suzy teased. "But seriously, if you go with us as my travel companion, my father will definitely look into you. But Darius? His ex-fiancée, Adrienne, took the jet to the Caymans with him twice as a gift from my mom. And she went to Japan with us the last time we went on vacation for Thanksgiving. Appa won't question if Darius's girlfriend is traveling with us to Korea. Probably wouldn't even care."

"Suzy, I can't—"

"Blah, blah, blah, it's uncomfortable, and you can't get involved with your clients, blah, blah, blah." Suzy nudged Jia's shoulder. "It's a great idea. Everyone will buy it because you and Darius already look at each other like you're DTF. Stop being stupid. Go with it. We've only got three weeks left." Suzy stood up. Eyed the paper on the table. Then slid it back at Jia. "Do you have a safe place for this?"

"Yes."

"Good. Don't tell anyone where it is. Including me." Suzy gave her a firm look. "I'll see you tomorrow at the heliport at Pier 6. Be sure to bring at least one nice outfit." Then she dashed from her seat, her feet flying over the leopard-print carpet as if she were being carried on the wings of the Greek god Hermes.

Hermès. It always came back to Hermès. Like an ouroboros eating its own tail. Proof that the things you wanted most were often the things that came back to bite you in the ass.

Jia stared at the mural of Old King Cole and raised her glass of sparkling water in his direction. "I know exactly how you feel, buddy," she murmured.

# OSSO BUCO

## *T Minus 21 Days*

It couldn't be helped.

Despite Jia's jet lag and the feeling that the edges of her composure were fraying, now was not the time to grant herself the rest she needed. They were leaving in a few short hours for the other side of the world as an alleged couple. It was time to get this over and done with.

It was time to talk to Darius Rohani.

Actually, it was time to confront him, though she'd rather eat a paper cup of stinking beondegi than do that. If she didn't release her anger, it might cloud her judgment, and she needed to be sharp. The richly appointed den of a Korean ajumma—especially a Seoul National University–educated one like Suzy's aunt—was no place for Jia to appear anything less than perfect.

Her knee bounced beneath the coffee shop counter as if it had a caffeine addiction of its own. She watched and waited for the exact moment Darius Rohani would show his deceitful face.

Naturally, Orlagh's death and the Caymans bank statement had taken center stage these last few days. But Jia had not forgotten to nurse her rage at Darius at a low simmer, as if she were braising meat. Osso buco. One of her favorite dishes to make on a chilly winter evening. Waiting for the exact moment for it to soften and fall off the bone.

In fact, that was a great analogy.

The first step to a perfect braise was to sear the meat on all sides, just like the finest chef would do. Jia's anger had seared into her on all sides. Been left to braise for long hours. Now she was ready to cut into it and watch everything fall apart.

The second he turned the corner in front of the coffee shop, Jia stood up.

He grinned as he walked inside, his gait easy, his posture confident.

Until he saw her. He stopped midstep and held up his hands. "Well, shit. You read my dossier."

Jia glared at him with the fire of a thousand suns. "File. It's called a file. A *lawyer* should know that." She marched to an empty chair in the far corner of the coffee shop and took a seat, as if she were an executioner leading her charge to the gallows. With a world-weary sigh, Darius followed her.

Jia's knee resumed bouncing under the table. "Very cute with your *Law & Order* comments. Motive is important!" she said in a voice that reminded her of a high-strung cartoon character. "If you really want to speak from a place of conjecture . . . blah, blah, blah."

"I know you're not going to believe me," Darius said as he dropped into a chair across from her, "but it didn't seem relevant at the time. Also"—he looked sheepish—"I was hoping you wouldn't notice, at least not at first."

"What?" Disbelief curled her lips into a sneer. If she didn't start to calm down, she really was going to look like a member of the Looney Tunes. "You must have thought I was dumber than a box of hair. It's always relevant to tell a *lawyer* you're speaking with about a legal matter that *you also happen to be a lawyer.*"

"I don't practice law," he said, as if he were saying he didn't care for blue cheese. "And I never thought you were dumb."

"You passed the New York State Bar. And you've kept your license active."

"I worked hard for it." Once more, Darius didn't miss a beat. "Again, I didn't think it was relevant to tell you at the time. I also thought you'd be less likely to trust me if you knew."

"How do you think I feel about trusting you now?" Jia stopped herself from shouting. "Also, I call bullshit on the relevance argument. You took the time to tell me—specifically—that you had an MBA from Fordham. What you failed to do is say you had a *JD*/MBA . . . and that you also once clerked for a Supreme Court justice. Tell me, does it make sense that someone with that kind of impressive résumé would then turn around and work for legal aid, making less than seventy thousand dollars a year?"

"That one's easy, too," Darius replied. "Frankly, I didn't love the idea of working for a firm. I interned at two of Manhattan's best ones. It wasn't for me."

"The lawyer with a heart of gold?" Jia's scorn would wither most men.

Pity that Darius Rohani wasn't most men.

"No," he replied with infinite patience. "The lawyer who thought he should be doing something to help other people. I had no debt. I've had a lot of help in my life. My plan was to work for a nonprofit for a few years and then get involved as a corporate counsel for a company with an ethos I could support."

Again, Darius managed to sound so reasonable. She hated him for it. It only served to make Jia's rebuke come across as deeply petty. Like the overreaction of a jealous girlfriend.

Jia shook her head like an Etch A Sketch. "No," she said. "You're not going to gaslight me, Darius Rohani. You had every opportunity to tell me you were a lawyer. As a professional courtesy, you should have done it. Now it makes you look as though you have something to hide. Which makes me want to dig even deeper to see what your actual motivations might be."

"Jia, I really don't know why you're so upset about this. I'll admit I probably should have told you. But, again, I work as a house manager and a personal assistant, not as a lawyer." His features turned quizzical. "Is there something more about this that's bothering you?"

A flush rose in Jia's cheeks. There was. There absolutely was. But the truth of it made her feel smaller than small. She wasn't ready to breathe life into it by speaking the words out loud. "Of course there's more to it. I walked away from that first meeting wanting to believe I could trust you. Now that has been completely shattered because you cherry-picked the information you wanted to give me."

Darius frowned. "I did do that. I admit it. It was ill-advised on my part not to go ahead and tell you, especially when I knew you would find out eventually. I'm sorry."

His quick admission of his mistake took the wind out of Jia's sails. If she had accused Zain of something like this, he would have DARVO-ed her to death, turning the situation around to make it seem as though she was the one with a problem. As if "normal people" wouldn't have taken offense to such an insignificant slight.

It was why Zain was so great at what he did. He possessed an innate ability to read people and take advantage accordingly. One of his favorite tactics was leaning into the widely accepted notion that when women are angry, they are crazy. It's difficult to argue with someone when they accuse you of being crazy. The more Jia pushed back, the crazier she sounded. As if she were making Zain's point for him.

Darius searched her face. "I think I know what's going on here."

"Do you?" she said through gritted teeth. "Enlighten me."

He pressed his lips to one side. "You like me."

If Jia were a lioness, she would have lashed out, her claws spread wide to wreak the most havoc. "Forget *Law & Order.* You're a regular Sherlock Holmes."

"You know I like you, too."

Jia exhaled in a huff. "Well, isn't that just great. Let me win this case, and we can run off into the sunset together, hand in hand, singing songs from Gene Kelly musicals."

Her stomach growled, and she groaned in response.

"Have you eaten recently?" Darius asked.

"No," Jia admitted. "Why, are you hungry?"

"I could eat."

"Eat a dick," she grumbled.

He didn't reply, and Jia put her head down on the table, exhaustion overtaking her. She abhorred how much the pain of her past relationship continued to haunt her. How it made her come across as so disgustingly weak and emotionally scarred. It brought up every childhood insecurity, making her feel as though she were thirteen again, awkwardly second-guessing every thought and feeling that flitted through her mind.

Her anxiety had spiked much more than usual in the last few days. After Fiona's accusation of murder, Jia had found herself questioning everything around her. Maybe the threat of violence had caused a fight response. Because Jia refused to be the kind of person who fawned or froze or flew.

She picked her head up to look around. No sign of Darius.

"I don't blame him," Jia muttered before putting her head down on the table again.

She knew what had set her off the instant she first saw it in black-and-white. It wasn't the JD/MBA from Fordham, though the revelation of its existence—and that he'd taken pains to hide it from her—had irked her for a solid five minutes.

No. It wasn't that at all.

It was three words. Three names, actually.

Chadwick, Holloway, and Moore.

CHM for short.

Darius had interned at the same law firm Zain worked at. Likely at the same time Zain had interned there, the summer before he was offered a job.

Which meant that it was possible Darius and Zain knew each other.

The legal community in Manhattan—especially among the top law firms in the city—was smaller than most people realized. Competition among them was fierce, and by the time most lawyers settled into their places, they generally had an idea of who their competitors were.

At the clack of a coffee cup striking the table in front of her, Jia lifted her head again.

"I don't do coffee," Darius said apologetically. "So I got us some tea and a few cookies. It seemed like a good moment for tea."

"Why don't you drink coffee?" Jia said, her voice sounding especially miserable.

"Because tea is better. And there's a tea for every occasion." Darius settled back into the chair across from her. "I can name you a tea to drink when you're sad. When you're tired. When you're happy. When you're sick. Tea is infinitely superior."

Jia sat up and eyed the steaming mug in front of her. "What is this?"

"A London Fog latte. It's something my youngest cousin especially enjoys. Earl Grey with milk and a hint of the best vanilla extract. Try it."

All the anger deflated out of her like a balloon, replaced by a cold squeeze of embarrassment. "Why did you choose this tea for me?"

"Because you look—"

"Like shit?" She pointed at her unwashed hair.

"No, you seem bogged down by the weight of the world," he teased gently. "Moving about in—dare I say it?—a fog."

"Ugh, take your dad jokes and go."

"Come on." Darius grinned. "Drink it. You'll feel better. If you want to talk after, we can talk."

Warily, Jia took a sip of her tea. "It's good," she admitted. "I would never order it. But it's nice."

He grinned wider.

"What are you drinking?" she asked.

"Chai. It's not the best one I've ever had. But it's good for comfort."

Jia wasn't ready to tell him how much she agreed with that statement. "Why do you need comfort?"

"Because you're the first girl I've been attracted to since ending my engagement. I'm nervous around you."

"Stop saying the right thing."

"Okay," he said. "Let's go for rigorous honesty, then. I needed some comfort because you freaked out on me back there. And I don't think it was just about me hiding my degree."

She swallowed hard. "You interned at CHM."

"Yeah. Seven put in a good word for me. He's worked with them for years. It didn't matter though, because I hated it. It's why I didn't want to do corporate law, remember?"

Jia picked up a stirring stick and prodded at the foam on top of her London Fog latte. "Did you work with a guy named Zain Tawfik?"

"The Egyptian dude from Columbia with the watch obsession?"

Jia grimaced. So specific. So accurate. "Yeah."

"I worked with him a couple of times. Not for anything significant."

She stirred her tea more vigorously. "He's my ex. We dated for five years."

"Ah," Darius replied.

"I'm still fucked up about it," Jia said. "Clearly. And you're the first guy I've liked since we broke up."

"The synchronicity." Another of his trademarked wry grins. "For what it's worth, this was his loss. Dude makes bad decisions. Corrects people when they mispronounce Omega and waxes his eyebrows. Every decent Middle Easterner knows that threading is the only way."

Jia managed a weak smile. "Darius, I work for your employer. Given your legal background, I'm sure you know that, best case, it's an ethics violation for us to date right now. Worst case? I get accused of not doing my job well or making a mistake because I'm distracted. I can't afford to be distracted. This case is too important." She paused. "Also, I've just told you I'm fucked up about my ex. You ended your engagement when?"

"Four months ago."

"Why?"

He paused before responding. "Ego."

She waited for him to elaborate.

"She hated that I was a mere house manager, and I hated that she judged me for it," he said.

Jia nodded. "Yeah. This?" She pointed to him and then back to her. "Is a disaster waiting to happen. Rebound city. Lawsuits galore."

"Obviously a terrible idea for us to even consider it," Darius agreed. "At least for now."

"Plus, you lied to me," she said. "Made me feel like a fool."

"It was more a lie of omission."

"A lie is a lie, Darius."

"Good to know."

"I plan on returning the insult one day. Right after I lead you on."

"Promise me that," he said. "Promise you'll lead me on one day. I deserve it." Darius leveled his gaze on hers. "And I promise I'll let you get away with it."

The intensity in his brown eyes drew her in. She wanted to plumb their depths. Expose every lie and sift through every truth. Rigorous honesty from someone who knew her pain on an intimate level? It was just the kind of drug she could get addicted to. Just the kind of drug she needed to avoid. "I promise to lead you on one day."

"Good," he said, his voice husky. He cleared his throat.

Jia cleared hers, too, and looked around. The moment was lost. It was better if they didn't try to find it again. They could be professional about this. Jia knew it.

"I should probably go finish packing." Darius stood up. "See you later?"

"Like we have a choice," she replied. "But because you owe me for the lie: Any pearls of wisdom before we travel halfway around the world with the nuttiest Park sibling?"

Darius laughed. His hands went into his pockets, and his expression sobered. "Watch out . . . for all of them."

"Meaning?"

"They all enjoy yanking the carpet out from under people. It may seem like they're united in their hate. Maybe they are. For now." Grim lines formed around his mouth. "But don't expect it to stay that way. Their father likes to be their one and only. He plays favorites. Divides to conquer. When they were younger, he would select a child. Confide in that chosen one and separate them from the other two."

Jia nodded. "I've dealt with my fair share of narcissists."

"It's not that simple." His frown deepened. "Even though all three of them know he's bad news, they crave his notice."

"They're still seeking his approval, even now?"

He shook his head. "It doesn't have to be his approval. It's more about getting any kind of attention from him at all. It's why Suzy is the way she is. She could never be better or prettier than Sora. And Minsoo was the smartest of the three. So Suzy decided to be the wildest."

Jia took a careful breath. "You're saying Seven has likely already recruited one of the kids to his cause." Suzy's suspicions about Minsoo were beginning to sound more and more plausible.

"I'm saying if one of them is hinting that their brother or sister is in cahoots with their father, then they're probably the one guilty of it. He could have promised them money or a seat on the board or a chance to follow in his footsteps, but the thing that will matter the most is the feeling he gives them. That they are in it together."

Jia's insides tightened like knots around a carabiner. "Thanks," she said. "See you later."

She watched him stride to the door, permitting herself to admire the view, but only for an instant. If a man didn't look just as good walking away from her as he did walking toward her, she wasn't sure that man was the right one for the rest of her life.

Then she began to figuratively kick herself.

Darius had essentially told her that the Park sibling most likely working behind the scenes with their father was Suzy. The exact sibling they would be traveling half the diameter of the globe with in only a few hours. The sibling to whom Jia had chosen to reveal the only ace up her sleeve.

Minsoo had said it in Scotland: people didn't take Suzy seriously when they should.

Jia closed her eyes. Tried her best to brush aside the piles of emotional detritus.

Darius considered himself an honorary member of the Park family. A sibling of sorts to Sora, Suzy, and Minsoo. He could be guilty of doing the exact thing he had just implied about the other three. Intentional misdirection. Sowing discord. Dividing and conquering, like Julius Caesar in Gaul.

Jia's nails dug into her palms.

What if Suzy, in true Benedict Arnold fashion, had insisted that Jia speak to her aunt in Korea before going to the Caymans so that she could warn her father and give him time to cover his tracks?

Now Jia was stuck with Julius Caesar and Benedict Arnold. Traveling around the world in their private jet to ask Seven Park's only sister if she could help them yank the rug out from under his feet.

"Fuck me," she whispered.

# ALTER EGO

At this point in the tale, it is possible this author might be on the receiving end of some frustration. Perhaps accused of not being more forthcoming with respect to their identity. Again, there are important reasons why. Nevertheless, this author does feel a sense of responsibility for keeping so much of themselves in the shadows.

For failing to promote anything close to rigorous honesty.

Please don't mistake this responsibility for shame. Lies are not—in this author's opinion—as terrible as their reputation might suggest. Lies are the things that make stories and people interesting. They are the lemons of life. The right splash incorporated with a deft hand, and the entire prospect brightens, drawing out the flavors and undercutting the muck and mire. The fat that often overpromises and underdelivers.

But too much lemon can turn sour on the tongue. Can burn and savor of bitterness. Which is why this author would like to practice that deft hand and introduce several choice details with respect to their identity. As to their truth?

Is that not in the eye of the beholder?

This author is a lover of James Bond films. The best Bond will always be the original. Not until recently did this author believe another actor could take on such a commanding role and make it his own. But this author admits that their favorite actor of the current day is Daniel Craig. A seeming man's man with a rugged affect and a dour countenance. Someone adept at wielding a weapon and more than willing to bloody his knuckles or ruin his impeccable suits . . . but also one who relishes a good cry and a moment dancing like a free-spirited buffoon while shilling for a liquor company. This author finds this duality a delight, for obvious reasons.

Not long ago, someone asked this author the reason for their appreciation of films that glorify vigilante violence and toxic masculinity, among other things. This author pondered this for some time before responding.

Movies of the James Bond ilk offer a peek at a life well outside the norm. One of glamour and danger and intrigue and excitement. One in which sex, beauty, and wealth are not just mere commodities but ways of life.

James Bond—and the Bond actor an individual is most drawn to—provides a window into the voyeuristic parts of a person's soul. The parts that crave an intimate kind of escape. Indeed, the parts that may have drawn our reader to this tale in question.

As humans, we all crave escape. Our reasons are both simple and complex, often at the same time. It does not matter how much we accumulate of any one thing, we will eventually be drawn to its counterpart. Too many thoughts, and we seek an empty mind. Too much salt, and we crave the sweet. Too much wealth, and we feel lured to a simpler life.

Of course, a lure is simply a lure. One that requires a choice. Much like the best kind of voyeurism or the telling of a skillful lie.

In that spirit—and in a hat-tip to all things Bond—this author would like to spin a yarn of the globetrotting sort. One whispered in the hallowed halls of Manhattan's upper crust, with its old money disdain for new money excess.

Of course, this author is speaking about the story behind the Gulfstream G650ER that has belonged to the Parks of Park Avenue for the last several years.

Contrary to popular belief, not everyone who slithers about in the realm of the ultra-wealthy purchases a private jet directly from its manufacturer. The waiting list for the model in question is a cool two years. If customizations are expected—as they often are when it comes to a plane with a fifty-million-dollar base price—the time frame becomes even more drawn out. Many of these additions and modifications are of such a particular nature, they require the work of an individual or a company specializing in such things, rather than the manufacturer itself.

The Park family's G6 jet was purchased from a Saudi oil sheikh who was lucky enough to be among the first to receive the model when it was made available to the public. The jet spent another eight months enduring a rigorous customization with a company based in Monaco, tasked with retooling its interior in an homage to the life and work of Gianni Versace, complete with twenty-four-karat gold plating, Greco-Roman busts of Medusa, priceless Byzantine art, a king-size bed strewn with black and yellow pillows fashioned from baroque silk, hand-stitched Vachetta leather accents, and Alcantara suede walls. Inlaid alabaster tables and honed Statuario marble sinks finish off a look that could, at best, be described as notable for its level of detail.

After the completed plane was delivered, the sheikh used it for three separate trips before tiring of it and turning his attentions to a superyacht designed by the inimitable Espen Øino.

Thus—much to the delight of Jenny Park, who could never shed her pedestrian excitement at getting something for a perceived deal—their family was able to purchase the barely used jet for far less than the cost of a new one. The loss the billionaire sheikh incurred as a result was of little consequence. And, of course, Seven relished the connection he was able to forge with anyone connected to the Saudi royals.

The Park family's garishly appointed G6 boasts a passenger capacity of twelve, accounting for the king-size bed hidden behind a wall toward the back of the plane. It possesses a top traveling speed of Mach 0.85 and the fuel capacity to fly 7,500 nautical miles without stopping, which means it is possible for it to travel directly from its private berth at a hangar in Teterboro, New Jersey, to Incheon, South Korea, on a single tank of gas.

Impressive, without a doubt. A fascinating, if outlandish, backdrop for our next scene of intrigue. But this author feels compelled to warn their reader.

Do not be fooled by the ostentatious or distracted by the absurd.

The first of several mistakes has been made. A mistake of choice, that cursed thing.

On the surface, it will not appear to be a mistake of the dire sort. The most definitive ones rarely are. These tiny missteps that go on to shape our futures are often the ones we see in retrospect, akin to the butterfly effect. How a tornado can form weeks later because a butterfly fluttered its wings. Chaos theory at its best.

And chaos at its best is an optimal time for mistakes to be made.

For those with questionable morals and dubious intentions to take full advantage.

Be watchful. Be wary. Trust is a fragile thing, and the truth may not always be in the eyes of the beholder. The truth does, in fact, lie. There would be no stories to tell if it didn't, and our world would be a duller, sillier place for it.

Fret not. This author will leave you with more than cryptic considerations. Not much more, but more. A tossed bone, so to speak.

Pay no attention to the man behind the curtain. He is not what he seems.

Neither is the curtain.

# A HEAD OF SNAKES

## T Minus 21 Days

Five minutes before the Park family's G6 jet was scheduled to depart Teterboro with its three passengers, their pilot received a phone call.

Jia should not have been surprised. She'd been warned not to let down her guard when it came to any of the Park siblings. Nevertheless, she could not conceal her dismay when Sora Park-Vandeveld sauntered onto the plane as if she had all the time in the world. Wearing a white fur hat, no less. Like a modern Anna Karenina, complete with a pearl necklace, suede gloves, and a vengeful gaze.

Without a word, Sora took the seat positioned farthest away from Jia, Darius, and her twin. Then she proceeded to open an electronic reading device and ignore their existence. Suzy rolled her eyes and shrugged. Darius appeared concerned for the duration of takeoff and ascent. Then he, too, seemed to accept the situation. He raised his thick eyebrows at Jia, as if asking her if she was okay. When she nodded, he produced a weathered copy of *The Left Hand of Darkness* and settled in for the journey.

Only Jia continued to harbor noticeable anxiety around the unplanned arrival of the most fearsome Park sibling. The one Jia felt certain she could never win over.

Why was Sora here? How had she known to come? And what was Jia planning to do when it came to telling yet another member of the backstabbing Park family about the Caymans bank account?

Not long after takeoff, dinner was served. Sora continued to ignore everyone, while Suzy, Jia, and Darius consumed their meals in relative silence. Dinner was sushi from Masa served omakase style, one course at a time. Jia had no idea how the Parks managed to have one of the most famous sushi restaurants in the city cater their in-flight meal, nor did she understand how the attendants were able to adjust for Sora's unexpected arrival, but every course was produced without question or incident. Flawless. Perfectly chilled. Maddeningly delicious.

All the while, they avoided dealing with the pink elephant in the pearl necklace.

Not long after dinner, Suzy yawned before making her way to the walled-off room at the back of the plane. Darius began to nod off soon thereafter, and the attendants dimmed the cabin lights to a warm glow and prepared a bed for him by flattening the seat across from Jia and producing a Tempur-Pedic mattress topper, Italian linens, and a snow-white Frette duvet stitched with the Mirae logo in black. A pair of carp swimming in an endless circle.

The entire time, Sora Park-Vandeveld did not move from her seat at the opposite end of the plane, nor did she utter a word.

Twenty minutes after Darius fell asleep, Jia's phone buzzed from where it rested on the leather seat beside her.

Umma: *You have arrived?*

*Not yet,* Jia typed in response. *The flight left only a few hours ago.*

Umma: *Okay. Please let Umma know when you arrive.*

*Of course,* Jia replied.

The three dots appeared, then disappeared, only to reappear once more.

Umma: *If you have time, you should try to see your emo.*

*Umma, I'm sorry, but I don't have time to travel to Gyeongju,* Jia wrote.

Umma: *I told her you were coming. She will take the train to visit you in Seoul.*

Jia sat up, exasperation heating her veins. *Please. I'm really sorry. I just can't set aside any time to spend with her. I'm here for work.*

Again the three dots bore testament to her mother's passive-aggressive guilt trip.

Umma: *I understand. But it is very sad that you will fly all the way to Korea and not see your family.*

Jia closed her eyes. Counted to ten in her mind. *I'm really sorry, Umma. We can go together to visit her soon.*

Umma: 알았어

With a soul-deep sigh, Jia put down her phone. She looked around, struggling for comfort amid the ongoing silence. Hoping to clear her mind, she focused on the bust of Medusa across the way, backlit by amber lights set into the suede wall, her head of snakes writhing in the shadows.

"Monstrous, isn't it?" Sora said.

Though Jia was startled, she didn't show it. "Well, she *is* a monster, isn't she?"

"Punished by the goddess Minerva for daring to have sex with her man." Sora aimed an unblinking stare at Jia.

Jia coughed and averted her gaze. That wasn't how she remembered it. "Right."

Sora's eyes roved around the cabin. "It's a visual assault."

"It's not that bad."

"It's a coked-out Miami nightmare."

"I'm sure it could be . . . improved."

"Unlikely. My mother doesn't want to lose access to the jet for the time it would take to fix it. And, of course, my father loves it. It's a manifestation of his inner self: a nightmare of monstrous proportions."

"But, like, make it Italian."

The edges of Sora's lips twitched. "He does love all things Italian."

The conversation faded to silence. Exhaustion was beginning to settle deep into Jia's bones. This week, she would be in three different time zones. In none of them was she likely to get meaningful rest.

"Call for the flight attendants if you want to sleep," Sora said. "They'll bring linens to make up a bed for you."

Jia eyed Darius's gently snoring figure. "And who knows when I may get another chance to sleep on a custom Tempur-Pedic mattress topper in a private jet?"

Sora made a face. "Don't get too excited. Tempur-Pedic is nothing special."

"Really? I love mine." At Zain's urging, Jia had splurged on a king-size, top-of-the-line mattress two years ago.

"Tell me that after you've slept on a Hästens 2000T."

Jia blinked.

"It's an ethically harvested horsetail mattress," Sora said. "Like the ones Tudor royalty slept on." She smirked. "Without the ethics, of course."

"That doesn't sound comfortable at all."

"If you have sixty thousand dollars lying around, I'll prove you wrong."

Jia laughed, then realized Sora was serious. "You've got to be kidding me."

"I never joke about sleep," Sora said. "And you look like you haven't slept in days. Get some rest while you can."

"I'm fine," Jia insisted.

"No, you're not. You hide it badly. You haven't been okay since you received those texts."

Jia swallowed down the hint of anger creeping up her throat. "I'm sorry."

"Don't be. I dislike it when people hide how they feel."

That comment surprised Jia. "Isn't it kind of requisite in the circles you run around in?"

"The only circles I run around in now are the ones with my kids."

Again, surprise flared through Jia. "I thought otherwise."

"You were meant to. Just because I'm wildly unhappy doesn't mean I want everyone to know it."

"I thought you said you dislike it when people hide how they feel."

"Which is probably why I'm wildly unhappy."

This fresh exchange with the Grand Gijibae unsettled Jia more than she cared to admit. She squirmed in her seat, still seeking a comfortable position.

"I'm telling you this because you need to know how much this matters to me," Sora said. "How much I need my mother to win."

Jia nodded slowly. Here was something she could understand all too well. In her mind, winning was always the only option. So she threw caution to the wind and said, "You need your mother to win against your father because you need to see a woman who was mistreated by her husband get justice."

"Or revenge. Which of the two makes no difference to me. I just need to see him lose."

"So the money isn't really your focus?"

"My money is eventually my kids' money, so it's of vital importance to me. But not without the pain. He needs to feel pain for what he did."

There was something to the adage that hurt people hurt people. Even if Jia finally understood something about her, Sora was still the scariest of the three Park siblings. But did her pain and her need for revenge make her trustworthy? Or would she toss aside her retribution for a chance to stick it to her siblings, especially the sister who had, quite literally, fucked their relationship beyond repair?

"I came on this trip because I need to make sure you don't screw this up with my aunt. Don't Worry, Be Happy Darius isn't vicious enough, and Suzy is a drunk clown." Sora's gaze darkened for a moment, then refocused on the bust of Medusa. "I need a head of snakes. Are you a head of snakes, Jia Song? Because if you are, I'll work with you. I'll do whatever you need me to do—fight whatever fight you need me to fight—to take him down."

Jia considered Sora for a minute. "I can be a head of snakes, if I need to be. But, for the record, that story doesn't end well for Medusa."

"Doesn't it?" Sora quirked a brow. "She was vengeance, even in death."

Jia squirmed again, then laughed. "Right." She glanced away, her eyes landing on Darius, who was still fast asleep, his head sideways on his pillow, his beautiful hands holding the edge of his duvet cover.

Sora must have noticed something in Jia's face, because she said, "You know, we were each other's first kiss."

"You and Darius?"

Sora nodded. "He was too sweet for me. Alex used to do sweet things. His mother is obsessed with the language of flowers. He used to send me bouquets with hidden meanings. Buy me bespoke chocolates and quirky jewelry I would never wear. Write me a haiku in a card. I never knew how to react to any of it." Her hard expression melted into sadness. "He doesn't do sweet things anymore."

Jia kept silent, the longing in Sora's voice causing her chest to constrict.

"It's true what they say, Jia Song," Sora continued. "Make sure you're with someone who loves you more than you love them. It's the only way to be happy. Or at least find a measure of peace." Then she pressed the button to call for the attendants to prepare her bed.

Jia didn't say anything. After Sora's bed was prepared, the attendants turned their attention to Jia's sleeping arrangement. They left the cabin lights on the dimmest setting, and Jia pretended to settle in for the evening, though her mind refused to follow suit.

Sora's parting words continued to haunt her.

Jia had always known that being able to buy her dream Birkin wouldn't bring her lifelong happiness. It had been about what the bag represented. The time and work and energy she'd spent making the impossible possible.

Money certainly made things easier. It greased wheels at Masa and opened doors onto private jets. But after just a short time in the Parks' company, Jia was further convinced of the fact that money did not bring peace. Money might buy her a sixty-thousand-dollar horsetail mattress, but it wouldn't silence the worries of a troubled mind, especially one troubled by deep personal pain, like Sora's.

It was both comforting and disheartening for Jia to realize that winning this case on behalf of Jenny Park and her three children wouldn't necessarily solve anyone's problems in the long run. Including her own.

Perspective. Moving about in a world of extreme wealth meant it was more important than ever that Jia consider the bigger picture. That she maintain her focus and not succumb to any distractions. Especially the beautiful one sleeping across from her.

The jet hit a mild patch of turbulence, and Jia watched her worn leather carry-on jostle, the zipper pulls and shoulder strap vibrating in time with the plane's motion. She'd been meaning to replace it for the last few months but hadn't found the time. Even in the dimmest lighting of the G6, it managed to look drab. To call her out as not belonging, like the holey socks her dad refused to throw away.

Her mind drifted again to that dark morning so many years ago, the day she'd first beheld Lexi Niarchos's gold-on-gold Birkin. At the time, Jia had thought Lexi must be on her way to fly in her family's private jet, which was likely housed in a private hangar similar to the one the helicopter had delivered Suzy, Darius, and Jia to earlier this evening.

Jia had thought Lexi looked so young and beautiful, with the promise of a perfect future looming on her horizon. A *Vogue*-worthy wedding to the son of a Greek shipping billionaire. Vacations on pink sand beaches and holidays on the white-capped mountains of Gstaad. But that engagement had ended. Followed by two more. Then a marriage with a record producer, who left a few years after she bore him two kids.

At least Lexi's revenge was sweet. She now ran a successful luggage company, specializing in luxury leather goods. A regular Jane Birkin, on her own terms.

But was she happy? What did this elusive pinnacle of earthly achievement even mean? Was it merely a moment to savor or something meant to last a lifetime?

Jia wondered if too much money might be the antithesis of happiness. Maybe it made it harder to find contentment. After all, everything in life couldn't be glitzy or polished to perfection. Real life wasn't meant for a curated highlight reel. Perhaps it was important to bear witness to both ends of a spectrum to appreciate the experience of either one. Like a superhero slogan about how the darkest nights gave rise to the brightest dawns.

For the Park family, this night looked to be especially dark. Maybe Jia should seek solace in what the future sunrise might bring. After all, if someone had told Jia that morning in her parents' bodega that she would one day find herself on a Versace-themed Gulfstream jet, cruising through the night nonstop from Teterboro to Incheon and dining on sushi prepared by a master Japanese chef, she would have died laughing.

Yet here she was, with her drab leather carry-on, dreaming about a Birkin.

Both ends of the spectrum.

Jia bunched her hands around her snow-white linens. Even if she didn't belong here, she could fake it until she made it. She'd more than earned the right to appear comfortable amid such excess, even if she wasn't sure she would ever truly feel that way beneath her skin.

As for the likelihood that one or all of the Park siblings might be plotting to backstab the rest?

Jia would take it in stride. She would do what Sora needed her to do and win. Life had taught her the best path was rarely the easiest one. If she couldn't win by being honorable or using her wits and wiles to get ahead, then she didn't deserve to win. Jia would do the necessary work to get there. She would make sure the right side won doing the right things.

# KANGNAM STYLE

## *T Minus 19 Days*

Jia was five years old the first time she disembarked from the plane at Gimpo International Airport in Seoul, after many long hours crammed into an uncomfortable seat. Revisiting this core memory was like reacquainting herself with an old friend. Their parents had saved for years before deciding to take all three of their young kids to Korea that summer.

The experience had struck Jia so profoundly because it had caused the most unexpected reaction. The second she walked off the plane clutching her small Keroppi backpack—a hand-me-down from her elder brother, James—she was overwhelmed by the strangest sensation.

When her mother saw her standing there, unmoving, she asked in English, "What is wrong, Jihae-ya?"

Jia looked up at her mother and squinted into the late afternoon sun. "I've been here before."

"No," Mihyun Song replied. "This is your first time in Korea. Only James has been here before."

Jia shook her head, adamant. "No. I've been here already. It smells like a place I've been to before."

Her parents had chalked it up to her general precociousness, but Jia had never forgotten that feeling. It struck her every time she deplaned in Korea.

It was like coming home. The first breath of air would flow into her blood. The tension would ease from her body. She would look around and believe, even if she didn't really know it for certain, that some part of her had lived here before.

The Gimpo airport of her childhood was a far cry from the new, glitzy hub at Incheon. Now she was greeted by the lulling strains of a string quartet. The restaurants framing the wide passageways were world-class, the food leagues above the dusty, sticky food courts of the west.

And Seoul itself? It changed every time Jia visited. Still, that feeling of coming home remained the same.

During the hour-long ride into the city, Jia did as she always did. She sat in the back seat of their chauffeured black Navigator and appreciated the sunset views. The hipped-and-gabled roofs of ancient palaces flashed along her periphery, bordered on all sides by gleaming skyscrapers. Mirrored surfaces reflected the many angles and colors of the sky, along with a slew of neon lettering. Cheerful cartoon figurines plied ordinary wares. Mouthwatering street food lined serpentine alleyways. Wide, multilaned thoroughfares stretched before her, bordered by granite walkways and punctuated by immense statues paying homage to a storied past.

The driver stopped at a streetlight beside a pojangmacha. For an instant, Jia considered cracking the window to take in the smell of the bubbling tteokbokki and the hot honey pancakes, the kimbap and the deep-fried dumplings. These humble tents or moving food carts—often situated on street corners where the soju was served like water—represented the best and worst of her parents' homeland: unbelievable food and unavoidable alcohol.

Jia's umma and appa were raised in a small coastal town with a post–Korean War perspective. Their notions of frugality, along with the importance of raising tall children with proper dental care, were shaped by their experiences of rebuilding their country from the rubble.

In less than fifty years, South Korea had become a veritable phoenix rising from the ashes. It was now a player in global economics, as well as a tastemaker throughout the entertainment world. Jia never tired of the thrill when she came across non-Koreans who were passionate about K-drama and K-pop. Ten years ago, if people had told her that one of WhitVo's senior partners—a Mormon from Utah, at that—would pay thousands of dollars to take his daughter to a BTS concert, she would have felt insulted by what she viewed as a tasteless joke. Now it felt like every It Girl on social media swore by a ten-step Korean skincare routine, dutifully sponsored by the mighty marketing machine of Mirae itself.

Jia was, of course, willing to acknowledge the good along with the bad. Everything had a price. South Korea had indeed become a glittering firebird, but the cost of its rapid ascent could not be ignored. The drive for exceptionalism meant that it also boasted some of the highest suicide rates. Alcohol abuse was rampant, and it clouded business interactions from the top down. In the last two decades, Seoul had become a premier destination for plastic surgery. Girls as young as fourteen were often gifted a popular procedure to "fix" their monolids by creating extra folds of skin above their eyes. Many women paid good money to have the bones in their jaws and chins shaved to make them appear less rounded. Such things had become de rigueur, rather than the exception. Jia's relatives in Incheon spoke at length about how much this culture of excess tainted the rosy portrait of South Korea, emphasizing its wealth gap and already problematic notions of class.

Jia had to admit, however, that she was more often proud of her Korean heritage than she was not, even if she struggled to identify with anyone who was raised there. For better or for worse, she felt Korean American, down to the marrow of her bones. Her parents' homeland shaped her as much as the concrete jungle of New York City did.

She was an amalgam of old and new, in more ways than one. But most importantly, here Jia wasn't just the Asian Girl. Bullies existed just as they did everywhere, but not once did she ever have to fear a group of boys would chase her around the swings yelling *ching, chong, ching* while tugging at their eyes.

That night, Jia slept a solid seven hours before awaking to a crisp dawn. Darius, Suzy, and Sora were waiting in the living room of the Park family's large, ultramodern high-rise apartment in Kangnam, a magnificent view of the Han River just beyond the floor-to-ceiling windows.

In jet-lagged silence, they made the short journey to Park Hyun Jung's residence.

When they arrived at one of Seoul's most fashionable and expensive addresses, Jia expected to meet the kind of posh Korean woman on the dramas that consumed hours of Jia's free time. An elegant older woman with perfectly dyed hair shaped in a low chignon, her skin like glass, her eyes tired but kind, wearing an outfit that epitomized quiet luxury long before Hollywood made it a thing.

Instead, the door to the Kangnam apartment opened with a rather tacky chime, almost like the theme song to a toddler's television show. The same kind of overly saccharine tune Jia had become accustomed to hearing whenever her mother's Cuckoo rice cooker began and ended its crucial daily work.

"Yah, illjeek watda!" the flustered woman in her late fifties admonished, her gaze directed at Suzy. Pink lipstick stained her front teeth, and her short, chin-length hair was graying at the temples and styled in a manner reminiscent of Judy Jetson.

"Yeah. I'm sorry, Como," Suzy replied in English. "I told Jia we didn't need to arrive so early, but she's one of those pahbos who thinks showing up on time means you're late."

"Americans," Como snorted in accented English. "You'll have to wait. The food is not ready."

Sora replied with an elegant flourish of Korean, complete with a clever joke that resonated in both languages. Como gave a hearty laugh before gesturing for everyone to come inside and remove their shoes in the sunken vestibule, her long navy outfit trailing behind her like a cape.

In fact, that was it. Something about Suzy's como reminded Jia of a warmer, less serious Maleficent. Like Maleficent's older sister, who didn't hate sunlight or abhor joy.

Jia bowed low while holding the basket of fruit she'd purchased from Shinsegae, one of the nicest department stores in the area. Then she introduced herself in formal jondaemal and hoped she didn't come across too obviously as the American-born Korean girl she was.

Como grinned at Jia and answered in a long and loud stream of Korean, which Jia struggled to keep up with, especially because of her saturi accent. A much-needed reminder that both Seven and Jenny originally hailed from the southern coast of South Korea, just like Jia's parents. Among Seoulites, the saturi accent was akin to an accent from Mississippi or Louisiana. Charming in its own right, but mocked by educated elites for being shamefully redneck. As if speaking in saturi indicated that a person was low-class for no other reason than the way they pronounced their vowels.

Jia decided that someone who came across as unpretentious as Suzy's como deserved the same level of consideration. "I'm not great at speaking anything except conversational Korean. My jondaemal is middling at best, and the only joke I know is one my harabugi told me when I was six."

Como's dark eyes sparkled. "I want to hear it."

Sora turned in place with slow precision and leveled a death stare at Jia.

Jia almost groaned. Why oh why did she have to be a smart-ass about her insecurities? And why oh why did Sora always make her feel like a wallflower sitting on the bleachers at a school dance?

She sighed to herself. "What did the fish say when he broke his bones?"

Blessedly, no one answered.

"Oh, my gashi!" Her grin was sheepish.

Complete silence. The kind of silence that made Jia want to shout "Whee!" while spiraling down the nearest drain. Darius looked at Suzy, as if asking her for help. Suzy shrugged. And Sora continued to glower at Jia as if she were a stain on her suede Loro Piana loafers.

"You know." Jia cleared her throat. "Because *gashi* means *fish bones*?"

"Oh!" Como laughed loudly and took the basket of fruit from Jia's hands. "That is quite funny. But don't worry; we can speak in English. It is good practice for me. My tutor will be pleased. I'm not as good at learning languages as Jeeyun, but I think it is good enough for us to understand each other."

"You speak beautifully," Jia said.

"Aigo, kuhjeemal," Como joked with another grin. "Come inside. I'm preparing everything for budae jjigae. Suzy's favorite."

"Hell yes," Suzy said. "Umma never, ever makes it. She thinks army stew is a Shakespearean tragedy, probably because of the baked beans. Como's budae jjigae is the thing I always crave after drinking too much. Spicy, sweet, and perfect, just like me."

"Your umma didn't want to come?" Como asked, her features hinting at a deeper sadness.

"I think it's just too difficult now," Sora said in a soft voice.

Como nodded, sadness seeming to overcome her for a moment. Then she ushered everyone inside. "I'll get the beers. Let's sit down and talk. I think this will be a nice afternoon."

Contrary to what Jia had thought prior to her arrival, she found herself inclined to agree.

---

Jia didn't present Como with the copy of the bank account information until halfway through the meal. In truth, she'd been angling for the right time and had considered asking to speak to her alone, in private. Sora and Darius still didn't know what Fiona had passed along on behalf of her mother, and Jia wasn't sure she was ready to reveal it to them. Especially now that her suspicions had risen toward just about everyone present.

But then, of course, there appeared to be no rule that Suzy didn't intend to break.

"Jia, show the thing to Como," Suzy demanded in the middle of lunch. "I'm dying to know what she thinks."

Jia pursed her lips. She thought she'd been crystal clear about this at the King Cole Bar. She glanced around the table. Sora continued eating her bowl of budae jjigae with the perfect manners of a Korean Stepford wife. Darius put down his chopsticks and eased back in his chair, his expression circumspect.

"Obviously, we know you have something important to show her," Sora said without looking up from her food. "Why else would we be here?"

Jia frowned at Suzy, who ignored her in return. Then she reached into her bag and removed the folder of papers, passing it to Park Hyun Jung.

As she sifted through the pages, Como's eyes narrowed. Then her nostrils flared, and she sucked in a breath. She glared at both Jia and Suzy over the Swarovski-embellished spectacles perched on the tip of her nose. "Will you tell me where you found this?"

Jia glanced at Darius and Sora, gauging their reactions. They remained quiet and still, though Jia could detect a faint buzz of curiosity around Sora.

She wanted to look at those papers. Desperately.

"I think it's best that I keep that information to myself for now," Jia replied. That was mostly true. But she also wanted to know how their aunt would respond to being thwarted in her attempt to gain information. If and how she pushed back would be telling. If the source didn't matter to her as much as the content, then Jia would begin to feel better about trusting her.

"Good," Como said. "I don't think you should tell anyone either."

"Como, does anything here stand out to you?" Suzy asked.

"Maybe," Como said, squinting as she parsed line after line of numbers. "Song Jihae, I managed my younger brother's money for many years, just as I still manage Jeeyun's. For decades, he trusted me. Then, maybe about ten years ago, he became friends with some wealthy men in Paris and London. Many of them did their banking in Switzerland and other countries famous for helping rich people hide money. They told him he was making too many mistakes. That my ineptitude was to blame." Como adjusted her spectacles and sighed.

"It is possible they are correct, in some way," she continued. "I do not feel comfortable helping him hide his money. Nor do I wish to engage in anything illegal. I always thought my brother should pay his taxes and declare all his income in America. He should feel responsibility to that country because it is in that country that he was able to make this dream real.

"He did not agree. Honestly, I did not expect him to. My brother and I have always been very different. When he took the management of Mirae's finances away from me, I was very sad, but I knew why he did it. Chilsoo has always wanted to be liked, especially by rich, important men. When we were children, he would steal part of the money my parents gave me for my schoolbooks to buy American shoes and American music. American gum and candy from the GIs. He wanted to be American so much that he did not care if we did not have the things we needed for school, as long as he could look or feel American." A bitter smile angled up one side of her face. "He never deserved a woman as good as Jeeyun. She should have left him many years ago."

The faint buzz around Sora rose to a discernible hum. She crossed her arms while Darius nodded in agreement, his features tight.

"I think we can *all* agree on that," Suzy said. "But . . . is there anything in these documents that might help us find where this money is now?"

Finally, Sora put down her chopsticks and bent toward her aunt to get a better look at the papers. Jia watched her take in their contents. Save for a thinning of her lips, she did not react. Darius maintained his distance, which either meant he didn't care or he already knew what Fiona had given to Jia. Neither option sat well with her.

Como replied, "When I stopped managing his finances, Chilsoo and Jeeyun possessed around two hundred and fifty million US dollars in assets. He had some of it in a bank account in the Cayman Islands. It is not this bank account here. The numbers do not match. So he either liquidated that account or made another one. Before he fired me, he asked me to help him with Swiss bank accounts and come with him to explore another set of banks in the Cook Islands." She cocked her head and raised the piece of paper before her so that it was only a few inches from her face. "Around seven months ago, he began a major renovation of his Paris apartment in the Marais. Some of these rather large deductions appear to be transactions moved from this account in the Cayman Islands to another bank account in Paris. One that I also do not recognize. It is possible that is the account Chilsoo used to pay for the renovations. Maybe the Paris apartment contains receipts for payments. We can match the dates and the amounts, if we find these bank statements."

Jia wrote furiously on her notepad. "That's a wonderful idea. We really appreciate your help with this."

"If you had showed this to Minsoo, I believe he could have told you these things, too," Como said. "You are not talking to your brother now?" She frowned at Suzy, then turned to Sora, accusation pitching her voice louder. "Park Sora, you are not taking care of your tongsangduhl. You are letting hate and anger make you a bad elder sister. Even if you hate them, you are still responsible for them. Your mother and I taught you better. They are your *family*."

Sora's jaw clenched. Jia could see the ripples pass beneath her flawless skin. But Sora did not protest. Another wash of sympathy coursed through Jia.

Sora's family had the same expectations that Jia's family had of her. For Jia to always be the bigger person. To take care of everyone and always do the right thing, even when no one took care of her.

As if he could hear her inner thoughts, Darius angled himself toward Jia. She felt a reassuring hand on her knee. Without thinking, she wrapped her fingers around his and squeezed.

"Why aren't you talking to Minsoo?" Como demanded of Suzy.

Suzy rolled her eyes. "We're not ignoring Minsoo. I promise. It's just that he's still chickenshit about standing up to Appa in any kind of direct way. You know how he loves the shadows. Plus, he's just really busy with work. We're all totally fine. Like, better than fine. I mean, when was the last time you saw me and Unyee having lunch together like this? Speaking of, may I have more budae jjigae?"

"Kuhjeemal." Como *tsk*ed again. "Don't change the subject. Stop arguing with your brother and sister. Or else you will end up like me."

"I would do just about anything to end up like you, Como," Suzy continued with an overblown smile. "No kids. No man messing up your life. No one to answer to except yourself."

"I enjoy my life, it's true," Como said. "But one day—when you have no relationship with your brother and sister, and the only family member who loves you in return is dying—you will know this ache. This ache of realizing no one exists in the world who knows you as they did. Who sees you and understands where you come from."

Jia chewed on the inside of her cheek as Suzy looked away.

Sora closed her eyes, her arms still crossed.

Darius squeezed Jia's hand again.

Como removed her spectacles to clean smudges off the lenses. "Something else to consider is this: My younger brother is very smart. He is excellent with people and gifted with negotiation. But he is not as good with numbers as he hopes people would believe, nor is he as organized. When he worked with me, he insisted on keeping paper copies of everything, as he did not trust the internet. If I had not been meticulous about filing these documents, he would have struggled to find them when he needed them most. But even more importantly, he kept a small notebook of blue leather, maybe the size of his hand, in the breast pocket of his suit jacket or coat. It contained the access information for all his accounts. He would use some ridiculous code or cipher, but my brother wrote down everything so he would not forget it. If he has many bank accounts all over the world where he has hidden their money, there would be a record of it somewhere. Probably with him. If you can find that record, we can figure out where he has moved all that money and how we can gain access to it."

Jia stopped writing, her mouth agape. Suzy had been right. Coming to see Como had absolutely been the correct thing to do.

Como inhaled through her nose. "The only other thing I will say is that many Swiss banks give their clients the option of keeping their statements at the bank for a year, rather than sending them out periodically, as many banking institutions do. But the client must pick these statements up in person once a year. Before my brother and"—she paused—"that woman moved from the Caribbean to France not long ago, they made a stop in Switzerland. I know this because he called me from a hotel there to tell me something. Something I am certain you already know."

The baby. He'd called to tell his sister about the baby.

"You thinking what I'm thinking?" Suzy said to Jia.

Jia met her gaze. "After the Caymans, we need to go to Paris."

"Well, *you* need to go to Paris," Suzy said. "I don't think I can be in the same city as my father and his slut. Not without destroying something."

Jia nodded, the wheels spinning in her mind. "It's beyond important that everyone at this table agree not to say anything to anyone—including Jenny while she's at the Park Avenue residence—about this trip to Paris. If your father gets wind of our plans, he may attempt to cover his tracks and hide any relevant information before we arrive. We have to catch him off guard and out of his element. When we do, he will make mistakes. We need to be there to catch them. Agreed?"

Sora leaned back in her seat, a hint of approval on her face.

Darius said, "I'll start putting together the travel plans."

"You can't fly commercial," Suzy said. "If you do, he'll have a few hours' notice."

"No company jet, Suzy." Jia continued to think. "This is a ridiculous question, but do any of you know someone whose private plane we can borrow without your father finding out about it?" Even as the words left her mouth, Jia knew a tiny version of herself was shouting into a void.

*Who* are *these people?*

"Of course we do," Sora replied as if Jia had asked her if she had any gum.

Suzy grinned. "Offhand, I can think of three people who would be thrilled to stick it to Seven."

"I'll handle the arrangements. Discreetly." Sora side-eyed Suzy, who blew a raspberry in response.

"Good." Jia took a deep breath. "Make plans for three days from now, so we have a chance to go to the Caymans first."

Como's husky laughter echoed into the high ceiling. She beamed at the twins. "It is good to see you both together again. I hated when you were angry at each other."

"Oh, I'm still angry at her," Suzy said. "We're just united in our hatred for Appa."

Sora scowled at her younger sister and said nothing.

"Park Sora," Como scolded. Then she turned to Suzy. "Park Sujin. It is time you forgave each other."

"No problem." Suzy laughed airily. "She can apologize first, since she's the unyee."

Jia could feel the silent fury seething from Sora and the tension emanating from Darius.

"Yah!" Como smacked Suzy's shoulder. "That's enough. Both of you need to spend time enjoying each other's company, like you did when you were younger. Go out tonight. Have fun! Take Jia to dinner or to the noraebang."

"No," Sora said softly. "I will not."

"If you don't," Como threatened, "I will tell your umma that you are fighting again."

Alarm flashed across Jia's face. If Jenny Park learned that her children were still at odds, she might call everything off. "I think it would be a great idea to go out tonight," she said. "It's been forever since I sang karaoke in a noraebang."

"All together," Como reiterated. "All four of you, including Darius, just to make sure you behave." She raised her eyebrows at Suzy.

"It was just a little bit of hash oil!" Suzy grumbled.

Jia smiled weakly. The stress and the mounting jet lag were already taking a major toll on her. A late night out in Seoul was exactly what she didn't need. But she refused to have Sora and Suzy's personal issues interfere with work. She was too invested.

There was no other option for her, except to win.

Como shifted her gaze between the twins. Suzy sent Sora a shit-eating grin before saying, "Yeah. Why not? I've always been the better singer anyway. You down, Unyee?" She emphasized the last word with the clear intention to provoke.

Jia held her breath and hoped Sora would refuse to take her sister's bait. Again, it was almost as if she could hear Sora counting to ten in her head.

Sora nodded, her expression cool.

That was . . . easy. Too easy.

Nothing good would come of this. Of that Jia could be certain.

Como clapped her hands. "I will make sure the arrangements are made." She beamed. "Song Jihae, I can't wait to hear all about your night enjoying our beautiful city."

Jia smiled brightly at Como, dismissing her growing sense that things were about to get a lot worse.

Tits up, as Elisa liked to say.

# YAMAZAKI 25

## *T Minus 19 Days*

Jia thought she knew what to expect.

When it came to the Park family, she was wrong, yet again.

For Jia and her friends and family, a typical night of noraebang in Seoul was almost like barhopping. If they wanted more of an artsy vibe filled with locals, they would go to the Hongdae neighborhood. For something more upscale, they might choose Kangnam. And if they wanted the most commercial atmosphere with typical clubbing energy, perhaps they would select Itaewon. Then they would decide which of the available karaoke hot spots had the best amenities and the lowest cover charges. If one noraebang failed to deliver, they would simply make their way to another one close by.

That night, at precisely 9:00 p.m., a matte black Bentley Bentayga pulled up outside the Park family's Kangnam apartment.

Jia's best Agolde jeans in a dark wash and a black silk top with a cream-colored wool blazer and a thick Acne Studios scarf had seemed like the perfect decision. Until she met the twins in the foyer a minute later.

Sora scanned Jia from the top of her intentionally tousled hair to the bottom of her pointed Balenciaga knife flats . . . and frowned.

Suzy snickered. "Going low-key. I like it."

Jia stopped herself from stammering. Suzy wore a long navy velvet dress with a mock turtleneck and a gray fur coat. A sapphire pendant flashed around her neck, contrasting with the rich texture of the velvet, perfectly showcasing the flawlessness of the walnut-size stone. Smaller versions dangled from each of her earlobes, her hair piled into a messy updo.

Sora wore a dress pulled straight off the runway. Elie Saab or Oscar de la Renta, if Jia had to guess. Even though the honey color was subdued, the cut of the long-sleeve Gatsby-style dress was daring, showing off her toned back and sharp collarbones. Her hair was gathered into a sleek ponytail, and the only adornment she wore, aside from her massive wedding rings, was an enormous diamond-encrusted Bulgari Serpenti bracelet, its coils wound around her wrist like a snake about to strike.

Sora Park-Vandeveld definitely had a theme.

Jia cleared her throat. "Are we going to the Oscars or to karaoke?" she joked.

Sora rolled her eyes just as Darius appeared from the hallway.

Jia bit her lip.

He wore a navy suit with a white button-down, the collar open on his tanned throat. A five-o'clock shadow darkened his jawline, enhancing its angles. Compared to the twins, he looked casual, save for the fact that the suit was clearly custom-made. Of course he smelled like the trap he was.

"Uh," Jia said. She warred with the desire to go change, only to remember that she had failed to pack a dress for a gala, since no one had told her she needed one.

Darius smiled brightly. "You look great."

"Thank you?" Jia attempted to return his smile.

"Try harder, Darius," Suzy said. "You definitely have better pickup lines than that."

"Maybe I don't." His reply was cool. "And maybe I don't want to use lines on Jia."

"Mm-hmm." Suzy hip-checked him.

"Just make sure they know she's with us," Sora muttered before putting on her Jimmy Choos and grabbing her snakeskin mini Kelly.

Soon they were being whisked a mere ten minutes away, to what appeared to be the rear entrance to one of Seoul's most exclusive five-star hotels. Without a word, the doors to the Bentley swung open, and Jia found herself following a slew of bowing attendants to a red carpet leading to a side door tucked beneath an emerald awning. The sky above Seoul resembled the velvet of Suzy's dress, the lights around them flashing like Indian sapphires.

In hushed silence, they made their way down two flights of stairs to what appeared to be an underground grotto designed for billionaires.

Jia caught the scent first. Like walking into an expensive hotel, the air perfectly chilled, suffused with the perfume of sakura blossoms and the finest green tea. The walls of the darkened grotto were constructed of honed and fluted Calacatta marble. The floor was lacquered cement, covered with glossy Persian rugs. They passed by a trio of flawlessly dressed Koreans seated on an ivory bouclé sofa. One of them nodded knowingly at Sora, who responded with a polite bow of her own.

All at once, the way they were dressed made sense to Jia. A night on the town meant they were here to see and be seen. People with the kind of money and clout the Park family must command in Korea could not afford to be seen in anything but their best.

A few moments later, they were led to a hallway of doors with warm sconces sending cascades of light down pale travertine walls. They were seated in a private room with three chaises covered in oatmeal-colored suede, arranged in a U shape, and adorned with silk-screened accent pillows. A circular coffee table made of rosewood with gold and glass accents anchored the space.

Jia looked up and realized that the black ceiling was hand-painted to appear as the heavens, replete with swirling galaxies and twinkling stars that flashed as though they were hewn from precious gemstones. Pale light emanated from behind the recessed ceiling, its ambient colors shifting in slow succession, lending the room an otherworldly glow.

Suzy settled on one chaise and yanked Darius down beside her. Sora arranged herself catty-corner to her sister, and Jia took the remaining chaise for herself.

Attendants flitted around them, asking questions in soft Korean. A whirring sound caught Jia's attention as two marble panels along the wall running parallel to where she sat opened in the middle to showcase a seventy-five-inch Samsung OLED television with a screen so thin that it appeared as if it were built into the wall.

Sora ordered food and drinks. In no time, the bevy of attendants produced an artfully arranged platter of fresh fruit sliced into swans and dragons and flowers, crispy rice squares with confit egg yolks and seared Wagyu, a charcuterie board with smoked meats imported from Spain and cheese imported from France, as well as an assortment of hand-cut crackers made in-house, a tray of Fauchon macarons, a full service of delicate osetra caviar with crème fraîche and chopped chives, and a bowl of fresh potato chips served alongside a sriracha, dill, and honey aioli.

And the alcohol?

Two carafes of Château Rayas Châteauneuf-du-Pape, a fifth of Beluga vodka served with freshly squeezed blood orange juice and sprigs of mint and rosemary, as well as a bottle of Pappy Van Winkle 23, a bottle of Yamazaki 25, a bottle of Moët & Chandon champagne, and a solid silver bucket filled with immense clear ice cubes embossed with a logo Jia did not recognize.

Suzy made a beeline for the crispy rice squares and crammed one into her mouth. "It was better last time," she said without pausing to chew. Then she poured herself a glass of Château Rayas to wash it down.

Darius took a crispy rice square for himself. "It's still delicious to me. I'll eat whatever you don't eat."

"Is that a promise?" Suzy waggled her eyebrows.

"Try harder, Sujin-ah," he replied without missing a beat. "You definitely have better pickup lines than that."

"Okay, I deserved that."

Darius handed the platter to Jia, who demurred. She was already exhausted, and it felt like hornets were swarming in her stomach. The last thing she needed was to eat something that decadent only to have it all come back up.

What she really wanted was to taste that Pappy Van Winkle 23. She'd tried Old Rip before and thought it was one of the best bourbons she'd ever had, with the exception of her tried-and-true favorite, Elmer T. Lee. But Pappy 23? She'd seen single pours of the stuff sold at bars for hundreds of dollars.

God only knew what this entire bottle cost with the markup at this high-end noraebang.

"Go ahead," Sora said, her expression amused. "Help yourself."

Dismay flashed across Jia's face. "What do you mean?"

"I can see you staring at the liquor," Sora said. "Help yourself."

Too tired to protest, Jia reached for the Pappy.

"Not that one," Sora scolded, a furrow forming along her brow. "I thought you knew better."

"What?" Jia said.

"The best thing on that table isn't the Van Winkle. It's the Yamazaki."

"I'm a bourbon girl, though."

"I don't care. Don't be predictably pedestrian and go for the whiskey everyone knows about."

"I know about Yamazaki."

"If you did, you wouldn't be going for the bourbon."

Suzy groaned. "Oh my god, you're being such a dick. Maybe Jia doesn't care what the most expensive bottle of liquor on this table is. Just because it's expensive doesn't mean it's better. You really can be such a basic rich bitch."

Sora ignored Suzy and reached for the Yamazaki herself. She poured two neat drinks into a pair of Baccarat tumblers, then handed one to Jia. She raised the other and didn't wait for Jia before taking a sip and humming to herself in appreciation.

Jia forced herself to relax, despite the mounting strain collecting in the air. It felt like a firecracker might shoot off at any point, without warning. She took a sip of the Yamazaki 25. "It's delicious," she said to Sora, though she never would have said anything to the contrary.

Suzy toyed with the giant sapphire around her neck and made a face. "God, I hate how everyone is so afraid of you," she muttered in her sister's direction. "I don't even get it."

Like a hawk homing in on its next kill, Sora shifted her attention to Suzy and opened her mouth to speak, her eyes glittering.

Darius snatched up the wireless microphone and stood in the same fluid motion. The seventy-five-inch OLED screen flickered to life, and he bounded in front of it with the energy of a circus ringmaster.

Jia plastered a smile on her face. "What are you going to sing?"

"Who cares?" Suzy laughed. "Just take off your shirt."

Darius shared a look with Jia. Past the cheerful veneer, she could sense his discomfort. This seemingly harmless outing was starting to resemble a loaded gun. And it was clear Darius would do whatever it took to keep anyone from pulling the trigger.

Jia did a quick search on the tablet the attendants had provided. Something she knew he would be able to sing. She pressed the first selection that came up in the results and immediately regretted it when the familiar violin chords emanated from the Bang & Olufsen surround sound speakers.

Darius's eyes widened. Then he shrugged and began to sing.

Jia braced herself for the next round of Suzy's bad jokes.

Perhaps she should have waited for another song from *Singin' in the Rain* to pop up in the selection window. In hindsight, "You Were Meant for Me" probably wasn't the wisest choice.

As Darius began to sing the refrain—his baritone as rich and perfect as Jia had remembered—Suzy threw one of the silk-screened pillows at Jia. "Oh my god, you're not even pretending anymore, are you?" She cackled. "Why don't you two just have at it right here?" She eyed her sister with a malevolent grin. "We like to watch, don't we, Unyee?"

The entire room froze, as if it had been doused in liquid nitrogen.

*Oh fuck,* Jia thought, her eyes squeezing shut. The song died on Darius's lips, even while the unaccompanied melody continued flowing from the speakers.

"Shut your stupid mouth, Park Sujin," Sora said from gritted teeth.

With that, Suzy sat up straight. "Finally," she said. "Let's do this."

"Suzy, no," Darius said. "Let's go for a walk." He reached for her hand, and she batted him away. His face drawn, he sat beside Jia, resigned to witness the inevitable.

"I want her to take her best shot," Suzy said as she and Sora faced off from opposite sides of the rosewood table. "It's time she let it all out. Let's see exactly what kind of bullshit lies she's been feeding herself for the last two years. I'm ready."

Sora's chest heaved. Up and down. Up and down. As if she were buying herself a precious moment to collect herself. Then she stared down her chin at her twin. "You're not even worth the effort," she said. "You traitorous bitch." For the first time since Jia had met Sora, she saw the telltale shimmer of tears. It rattled Jia even more. Almost like watching a storefront mannequin start to sob.

"I'm not worth the effort?" Suzy retorted. "But this twenty-five-thousand-dollar Japanese whiskey is?" She reached for the open bottle of Yamazaki 25 and stood, returning her sister's dead-eyed stare without flinching.

Sora said nothing, though her body started to shake.

Then, as if Suzy were pouring gasoline on a fire, she tipped the bottle of Yamazaki over and began emptying its contents onto the Persian silk rug.

Jia swallowed a scream. Darius went rigid beside her. She could sense his struggle. His desire to do as he always did and take the wheel to prevent this tailspin from turning into a full-on crash.

Jia could bet he'd saved them countless times in the past. But enough was enough. Maybe Suzy hadn't gone about it in the best way, but maybe it was time for the twins to finally have it out. Maybe then they could start to heal.

And maybe then they would be able to stand together and provide each other the support they both desperately needed.

Suzy continued letting the ridiculously expensive whiskey flow from the bottle to the floor in torturous glugs of liquid gold. "I'm not worth it, eh? What makes you think you can say that to me, the only person on this planet you *shared a womb with*? What makes you think you can just treat me like garbage and ignore me and blame me for something that's just as much his fault as it is mine? Why would you forgive Alex and not me? Make it make sense, goddamn it!"

Sora stood. "Don't fucking say his name."

"I'll say whatever the fuck I want." Suzy shook the bottle to empty every last drop. "You're not the boss of me." Then she let the brown bottle fall to the Persian rug, where it landed with a wet thud. "What?" she sneered. "Are you going to chuck some more Pellegrino at me?"

As if in a trance, Darius reached for a house-made potato chip, and Jia caught his hand, even though a part of her desperately wanted to sit back and take in the spectacle as if she were part of a paying audience.

Sora's fingers balled into fists. "Forgive you?" she said. "Forgive *you*?"

Her laughter sounded manic. "Everyone keeps talking about forgiveness like it's some kind of rule or law. How can I ever forgive you when you have no idea what you took from me? The trust and the safety you stole from me. And my *kids*?" she continued, her words filled with unmitigated pain. "How could you do that to them? They love you so much, and now I can't stand it when they ask about you or say they miss you. It makes me want to die." She pressed a palm to her cheek to catch the stream of newly fallen tears. "Is that what you want to hear?"

Now tears streaked down Suzy's face, too. All the fight seemed to leave her in a single tremulous breath. "I-I-I didn't know what I was doing."

"Fuck you," Sora said. She straightened and forced her shoulders back. Swiped away the tears collecting on her chin. "You're lying, just like he is. You think because we shared a womb, you're entitled to everything that is mine. Get your own life, you fucking whore. You can't have mine."

Something tightened in Jia's chest.

Suzy collapsed onto the chaise, her body consumed by racking sobs. "I'm sorry, Unyee. I'm so sorry. I know I shouldn't be asking for forgiveness, but I need you to forgive me. I'm a mess without you. I can't paint or sculpt or sleep. I can't do anything. You and Xander and Colette . . . you're everything to me." She clambered to her knees, her hands clasped like a character from a K-drama. "Please. Please forgive me. I'll do whatever you want if you'll just forgive me."

"Then go off and die," Sora whispered. "Maybe then I'll forgive you."

At that, Suzy stumbled to her feet and fled, her sobs getting louder. Without hesitation, Darius took off after her. Jia knew without being told that Darius would take care of Suzy. Not because he was paid by her family to do so but because he was a good person. Or at least, in that moment, Jia desperately wanted to believe he was.

The instrumental soundtrack to *Singin' in the Rain* continued emanating from the speakers. Sora patted her face with both hands and smoothed her sleek ponytail. In a few deft motions, she appeared perfect once again. Then she began to spear pieces of fruit with careful precision, dismantling the artful arrangement a single bite at a time.

Jia swallowed. "Do you need—"

"No talking," Sora interrupted. "Not for at least ten minutes."

With a sigh, Jia eased back into the chaise and stared up at the ceiling. The wash of colored light switched from a pale blue to a delicate violet before warming to red, as if in warning.

The second the colors faded from red to orange, Sora's phone dinged. Without hesitation, she picked it up to read the message, ever the vigilant mother.

In the pocket of Jia's blazer, her own phone buzzed. She reached for it, just in case it was Ben or someone at the firm.

The second she saw the sender's name, her heart stopped. She stood, fighting a sudden wave of unsteadiness. Then her heart restarted, careening around her chest like a pinball.

When Jia looked up from reading the email, Sora was watching her with that same hawklike gaze.

Sora had read the same message only a moment before Jia had. Jia knew it because she'd seen the list of recipients. Did she know what this meant? Did she have any inkling how this message had unmoored Jia, leaving her resolve in tattered shreds at her feet?

Jia looked at Sora and could not stop herself from silently imploring, *Will you help me?*

It was shameful to even make the request, especially because Sora likely had no idea why Jia needed help. She couldn't know, unless she'd immersed herself in Jia's life story as Jia had with the Park family.

The Grand Gijibae shrugged. Then returned to spearing pieces of fruit.

Jia's phone fell from her trembling hand onto the floor. How could they do this to her? How could anyone be so cruel? It didn't make sense.

But then of course it did. She should have expected nothing less from either of them.

Seven Park had requested for Jia to meet with him at his attorney's office to discuss a possible settlement offer, as soon as possible. The email entreaty had been made by Seven's attorney. It was polite. Professional.

And it landed like acid thrown against a wall.

Seven Park's attorney at CHM was none other than Zain Tawfik.

# GRAY ROCK

*T Minus 17 Days*

Jia was familiar with the main conference room at Chadwick, Holloway, and Moore. She'd walked by it countless times, usually at night, on her way to have a late dinner with Zain. She'd stop by his favorite restaurants and pick up their standard orders before bringing the food to him at work. Sometimes he would do the same for her. When they were deep in the trenches working hundred-hour weeks, it was often the only time they had together.

This was Jia's first time sitting at CHM's conference table as an attorney of record.

She'd had two days to prepare for this meeting. Well, a day and a half. And still she felt off-kilter, as if she had just disembarked from a roller coaster.

None of the Park siblings had agreed to accompany Jia to this meeting. And why should they? Clearly not even one of Seven Park's children wished to spend a second more than necessary in his presence. One of two things on which they could all agree. The other? That there was no chance in hell they would be willing to accept any kind of settlement. Not with the revelation of the Caymans bank account. And not without pursuing their chosen course of action to the bitter, bitter end.

Of course, none of this precluded the possibility that one of them had told Seven about the papers Orlagh Campbell had pilfered before her death. Maybe the news had scared him, just a little. At least enough to try for another settlement. Perhaps that same traitor had been the one to tell Seven about Jia and Zain Tawfik.

Jia replayed her conversation with Darius at the coffee shop and winced.

Anyone could betray anyone. That much was true. But the idea that Darius might have weaponized Jia's pain was a cruel blow. Maybe it wasn't him, though. A PI could have provided any member of the Park family with a file about her.

Regardless of the hows and the whys, Seven Park's three children had decided they wanted to hear what he had to say, if for no other reason than to "spit in his eye," as Suzy put it. Which was the reason Jia was here first thing in the morning, dressed in her finest armor, ready to do battle.

She'd eaten dinner last night at Elisa's house. Rice and tostones rellenos, her favorite. In fact, she'd fallen asleep on Elisa's sofa, not long after consuming more than half a bottle of wine. She'd needed Nidhi and Elisa's company even more than she'd needed the liquid courage to face Zain today, with no one in her corner but Jia herself.

And why should anyone be? Jia was a goddamn professional. It was pathetic that she'd even thought to ask Sora. She did not need anyone fighting with her, for her, or beside her. She was more than enough. It didn't matter that Seven Park had chosen Zain as his attorney for the clear purpose of messing with Jia's head. There was no way it could be a coincidence. Zain didn't even work on cases like this. He was strictly M&A. And, of course, he'd agreed to Seven's request. He'd probably convinced himself he was doing the right thing by Jia. Forcing her to realize, in his slyly cruel way, that they were better off apart, at least until the next time he needed to remind her of everything she'd lost.

Like Jia had said to Darius, she'd dealt with her fair share of narcissists. It was time for her to confront her pain. To face it and overcome it. In fact, that was the angle she'd chosen to take today, despite all the warnings Gail had given her over the years of therapy they'd shared.

Today, Jia was most definitely channeling rage to get her through. A frigid kind of rage, à la Sora Park-Vandeveld. A rage that burned on contact, like dry ice.

Zain would not see her laid low. Seven Park would not win this round, no matter how many dirty tricks he had up his sleeve.

The richly stained double doors swung open, and Zain glided into the room, handsome as ever, his pale gray suit perfect, his collar and shirt-sleeves starched, his white teeth immaculate. Beside him strode a slender Korean man around the same age as Jia's dad, wearing tan chinos, a blue button-down, and a charcoal V-neck sweater. His full head of black hair was likely the work of a doctor skilled at hair transplants and the deft hand of a colorist. It gave him the appearance of youth and vitality, despite the signs of aging around his eyes.

The large face of Seven Park's Audemars Piguet watch flashed as he sat down. That particular model was a special order. Jia knew it had to have caught Zain's eye. Perhaps the two men had bonded over the workmanship of such fine watches. Had shared their admiration for John Mayer's collection and obsessed over Paul Newman Daytonas and statement pieces that just a handful of other people would recognize or appreciate.

The only reason Jia knew anything about watches was the five years she'd spent on Zain's arm, in addition to the four years they'd moved in the same law school circles. Nine years of Jia's life, a kaleidoscope of memories now.

Those five years with Zain were the first time in Jia's adult life that she'd trusted another person to see her and value her above all else. Maybe it was the curse of being the middle child, but even her own brothers used to joke that if there was a house fire, Appa would grab his eldest son, and Umma would save her baby . . . but Jia would be able to make it out on her own because she was Jia. Everyone had laughed when James had first said it. Even Jia had managed a half-hearted giggle, though the words had struck her like a kick to the stomach.

They'd thought they were complimenting her resourcefulness. In fact, she'd hated their chorus of laughter so much that its recollection still brought tears to her eyes.

They'd made a joke of the fact that Jia was precious to no one.

She steeled herself and sent Zain a frigid look from across the long polished oak table.

Jia Song was precious to herself. And today, Zain Tawfik would see that.

"Hello, Jia," he said, his grin warm, his expression affable. "It's been a long time."

"Right," Jia said, her tone flat.

Zain turned toward Seven Park. "Mr. Park, I'd like to introduce you to Jia Song. She and I have known each other for many years. We attended law school together, and she's an excellent attorney. I believe she was recently made a junior partner at her firm."

"Congratulations," Seven said with a kind smile. "It's wonderful to make your acquaintance, Ms. Song, though I wish it were under different conditions." He spoke with the barest hint of an accent, his presence commanding. He had the kind of lines around his mouth that suggested he possessed an excellent sense of humor or a proclivity for shouting.

"Of course," Jia said with a level gaze.

"I understand you've been speaking to my family with respect to my initial settlement offer."

"Yes."

He shifted in his seat. "In the interest of moving toward a quick resolution, I reached out to Zain to see if he could help facilitate an agreement that would be beneficial to everyone."

Jia said nothing. Seven caught himself before frowning, then looked at Zain.

Zain sent Jia another winsome smile. The same smile that had brightened so many of her days. "Look, there's no easy way to say this, but—given Mrs. Park's unfortunate diagnosis, dragging out this matter isn't the best idea for any of us."

*Us?* Jia smirked and crossed her arms. An interesting tactic, to make it seem as though everyone was on the same side.

"Mr. Park doesn't wish to put the mother of his children under any further duress," Zain continued. "To that end, he wanted to revise his initial terms."

"Great," Jia said. "That's why I'm here."

Immense satisfaction flared through her as Seven shifted in his seat again. Nothing about this interaction was proceeding the way he had planned.

He'd hoped to unsettle Jia by forcing her to engage with her ex. To rattle her and turn her vulnerabilities into kindling.

It wasn't the first time Jia was grateful for Gail. Nor was it likely to be the last.

Jia had known even before she'd decided what to wear this morning that it was time for her to be a gray rock. Gail had offered her this tactic whenever Jia was forced to deal with a toxic person. To be completely uninteresting. Unresponsive and unemotional in the face of direct provocation. To make it difficult for anyone to read her or take advantage of her.

Zain took a steady breath. Checked in with his client a final time. Seven Park shrugged off his irritation by passing Jia a look of fatherly approval. "Jia, I hope you will do whatever you can to convince the mother of my children—whom I truly loved—that her limited time on earth should not be spent arguing over such unsavory matters."

The irony was the fact that his future ex-wife felt the same way. Jia wondered if it would make a difference to Jenny Park to see her husband take such skillful advantage of her worst fears. That most human of weaknesses. Her mortality.

"I'm listening," Jia continued without making eye contact with either of them.

"Mr. Park is willing to offer twenty million dollars of the twenty-five million currently in their joint accounts, as well as the deed to the Park Avenue residence, free and clear." Zain paused for effect. "Additionally, he would be willing to transfer company stock to each of his children. Ten million dollars of preferred shares to Sora, ten million to Suzy, and ten million to Minsoo. Given Mirae's current growth, in fifteen years, that will likely amount to a small fortune."

Jia said nothing.

"Lastly," Zain said, "he is willing to continue paying for all the operating expenses of the Park Avenue residence for the next five years, regardless of who lives there."

"I see," Jia said. She flipped closed her leatherbound notepad. "I'll convey this to my clients." Then she stood.

Flustered, Zain stood as well. "Jia, I don't think—"

Seven Park's laughter was low. Begrudging. "Well done, Song Jihae," he said under his breath.

"Pardon?" Jia replied while sliding her notepad into her Prada tote. Though she remained outwardly calm, her pulse kicked up, her nerve endings tingling.

"I held a grenade in my hand," Seven said, extending his open palm. "Zain was the pin. But today I learned that my grenade doesn't have any gunpowder in it."

Something unseen trickled down Jia's spine, causing her to shudder. *A family of murdering thieves.* She stood straight. "I think war metaphors are probably not conducive to any kind of agreement."

"I don't wish to be at war with anyone," Seven said.

"No," Jia said. "You just hope everyone will play dead . . . until they actually are."

Zain flinched at that. In his reaction, Jia saw a glimpse of his humanity. He hadn't always been a monster in her eyes. She wanted to cling to that memory, even now. That all those years together hadn't been a total waste. Instead, she held Seven's gaze.

"Nothing good will come from pursuing this," he said. "I will not leave the mother of my children to die with nothing, but if Sora, Suzy, and Minsoo continue down this road, I will not hesitate to cut them off completely."

"I will convey your threat to them as well."

"It is not a threat. It is a promise. I have taken great pains to grant them space for their anger. To let them hate me, even. To ignore me, even though everything I have ever done I did for them. To give them this extraordinary life they now take for granted. For years, I worked like a dog to feed and clothe and provide the best of everything for all of them. They are ungrateful," he said in a quiet voice. "They resent me for finding the happiness they still struggle to achieve on their own, even with every advantage money can buy."

"Providing for your children isn't a favor to them, Mr. Park. It's your job as their father."

"That's the American way of thought." His scowl reminded Jia of Sora. "I'm disappointed that you don't know better."

"Okay," Jia said. "I think I'm going to go."

"If they do not accept this offer by nine o'clock this evening," Seven said louder, "then I will rescind it. When the time comes, they will be entitled to nothing. If they wish to retain any of their rights to Mirae, they will do the right thing, for all of us." He stood and walked toward Jia, his gait slow. Purposeful. Though he was the same height as Jia in her three-inch heels, she felt as though he were looming over her. She fought the urge to take a step back.

"Everyone took great trouble to be here this morning," Seven continued. "I know you were in Seoul less than thirty-six hours ago. I flew commercial overnight from across the Atlantic." He turned toward Zain, who still stood beside the conference table, his expression aloof. Belying the swirl of emotions beneath it. "And, at my specific request, Mr. Tawfik left his engagement holiday early so he could help me deliver this offer."

All the sound in the room seemed to muffle as if Jia had stuffed her head into the collar of a thick sweater. She looked at Zain again and despised him for the sympathy in his face. The hint of protectiveness. How dare he play that card? As if the prospect of trapping her heart under his foot hadn't dawned on him until now.

As if he hadn't known exactly what he was doing when he acquiesced to Seven's request.

"You should congratulate Mr. Tawfik," Seven continued blithely. Then he aimed a wide smile at her, as if it were the barrel of a gun.

Zain wasn't the pin at all. This was. And Seven Park had waited until its explosion would cause the most damage.

Jia hated herself in that moment. Hated how much she wanted to fall to the floor and cry. To let Zain crush her beneath his Italian shoe and succumb to all the pressure and the pain, all the anxiety and the fear and the exhaustion, and cry until there was nothing left of her for anyone to pity. Until she'd vanished into oblivion.

Zain was engaged. Six months after ending their five-year relationship, he'd found someone else to build a life with. It didn't even matter who it was. He'd fully moved on, and Jia was still here, her heart aching and her mind trapped in a vortex. She wanted to walk away. But Seven Park was blocking the path. Jia tried to change direction, one of her ankles wobbling. She caught herself and closed her eyes, forcing herself to stand tall.

The double doors burst open. Sora and Suzy Park stormed into the conference room like a pair of Korean Avengers, dressed to the nines.

"Bangawo, Park Chilsoo," Suzy said, her eyes wild.

Seven swiveled toward his daughters. "You are late."

"No, we aren't," Sora replied coldly. "We're not here for you. We're here for her."

Suzy looked at Jia. "Come on, Columbia. Get your shit. Let's go."

Jia's hands balled into fists. If the backstabbing Park twins could get it together to face their father for her, the least she could do was make their efforts worthwhile. Jia remembered the way Sora had first looked at her. Like a pulae. She sent the mirror of that image to Seven. "This was a profound mistake, Park Chilsoo-shi." Then she made her way around the opposite side of the table toward the door.

"Song Jihae," Seven said with another merciless grin, "be sure to tell your clients that this is the last chance they have to protect their inheritance. If they don't agree to my terms by this evening, there will be nothing left for them."

"I'll make it easy for you, Appa," Sora said in an equally deadly voice. "We don't need until tonight. Even if Minsoo and Suzy agree to your terms, it won't matter. I won't sign off on it. I won't settle for less than everything."

Suzy helped Jia into her coat.

"Ms. Song was right," Sora continued. "This was a profound mistake."

"That's the last time you fuck with us, Dad," Suzy said. "When you look back on this moment, it will be with nothing but regret for everything you lost, which is a whole lot more than money." Then she looped her arm through Jia's, and the three of them left the conference room together.

Not once did Jia look back at Zain.

A steady drumbeat echoed in her ears as they walked out of CHM. Jia glanced sidelong at Suzy, who still held fast to Jia's arm, her delight evident in the way her curls bounced with each stride.

"Darius?" Jia asked under her breath.

Suzy shook her head. "Sora."

Jia's features registered her shock, though she kept silent.

Suzy pulled her closer, until their shoulders were touching. "Remember? I said I would do anything if she would forgive me. She said she might consider it if I came with her today. Couldn't convince Marky though, the little chickenshit." She rolled her eyes. "Besides, it's high time we stood up to our dad, face-to-face. He needed to see that."

"I recognized Zain's name from your file," Sora announced without turning around. "I hope he steps on Legos with his bare feet for the rest of his life."

Jia stared at the back of Sora Park-Vandeveld's haughty head.

And marveled for just an instant.

# IN TERRORUM

We have reached an impasse, dear reader. For this author can no longer remain a casual witness to these happenings. Perhaps it is because I have been afforded the luxury of hindsight. Perhaps it is because these circumstances have become too personal in nature.

Perhaps it is because I am angry.

Naturally, it is rewarding to hear about the happenings of that morning in the conference room at CHM. A moment in time when good appears to triumph over evil and our charming heroine learns she is worth fighting for.

But, as I mentioned earlier, we often delight in spectacle at the expense of another person's suffering. I do not relish suffering of any kind, despite what one may think. And it is all too easy to dismiss the pain of a lost love as the pain of a diminished person—the sorrow of a pathetic soul—rather than what it truly is.

Loss and grief are the price for living and loving. And when grief comes to take its pound of flesh, we fight back, for we do not wish to suffer. When instead we should hand over our payment, gladly.

A man like Seven Park may never know the satisfaction of paying for his losses, for the losses he holds most dear are nothing but numbers on a page, not the anguish of a broken connection or the cold solace of memory.

Maybe he should have stopped while he was ahead. Maybe he never should have claimed that he did everything for his family. That he truly did love the mother of his children. If he did love her, then he never would have tried to destroy her. He never would have sought to cause pain to any of them.

For that, perhaps he will learn a lesson of his own. Or maybe he will merely see that life is as it has always been for men like him.

Kill or be killed.

# BODEGA NIGHTS

## T Minus 17 Days

Today would go down as one of the most interesting days in Jia's life.

A series of full-circle moments, in more ways than one.

She'd begun the day feeling like an empowered—albeit nervous—attorney at the CHM offices, ready to do battle in her finest armor. In an instant, she'd nearly been reduced to a mewling mess. Only to be rescued by the most unlikely of saviors, who, days before, had been mortal enemies.

The three of them had gone their separate ways after the encounter at CHM, but the adrenaline had remained with Jia through her solo lunch at one of her favorite vegetarian restaurants in Koreatown.

Jia knew how Sora felt about men who wronged women. How important it was to win. But why would Sora have asked Suzy for help, especially after what had transpired that night at the noraebang in Seoul?

Was it possible that Suzy actually had managed to crack through Sora's icy exterior?

Jia often thought demanding forgiveness from someone was an act of selfishness. An injured party being forced to reconcile with their tormentor, regardless of their true feelings, all to honor some higher moral calling. She'd heard people argue that forgiveness was an act of unburdening, but she didn't buy it. Especially when she thought of Zain.

Maybe it was selfish of her, but she had no intention of forgiving him for what he'd done today. Especially if forgiving him meant unlearning one of her life's greatest lessons: Loving someone unconditionally was an act of idiocy. No one in the world should be allowed to do or say whatever they wanted to someone and then expect forgiveness.

After lunch, Jia had begun making her way back to her office when she'd received a series of panicked text messages from her mother. Both her parents had prior commitments later that night. Commitments they couldn't break. Their nighttime employee's wife had just gone into labor, which meant no one was available to manage the bodega that evening.

Could Jia help?

With a single question, she was ten years old again, trying to hide from her classmates while they bought gum from her parents as she swept the bodega floor. Immediately, Jia's mood had soured. She'd stifled a dozen retorts. Wondered if her mother had even thought to ask Jason or James. The next second, guilt had washed over her.

She always had this reaction when her parents asked her to help at the bodega. It was irrational. Jia knew it. She'd spent entire sessions with Gail discussing how much she abhorred setting foot inside her family's bodega, much less being forced to work there.

Everything the bodega represented—all the good and all the bad—knotted her emotions into a tangled web that she'd only begun to take apart.

But she hadn't protested when her mother asked, despite her strong desire to do so. She'd agreed to manage the space until 10 p.m., despite her severe jet lag and the fact that she was traveling at 2 a.m. that night on a borrowed private jet to the Cayman Islands with Darius, posing as a couple on a supposed holiday.

Jia couldn't shake a lingering sense of foreboding. Probably because of how she'd begun the day at a career pinnacle only to end it right back where she started.

She almost laughed at herself that evening when she caught her reflection in the bodega's curved mirror positioned to prevent shoplifting. Jia was sitting on the same rickety stool with uneven legs, behind the same worn register with sticky keys, at the same cracked Formica counter where she'd first met Lexi Niarchos and her Birkin.

Jia looked at the faded wall clock. The one her father had gotten for free when a local school had given away used items prior to a much-needed renovation. 9:18 p.m. Less than an hour before her mother planned to relieve her.

She glanced around the small bodega. A feeling of begrudging fondness—one strongly attached to memory—washed over her. Everything about this place was familiar to Jia, from its damaged floor tiles to its fluorescent lighting, down to the scents of produce and plastic and the musty smell of corrugated cardboard boxes. Too familiar. That same light near the refrigerated section that still flickered on occasion, even though Jia had said she would send an electrician to fix it six months ago. Her father had refused, and a weary Jia had let the matter go.

Why wouldn't they just take some money to fix the place up a little bit? Her parents were happy to have her help with things like Umma's teeth or Appa's knee surgery or Halmunni's copays or working random nights at the bodega, but they frowned whenever she offered them money for things they arbitrarily deemed unnecessary or wasteful, only to continue complaining every chance they got.

Sometimes it felt like she couldn't win with them.

She hated being here. Every time she set foot inside the small, cramped space with its familiar smells and the ringing bell over the door and the never-ending list of things that needed to be done, hate boiled through her blood.

The bodega represented everything Jia had failed to deliver so far. She wasn't financially secure enough to tell her family to sell it. Not yet. Her parents needed its income to support themselves and provide care for Jia's ailing grandmother. Her mom and dad would never agree to put Halmunni in a home. Like most older Korean immigrants, it wasn't an option for them.

Her entire life, her parents had cared for Halmunni and Harabugi. Though they would never admit it, it was often at great cost to Umma and Appa's comfort. More than anything, Jia wanted to give her parents the retirement her harabugi had never had. Harabugi had worked every day until he died. He'd loved to talk with Jia about all the places he wanted to go. Far-off destinations he'd read about in books. Pictures he'd seen on the internet or amid their shared love of history, with all its lessons. Places and things he'd never had the chance to see.

When Jia made senior partner, she would have enough to tell her parents to sell the bodega. She could comfortably provide for them and for herself without any worries.

But until that day, her parents would have to work in this tiny, disheveled room, serving people who didn't see them, their reflections forever distorted in a curved mirror.

Jia wanted bigger and better things for herself and her family. Proving that she could honor her grandfather's final request had become her sole focus in life, especially after the hazy future she'd dreamed about with Zain had been doused by cold reality.

Jia Song didn't need anyone to make her dreams come true. She would do it herself.

She could almost see it, as if the finish line were within reach. She fought back a wave of desperation. Like her soul was stretching out a metaphorical limb, fighting for every inch.

The bell above the door dinged, and Jia was startled from her reverie.

Umma hurried into the bodega, tearing off her coat as she walked. "Did you eat?" she said in Korean without pausing.

"Not yet," Jia replied in English as she hopped off the stool to take her mother's coat. "I had a big lunch."

Umma reached into her large bag and pulled out two containers. "I brought some of Halmunni's kimbap. Eat." She plopped the Tupperware onto the counter along with two sets of wooden chopsticks.

Jia stifled a sigh. "I should probably go. I don't really have time to eat." She moved to gather her things, but her mother blocked her, her eagle eyes sharp.

"Why do you look sick?" Umma demanded. "So thin." She *tsk*ed. "And your skin looks horrible. Are you not washing your face?"

"Last time I was too fat, this time I'm too thin. I'll just wait for the next time." She forced a grin. "Maybe then I'll finally be perfect."

"You need to eat." Umma popped open one of the containers.

"Umma, I really don't have time."

"I'm early. Just eat, and then you can go."

"I have to catch a plane at two."

"That's many hours from now. Eat." Umma arched one of her microbladed brows, a gift from Jia last Christmas.

"Not two in the afternoon. Two at night."

Her mother snorted in the tradition of Korean ummas everywhere, long and dry, almost like an extended scoff. "What kind of flight is at two in the morning? Go later. You need to eat and get some rest."

"I will. As soon as this case is over." Jia attempted to grab her tote bag and her Moncler puffer coat.

"Umma is worried about you." Her mother frowned. "Please travel later and get some rest. You've been working so hard. I'm sure your boss will understand that you need to sleep."

"Not likely."

"You work too hard."

"I have to if I'm going to make partner."

Confusion tugged at her mother's brows. "I thought you just made partner."

Jia closed her eyes and counted to ten in her head while shrugging into her coat. "It's the next kind of partner. Don't worry about it." She tucked her tote under her arm. "I'll see you later." She turned to walk toward the door.

"Yah, Song Jihae!" Umma yelled in that same way she always had, with her voice pitched to the ceiling. It never failed to halt Jia in her tracks. "I told you to eat. Are you really not going to listen to your umma?"

Jia swallowed. Then she pivoted and snatched the wooden chopsticks from the counter. Before another word was spoken, she crammed two pieces of kimbap into her mouth to prevent herself from starting an argument with her mother. One she had neither the time nor the patience to have at this moment.

Temporarily mollified, Jia's mother broke apart the other pair of wooden chopsticks and began to eat as well. "I saw Ara's mom today."

"Mm-hmm."

"She told me Ara got engaged last month."

Relentless, as usual. "Good for her," Jia said around her mouthful of rice. "Did she also make junior partner?"

"She said Ara was really happy. She asked if you were happy." Umma paused to open a can of cold grape Sac Sac for Jia. It had been one of her favorite drinks as a child. The tiny bits of real grape had delighted her. "I told her I wasn't sure."

"Tell Ara's mom I don't have time to worry about being happy. Once I'm done with my work, then I can worry about that shit."

Umma's voice dropped. "All the work you're doing, Jihae-ya. It doesn't matter what kind of success you have if you aren't happy. If you don't have peace inside yourself."

"Jesus," Jia whispered. "I have great friends and a great job, and all my family members are close by and in relatively good health. I'm fine."

"Those are all things outside you. I am not worried about those things. I am worried about what is going on inside you." Umma used her chopsticks to point at Jia's heart.

Jia put down her own chopsticks. No matter how hard she tried, her mother would never understand her. Never truly hear what she had to say or see the world through her eyes. "Look, Umma." Her expression softened. "I know you're worried about me. But I'm really fine. I just need to rest. I'll do that as soon as I'm finished with this client."

"There is always a client. And then another and another."

"And I'm glad!" Jia raised her hands in the air. "You'd rather I not have any clients?"

"I'd rather you live a life of balance."

"Like you?" Jia said. "You worked all hours of the day every day for most of my life."

"I did that so you wouldn't have to."

"Okay. Sure." Jia wiped her mouth and tossed her chopsticks into the nearby trash, despising how—on top of everything—she felt guilty for causing her mother to worry. It felt like nothing she did would ever be good enough for her mother, like she was destined to be a disappointment in one way or another. "I'm sorry I'm not living my life the way you think I should be living it. Thanks for the kimbap. Tell Jason and James the next shift is on them."

Umma flinched. Guilt spread through Jia like wine across a white rug. But she kept silent and steady, as she always had. Her feelings were her own, and she didn't want the burden of sharing them with her mother. The shame of needing her solace or the sadness of realizing Umma could not provide the comfort she wanted.

With a nod, Jia kissed her silently judging mother on the cheek and raced into the bracing wind, the bell above the door cheerfully chiming behind her.

# THE SPIDER AND THE CIPHER

## *T Minus 16 Days*

When the Cayman Islands first came into view, Jia gazed at them from the window of their borrowed Learjet 60—supplied by Minsoo's mentor, a recently retired hedge fund manager—for a solid two minutes. She'd never arrived at a tropical destination when it was still dark outside. It was strangely mesmerizing to watch the shadows emerge from the dark sea below. There was a hushed sense to their arrival, almost as if Jia and Darius were clandestine agents on a secret mission.

Actually, they kind of were, if Jia stopped to think about it.

She'd always had a thing for spy novels.

After they landed at the private terminal, they were whisked in a Lincoln Town Car along winding two-lane back roads. Though Jia's mind was still murky from the two hours of restless sleep she'd managed on the four-hour journey south, the smell of the sea and the tinge of sand in the air seemed to settle her. She watched as tilted palm trees flickered past the window. A fleece of soft clouds stretched across the night sky. They drove through a small town with humble dwellings before larger homes began to emerge on the horizon, their umber-colored tile roofs and tan stucco exteriors stark beneath the light of an almost full moon.

Jia's pulse ratcheted up as they paused at a manned gate and waited for permission to enter the exclusive beachfront community on the famed Seven Mile Beach, where the Parks' mansion was located. Darius had assured her there was no way Seven could have had any advance notice of their arrival. As an extra precaution, the pilot had filed the flight plan at the last possible second. None of the house staff had been informed of their visit, which should provide an ideal window for Darius and Jia to search the home in private. If everything went according to plan, by the time Seven Park learned that Darius had taken his unnamed girlfriend to the Caymans property, it would be too late for him to order any member of the staff to hide anything important.

As Jia had discussed last night with Ben Volker, the thing they needed most now was proof. Something they could give to their forensic accountants. A starting point. A trail of breadcrumbs. Anything. The single account Orlagh had provided had been liquidated five weeks ago, and nothing in the three pages tied its contents to Seven Park, save for the testimony of a dead woman.

Without clear proof, they would not be able to pressure a man like Seven into capitulating. Almost half the month Jenny Park had given Jia had already passed. Which meant she had only sixteen more days to make this case work for Whitman Volker. To show the senior partners that she belonged among their ranks.

That she could be the head of snakes they all needed.

The Park family's white stucco waterfront residence loomed three stories high, its floating glass railings gleaming in the moonlight. When Darius turned the key in the ornate, lightly stained front door, a light flickered on in the darkness above them.

"Motion detection," he said softly, as if he'd expected it.

"What does that mean? Will it call for someone?"

Darius shook his head. "Theoretically, no. But an elderly caretaker named Rolando lives only ten minutes away. I wouldn't worry about him. He's been here forever and knows me well. He won't ask questions or bother us unless we need something. But it's possible Svetlana might get a notice that we've set off the motion detection. Once I turn off the alarm, she'll probably know someone is here. If she's working with Seven—which I think we all suspect—she'll be here as fast as she can to see what we're doing."

Jia worried her bottom lip between her teeth. "That gives us what, like an hour?"

"Thirty minutes to an hour."

"Jesus."

"I know." Darius pushed open the door. "We should start with the primary bedroom and the office."

---

At first Jia tried to clean up after herself as much as possible. If she moved aside books or lifted clothing from inside dresser drawers, she spent a few seconds attempting to make everything appear as undisturbed as possible.

Twenty minutes later, she ceased with all pretenses and began casting things every which way and pushing on rows of books lining the three walls of the home office to see if there was a hidden safe behind them. When Jia couldn't find anything, she moved toward the primary bedroom, where Darius had been searching since their arrival.

The closet just beyond the spa-like Japandi bathroom was immense. One section of it was filled with menswear. Expensive Bermuda shorts and pressed linen trousers and an enviable collection of Brunello Cucinelli loafers and Bruno Magli sandals. The remaining three-fourths of the space were chock-full of colorful women's clothing. Beachwear and frothy flowing dresses with loud patterns and low necklines.

Jia knew without being told that none of this belonged to Jenny Park. The sample-size gowns and the towering heels and the lacy pink lingerie were undoubtedly the property of Annika Bergström, Seven's thirty-four-year-old paramour. But that didn't preclude her section of the closet from being searched. In fact, it only hastened Jia's efforts. Soon she began shoving aside rows of garments and lifting hems and moving unopened boxes of Louboutins and Gucci espadrilles and Prada loafers and strappy Amina Muaddi sandals.

When Jia knocked over five boxes of glittering Mach & Mach heels, she muttered a Korean curse word. She bent to restack the shoes, only to discover a metal door about the size of a microwave concealed inside the corner behind them, its flush-mounted cover painted to match the earth tones of the suede wall.

The small metal door had a black handle and a tiny keypad.

"Darius," Jia said, her skin prickling. He didn't answer immediately. "Darius?" she repeated even louder.

He joined her in the closet the next instant. They shared a knowing glance. He looked at his watch. "Svetlana could be here any minute."

"Birthdays," Jia said. "Start with birthdays." She pulled up the list she'd created on her phone during the flight from Teterboro, but Darius had already begun typing in six-digit codes.

"It's not Seven's birthday," he muttered. "Let's try Annika's." Again they were met with a red light. They proceeded to enter the birthdates of the three Park children. None of them worked either.

"He might just be the kind of self-satisfied prick who uses his ex-wife's birth date," Jia said. She reached over to type out the six numbers and held her breath. Still, it didn't work.

Darius then attempted to input the house number of the Park Avenue address, followed by the numbers for all the other residences Jia provided from her list. Red light after red light.

He raked his fingers through his hair.

"Do you know the address of the first dry cleaning place they ever owned?" Jia asked out of the blue. Perhaps it was because she'd just spent a fretful evening at the bodega, but it was still on her mind. The location of her parents' first bodega had always been a point of pride for them, long after they had sold it for a bigger and better spot. It represented their first chance. The beginning of their family's new chapter. A springboard for all their dreams to come.

Darius closed his eyes and sucked in his cheeks. "I can't recall the actual address, but I believe it was in the 160s."

Jia scanned the list on the note in her phone.

Mirae Dry Cleaning, located at 823 164th Street.

She bent closer and pushed in the digits 823164.

The green light flashed. The safe trilled. Her breath tight in her lungs, Jia pushed down on the lever, and the safe door opened.

Again they shared a look, not even daring to show their excitement.

Inside the safe they found boxes of jewelry from Cartier, Bulgari, and Van Cleef & Arpels. Several stacks of cash in US dollars, as well as euros and won. Two bars of gold bullion. A small velvet pouch with loose gemstones. A worn paperback copy of Ayn Rand's *The Fountainhead*. A single manila file folder was propped on one side of the safe. Jia withdrew it. When she opened the file, a thin book about the size of her hand, bound in navy leather, slid out.

Jia flipped it open.

It was filled with tiny lettering, handwritten in blue ink. Each page began with a series of numbers separated by dashes, followed by what appeared to be columns of deposits and withdrawals. On several of the pages, Jia noted seven- and eight-figure sums in both columns. She gave the small book to Darius, her adrenaline reaching a fever pitch.

"This is Seven's handwriting," he confirmed.

With the back of her wrist, she swiped at a line of perspiration forming above her lips. "Do you think this could be the book Como mentioned?"

"Maybe. I'm just surprised that Seven would leave it here and not keep it on him." He continued turning the pages until he flipped to the very end. Understanding dawned on him. "This one is old. On the back, it's dated for 2019."

"Is it possible he's still using the same accounts?" Jia asked. "We can take this to our forensic accounting team. It might even be possible to break whatever code he uses."

"It looks like a book cipher," Darius mused before glancing at the copy of *The Fountainhead* still in the safe. "Seven Park, you're a basic bi—" Then he screamed and dropped the blue notebook as if it had scalded his fingers.

A spider scurried from beneath the pages onto the herringbone oak floor before vanishing under an upturned box of glittering slingbacks.

Jia grinned. "Looks like Seven Park isn't the only basic bitch among us."

"I hate spiders, okay? Snakes I can deal with, no problem. Some of them are even cute. But spiders?" He fake shuddered.

"It was small. Barely the size of my thumbnail."

"Fuck that. Did you hear about that guy who got bit on his toe during a cruise and woke up one morning to *spider eggs hatching out of his foot*?"

The chime on the front door sounded. Without a word, Darius crammed the notebook into the breast pocket of his linen blazer while Jia slammed the safe shut. Then they raced to the hallway beyond the primary suite and slowed to a casual stroll before entering the main living space.

An elderly man with white hair, leathery skin, and a slight stoop blinked at the sight of them. "Mr. Darius?" he said. "I am sorry no one was here to greet you. We did not know you were arriving."

"Please don't be troubled at all, Rolando," Darius replied smoothly, despite his harried appearance. "Jenny asked me to retrieve some jewelry she thought she left here the last time she came, and she offered to let me bring my new girlfriend."

"Certainly, sir. Certainly." He paused as if he were noticing the sweat on Jia's brow and the way Darius's chest rose and fell in rapid succession. Then he peered behind them at the corridor leading to the primary suite and chuckled to himself.

*Dear God*, Jia thought. Well, if that was the worst thing Seven heard about what Darius and his new girlfriend did in the Caymans house, then so be it. She could be the floozy for one day.

"This is my girlfriend, Jessica," Darius said, nodding at Jia.

Jia smiled brightly. "It's lovely to meet you, Rolando."

"Pleasure, miss. Can I bring you anything to drink or eat? It might take a moment, but I'll be happy to put something together for you."

"Not at all," Darius said. "We'll be out of your hair soon, right after we grab Jenny's jewelry. Our plan is to go to a nearby all-inclusive."

Rolando looked puzzled. "You will not be staying here, then?"

"No, no," Darius replied. "Since we didn't give you any warning, we thought it best to handle everything ourselves."

Rolando frowned. "It is no trouble at all, Mr. Darius. Svetlana will be here in fifteen minutes. I am sure she will be happy to provide anything you might need."

Darius smiled. "Thank you, Rolando. But please don't worry. I'll just collect the pieces, and we will be on our way."

"Certainly, sir," Rolando said.

Jia and Darius returned to the hallway leading to the primary bedroom suite. They hastened through the space, trying to restore everything to its former appearance. In the office adjacent to the bedroom, Jia pushed shut a drawer that was still ajar. Her fingers brushed over the handle of the drawer above it. On a whim, she tried to tug it open, but it wouldn't budge.

She shouldn't be wasting precious minutes of the little time they had left trying to open it. But what if the navy notebook wasn't enough? What if all the accounts inside it no longer existed? What if the code wasn't a simple book cipher with *The Fountainhead* as the key? What if Zain claimed that the information included was from years ago and no longer relevant to the family's current financial situation?

Jia needed something more than a handwritten log from 2019.

"Can you get me a butter knife from the kitchen?" she whispered as Darius entered the office.

"Not without Rolando seeing me," Darius replied under his breath. "Hang on. Let me see if there's anything in the bathroom."

While Darius searched, Jia tugged harder on the handle. Then she yanked open the long middle drawer of the desk and rummaged around until she found a letter opener. She wedged it in the space between the drawer and the desktop and pulled. Nothing happened. Kneeling, Jia started wriggling the letter opener back and forth while yanking on the handle.

Darius returned with tweezers and a teasing comb with a thin metal handle. "Hurry."

Jia jammed the letter opener back into the space above the lock. With careful leverage, she worked the space a little wider before sliding the metal handle of the teasing comb at a perpendicular angle near the latch.

"Were you a master thief in a past life?" Darius joked.

"No," she murmured. "But I had to break into my house when I was a kid a few times. My brothers would intentionally lock me out if I ever snuck out with my friends. They wanted me to have to wake up my parents so I would get in trouble. Always kept a pocketknife and some nail scissors handy"—she used a bit more force—"just in case."

The lock clicked. Jia yanked open the drawer, her expression one of sheer disbelief.

On the very top—not even concealed—were bank statements from two accounts in the Caribbean. These were dated from less than three months ago, likely from the last time Seven had been here. One set of papers contained the same bank account number as the one Orlagh had provided. The updated account balance was over two hundred million dollars. A second account at another bank in the Bahamas held just under sixty-five million dollars.

Both these accounts could now be tied to the Park family. Darius could testify under oath that they'd found them in one of the Park family's residences.

Which meant they could be linked to Seven Park.

Jia and Darius stared at each other, unblinking. Then a throaty female voice called out from beyond the hallway. "Darius?"

"Here," Jia said, frantically looking around. The documents would not fit inside any kind of pocket. Briefly she considered stuffing them down her shirt. "Put these in my tote bag by the closet. In the zippered pouch on the front." She fluffed her hair. "Say you were in the bathroom."

Then Jia strode out of the primary bedroom with a Cheshire cat grin, coming face-to-face with a very tall, slender blond woman in her mid-to-late forties. She was neatly dressed in a white linen shirt and white jeans, her shoulder-length hair pulled back in a low bun.

The woman did not attempt to hide the look of suspicion on her face as she scanned Jia from head to toe.

"Hello," Jia began. "My name is Jessica. I'm Darius's girlfriend. He's picking up some jewelry for Mrs. Park."

"Hello," Svetlana began, her Russian accent slight, her blue eyes alert. "Welcome to the Caymans. I am wondering why no one told me you were coming here?"

"It was a last-minute trip. Mrs. Park asked Darius just last night. A friend of hers was already taking his jet, so we hitched a ride," Jia blabbed. "She said she thinks she left some pearl earrings and some kind of brooch here or something."

"I see."

Jia walked past Svetlana, who turned in her direction as Jia led her farther away from the primary suite. She fanned herself. "It's so hot here, even in the morning! Is there any way you could point me toward something cold to drink?"

Svetlana stared at Jia. Then she looked behind her, searching for Darius. "I would be happy to get some ice water for you. Please wait here."

"Oh, I'll come along. I'd love to see the kitchen. Maybe hear a little more about the home. The view is just spectacular. What was the name of this beach again?" Her pulse continued to trill in her veins as she sauntered down the hallway.

Though the housekeeper hesitated, she joined Jia, who maintained a steady stream of chatter the entire time.

Jia hoped she was convincing enough. All they needed to do was get out of the house without raising any undue suspicion. If they could leave with their documents and the navy notebook, thcy would be well on their way to convincing Seven to stand down or, at the very least, come back to the table with a far more substantial settlement offer. They might even be able to convince Zain and the higher-ups at CHM that a longer, more protracted dispute would prove far too costly for them.

Jia could almost see the finish line.

And this time there would be no question about whether she belonged there.

# MISSING THE MOMENT

## *T-minus 16 Days*

Jia texted Ben Volker the second she and Darius sat down in the Lincoln Town Car Svetlana had called to take them to the nearby all-inclusive hotel.

*I have it*, she wrote. *Corroborating evidence for the forensic accountants.*

He replied less than a minute later. *Send everything to Kurt as soon as you can.*

Her body trembled with excitement.

As the Lincoln Town Car pulled away from the house, Darius and Jia continued staring straight ahead, Jia's fingers tapping on the pebbled black leather of her tote, Darius's knee bouncing at a frenetic pace. They didn't dare say a word to each other, as the driver could have been instructed to report back on any of their exchanges.

Darius's phone chimed once on the drive. After reading the text message, he showed it to Jia, who simply nodded.

Jenny Park wanted to meet with her at the Park Avenue residence when they returned later today.

"Almost there," Darius said as the driver made the turn into the roundabout leading toward the entrance of the resort.

They thanked the driver and collected their single rolling suitcase, along with Jia's tote. At the house, neither Jia nor Darius had taken their eyes off the tote for more than a few minutes. And they'd never left Svetlana alone with it, even for a second. Jia had been itching to check the paperwork inside it ever since Svetlana's arrival, but the housekeeper had been just as vigilant as they had been. She'd been watching them the entire time.

There was no possible way either of them could have had a chance to go through their things. Nevertheless, Jia had seen Darius—on more than one occasion—run his hand along the inside of his jacket pocket.

Jia and Darius walked past the check-in desk toward the restaurant to the right of the open-air lobby, with its lazily circling fans and its dark polished floors and its soothing steel drum music. After ordering drinks, Darius removed the small notebook. His shoulders slumped in relief.

With a long exhale, Jia lifted her tote and unzipped the front pocket. When she saw the papers and the copy of *The Fountainhead* stuffed inside, she almost let out a cheer.

Here was the proof they needed to corroborate the information from Orlagh. The notebook and the paperback could offer the final key to deciphering everything. She was going to win this case.

Jia pulled out the papers. And froze. "No," she whispered. "No. No. *No.*"

"What?" Darius's eyes went wide.

Jia flipped through every piece of paper, panic causing the hairs on the back of her neck to stand on end. "They're all blank," she said in a hoarse whisper. "Someone switched them. Everything is gone. But . . . but *how*?"

Darius dragged a palm over his face, his expression one of utter defeat. "Rolando. It had to be Rolando. He's the only person with the opportunity."

Suspicion caused Jia's toes to curl inside her Chloé sandals. "Are you sure you put the papers in the tote?"

Darius stared at Jia in silence for a moment. Anger clouded his features. "Unbelievable. You still don't trust me."

"Would you?" she accused, though she sounded miserable.

"What have I done or said that could possibly lead you to believe I'm going to betray Jenny?"

"Maybe you don't have to do or say anything. Maybe it's just that you're always in the right place at the wrong time. That anything I share with you winds up being turned against me before I can blink."

"You sound paranoid." He glared at her.

"I'd rather be paranoid than dicknotized."

"What?"

"Like . . ." She waved her hands. "Like completely lost in your bedroom eyes and your beautiful hands and your . . . just *you*!"

Darius stood up, the hurt on his face plain. "Listen, Jia," he said. "If I were you, I would trust my instincts." He reached into his wallet and produced a hundred-dollar bill. "My instincts told me the moment I met you that you were special. I really hope I'm not wrong."

"My instincts told me you were too good to be true," Jia retorted. "And everything good in life comes with a price. Maybe I'm not ready to pay it."

"Right," Darius said. "When you start calling into question every good thing that happens, you wind up missing the moment because you're stuck in the past or worried about the future. I don't have time for that." He placed the money on the table to cover their drinks. "Whenever you're ready, I'll meet you out front to go home."

They traveled the entire way back to New York in silence.

# I CAN'T STAND THE RAIN

## T Minus 16 Days

When Jia rolled up to the front of the Park Avenue residence six hours later, she was alone. It was raining, the sidewalks gleaming in the late afternoon light.

On normal days, she preferred the rain, just like her grandfather had. They'd shared a long-standing love of it. She prided herself on being odd like that, as if it were a badge of honor. But not today. Today the sky reflected the way she felt. Miserable and in need of a good cry.

Ben Volker had texted her twice. Left her a voicemail.

She hadn't returned any of his messages because she wasn't ready to face her failure.

*Failures*, she should say. Today seemed rife with them. Now Jia was set to meet the Park family's dying matriarch and confess that, despite all the globe-trotting and intrigue of the last two weeks, she had precious little to show for it.

Jenny Park was probably going to fire Jia when she heard what had happened. The story sounded far-fetched on its own. But coupled with her many failures?

Jia would fire herself, too, without question.

Darius had given the blue notebook and the copy of *The Fountainhead* to Jia before leaving the hangar at Teterboro. He'd taken the rest of the day off. His face before he got in the taxi still haunted her. It looked cold and remote. Masking his feelings in a manner completely unlike him.

Her phone vibrated in her hand.

Umma: *Are you home? Do you want to come to dinner?*

*I don't think I can,* Jia typed back. *I'm sorry.*

Umma: *But you usually come for Sunday dinner.*

Jia ignored her mother's response and heaved open the door of the black Lincoln Navigator. "Let's get this over with," she muttered to no one.

She angled herself through the rain toward the crimson awning above the entrance of the Park Avenue co-op. A man in a Yankees hat with a tan trench coat passed by her, singing, "I can't stand the rain," under his breath, the black band of his Bose headphones dangling beneath his jaw.

Jia had to agree with him. This was a good day for some old-school Missy Elliott.

She rode the elevator to the penthouse in the company of Anthony, the cheerful doorman she'd met with Suzy two weeks back. It felt like a lifetime ago.

Celeste answered the door to the apartment because Darius wasn't there to do it. Clearly, Jia had done enough damage to warrant his avoidance of her. But was it for the rest of the day, or forever?

She shucked her dripping raincoat, then followed Celeste into the same sitting room with the Hyewon painting and the floor-to-ceiling windows overlooking Central Park. The same space where they'd shared lunch together the day she'd first met Jenny.

Jenny was sitting in her spot on the couch, wearing a dove gray tracksuit and ivory cashmere socks. She looked smaller, as if she'd lost more weight. Her short silver hair was soft and unbound. When she saw Jia, she closed the book she'd been reading. From the look of the cover, it appeared to be a historical romance. A beautiful woman with pink cheeks and full lips, her long tresses blowing in the wind, stared adoringly up at a stunning man with gleaming chest muscles and an expression of fierce protectiveness. Like an adult version of a Disney fairy tale.

Something about seeing Jenny holding this book made her want to cry even more.

Jenny studied Jia for a moment. "Are you all right, Song Jihae?"

"I'm fine," Jia replied quickly. She sat across from Jenny and attempted to smooth her wet, disheveled hair. "I hope you weren't waiting long."

"Not at all." Jenny placed her book on the marble coffee table between them. "I appreciate you coming to see me on such short notice. I thought I should try to speak with you while you were still in town. You are leaving again soon, is that right?"

Jia nodded. In two days, she was supposed to be flying with Sora and Darius to Paris, on a GV jet Sora's father-in-law, Chip Vandeveld, had arranged for them by calling in a favor with one of his Princeton buddies.

"May I ask about our progress?" Jenny's voice was soft. Kind. Patient.

A stinging sensation formed at the bridge of Jia's nose. She tried to blink it away. "We've made some progress. But we're still hoping to find concrete evidence of these hidden accounts, as well as a way to tie everything back to Sora's father."

"And my children are working well together?"

"They are." It was mostly true. Jia thought of the way the twins had stormed into the conference room at CHM and found herself close to smiling for the first time since this morning.

"I am glad to hear it." Jenny eased back into the cushions, a grimace rippling across her face. "Just as I am glad to hear that things are moving in a forward direction."

Jia didn't want to lie. "Please, I don't want you to misunderstand. We have definitely encountered some difficult setbacks."

Jenny nodded. "Orlagh." She closed her eyes. Her chin trembled ever so slightly. "Her daughter will not return my calls."

"She made it clear she didn't want to hear from any of us again," Jia replied.

"Orlagh was a lovely soul who deserved far better than that. What happened to her will haunt me even after I die." Jenny spoke plainly, without emotion. If someone wasn't watching her face—wasn't there to witness the telltale trace of tears—they would not realize how much Orlagh had meant to her.

"Of course," Jia said. "I'm so sorry for your pain."

"My pain is not of consequence." Jenny opened her eyes and patted the tears away with her palm in a prim gesture that reminded Jia of Sora. Then she turned to gaze out the large windows that looked out onto Central

Park, and for a few moments, they listened to the wind throw rain at the glass. "Today I met with hospice care for the first time. They will begin coming here soon."

Jia's eyes widened. She thought they'd given Jenny until the summer. "I'm . . . sorry." She couldn't think of what else to say.

"Don't be," Jenny continued, her gaze still focused on the window and its gloomy view of Central Park. "There are many other things to be sad about. That should not be one of them."

"Is there anything I can do?"

Jenny nodded. "You are doing it. You are giving my children a reason to unite. A cause to fight for together. For them, I will do anything."

That same unease snaked through Jia's stomach. "I don't want to lie to you and tell you we will make it work. The most I can do is promise that I won't give up until you tell me to give up. That I will do everything in my power to get to the truth and seek justice for you and your children."

"Good," Jenny said. "Your honesty is the reason I chose to work with you. Never lose that quality."

"Thank you," Jia said softly. The burning feeling on the bridge of her nose reignited.

Jenny sighed. "I am . . . so tired of living this way. But I am ready for the next step. It is time to make my apologies and say the things I've felt but have struggled to articulate for many years." She stopped to take a halting breath, then turned back to Jia. "I've made many mistakes in my life. Most of the ones I cannot seem to forget are the ones with my children . . . and with their father. I don't want to continue making these mistakes, Jihae-ya."

The endearment at the end of her name—the familiarity of it—caused Jia's shoulders to drop and her voice to catch. "I—I understand if you don't wish to pursue this matter anymore."

Jenny shook her head. "No. I promised you one month. I will not go back on my word. When my kids were younger, I didn't always fight when I should have fought. But I want them to see me as strong. As the kind of person who is willing to fight for what is right, even when it is difficult." She shivered before reaching for the throw blanket near her feet. Jia helped her spread it across her legs.

"I asked you to come here today for two reasons," Jenny continued. "First, I wanted to let you know that I will be leaving for Greece tomorrow. Before hospice comes, I want to spend two weeks in one of my favorite places in the world. Hopefully, my children will join me at some point. If you need anything from me, you are welcome to contact me there or visit whenever you wish."

"Thank you," Jia said.

"Secondly, I wanted you to know that you have my full support. I suspect things have not been easy for you these last few weeks. One of the mistakes I made as a parent was not telling my children how much I supported them, even if I didn't always agree with what they were doing." She smiled a tired smile. "Facing the end of my life has reminded me that we are not always given the gift of time to correct our mistakes. I would like to do that, from today forward. I hope to do that with each of my children, who are all so wonderful and unique, yet so troubled and . . . terrified." She winced again. "I wish they could see that all I want for them is the space to dream."

That caught Jia off guard. "The space to dream?"

Jenny looked at Jia, her gaze steady. "Dreaming is essential to life. If we cannot dream, we cannot believe. If we cannot believe, we cannot trust. If we cannot trust, then we cannot live a life of meaning."

Jia worked through the knot in her throat. "Have you found the space to dream, even after all of this?"

"Yes," Jenny said. "I have found my peace. In order to have the space to dream, we must find our peace."

"How did you find it?"

Jenny leaned forward, her voice dropping. "By forgiving. Others, of course. But myself, most of all."

"But . . . forgive yourself for what?"

"For all the things I did . . . and all the things I failed to do. For not trusting myself. For loving and hating in all the wrong ways."

Again Jia fought back tears. Jenny's words were striking too close to home. "I . . . don't know if I can do that."

"You can. If you want the space to dream, you will."

Jia nodded. Tears filled her eyes. "I'm sorry. I have to go." She stood up and raced from the room, though she knew it was the height of rudeness. She bit the inside of her cheek to keep from sobbing as the elevator fell back to earth. Then she spent a moment trying to collect herself before making her way through the perfumed lobby and back into the rain.

Her phone rang.

Without thinking, Jia picked it up.

"Jihae-ya?" her mother said. "How come you didn't respond to Umma's message?"

Jia's voice shook. "I can't come to dinner tomorrow. Please just understand. I'm sorry I'm such a disappointment. I'm sorry I never do the right thing. I'm sorry. I'm sorry. *I'm sorry.*" She sobbed.

She was met with silence. Not unsurprising. She so rarely shared her innermost thoughts and feelings with either of her parents.

Jia sobbed louder. "I'm sorry, Umma. This isn't your fault. I—"

"No," Umma said. "Don't apologize." She hesitated. "I think maybe . . . I have been the one to fail you."

"What?" Jia stopped short, the rain cascading around her.

"I thought about this all day. Appa and I put too much pressure on you. Everyone did. Even your harabugi."

"No." Jia shook her head. "Harabugi always believed in me. He made me believe in myself."

"But we made you believe it wasn't okay to fail. Jihae-ya, we all fail. When we fail, we learn."

Tears coursed down Jia's cheeks. "Umma, I can't fail. I've worked too hard. There is too much on the line."

"No. There isn't. No matter what happens, you will be okay. Your family will be okay. It is not your responsibility to fix everything. I am so sorry you think it is."

Jia cried louder, body-racking sobs that caused a woman dressed in what looked like a polka-dotted space suit carrying a hot-pink umbrella the size of a SmartCar to steer clear of her.

Her mother sniffled, and Jia realized she was crying too. "Cheongmal meeyanae, nae dahl," Umma said.

*I'm so sorry, my daughter.*

"It's okay," Jia said. "It's okay, Umma."

"I'm sorry you ever thought you were a disappointment. You . . . are the light of my life."

With that, Jia looked up into the rain and cried with her mother on Park Avenue.

# SUPERCAR DEATHMATCH

## T Minus 15 Days

Even after the catharsis of a good cry, part of Jia wanted to give up on the case. She wasn't sure she could continue hitting wall after wall and still bounce back. Nor could she stomach feeling like Seven Park was three steps ahead of her in every way that mattered.

Mostly, she couldn't stand the idea of failing Jenny Park in the two weeks they had left. She understood now, more than ever, why so many people stayed around Jenny for so many years. It had confused her at first. She wasn't enigmatic like Sora. Nor was she dramatic like Suzy or pragmatic like Minsoo.

Jenny was real. Broken, but not destroyed. The romantic in her hadn't died when the former love of her life had turned his back on her. The simple strength of that choice was not just an inspiration. For Jia, it had become an aspiration.

The evening after Jia had met with Jenny, she'd called Nidhi to tell her she wanted to give up. Nidhi had said they would be over in an hour. Sure enough, Jia's best friends had arrived at her place after midnight, armed with mochi doughnuts and green tea ice cream from their favorite shop on Thirty-Third Street, ready to give her a loving figurative slap upside the head.

"If you give up on this case now, how will you feel after Jenny Park dies?" Nidhi had asked between bites, all three of them sprawled on their stomachs across Jia's unmade bed.

"Like shit," Jia had said. "But I already feel like shit, so . . ."

Elisa had clucked through her teeth. "So pick your poison. Do you want to feel like shit after trying, or do you want to feel like shit after giving up?"

Jia had groaned. "The first one. I guess."

"Then stop acting like a lamp without any oil," Elisa had said. "The Jia Song I know loves to win."

"All she needs is a good reason," Nidhi had finished. "This time, find a better one."

That directive had replayed in Jia's mind all night, long after her friends had left.

Since the day she'd first started working at Whitman Volker, she'd wanted to be Emily Bhatia. No, she'd wanted to be better than Emily Bhatia, because when Jia got to the top, she would be looking out for the ones like her. The hungry young women with the kind of much-needed perspective that would reshape the legal field for decades to come.

Jia had taken on this case because she thought it would get her up the ladder faster.

But Nidhi was right. She needed a better reason.

She had one now. Now it was personal. Jia wasn't going to win this case for the accolades or for the sake of justice or for the billables.

She was going to win this case because it mattered to her. Maybe it mattered in the same way it mattered to Sora, who wanted her pound of flesh. Or to Suzy, who craved attention. Jia still wasn't certain about Minsoo, or if he was even someone she could trust, but she had to believe his mother mattered to him. He couldn't be so heartless.

Jia didn't know when this family's predicament had come to matter to her in a personal way. It wasn't solely because Seven had recruited Jia's ex to his cause.

Perhaps her reasons didn't signify. Perhaps it was just because Jia cared about Jenny. Or maybe it was because the lure of becoming the next Emily Bhatia had lost a bit of its luster. Striving to be perfect was exhausting. And Jenny wasn't perfect. She was flawed and real. Broken, but not destroyed.

Jia could do flawed and real.

She didn't know the right path forward, but she wouldn't stop until she found it. Proof of Seven's lies was out there. If she'd managed to find it once, she would find it again.

But before she left for Paris, she needed to speak to Minsoo. Among all the siblings, he was the one well-versed in financial matters. It was his chosen field of expertise. But more importantly, Jia wanted to spend one-on-one time with him, if for no other reason than to glean his true motivations. She still wasn't sure she could trust him—or any of them, for that matter—but she needed to stop wasting time hedging her bets.

Gail always said it was better to give people the benefit of the doubt. In her most soothing voice, she would ask Jia why anyone would want to worry about something twice. *Worry about it when it happens,* Gail would say, *instead of obsessing over every possible outcome beforehand.*

The only problem with arranging to speak with the youngest Park sibling?

Minsoo Park was a busy man.

Which was why Jia had agreed to meet him in a random parking lot in Queens at 8:30 that bright morning. Yesterday's early spring rain had washed away the dirt and debris. The air smelled like damp earth. Before her grandmother's diabetes had begun to limit her mobility, Jia's halmunni had enjoyed gardening in the small plot of land behind their house. Her hands always smelled like damp earth, even after she washed them well.

Now Jia filled her lungs with the scent. It reminded her of home.

Then she made her way past the trees into the parking lot . . . and halted in her tracks.

Countless sports cars in an array of colors were lined up at an angle along the perimeter of the lot. Some had their doors thrown wide and their hoods propped open. Oglers gathered around, snapping pictures with their phones. Occasionally an engine would rev, which would then prompt one of the strangest displays of peacocking Jia had ever witnessed. A chorus of growling, screeching, and popping would follow until, finally, the noise would die down as it had begun. Inexplicably.

This gathering didn't resemble a scene from a movie of the fast and furious variety. No riced-out Skylines modified for drifting or old-school Chargers with gleaming ram air intakes were anywhere to be found.

It was like the parking circle in front of a casino in Monte Carlo. Ferraris, Lamborghinis, Bugattis, Porsches, McLarens, Aston Martins, and several models Jia didn't recognize.

This was apparently a meeting place for some kind of supercar club.

Jia lowered her sunglasses and squinted into the light until she spotted Minsoo standing beside a gleaming black Porsche with a massive spoiler.

She jogged up to him still trying to erase the peevish look from her face.

Why couldn't these people have a normal meeting with her in a normal place?

"Hello, Jia," Minsoo said, looking up from his phone.

"Hi." She attempted a smile. "I hope I'm not interrupting your supercar club party."

Minsoo pocketed his phone and braced a hip against his 911 GT3 RS. "It's not a supercar club." He opened the passenger door to the Porsche. "Ta," he said, grinning.

The little shit was enjoying this. Darius was right. All the Park siblings liked yanking the rug out from under people.

"You know I'm older than you, right?" She cast him an arch glance.

"Do you want me to call you noona?" He laughed. "Bahlee ta." He gestured toward the open car door with a tilt of his head.

Jia didn't appreciate being told what to do. But she did like how easily he spoke to her in banmal. It surprised her. With his perfectly pressed slacks, polo, and boat shoes, Minsoo Park didn't appear to be the sort of guy who would forgo formality so readily.

With a good-humored glare, Jia got into the Porsche. A moment later, Minsoo slid behind the wheel in a single smooth motion and closed the door. "I thought it was better if people assumed we were friends, rather than a client with his attorney." He checked his Panerai watch. "We should be heading out soon. You're good until after lunch, right?"

Jia cut her eyes at him. "Yes, my schedule is clear until dinnertime."

He fiddled with some settings along the steering wheel. "No motion sickness issues?"

"No. Why?" Her suspicions began to peak.

"We're going to be taking a nice jaunt to Fire Island this morning."

"What?" Jia gasped. "That's hours away from here."

"Only two." This time his grin was boyish. It softened his features in an endearing way. "Besides, it will give us a chance to speak without worrying about who might be listening."

"Why Fire Island?"

Minsoo shrugged. "It's a beautiful drive, first of all. Lots of winding roads and charming towns. The trees should be starting to bloom. Secondly, this is what we do."

"You and this supercar club routinely make unnecessary long-distance drives on random Sundays?"

"It's not a supercar club. It's a collective of car enthusiasts."

"Potato, tomato," Jia returned.

He smiled with all his teeth, and it touched his eyes, making them scrunch at the edges. Jia was struck by how young he looked. Young and carefree. She couldn't remember a single time she'd thought of either word in front of Minsoo Park.

"Are you ready?" he asked.

"It's not my first time riding in a fast car." It wasn't a complete lie. Her brother James had long been a car enthusiast. An original Dominic Toretto fanboy. Jia had been in a fast car before. But she'd never been in one that cost several hundred thousand dollars. She looked around the inside of Minsoo's undoubtedly custom Porsche. Admired the caramel suede and the carbon fiber and the hand-stitched leather. Then she heard the car beside them fire up. Listened while the driver revved the engine until twin flames burst from the back of it.

"Honestly, I'm surprised you're not driving that," Jia remarked.

"The SVJ?" Minsoo sniffed. "I have a Lambo."

"Isn't that the fastest one you can have?"

"If you say so," Minsoo said. "I already went through my Lambo phase. I'll take this car any day."

"I've ridden in a Porsche before. One of my law school buddies has a Boxster."

He groaned. "The sacrilege. As a point of fact, you haven't ridden in an actual Porsche before." His dark eyes glittered like black diamonds. "This is one of one. You're in for a treat." He pushed the ignition button, and the car hummed to life. The next instant, it zipped from the curb with an anticipatory growl.

Jia's heart flew into her mouth when Minsoo pulled onto the street. Then it plummeted the next second. She was pretty sure the entire contents of her stomach—a croissant and a café au lait—were hovering in the back of her throat, just waiting for a chance to be set free.

"Like it?" Minsoo smiled at her as he switched gears again and mashed his foot on the accelerator. The Porsche responded with a low purr, trees flying by on either side at frightening speed.

Jia was tempted to say no. "I'm pretty sure I'm going to be sick," she replied. "But I don't hate it."

"Just keep that thing on you." Minsoo glanced down at the motion sickness bag on Jia's lap. "This leather is not for puking."

She watched the fire-engine red Ferrari in front of them take the curve ahead at a breakneck pace. Minsoo followed suit, the fleet of supercars around them revving and blasting their engines in a single sonorous roar.

The SVJ from earlier passed Minsoo on the left, then gunned forward, a pair of wicked blue flames bursting from its exhaust pipes. The sound caused Jia to shiver.

"Nothing quite like a screaming Lambo. But still not good enough, Akin," Minsoo said under his breath. He kicked his Porsche into high gear, and the black car glided over one hundred miles an hour before passing the bright green Lamborghini with the ease of a silk strap falling off a shoulder.

---

For the first hour of the drive, they managed to keep the conversation light. Almost as if they were still trying to feel each other out. Now it was time for Jia to get to the meat of the issue.

"Do you still think it's worth going to Paris?" she asked him without preamble.

Minsoo eased the wheel left, and the Porsche leaned into the curve with a growl. "Yes, I do."

"But your dad knows we were snooping around the Caymans house—wouldn't he take the time to protect himself in Paris?"

"Not necessarily," Minsoo said. "If he thought you had found something truly important, he would have lashed out by now. He's not the type to stay silent when he's scared. He likes to bully people when he's worried. It makes him feel strong."

"So he's not scared of us." Jia watched the trees blur through the window.

"That's a good thing. Also I don't think he would expect you to show up in Paris so soon after what happened in the Caymans. It's brazen of you to even try. He believes he has us on the ropes after those papers were taken from your bag."

Doubt grew in her mind—the question of whether Minsoo was a double agent whose true loyalty remained with his father. It had started that day in Falkirk and solidified the morning Suzy and Sora had rescued her without Minsoo in tow. Why hadn't he come with them? A show of solidarity would have been important. Was it more than what Suzy had said about her brother being too chickenshit to stand up to their father in a direct way?

Had he chosen his side long ago, while continuing to play a part?

"Suzy told me what happened," Minsoo said. "I'd bet it was Rolando, too. My dad is good at getting people to do his bidding. I'm sure he enjoyed sticking it to you like that. He'll be expecting you to lick your wounds for a while."

"You mean *our* wounds, right? He's sticking it to all of you when he does things like that."

This time, Minsoo kept silent for a beat. "I'm used to it."

Jia considered his response. Asking a few soft questions was a good way to get him to lower his guard. "Going to Paris is still a gamble, don't you think?"

"All of this is. But we're running out of time. Do you have a better idea?"

"No," Jia admitted. "I agree that he's the type to keep the most damning evidence close to him. Is it true that he's not that organized? Your aunt mentioned that she was the one to file his papers when she worked with your dad."

Minsoo lowered the volume on the jazz clarinet crooning from the speakers. "I can't speak to how he is now, but I do remember him being the kind of person who hangs on to paper copies of everything, like a weird kind of pseudo-Luddite."

Jia nodded. "Then we'll give it a try and hope for the best. Maybe we'll catch him in a mistake." However unlikely she thought that would be.

"I already sent PIs to watch over the apartment in Le Marais. They said both he and Ani are still there, acting as if everything is copacetic. Nothing about their schedules or the staff's routines has changed. Once you arrive in Paris, I'll send the contact info for the PI in charge to Sora. His name is Hugo. He'll let you know the best time to go inside, when no one else is there."

"Thank you." Jia watched Minsoo as he navigated the winding roads with the ease of a Formula One racer.

"You're trying to decide if you can trust me." Minsoo kept his eyes trained in front of him.

"I'd be foolish if I didn't at least consider it."

"Honestly, you're right to worry." He quirked his lips. "About forty-eight hours after we first met with you in your office, my father offered to make me the next CEO of Mirae. He made a big production out of it. Like, prodigal son stuff."

Jia froze, her heart thundering in her ears. "What"—she cleared her throat—"what did you say to him?"

His cheeks hollowed. "I won't lie. I did consider it. But after what he did to Mom . . . I couldn't do it."

"How would he have known about our meeting so quickly?"

"Suzy is nuts about a lot of things, but I do think she's right about the staff at Park Avenue," Minsoo said. "Probably at least one or two of the regulars are being paid by my dad on the side to report back to him. Look through the mail. Sift through the trash. Listen in on calls and meetings. That kind of stuff."

"What the fuck?" Jia shook her head.

"It's not that uncommon, sadly. It's why rich people always say good help is hard to find."

"Yuck. Please don't ever say that again. You sound like a tool."

Minsoo laughed. "Probably because I am one. Remember? I considered siding with my dad, despite everything." He drove in silence for a few minutes. "All I've ever wanted is for him to treat me like I'm his heir. Like I'm the one destined to have it all."

Jia couldn't stop herself from frowning.

"I know, I know," he continued. "It feels disgusting coming out of my mouth, but it's true. Most of my adult life, my father has treated me like I'm an experiment gone awry. When I was younger, he always told me everything was for me. He would show me the plans for the next business he wanted to build, or he would take me to the site of something while it was under construction. He said he was raising me to take over one day, and that he knew I was tough enough to fill his shoes."

"He thinks he's the hero, when he's really the villain."

"Isn't that the case with all villains, though?" Minsoo said. "Once he realized that my sexuality wasn't a 'phase,' he stopped talking to me like that or taking me with him to show off his work. My entire adult life, all I've ever wanted from my dad was for him to treat me like that again. Even though I know it's supremely fucked-up and wrong. Trust me. I've been to enough therapy to know how messed up all of this is." He breathed deeply, his expression tinged with regret. "How messed up I am."

His grip tightened on the steering wheel until his knuckles went white. "When Mom first got cancer, I saw him pull away, and I thought he was just struggling to cope, like I was. I get that he wasn't happy. I see why he wanted to move on." A wry look settled on his face. "We're more alike than not, after all.

"Then, after her double mastectomy, she went into remission, and I thought everything would go back to normal." He flexed his fingers along the wheel. "To be honest, I wasn't surprised he cheated. But I didn't think he would flaunt it like that, especially with someone half his age. Then the cancer came back, and Annika got pregnant, and he just . . ." The Porsche's engine roared, and Jia's skull flew back into the headrest.

"What kind of guy does that to his dying wife?" Minsoo whispered, the odometer continuing to climb. "What kind of person tries to steal everything from the mother of his kids when she's fighting at death's door?" He clenched his jaw. "I've worked in finance for most of my career. Morally bankrupt men are a dime a dozen. But this? Even the most reptilian guy I work with wouldn't know what to say about Seven." He spoke faster and faster. "Because that guy, that sleazebag with the secret uptown and downtown sex pads, still takes care of his family, without question. He wouldn't take a dime from his wife. And he would never, ever take anything from his kids." The muscles in his neck rippled, fury coursing through his body. He mashed down on the accelerator again, and, for the first time, Jia felt afraid.

Minsoo took the next turn far ahead of the pack. "And now my mother . . . is going to die feeling like a pile of discarded trash." He swallowed. "It took me forever to be able to say those words out loud. *My mother is going to die.* For months, I couldn't even say it. I couldn't try to fix it like Sora did, with all her calls and connections and second opinions. I couldn't try to feel it like Suzy did, over and over again, wallowing in her pain. I couldn't—I can't—*I can't do anything.*" He slammed his palm against the steering wheel the same instant the car struck a puddle of standing water. Jia felt the tires start to slip, the trees streaking past them like stars in hyperspace.

The next instant, the back of the Porsche careened to the left. Jia screamed as the car began to spin. She grabbed hold of the handle above her window and watched the world revolve around her almost as if it were in slow motion.

Thankfully, the Porsche skidded out on a patch of dirt shoulder, a cloud of dust settling around it. The rest of the supercar fleet slowed to check on them. Minsoo waved them on with a rueful smile. Then his features sobered.

Jia reached out a tentative hand to rest on his shoulder. Beneath her fingers, she could feel the tension as if it were a rubber band about to snap.

"I'm sorry," Minsoo whispered. "That was . . . really reckless."

Jia's pulse was still thudding in her veins. She wanted to yell at him like a noona would. She also wanted to urge him to talk more. It was clear he needed it. But—even after everything she'd just witnessed—she still didn't trust Minsoo Park. His quiet volatility surprised her. It seemed incongruous with the picture of him she'd had in her mind.

She needed to distract them from what had just happened. "If we find something helpful in Paris, what would your next play be?" she asked in as nonchalant a tone as she could manage. "I'm asking because of your background. Is it better to follow the number trail or try to settle?"

Lines gathered along Minsoo's forehead. "If we find a way into any of those accounts, I will drain them myself, without question," he replied. "I've already set up legal shell corporations and offshore accounts for that exact purpose. Good luck to Seven if he tries to sue us."

"If you can't get into the accounts, would you try to settle?"

Minsoo pondered. "He won't settle if we come to him because he will think we have the weaker position."

Interesting. "So when he reached out to us about a settlement, he believed he was in the weaker position?"

"I told you he doesn't stay quiet when he's truly scared." Minsoo glanced sidelong at her. "I don't think we should try to settle. Not until we have the clear upper hand. The only way I've gotten my father to agree to anything is by playing devil's advocate and almost tricking him into doing the opposite of my suggestion, which is actually what I wanted him to do in the first place. Does that make sense?"

It did. But it was so convoluted. As if Jia were knowingly agreeing to play a game with someone who'd stacked the deck against her. "What would you do if you were me?"

"Probably run, but your firm wouldn't let you, would they?"

Jia said nothing.

Minsoo nodded. "When I was a boy, my father used to tell me I should have three faces: one to show the world what it wanted to see, one to show myself what I wanted to see . . . and the last one? The last one he told me I should never show anyone, not even myself." He turned to Jia. "My true face. The monster in us all." He paused. "My father's true face isn't just monstrous. It's evil."

All at once, Minsoo's behavior made sense. "You're genuinely afraid of him."

He hesitated a beat. Then he nodded.

*A family of murdering thieves.*

Jia listened to the idling engine and considered Minsoo Park in earnest. "I'm sorry. I know it's silly of me to apologize for something someone else did. But it's the best I can do right now." She offered him a weak grin. "Flawed and real, at its best."

"I think I can work with that." A half smile curved across his lips.

Jia still wasn't sure she could put her full faith in anything Minsoo had to say. After all, he'd admitted to contemplating his father's offer to switch sides and to being more similar to Seven than not, which was alarming in its own right.

Which of Minsoo Park's three faces was he showing her now? Most importantly, where did this leave Jia with respect to their next move?

As much as she wanted to avoid it, it still sounded like going to Paris made the most sense, despite how complicated everything was. Minsoo was right: Jia didn't have the time to be indecisive. She needed to make every day work for her. If they could manage to pull off this trip and find something pertinent to the case, perhaps Seven would come to them with a revised settlement.

This time Jia would be sure she was the one holding the grenade.

# ANIMUS NOCENDI

Of late, I have spent a great deal of time contemplating what makes a hero and what makes a villain. Inevitably, my mind returns to the same thought: it is all a matter of perspective. A villain is said to be the hero of their own story. But if that is true, are there no real villains to be had? Or do villains only exist in service to a cause? Because history, I've been told, is often written by so-called heroes.

Is the idea of good versus evil nothing more than a construct?

Maybe villainy lies in the intent. If there is intent to cause harm, then the answer reveals itself. But what, then, constitutes harm? Our heroine believes a lie to be a lie. However, there are lies made from a place of love. Lies made not with the intention to harm but with the intention to help.

Ultimately, perhaps the intention does not matter if harm is done.

Or perhaps, as always, it depends on the skill of the so-called hero telling the story.

After all this time spent together, I am vain enough to hope I am not seen as a villain. I hope I have earned the barest measure of trust, though I have suggested on more than one occasion that I may not deserve it.

I regret to say that I have fulfilled my role in this tale and will now make my exit. But before I go, I wish to leave you with a parting note about the power of stories. I've made it clear on several occasions how enamored I am with words of all kinds from all languages. This naturally extends to my love of stories.

But then, who isn't a lover of stories? Even the people who proudly attest to never having read a book after completing their schooling (the unmitigated horror!) are in truth fans of stories, for they are the stuff of life.

Stories propel the shows and the movies and the video games we crave as both entertainment and solace. Stories charge us with the strength and the fear and the hope that we all need to overcome hurdles large and small.

And, yes, we do need fear. For fear, not hate, is the other side of love.

The feelings we experience when we are afraid . . . are they so different from the ones we feel when we are in love? That heady rush. That inability to control the rapid pace of our hearts. That tightness in the chest and along the skin. As if something within us is begging to be set free.

When humans hate, it is not from an absence of love. Where there is hatred, there must be love. For hatred cannot be sown from an absence of feeling.

Strong hatred is often a product of strong love.

I remind myself of this fact daily. Just as I contemplate my desire to do harm and whether it makes me a villain or if I am, as they say, simply the hero of my own tale.

Speaking of intent to harm, I have recently learned of a new word that delighted me when I first heard it. Unsurprisingly, it is another German word.

*Backpfeifengesicht.*

Is it not delightful? Find a friend who can pronounce it. It is a glory to hear.

Its meaning—as well as its intent—is no less a source of delicious delight . . . or perhaps of hateful villainy. As always, the power to choose remains with you.

It means: a face that begs to be slapped.

# PONT NEUF SOUS LA PLUIE

*T Minus 13 Days*

Jia had been to Paris exactly once in her life, the summer she'd backpacked through Europe with her two best friends. Even in a veritable sea of sights and experiences, Paris had stood out. It wasn't just the buttery sauces and the abundant bakeries, the scent of melting sugar and fresh bread wafting from every street corner. Nor was it the snooty citizens, turning their noses up at her halting attempt to speak their language.

It was the feeling she had while she was there.

If there was any place on earth where time truly stood still for her, it was Paris. It was the only city where Jia had, up until that point in her life, enjoyed a meal that lasted until dawn. Where she walked into a museum and lost herself for hours, never once checking her phone or the time.

In her youth, the city had come to epitomize everything she worked for and dreamed of. A place that embodied sophistication, from the beauty of its streets to the deliciousness of its cuisine.

The home of Hermès.

This past year, Paris had lost a great deal of its appeal, at least for Jia. In fact, six months ago, she had sworn she would never go there again.

The mere thought of the city—of the Eiffel Tower sparkling beneath a starry sky, the strains of a far-off accordion sighing in the distance, and spring rain falling on the Pont Neuf—brought a stab of pain to Jia's chest.

Four months before she and Zain ended things, he'd asked her one night at dinner where she thought the most romantic place for a guy to propose would be. She'd twisted the napkin in her lap, her entire body filled with irrepressible anticipation.

Zain was asking Jia where she wanted him to propose.

Which meant . . . he wanted to propose.

"Hmm," she'd replied, her expression coy. "I suppose—if someone were thinking about proposing to me—I'd have to say Paris."

Zain had rolled his eyes, though he'd been amused. "Don't tell me. Beneath the Eiffel Tower, at night. Followed by a romantic stroll along the Seine."

"No." Jia had shook her head. "In the rain. Early spring. Dusk, in the middle of the Pont Neuf."

"In the rain?" he'd argued, feigning distaste. "Why the hell would you want someone to propose to you in the rain?"

"Because all my best childhood memories have to do with the rain."

"More Gene Kelly nonsense," he'd teased.

She'd shook her head again. "It's not just that. To me, rain represents so much. Sure, it's about washing something clean, but it's more about being totally uninhibited. As if the rain is washing away every ounce of pretense. Only children really like to stand in the rain. When someone proposes to me, I want to look up at the sky and say, 'Do your worst. No matter what storms you send our way, we're a team. Forever.'"

With a smile, Zain had nodded. "I don't hate it. And why the Pont Neuf?"

"Because it was always considered the heart of Paris. And a bridge is a joining of two fixed points. What can I say, I'm a sap for symbolism."

Zain had laughed at that. Then they'd gone on to joke about rings and diamonds and other glittering things that had seemed so far away but all at once, with a single question, appeared within reach.

For a blink of time, Jia thought she saw her future, clear as the morning sun.

Now, as Jia gazed out the window of their white Cadillac Escalade at the Eiffel Tower, she grimaced. Everything about this trip set her teeth on edge.

In front of her to the right, Sora Park-Vandeveld texted someone, her back ramrod straight. She'd been in a foul mood since they'd landed, and—judging by the vicious way she was typing—the person on the other side of that conversation was to blame.

Seated in the captain's chair to Sora's left—directly in front of Jia—was Darius Rohani.

They still hadn't spoken more than five words to each other since the Caymans. He'd barely acknowledged her on the long transatlantic flight, and she'd been happy to return the favor.

When Darius had arrived at the private hangar with his rolling suitcase in tow, Jia had almost asked why he'd bothered to come. The pretense of their relationship was no longer necessary. The jig was up. They weren't likely to pull off the same ruse on any member of the staff at the Paris apartment. In fact, she would much rather have had Suzy's company than Darius's on this trip, but Suzy had reiterated that she couldn't stomach being in the same city as her father and his pregnant paramour.

In any case, it didn't matter. Jia worked for the Park family. If they thought Darius should go to Paris with them, it was none of her business to question it.

Sora stopped typing. Then she held up her phone between her thumb and forefinger as if it were a soiled napkin. Without a word, she dropped the offending device between the seats.

Darius glanced down at it. Considered her for a moment. Then quietly reached for her phone and tucked it in the pocket of his coat.

Anger seethed through the small space like simmering water, just waiting to be raised to a boil. Jia closed her eyes. Only a fool would fail to recognize Sora's bid for attention.

Who would cave first?

Darius breathed in deeply, as if steeling himself. He looked over his shoulder at Jia, a question in his gaze.

She shook her head, almost imperceptibly, as if to say, *Hell no. This one's on you.*

He scowled, then rubbed his right hand along the back of his neck.

A wave of leather and oud hit Jia in the face. Damn it.

"Do you want to talk about it?" Darius asked Sora.

"Not really, no," she said through clenched teeth. "But it seems I have no choice." She leaned forward to address the driver. "We won't be going to the Marais after all."

"Oui, madame," the driver said in accented English.

Darius pressed his lips to one side. "He won't leave?"

"No. Hugo said they were still at the apartment. Seven probably doesn't want to inconvenience his pregnant whore," she fumed. "Even an invitation to that stupid flower show didn't seem to catch her attention." Sora kicked off one of her Aquazzura heels and flexed her stockinged foot. "That sort of ridiculous society event is just the kind of thing that makes Ani salivate. And I went to a lot of trouble to get them on that guest list. Delphine is going to be ticked off at me for wasting those tickets, not to mention my mother-in-law. I so rarely ask her for favors. Of all the things, they had to fuck me on this." She tugged at the oversize collar of her navy cashmere Max Mara coat.

"You can't control what other people do," Darius said gently. "If they don't go, it's not your fault. We'll figure out another way to get into the apartment."

Sora sent Darius a testy look. "Did I ever mention that you can be really patronizing?"

"Many times," he said without missing a beat.

The driver cleared his throat.

"Yes, Serge?" Darius responded.

"I am so sorry for the interruption, monsieur, but what is our new destination?"

Darius thought a moment. "I suppose we could go to the secondary location in Montmartre, if that's—"

"No," Sora interrupted. "À l'Hôtel de Ville, s'il vous plaît."

"Oui, madame," Serge replied. The next second, the Escalade made a crisp turn right.

"Sora?" Darius said quietly. "We can't check into a hotel. If we do, your dad will know we are in Paris."

Sora rolled her eyes. "I'm not checking into a hotel. I'm going to that flower show and buying something rare and expensive for my mother-in-law, as a thank-you for getting us the tickets."

Jia could hear Darius's mind whirring. Sora was in no mood to brook protests. Whatever he said next would have to be posed delicately. "Sora, we can't show our faces at a Paris society function," he said. "Again, your father will know we are here within the hour."

"The tickets are under their name, you fool, not mine, and I won't talk to anyone." Sora donned her sunglasses and pulled her large mink hat low onto her brow. "No one will recognize me."

Jia almost laughed. It came out like a snort.

Sora glowered at her. Jia met Darius's gaze and could see a hint of amusement in his features. It was the first time he'd looked at her with anything besides anger or hurt since the Caymans. Something eased in her chest.

"Maybe Darius is right," Jia said gently. "Is there something else we could pick up for your—"

"No," Sora said through gritted teeth. "I'm going to that flower show, and you two can either sit in the car and wait like self-righteous assholes or you can keep me company. But I'm not wasting those tickets."

"I can wait in the car," Jia said.

Sora pursed her lips. With her large fur hat and oversize Chanel sunglasses, she resembled a caricature of herself. "Why?"

"There are only two tickets, right?" Jia blinked.

Sora harrumphed and faced forward again. "No one says no to me."

As usual, Sora Park-Vandeveld was right.

In no time at all, Sora, Darius, and Jia were permitted through the cordoned-off entrance and led through the main building into a courtyard situated in the center of the massive French Renaissance château.

Jia almost halted in shock at the sight before her.

"It's wonderful, isn't it?" Sora said, her breath puffing around her face like smoke from a cigarette. "One of my favorite places in the city. They used to hold public executions here."

Jia held back a quip.

Contrary to its name, the Hôtel de Ville wasn't a hotel at all. It served as Paris's city hall, the grandeur of its design a fitting reflection of its long, sordid history. The immense courtyard had been transformed into an ice-skating rink. Bright red carpeting formed a maze of pathways across the ice, all intended to display an array of stunning flowers and elegant arrangements, exotic blooms and hothouse varietals, positioned on tables with up lighting, as if each blossom was a work of art in its own right.

A rich floral perfume hovered in the chilly air, the lulling strains of a chamber ensemble echoing into the twilit sky. People with entirely too much money milled around the space, their jewels flashing and their furs gleaming.

Once again, Jia was woefully underdressed in her warm wool slacks and dark sweater. Even her camel Sentaler coat wasn't enough to conceal that she was out of her element.

She and Darius followed Sora through the red-carpeted labyrinth in silence. Jia wanted to ask how long he was going to be mad at her. But she refused to make the first move.

True to her word, Sora did not speak with anyone. She kept her mink hat low and continued wearing her sunglasses the entire time. She paused before a display of golden daffodils alongside enormous branches of white orchids, the snowy blossoms drooping under their own weight. One arrangement had been placed in a chinoiserie vase, which was likely worth a fortune on its own.

With a gloved hand, Sora leaned to cup one of the orchids and breathe in its scent, careful not to touch a single petal. She smiled to herself in appreciation.

"It's beautiful," Jia said softly.

"I've always liked orchids," Sora replied. "They're temperamental. Often difficult to cultivate. Most people give up on them or toss them the second their blossoms fall."

Jia recalled what Sora had said about the language of flowers. "Do they have a particular meaning?"

"Most often they are associated with sincerity. If you wanted to offer someone a heartfelt apology, a white orchid isn't a bad choice. But different flowers mean different things depending on one's culture." Sora eyed the nearby daffodils with distaste. "My father and his whore sent a bouquet of these for my birthday last year. They are supposed to be flowers of forgiveness. Ironically, their scientific name is *narcissus*. I burned them in our fireplace. Alex was . . . displeased by all the smoke." Anger clouded her expression, her chin jutting out. "I don't care how many times she tries to win our forgiveness. I'll never forgive her. Or him, for that matter." She narrowed her eyes and wrapped her coat around herself even tighter. "I'm so sick and tired of people talking about forgiveness. You'll notice, it's always the ones who don't deserve it."

Jia was inclined to agree. She caught Darius watching her, though he kept his distance.

"One of these days, I'm going to hit Seven. In the face," Sora said. "Then he'll finally know what it feels like." The last sentence was in soft Korean. Almost like an afterthought.

Jia chewed on the inside of her cheek. As always, it was interesting to witness Sora display any vulnerability. Maybe her emotions were closer to the surface because they were in Paris. Or because they were at a flower show that reminded Sora of her husband and mother-in-law.

Usually she seemed so self-possessed. Even at the noraebang—while saying horrible things to her twin—Sora's makeup remained intact. Not once did she raise her voice. And then she ate all that fruit, as though she were unbothered. But Jia should have known better.

All the Park children contained reservoirs of feeling, hidden deep within them.

"My father hit me in the face once," Jia blurted. She didn't know what possessed her to reveal this fact. Only that some part of her wanted to help, in whatever small way.

Both Darius and Sora turned in tandem to look at Jia.

"It happened just before my fourteenth birthday, not long after my harabugi died," Jia continued. "My grandfather and I were really close. He was kind of like my living, breathing guardian angel. Whenever my parents wanted to yell at me when I was little, he would put me on his back and ubbuh me to safety." She smiled to herself. "He would pretend to be a train when he did it. Like, even with a *choo choo*! I'm not sure why he did that. It didn't make any sense." A knot gathered in her throat. "Anyway, after he died, I was a brat about it. Instead of dealing with my pain in a healthy way—which, for the record, wasn't really modeled for me by my parents—I started to act out."

Sora turned around fully, her lips pressed together.

"I started arguing with anyone and everyone," Jia said. "I think in hindsight my behavior was pretty normal for an almost-fourteen-year-old. But after a few weeks of having to deal with my sustained brattiness, my dad decided he couldn't take it anymore." A spark of hesitation flickered in Jia's chest. She already regretted starting this story.

She didn't mind if Darius knew about something so private from her past. But Sora? Did Sora deserve to know?

This tiny moment in time had come to hold a greater meaning for Jia. In many ways, it had taught her what it meant to be strong. To be a woman. To know, deep in her soul, what she was worth. It had been the memory she clung to in her moments of weakness after her breakup with Zain.

This memory had given her the strength to finally say no.

Jia hated how much and how often she thought of Zain, half a year later. How a completely unrelated thing would happen and conjure, in the quickest flash, a flurry of emotions. Never the good ones.

But she figured, at the end of her life, there would be a handful of moments—a select few memories—that came to shape how she saw the world. For better or for worse, heartbreak had to be one of them. In heartbreak, Jia learned how to truly feel. And when she learned the depth and breadth of the feelings inside her, she realized her own strength. Her own capacity to love.

The deepest love brought with it the deepest pain. That was the trade.

Jia wasn't entirely sure if it was worth it. Not yet. But she knew she would rather experience a life of love and pain than a life without either. Everyone everywhere had their own heartbreaks. Their own broken records. It was what made humans truly human. And it was the way Jia learned to see through the eyes of someone else. There was connection in that pain.

"Please," Sora said softly as the strains of chamber music lilted around them. "Go on."

"It happened while we were cooking dinner," Jia said. "My mother asked me to do something insignificant. So insignificant that I can't even remember what it was. Maybe set the table or serve the rice or get her some kind of pot from above the fridge." Her voice grew small as her mind drifted back. "I had been reading a book. *The Witching Hour* by Anne Rice. If you've ever read it, you know how hard it is to tear yourself away from any of Anne's stories. Anyway, I didn't answer the first time my mother asked for help.

"The third time my mother asked, I said, 'I'll get to it. We're not even eating for another twenty minutes. Where's the fire?'" Jia paused to clear her throat, her expression hardening, even though she was staring into the space between Darius and Sora, unwilling to look either of them in the eye. "I didn't even see my dad before he hit me. It was the most unexpected thing. He slapped me, openhanded, across the cheek, and it knocked me from my chair, not because it was so hard but because I just didn't see it coming.

"My huge paperback of *The Witching Hour* flew from my hands. I covered my cheek with my palm because it was smarting, like I had sat too close to a fire. I glared at my dad and was just about to say something snide to prevent myself from crying when my mom shouted, 'Stop!' Then she came from around the kitchen island, her hand still wrapped around the knife she'd been using to chop vegetables. But instead of saying something to me, she, like, stalked toward my dad. 'If you *ever* hit my daughter like that again, I will kill you,' my mom said. Then she finished it with a loud, 'Arasuh?' My dad didn't even hesitate. He nodded. His eyes were huge. He understood her, fully." Jia exhaled in a huff, her gaze settling on a nearby arrangement of Black Magic roses, deep pink dahlias, red snapdragons, and purple delphiniums. "My dad never hit me again, and we're totally fine now. But it wasn't until much later—when I was applying to law schools, actually—that I really understood what a pivotal moment that was for me. It made me appreciate my mother in a new way. She fought to protect me, even from her own husband. A man who was fifty pounds heavier than she was and at least six inches taller." Jia cleared her throat again. "She taught me never to allow any man—no matter who he was—to think he could bully me into obedience."

Silence filled the space between them for a moment.

"Did you ever say anything to your mom about it afterward?" Darius asked softly, unmistakable feeling in his voice.

Jia laughed. "I'm Korean, remember? It's like Emotional Fight Club. We let those moments sift through our fingers like handfuls of sand." Then she glanced over at Sora and sobered immediately. Pain was etched all over her face.

Jia realized she needed to say something. Anything.

Because in that instant, she knew. Jenny had said she needed forgiveness for all the things she'd failed to do. That she didn't fight when she should have fought. It was clear no one had spoken out for Sora. No one had protected her. Suzy had said their mother would do anything for them. Jenny had echoed the sentiment during their last conversation.

But it wasn't true. They'd lied.

Jenny had failed to save Sora. Many times, from the looks of it.

Jia didn't want to be a member of Emotional Fight Club right now. Even if it caused Sora to lash out at her, she wouldn't let this moment sift through her fingers.

With a determined set to her brow, Jia reached for Sora's hand. Sora's upper lip started to curl in warning, like a cornered animal.

"Hey," Jia said. "Are you okay?"

Sora almost yelled at her. Jia saw her catch herself. Her hand felt limp in Jia's fingers. She swallowed again. "No," she admitted. "I'm not." A V formed at the bridge of her nose, behind the Chanel sunglasses. "But it's nice that your mom fought for you."

Jia nodded. Then quietly added, "I'm sorry yours didn't."

"It's fine," Sora said. She tried to pull her hand away.

Jia grasped it tighter. "No. It's not."

Sora fought back another urge to lash out. It was clear she wanted to. Instead she squeezed Jia's fingers once. Nodded. Then withdrew her hand.

Darius said nothing throughout this exchange. He seemed to know when his input was needed, and when it was more than enough for him to simply bear witness.

Jia liked that about him. It was . . . different from most of the guys she knew.

Sora cleared her throat and turned her attention back to the stunning orchids in the chinoiserie vase. "I'm going to buy this for my mother-in-law. A sincere gesture of appreciation." She eyed the daffodils with disdain. "Purple hyacinths are better if you're going to ask for forgiveness."

Jia smiled. "I'll remember that."

Darius shifted closer to them. He placed a gentle hand on Jia's arm. It was the first time he'd touched her since their argument in the Caymans. "Are you ready to go?" he asked Sora. "If so, I'll ask Serge to pull the car around and we can make our way to Montmartre."

"I hate Tiffany's place," Sora grumbled. "It's like some kind of Gertrude Stein worshipping, expat bohemian nightmare. Interior design à la Frankenstein's monster."

"That's . . . a lot." Jia grinned.

"So is Tiffany," Darius said. "But she did offer to let us stay there if we needed a place to lie low until Seven left the apartment."

Sora sniffed. "We could just go to the Ritz."

"We can't check into a hotel, and the suite isn't available," Darius replied. "They're fully booked right now because of that Louis Vuitton exhibit. Unless you want to throw caution to the wind and share a regular double room."

"Just because Jia told me one sob story and held my hand doesn't mean I like her now. At least, not *that* much." Sora sniffed again and turned back toward the Hôtel de Ville to glower at an architectural marvel in one of the most beautiful cities in the world. "If Seven and his whore don't leave the house tonight for dinner, I'd like to eat at Maison. Please make sure Anouk and Sophie are invited."

"Already made a reservation. And already messaged Anouk's PA."

Could anyone in the Park family function without Darius Rohani?

"Jia, it's not like you have anything better to do, so you might as well come with us," Sora said. "It's my favorite restaurant in Paris, which means it's my favorite place to eat in the entire world."

Jia sighed to herself. Perhaps she'd committed the cardinal sin among professionals in her field by oversharing with her clients. But breaking through the Grand Gijibae's frigid exterior was a step in the right direction.

# BLUE LOBSTERS AND HERMIT CRABS

*T Minus 13 Days*

Eating a meal in Paris with one of the heirs to an almost-billion-dollar fortune, it turned out, was a lot like Jia had expected it to be.

Sora spoke perfect French. Naturally. The chef de cuisine, a young Japanese man named Guillaume Kaneshiro, came out to greet their group in person before the second course was served. A bottle of Château Margaux arrived at their table less than five minutes after they sat down. The footprint of the dining room was small, its clientele exclusive. Jia knew without being told that they were sitting at the best table in the house.

Every course was served with perfect panache. Nothing too overblown. At Maison, the food spoke for itself.

At no point did Jia order anything. In fact, she was pretty sure no one did. After the wine was uncorked, a small plate of iced poached oysters with a seaweed and citrus granité was set in front of her. It was followed by an artichoke soup and a brioche layered with caramelized maitake mushrooms. Then foie gras with toasted milk bread and yuzu gelée. Jia lost count of how many delicious things she was eating somewhere between the pan-fried blue lobster with imperial beluga caviar and the grilled Wagyu with buttery sea urchin sauce.

Words alone couldn't do justice to the dessert. Something with strawberries, shiso, and umeboshi served alongside a sponge cake floating in a sea of frothy cream. The chef's Japanese influence was subtly worked into each dish to create something wholly unique. A cuisine Jia had never had before and was certain she would never have again.

All the while, a server stood in the wings, ready to rearrange her plate or refold her napkin or pour another measure of chilled water at the exact moment she needed it.

Even though this would go down as one of the most beautiful and memorable dinners of Jia's life, the thing that astounded her most was how much Sora Park-Vandeveld smiled and laughed.

Jia's French was limited at best. The work of her perfectly adequate public school in Queens. She didn't understand most of the conversation taking place between Sora and her Parisian friends, Anouk and Sophie, who bore an uncanny resemblance to the Hadid sisters. Regardless, Jia didn't feel comfortable breaking their flow with her Flushing High French.

Which made her doubly thankful for the wordless conversation she shared with Darius for most of the meal. Something had softened in him when she told the story about her father. His shell seemed to crack further during the two hours they spent at Maison. Jia was sure the wine and the poached oysters didn't hurt.

*This is . . . a lot*, Jia said to Darius without speaking.

Darius puckered his lips, almost as if he were kissing the air while he thought. It was distractingly attractive. *This whole family is a lot. I just enjoy the food in these moments.*

Jia arched a brow. *And wait for the other shoe to drop.*

*What other shoe?* Darius grinned. *I never understood that expression.*

*Oh, just eat your Wagyu.* Jia rolled her eyes.

*Tout de suite.*

Watching Sora with Anouk and Sophie—absent the permanent pole up her backside—made Jia realize that all the Park siblings were kind of like hermit crabs. Each of them carried a burdensome shell wherever they went. But that same burden also served as a refuge.

They wouldn't come out of their shells unless they were certain they were safe.

Jia glanced at Darius and caught a reflection of herself in the mercury glass vase of floating flowers in the center of their table. Her face startled her for an instant.

She looked almost at peace. Like a person who might be starting to trust herself, not just with the things outside her, as Umma had said, but with the things inside her as well.

Maybe everyone was a hermit crab, waiting for the right moment to feel safe.

Twice in the span of twenty minutes, Jia heard Sora cackle with glee in a way that reminded her a great deal of Suzy. Jia could almost see them as little girls. Twins thrilling in each other's company.

It figured that Sora felt safest with the world's most notoriously snooty people.

Sora bent closer to Sophie to hear what sounded like the beginning of a dirty joke or a nugget of delicious gossip. The sommelier poured Anouk more godforsakenly expensive wine, which she swirled around in her glass, pausing to admire the legs before launching into a conversation with him about the abysmal weather in the Rhône Valley this year. At least that's what it sounded like to Jia.

Once she was certain the other members of their dinner party were appropriately preoccupied, Jia slid her chair a few inches closer to Darius's and whispered, "Any word on Seven and Annika's whereabouts tonight?"

"I haven't heard from Hugo in almost an hour. Last I checked, they were still at the apartment. But don't worry too much. From what I can tell, Annika is an on-the-go kind of person. Enjoys seeing and being seen. That's why she loves Paris. Even if they stay in tonight, they won't be at the house multiple days in a row."

Jia considered this. Then lowered her voice even further, forcing Darius to lean closer. She could see the line of his jaw in the shadows. Smell the way his cologne mixed with the mouthwatering perfume of the restaurant. "No chance he would have recent bank statements in a safe with the same password though, right?"

"Your guess is as good as mine. Seven isn't foolish. But he's also far from perfect."

"Quels secrets d'amour partagez-vous?" Anouk said, her index finger running along the rim of her wineglass.

It took Jia a second to realize Anouk was speaking to her. She looked up, alarm on her face. "Secrets?" she said weakly, picking out one of the words she readily recognized.

Darius pulled back in a single fluid motion. With a bright smile, he said, "It's all Greek to me."

Sora was studying them, her head cocked to the right in consideration, her eyes luminous from all the wine. "Anouk wants to know what lovers' secrets you two are whispering about," Sora said. "I told her you weren't lovers. Right? Because it would be highly inappropriate, given our current situation."

"Highly inappropriate," Jia agreed, her voice almost shrill.

"Good," Sora said. "None of us needs that kind of distraction." Her words dropped to a lower register. "Especially when we're dealing with something this time-sensitive. This mind-bogglingly important."

Jia swallowed as Sora stared daggers at her. Though Jia agreed it was highly inappropriate for her and Darius to have any kind of romantic relationship right now, it surprised Jia to see how much Sora disliked even the suggestion of it.

She remembered how Sora had told her in passing that she and Darius had shared their first kiss. Was it possible Sora had feelings for him? Maybe Sora was like all the stereotypically wealthy wives of the Upper East Side. Married to money, of course, but canoodling with the help, especially while on vacation.

Jia grimaced. She needed to stop watching reruns of *Sex and the City*.

She was about to change the subject when all the color leached from Sora's face, only to be replaced by outrage.

"Well, well, what a coincidence!" a jovial male voice exclaimed from behind Jia.

She turned. Stopped herself from gasping.

Seven Park was standing two feet away, arm in arm with a stunning brunette around Jia's age.

"Sora-ya, it's good to see you," Seven said. "We haven't shared a meal together in such a long time. Appa missed having dinner with his eldest daughter more than anything." He beamed. Then, seamlessly, he gestured to the servers standing in the wings. Less than five seconds later, two more chairs were brought to their table.

Jia's fingers twisted around the linen napkin in her lap. She eyed Sora from across the table, but Sora's features had turned blank. Unreadable. She'd climbed back into her shell.

"Song Jihae." Seven sat beside Jia, his smile widening. "When did you arrive to Paris?"

"I think you already know the answer to that question, Park Chilsoo-shi." Jia smiled back at him, despite the anger spreading through her body with the speed of a forest fire.

How did he know they were here? They'd taken every precaution. Secured a private jet with no ties to the family's business. Gone through customs at a small airport on the outskirts of the city, famed for its discretion. The only people who knew they in Paris were Sora's friends, Tiffany, Anouk, and Sophie—and Hugo, the French PI from the firm Minsoo had contracted.

Jia locked eyes with Darius, who had been hovering over his phone since Seven's arrival.

His expression was grim. He tilted the screen toward Jia to reveal a series of text messages he'd sent to Hugo.

None of them had been answered. Jesus Christ.

How the fuck had Seven gotten to Hugo?

Seven's eyes gleamed. He gestured to the brunette seated to his right. "Jia, I would like to introduce you to my fiancée, Annika Bergström."

Across the table, Sora scoffed.

Annika—who could easily still be the Abercrombie model Suzy had mocked her for being—leaned over Seven and put her hand out to Jia with an easy smile. "I'm Ani," she said. "It's so nice to meet you, Jia. Seven speaks so highly of you."

"I'll bet he does." Jia gestured to the server for some more wine. Nothing less than the finest varietal of liquid courage for her tonight.

"Darius," Ani continued with another beautiful full-lipped smile. "It's been ages."

"Yup." The nervous grin on his face looked as if it would be etched there for all eternity. "Ages."

"Isn't this nice?" Seven remarked with an air of supreme satisfaction. "How fortuitous that we decided to come to Maison tonight, my darling Ani. Now I can share a meal with my beloved family. I'm a lucky man."

"Are you happy?" Ani said, her blue eyes bright, her gaze affectionate. She placed her left hand on his right, displaying an emerald-cut engagement ring half the size of Jia's thumb.

Seven nodded. "So happy." He wrapped his fingers around hers.

"You know." Ani turned to everyone else at the table. "I think it's so important to chase your happiness. We're made to believe that getting there is such an easy thing—that happiness is a simple choice, or that it just falls in your lap if you're lucky, or that it's a reward if you're diligent or patient or pious. I disagree. Happiness is something you have to fight for. I think if there's something you want in life, it's up to you to make it happen."

"Hear, hear!" Seven said.

"Keegah makyuh," Sora muttered under her breath.

Jia was inclined to agree. This was some serious bullshit.

Sensing the brewing storm, Anouk and Sophie stood with awkward suddenness. They made their murmured apologies in a mixture of French and broken English, before tripping over themselves to gather their things. Just before leaving, they exchanged looks of pity with Sora and breezed toward the entrance of Maison in a flurry of silk scarves, Celine belt bags, and cashmere coats.

After they left, Ani hailed a server and proceeded to speak to him in excellent French. While they discussed her pregnancy-related food restrictions, Jia took a quick glance at her midsection. The loose-fitting cream-colored sweater with its large funnel neck was chic and weather appropriate. At first, it was difficult to see any traces of a baby bump, but when Ani twisted in her seat, Jia noticed it, cleverly concealed under all her couture.

"Jia," Seven asked after approving the new bottle of wine the sommelier had produced. "I know you attended Columbia for law school. Did you also go there for college?"

Jia blinked. There was no way Seven Park didn't already possess the answer to this question. He definitely had files on everyone at this table, including his own daughter. What was his angle? Why would he ask her such a predictable Korean-parent question? Was he trying to belittle her?

She wanted to ignore him or volley back with a cutting retort.

Instead, she decided to be a gray rock. "I went to college at NYU."

He nodded. "It's an excellent school. I'm sure your parents were very proud. Just like I was proud of my Sora for going to Harvard."

Yuck. This guy never made it to the next level of Passive-Aggressive Immigrant Parent. He was still stuck in beta mode.

Then he said, "Ani also went to Harvard. She speaks five languages and has a PhD from Berkeley in molecular and cell biology."

Ah, right. He wanted to create an opportunity to brag about his mistress.

What a performative jackass.

Of course, Jia wasn't surprised to hear about Ani's degrees. She'd read about them already in Seven's file. If memory served her correctly, there was overlap in the time Ani and Sora were at Harvard, which was probably another reason for Sora's palpable disgust.

Even if Jia hadn't already read about Ani's impressive achievements, she would not have been surprised to learn of them now. Nothing about Annika Bergström indicated that she was a stereotypical homewrecking second wife. She clearly had more to offer than her beauty and youth. Her attention was sharp. Her statements were pointed. She riffed off Seven's toxicity as if they were a match made in heaven. And she was quick to cause discomfort before it could be directed her way.

Jia sucked in a breath.

Ani and Seven were, in fact, great together. Both of them were clever bullies.

Jia squared her shoulders and looked Ani straight in the eye. "I have no idea what getting a PhD in molecular biology entails, but congratulations on your many, *many* achievements." Then Jia looked down at Ani's ring and smirked.

It was catty. Ridiculously so. But Jia didn't want to be a gray rock anymore. Just for a second, she wanted to shine like an emerald-cut diamond. In her experience, bullies were countered best by two things: a deep sense of justice and unshakable confidence. The kind of confidence that communicated, without words, that Jia would spit hot sauce in someone's eye if they dared to cross her.

Though Ani kept smiling at Jia, her expression sharpened. "Telomeres. My dissertation was on telomeres as being a potential key to unlocking the fountain of youth." She propped her elbows along the edge of the table and batted her eyelashes at Darius.

"Interesting." Darius mirrored her body language, and Jia almost fell in love with him for it. "I'd like to hear more."

Pride flared through Jia. Darius saw what she saw. Knew what she knew.

And he also refused to back down.

"Essentially," Ani began, "telomeres are like the endcaps on a strand of DNA. They protect the chromosomes housed within. As we age, these telomeres shorten, making it harder to protect the DNA strand during cell division. If we were to, say, find a way to prevent this shortening from happening on a cellular level, we could perhaps uncover a way to prevent aging."

"Most of those studies were debunked," Sora said through gritted teeth, her eyes flashing.

"They are still in their infancy, for sure," Ani replied coolly. "But the work itself is promising. It deserves more than petty disdain." She pressed her lips into a moue. "In fact, if I remember correctly, telomeres interested you a great deal when we were at Harvard."

"I was young and stupid back then," Sora said. "I know better now."

Ani laughed. "I never thought I would hear the great Sora Park admit to stupidity of any kind."

"I had to have been embarrassingly dense, or else I never would have introduced my slutty roommate to my cheating father."

Good God.

Roommates? Jia racked her brain trying to remember Sora's file. There was no way she could have missed something that important.

"Don't freak out, Jia Song," Sora said as if she could hear Jia's thoughts. "*Ah-nee*," she mocked, "wasn't born Annika Bergström. Bergström is her grandmother's maiden name. When we met, she was skinny little Annie Schmidt from Milford, Connecticut." She smirked. "It appears that stolen money can help you change your name so that it no longer rhymes with *shit*. A shame it can't also buy you a soul."

"Careful, Sorina Sorina. You'll scare away our guests," Ani said softly.

Jia felt Darius's hand on her knee. "Close your mouth," he said under his breath.

She snapped her lips shut. She hadn't even realized she was gaping like a cartoon cat who'd just been hit by an Acme anvil.

"Woori kun-dahl," Seven said to Sora. "Why didn't you bring my grandchildren to see me?"

Sora sneered at him.

"Song Jihae," Seven continued with a sad sigh. "Did you know I haven't seen my only grandchildren in almost eight months? It is so difficult to be kept away from the ones I love. My little angels, whom I would die for."

"If you would die for them, then maybe you should have called on Xander's birthday," Sora said in a vicious whisper.

"I did call." Seven didn't miss a beat. "I left a voicemail."

"No, you didn't," Sora said.

"You shouldn't lie, Sora-ya. It sets a poor example for your kids."

Sora exhaled. Closed her eyes. Just like that day at Whitman Volker, Jia knew she was counting to ten.

"Some more sparkling water and your best bottle of Louis Latour Grand Cru, please," Seven said to the approaching server without even looking his way. Then he turned to Ani with an aggrieved look. "Sweetheart, didn't you hear me leave a message for Xander?"

"Of course I did," Ani replied. "I would expect nothing less. You're such a wonderful grandfather, yuhboh."

*Yuhboh?*

Jia cringed. It was probably the same old-fashioned term of endearment

Jenny had used for Seven not long ago. And it struck them all like an unseen punch to the gut.

Sora's eyes flew open. "Don't. Just don't." She sent Ani a glare that would have melted the sun.

Ani turned to Sora, her expression kind. "Don't what, dear?"

"I can take it from him," Sora said. "But I can't take it from you."

"You're going to need to be more specific, sweetie." Ani squeezed a lemon wedge into her newly poured glass of sparkling water. "Take what?"

It was said so carefully, so softly, that only those sitting around the table would be aware that it was a call to war. A drumbeat sounding from the hills. A knife sharpening on a whetstone.

Jia's body went rigid.

Seven continued drinking his wine, his amusement plain.

Jia watched Sora battle with herself. Then she stood. Collected her things. She didn't wait for Jia and Darius to join her. She began walking toward the exit, her head high.

Confident. With a deep sense of justice. The perfect response to a clever bully.

Jia shook her head. No. She would not admire Sora Park-Vandeveld. She refused.

As Sora passed by Ani and Seven, Ani stood up.

Stepped into Sora's path.

And pulled her in for a hug.

Everyone at the table braced themselves. A collective hush fell around them.

Sora murmured something in Ani's ear.

The next second, Ani slapped Sora across the face with all the vim and vigor of a soap opera star. Sora stumbled to the floor. Everyone but Seven jumped to their feet. Before Sora could launch herself at Ani, Darius and Jia pulled her out of Maison without a second thought.

# CLEAR AS WATERFORD CRYSTAL

## *T Minus 13 Days*

They burst into the Park family's apartment in the Marais like a tornado.

Fueled by unapologetic rage, Sora pushed past the startled maid, who wore a black dress and a frilly white apron, like a stock photo of herself. In shocked French, the maid called out to a string bean of a man who ran from the kitchen. The next second, the string bean was on the phone.

"The office is this way," Sora yelled over her shoulder as she cut through the center of Seven's newly renovated Parisian apartment, its parquet floors, twelve-foot-high ceilings, ornate nineteenth-century panel molding, and solid marble mantel juxtaposed with starkly modern interior design. Even the antique chandelier in the foyer had been given an updated look, its surface repainted a lacquered blue to match the large pop art canvas hanging near the entrance.

Jia and Darius followed Sora as she sped toward the end of a hallway lined with shiny black doors. They crossed through a large primary bedroom, and Sora shoved open a narrow door off to the right.

Then she stopped short. Jia and Darius looked past her into the office.

Every usable surface was covered with neat stacks of paper. The desk. The velvet fainting couch. Half the floor. The tops of the cabinets beneath the bookshelves and even the Second Empire credenza.

"No," Sora whispered, her voice shaking. She pushed her way inside and began flipping through the stack nearest to her. "He can't win. He can't win. *They can't win.*"

It was clear as Waterford crystal that Seven had done this intentionally.

He probably hadn't wanted to throw away any of his papers or take the time to organize them. So he'd done what law firms like Whitman Volker routinely did when served with a subpoena.

He'd buried them in paperwork.

There was no way Jia or Sora or Darius could find anything useful before Seven Park had them removed from the premises.

He'd beaten them. Again.

"No," Sora cried out. "No, no, *no*!" Then she screamed and shoved over the stack of paper beneath her hands.

Jia's chest heaved. She stared at Darius, who looked as lost as she felt. Then she closed her eyes and counted to ten. It didn't matter if Jia had less than two weeks to prove the impossible. She wasn't going to back down. Seven Park wouldn't win this round. He thought he knew them. But Jia had learned a thing or two about him as well.

She opened her eyes. Then she grabbed a file box from the bookshelf to her left and dumped its contents onto the floor.

"Take something from the middle of every stack of paper," Jia said to Sora and Darius. "I don't care what it is. Don't take the time to look at it. Put it all in here." She handed Sora the box. "When it's full, find another box. And make an absolute mess doing it."

"Jia," Darius said, "we have no idea what—"

"I know." Jia's voice was more breath than sound. "We have no idea what's on all these papers."

*And I'm betting he doesn't either*, she conveyed without words.

Understanding settled on Darius's face. "Grab anything with numbers on it," he muttered. Then he turned to the bookcase and began searching for something.

For the next few minutes, Jia and Sora tossed stacks of papers into three large boxes without pausing for breath. It took Darius some time, but eventually he found a first edition of *The Fountainhead* sitting high on a corner shelf.

"It's signed," Darius announced as he tucked the book into his belt and buttoned his coat.

Jia nodded. "I would expect no less. Now let's get the hell out of here."

They each grabbed a full box and marched toward the door, ignoring the protests of the two maids and the string bean, who kept trying to step into their paths to slow them down.

"By the way," Sora announced as they neared the entrance of the apartment, "that Lichtenstein is fucking heinous. Do you hear me, Annie Schmidt?" she yelled at the security camera mounted above the front door. "You still have the taste of a Bavarian milkmaid."

They lugged the boxes into the elevator and hailed a cab on the street, like normal people. After tossing everything into the trunk, all three of them piled into the back seat, sweaty and furious and trembling from the effort.

As the cab lurched away from the curb, they saw the flashing lights of approaching police cars.

"Just in time," Sora said, her voice hoarse.

"Praise Satan and all his minions," Jia murmured.

Darius looked at Jia and started to laugh. Shocked by the sound, Jia just stared at him. Then she started to laugh, too.

Sora's lips twitched. "I need a drink."

---

"How is she so fucking heavy?" Jia whispered two hours later, as she and Darius struggled to carry a completely inebriated Sora Park-Vandeveld along the narrow thoroughfare leading up to her friend Tiffany's bohemian apartment in Montmartre.

"It's probably the contents of four bottles of wine sloshing around inside her hundred-and-ten-pound body," Darius grunted back.

"We should have stopped her." Jia hoisted their burden higher. When Sora's head threatened to snap back, Jia caught it.

"No one was going to stop her from drinking herself silly. She's more than earned it. And what the hell is the deal with these tiny-ass roads?"

"Well," Jia panted, "they were likely designed before the advent of—"

"Rhetorical, Song."

"Bite me, Rohani." Jia's knees almost buckled out from under her.

"We can't do this. Take her coat and her bag."

"What are you—"

"If you ever tell her I did this," he said as he bent over to reposition Sora, "I will inform everyone I know in the legal community that you farted loudly at a three-star Michelin restaurant in Paris and tried to blame our server."

"What the hell? I definitely did not do that!"

"Doesn't matter. I take my cues from our politicians. Once I say it, it becomes true." Darius passed Sora's Saint Laurent Manhattan bag and long Max Mara coat over to Jia before throwing Sora's limp body over one shoulder. Then he grunted loudly before racing uphill as fast as he could.

Jia ran after him.

At the top, Darius turned around, panting. "The key is in my back pocket."

"You're literally asking me to grab your ass," Jia mumbled.

"Take your time," Darius said through clenched teeth. "I'm only balancing a fire-breathing dragon on one shoulder."

Jia slid her hand into his back pocket. Why, oh why, did Darius still smell so good even dripping with sweat?

The gods really wanted to test Jia.

"Why are your pants so tight?" she demanded.

"Ask *GQ*." He squirmed. "Stop trying to tickle me."

"I'm not. I—it's stuck, and I—oh! Got it." Jia withdrew the key, her cheeks flaming. When she met Darius's eyes, she could see the flush on his face, clear in the light of a bright moon. For a blink of time, they shared a look, his chest heaving.

It could have been the recent exertion. It could have been the fact that they were standing so close to each other. It could have been any number of things.

They both averted their gazes the next instant. Then they attempted to maneuver through the narrow double doors of the building, intent on making their way to the elevator.

In that exact moment, Sora woke. She lifted her head . . . only to have it strike the doorjamb with a loud thwack.

"Yah!" she yelped. "Eegae moosun . . . what the—what is going on?"

Darius brought her inside and propped her against the wall of the building's entryway.

Sora rubbed her head. "How dare you," she slurred. Then she began to droop slowly toward the checkered tile floor.

Jia rushed to her side before she could fall.

"Yah!" Sora shouted again when Jia pushed her back against the wall with a forceful thrust. Sora's hair was in her face. She brushed some of it aside to peer at Jia. Then she snickered. "Oh. It's just you."

"Yes. Just me."

"Gijibae." Sora blew a dark curl off her lips. "I never liked you."

"Really? I'm so surprised to hear that."

Darius leaned in to check Sora's pupils and run his palm on the back of her head to make sure the blow wasn't serious.

Sora bared her teeth and wagged a finger at him. "But you . . . it's been a long time since I was drunk around you."

Darius nodded. "Look at me. Just hold still."

"The last time I was drunk with you, I told you I liked you."

"I remember."

"Why didn't you kiss me again? I said you could. If you'd kissed me, I would have slept with you."

"I don't shit where I eat."

Sora scoffed. "You were barely twenty. How would you know to worry about that?"

"Because I grew up poor."

"So did I."

"My poor was different from your poor."

"Cry me a river." She sighed again and began to slump onto the floor. "I should have just married you anyway."

"I didn't ask you to marry me," Darius replied as he heaved her back up. "And you sure didn't ask me."

Sora flung more sweaty strands of hair off her face. "I probably would have been so much happier. You would have loved me more." Then she pointed a finger at Jia. "Don't marry a rich white man, Jia. He'll make it seem like he wants to let you in. Make you one of them. But you're never let in. Not really. You wind up becoming the perfect, frigid wife, who won't let her husband touch her, much less have sex with him. And my kids?" Sora's laughter sounded like the beginning of a sob. "Who knows if they'll be treated the way their peers are treated. The way they deserve to be treated. That's the part that really guts me." She seemed to sober for a second. "If I had married Darius, then I would be the one with power. That's always better. I would be the one opening doors for him. No one would look at me as if I were the one who didn't belong."

"It's usually better to be the one with the power," Darius said, his tone a touch peevish. "But maybe we should be trying to burn down the whole thing."

"This gijibae agrees with you, Darius." She pointed a drunken finger in Jia's direction. "An idealist."

"I'm a realist," Jia said. "And I really am done with this."

"Hey, gijibae." Sora glared at her. "You're done with this when I say you are."

"No," Jia replied. "I may work for your family, but I don't take orders from a drunken gijibae in the middle of an existential rant, no matter how much money she has."

"Did you just call me a gijibae?" Sora hiccupped.

"Just saying what everyone is thinking."

Sora grabbed Jia by the collar and hauled her closer. "Say it again."

Jia knew it was foolish. Like goading a tiger. But after everything she'd had to deal with the last few weeks, she was tired. So tired. Of worrying and walking on eggshells and not sleeping and living with the fear of what might happen if she failed. "Gijibae," Jia said. "I called you a gijibae. And I'm going to let you in on a secret: a lot of people would agree with me."

Sora's eyes clouded over. Then began to swim. She started to raise her voice. Darius tried to step between them. Attempted to pry Sora's fingers from the collar of Jia's coat.

The next instant, Sora Park-Vandeveld, the Grand Gijibae herself, projectile vomited eight-hundred-dollar wine all over them.

In silence, Jia and Darius took turns taking showers. Jia went first, mostly because she didn't know how she would fare thinking about the fact that Darius had been in this bathroom only a moment ago, letting the water trickle down his bare skin.

Jia couldn't think about that. Not right now.

Not when she so badly wanted some kind of meaningful comfort.

Sora's words haunted her. On the outside, Sora appeared to have everything. But on the inside, she was obviously a wreck. The fact that her seemingly perfect life—her beautiful children and her perfect home and her gorgeous husband with all the pedigree and privilege the world could offer—wasn't enough to make Sora feel loved and at peace with herself depressed Jia beyond measure.

Of course, on a logistical level, everything Sora had said made sense. A happily married husband didn't get drunk at a Halloween party and have sex with his wife's twin. And a happily married wife didn't lie about it to keep face.

But part of Jia had been rooting for what Sora represented. For what someone like Sora had managed to accomplish. The actual dream, in all the circles of Korean aunties from all walks of life, who fretted about their daughters' prospects. The same saga, for generations upon generations. Sora had the looks and the education. She'd married the ideal man—a doctor!—from a prestigious family. She'd given birth to a healthy boy and a girl.

On paper, Sora Park-Vandeveld had everything. And nothing.

Maybe lasting happiness was just like lasting peace. Illusory.

Jia sat on the couch in the darkness, waiting for Darius to finish his shower. She'd found some tea in the cabinets and made them each a mug. Mariage Frères. A blue tea that smelled like honey and bergamot. Mostly she'd chosen it because she'd never had a blue tea before.

When Darius walked out of the shower, his black hair wet and his gray T-shirt clinging to his torso in the places his skin was still damp, Jia stood in a rush. "I should find a hotel, since there's no need for us to hide out anymore."

"It's almost two in the morning, Jia," he said softly. "There's more than enough room for you here."

Jia shook her head. "I can't stay here with you, Darius. Not right now."

He noticed the two mugs of tea on the worn wooden table. "Let's just have some tea and go rest . . . in our own rooms."

Jia's head continued to shake. "No. I really think I should leave." She turned to the door. Her hand was on the latch when she felt him behind her. He wasn't touching her. But she could sense his heat. His nearness.

"Don't go," he whispered.

"They don't have chai here," she murmured without turning around, her voice shaking. "I need . . . chai."

"So do I. Badly."

Jia's fingers clenched around the doorknob. Darius's hand came to rest on hers, his touch as light as a feather. He pulled her fingers away from the door and didn't let go. She felt his breath brush across the nape of her neck. It sent a shiver down her spine.

Darius took a step closer. She leaned back, until her shoulders were barely in contact with his chest. Jia wanted to tilt her head. To let it rest on him. Feel the warmth of his body against hers. Her heart wasn't pounding. It was a steady and fervent beat, loud in her ears, heightening her senses.

Darius brushed the tip of his nose along the shell of her ear. He exhaled gently, and Jia turned her head toward his. The only places they continued to touch were where his fingers threaded through hers.

The steady beat of her heart became an ache. An ache that spread through her body and pooled low in her stomach.

"I want you," she whispered.

"I know."

"Help me." Jia swallowed and worried her lower lip between her teeth as if she could pretend it was Darius's mouth. "Distract me." She thought about their practice of rigorous honesty. How much closer it had brought them, though that was never the intention.

*Liar.*

Jia lifted her chin. Darius pressed the side of his jaw against her temple. Their fingers continued twisting together in a slow, sensual dance. "Tell me something true." The longing in her words was palpable.

"I want to take you to my room."

"And?"

"I want to unzip your dress. Slowly. Watch it fall to the floor."

Jia's breath hitched. She took their entwined fingers and pressed her own hand into the skin of her thigh. Darius's grip tightened around hers. His lips nipped along the side of her neck.

"And then?" Jia asked.

He whispered in her ear in a language she couldn't speak. Yet she understood. Jia's head fell back, her shoulders trembling. She dragged their joined hands up her leg, taking the hem of her dress with them. Then she touched herself. He pressed her hand harder, tighter, higher. As if it were his.

With a ragged gasp, Jia turned around to kiss him.

He stopped them both, his chest rising and falling in tandem with his heartbeat. He braced his forehead against hers. "Do you trust me?"

Jia's breath caught. "I—I want to."

"Jia," Darius whispered. "I can't. Not like this."

"I know." Then she pushed him away and fled to her room.

# THE *MARADO*

## T Minus 12 Days

Jia was the first to wake from a fretful sleep the next morning. It was still dark outside. She'd set her alarm intentionally for 6 a.m. so that she could call Ben Volker and update him on everything that had transpired last night.

Even though it was after midnight in New York, Ben picked up on the first ring.

"Where are we now?" he asked crisply.

"We managed to get into Seven Park's study in Paris."

"Did you find anything relevant?"

She hedged. "We took a lot of papers, but it's too soon to be definitive about anything."

"Have them couriered back to the city immediately. I'll put some first years on it."

Jia steeled herself. "I don't think that's the best move at this juncture."

"We don't have time to debate this. Because of your *agreement*"—he pronounced the word as if it were an elegant curse—"with Jenny Park, we have less than two weeks left, and, quite frankly, we don't have much to show for it."

Jia knew she was toeing a line by going against him now. But she wanted to trust her instincts. "I believe now more than ever that we have a mole in our ranks. If we courier everything back and share this information with the first years, there's a chance Seven Park will find out what I'm trying to do. I can't take that risk. Like you said, I don't have the luxury of time. I need to keep my plans close to the chest."

Ben paused. "What are you trying to do?"

Jia took a deep breath and told him everything she'd worked through last night, when she should have been sleeping. Everything that had happened, and everything that she planned to do moving forward.

Well, maybe not everything. She did leave out the part where she'd almost had sex with the Park family's house manager.

"All right," Ben said when she was finished explaining. "I don't love this idea. But . . . I'm going to trust you on this, Jia."

"Thank you, Ben."

His voice lowered. "I don't need to tell you what's on the line if this doesn't work out."

The tension in Jia's stomach pulled tighter. "I understand."

"Good luck." He hung up.

After changing into a set of cream-colored sweats and throwing her air-dried hair into a low bun, Jia left her room and made her way into the retro fifties kitchen to find Darius sitting at a wrought-iron bistro table. The scent of something familiar lingered in the air. On the stovetop was a small simmering pot, and between his hands was a steaming mug.

"Is that . . . coffee?" Jia teased to mask her discomfort. She could still feel the way his five-o'clock shadow had scraped along her jaw. Rough and soft all at once.

"I caved. I needed something stronger than tea." He shoved his palms into his eyes. "I feel terrible."

"You need Advil and something spicy to eat." Jia poured herself a cup of coffee from the French press on the counter. She sat down at the table and took a sip. "This is awful."

"I don't know how to make coffee," Darius replied. "But you look a hell of a lot better than I feel, so maybe I'll take your advice about the spicy food. I could try adding some chili flakes to the soup, but it's Jenny's recipe, and I'm not sure she would approve."

"Soup?" Jia eyed the simmering pot.

"I made some congee."

She wandered over to the stove and lifted the lid. "You made . . . jook?"

"You've been a little worse for the wear recently. I'm not sure when the last time was that you had a full night's sleep." He shrugged. "I figured you could use a pick-me-up."

"You . . . made jook for me?"

He took a sip of his coffee and made a face.

Jia used a spoon to taste the congee. The same congee her mother had made for her when she was sick as a child. The taste of the slightly sweetened rice porridge with a touch of toasted sesame oil warmed her bones. "Will you marry me?" she whispered without turning around.

"No." He laughed softly. "We barely know each other."

"I wasn't talking to you. I was talking to the jook. We've been intimate for years."

He continued laughing.

Jia brought over two bowls of jook and passed one to him. "Thank you. Really." She wanted to say more, but something caught in her throat when he looked at her.

"Are we okay after last night?" he asked, one of his hands coming to rest on hers.

"I am if you are."

"Rigorous honesty?"

"Right." Jia cleared her throat. "I'd . . . be better physically if we'd both gotten what we wanted last night. But I'd also be a wreck emotionally."

"Same," he said. "But I'll rally." He held her gaze. "And I'll wait for the right time."

*I'll wait until you trust me.* He didn't say it, but Jia knew he was thinking it.

"We can't afford to make any mistakes," she said, "not when so much is on the line."

Darius removed his hand from hers and nodded. "Do you have a plan?"

"I think so." Jia pushed up the sleeves of her sweatshirt and lowered her voice to a whisper. "We need to get these boxes out of Paris as soon as possible. Ideally, I'd like to take them someplace where Seven can't find out what we're doing with them, in case it amounts to a whole lot of nothing. I'd rather he be kept in the dark as long as possible."

Darius nodded. "Where do you have in mind?"

"I don't know." Jia sighed. "I feel like he has eyes everywhere. Security cameras, motion-activated what-have-yous, a staff of spies, PIs on the take. I want as few people as possible to know what's going on because it's apparently the work of a moment for him to uncover what we're doing."

"Which means we probably have a mole," Darius said quietly.

"I agree. There's no way he could manage this level of duplicity without help." She tapped her fingers on the table. "We also don't have time to be paranoid about it, but I want to take precautions where we can. Unfortunately, I'm not sure where the best place to go might be, unless you know of a hut somewhere on a remote island with difficult access. Preferably a single road. And no possible chance of unwanted visitors."

"Well, I don't know about a hut, but I can think of something close." Darius canted his head. "A place with limited staff and challenging access." He took another sip of his coffee and shuddered. "I think we should take the boxes to Jenny in Greece. The *Marado* is anchored there, about a mile off the coast of Crete."

"The Park family's yacht?"

Darius nodded. "If we switch off the security cameras and keep a barebones crew, we can make it pretty difficult for Seven to find out what we're doing."

Jia leaned back in her seat and considered. Darius could be the mole. That was entirely possible. A mole trying to steer her in the precise direction he needed her to go. It was the reason she still couldn't trust him. Not yet. She found it hard to believe Darius would ever betray Jenny, but she hadn't known him that long. "I don't hate it."

"What are our plans after that, by the way?"

Jia paused to eat more of her congee. She was running out of options. There was one surefire way to be certain Darius Rohani wasn't the mole.

It was to put faith in her instincts. To trust him and him alone.

To make a bed with her potential enemy and lie in it.

She almost wanted to laugh at the thought, but her anxiety threatened to eclipse her. She could feel it churning in her blood, spreading like a sinister virus. Jia clenched her jaw. She wouldn't succumb to it. It was time to make her choice.

It was time to start trusting herself.

"Jia?" Darius pressed. "What's the plan?"

"We fake it until we make it. We wait a few days after we arrive in Greece, just to make Seven antsy. Then we act like we've found something important. I hint at a significant discovery to my boss, and you tell the Park kids we've uncovered the smoking gun and are days away from chasing down Seven's money trail." Her hands turned into fists. "Then we wait for him to come to us."

"You're trying to trick him into settling?"

"I have it on good authority that Seven won't settle unless he's afraid. I want to make him so afraid that he's willing to give us at least half the keys to the kingdom. His fear is going to cost him. Dearly."

"Calling his bluff," Darius said. "It's bold."

"It's the best I can do. He's one step ahead of us all the time. I want to see how he acts when he's completely in the cold." She bent over her bowl of jook. "And I don't want anyone but you and me to know the truth. Deal?"

Darius's eyes widened. He understood what she was saying.

Jia was going to try to trust him.

Darius drained his coffee cup. "I'll make the arrangements. He won't be surprised that we're going to Jenny in Greece. Suzy, Sora, and Minsoo will probably be there at some point, too. We can transport the boxes to the *Marado* ourselves if we charter a speedboat."

Jia nodded. "And then . . . we wait."

# IN ARTICULO MORTIS

I told you I would leave you.

I lied.

As we near the end of this tale, I find myself mourning. Not merely for the losses already incurred but for the ones to come. The ones from which there is no escape.

Soon, Jenny Park will die. That is an inevitability. Nothing can stop it from happening, no matter how much her children or her friends or her loved ones may wish it were not so.

Jenny's impending death has cast a perpetual shadow on this story. I find myself angry that someone so beloved would have to die to bring her fractured family together. That is the point of this account, after all. To bear witness to the things we must lose on the journey to find ourselves.

So I have returned, for the briefest time, to beg for your forgiveness. I cannot allow Jenny Park to perish in such a sad and ignominious manner. Perhaps she was, admittedly, a bit boring. Living an all-too-predictable life. Perhaps she did make craven mistakes, especially with her children. And most definitely with her husband, who was not always so terrible. There was a time, in fact, when he could have saved their marriage, if she had allowed it.

Regardless, she deserves a chance to be heard, especially at the end.

Maybe hers was not an exciting life. But it was not a bad one.

In the end, I hope Jenny Park can hold her head high and see that she was loved.

Not by me, of course.

No one who truly loves Jenny Park could do what I have done to her. I am certain you have suspected it for some time, dear reader. But I must confess it nonetheless.

I am the betrayer. I am the mole.

I am the one who has made certain our dogged heroine, Jia Song, cannot and will not succeed, no matter how hard she tries. I have lied, left notes, stolen documents, shared privileged information, and behaved traitorously at every turn. From the beginning, I have been there, like a snake, waiting to deliver a lethal strike to each of her admirable attempts to right this wrong.

I have sabotaged Jenny Park, a person I should have loved and cherished as she tried to love and cherish me, despite her many mistakes. It is unforgivable, in several respects. I have lied to her and stolen from her and left her to cry herself to sleep, cold and alone with nothing but her pain.

I hope you forgive me, dear reader. Despite my monstrous choices, I hope I am not your villain.

But I must admit I always intended to harm her. Alas.

An omelet cannot be made without breaking a few eggs.

# TRUTHFULLY

## *T Minus 8 Days*

Jenny Park knew she'd made a mistake the moment she decided to take the short journey from her olive tree estate in Crete to the *Marado* late that evening. Though it was anchored only a mile offshore, it wasn't the right night to be at sea. The wind was too strong, the water far too choppy. Beneath her feet, the yacht buoyed about, small waves cresting against its sides and sending sprays of water onto the deck.

This was neither the right place nor the right time for a confrontation.

But there would never be a good time to do what she had to do. To say what she had to say.

Chilsoo had come to Greece. At first, she hadn't believed it. Her heart had leaped when she heard he was coming, in that terrible way the heart betrays itself when it comes to love. But of course, he hadn't come to see her. Even knowing how limited her time on earth was, he still did not have the courage to face her. He'd gone to their outrageous excuse for a boat, intent on speaking with their children, who'd gathered in Greece two days ago to spend the last vacation of her life together.

Chilsoo hadn't come to see her. He'd come to argue and bully their kids about the money.

The money, the money, the money. If Jenny could change one choice she'd made during her life, it would be about the money. Instead of buying them freedom, it had become an anchor around their necks.

Chilsoo shouldn't have come to Greece. He should have been smart enough to see through Jia Song's plan. But he'd taken whatever bait she'd offered. He'd allowed his fear to best him. As much as Jenny hated to admit it, she was glad he'd been so weak. She was running out of time, and she had spent far too long waiting in the wings, hiding her pain and granting him the grace he didn't deserve.

She'd gathered her strength before making this journey. She'd fought for the willpower to do what needed to be done. And she'd arrived at the boat without any fanfare, much to the surprise of her kids, who'd protested and insisted she immediately retire to her stateroom to rest.

Jenny was done with resting.

She checked her watch. Before, when they'd come to Greece together, she and Chilsoo would take an evening stroll along the deck of the *Marado* at the same time every night. This yacht that he'd christened to honor Jenny's mother and celebrate the strong women of her family, the divers who'd defied death to provide for their families.

She waited belowdecks for him, lingering on the first step leading upward.

Jenny loved the water, but she'd never enjoyed boats. Truthfully, she didn't think her husband did either. He loved what boats represented. The statement they made.

Chilsoo had been like that all his life. A showman through and through. When they'd first met in Busan many years ago, it was what had drawn Jenny to him. He was the kind of young man who moved about the room like the sun. And when the sun shone on her, Jenny had felt truly seen, for the first time in her life.

Jenny took a deep breath and started up the steps, her hand clutching the polished wooden railing.

She'd been so weak for so long. The cancer had done more than steal her vitality. For too long, it had taken her will to live. It had eaten at her from the inside, hollowing her, leaving her with nothing but skin and bones. Jenny had watched her face shrink and shrivel. In the mirror, she'd seen a haunting memory of her own mother, who'd perished from lung cancer.

The greatest of ironies. Her mother had not smoked a day in her life.

But her father had smoked unfiltered American Marlboros until the morning of his death, though it wasn't cancer that took him. Jenny always believed he'd died of a broken heart, almost a year to the day after his wife had passed.

That was the kind of love she'd wanted for herself. The kind of love she thought she'd had. Maybe it wasn't passionate anymore, but it was loyal. Steadfast, despite all.

But when the doctors had deemed her cancer terminal, her husband had stopped seeing her.

The sun had moved on to shine elsewhere.

Jenny made it halfway up the stairs, the boat rocking beneath her feet, causing her stomach to churn. She gritted her teeth. Remembered all the nausea, all the suffering, all the shame of these last few years. Of hiding from her kids when she needed to go to the doctor, because she hated them seeing her like this. Of getting up from bed in the middle of the night and struggling to make her way to the bathroom without help.

She wouldn't ask her husband. Even then, she knew he was disloyal. And she would never ask for help from a man who couldn't keep his family.

If a man couldn't keep his family, he couldn't keep anything.

Jenny took a deep breath and continued climbing.

A purple sky came into view as she neared the top, her body swaying from the motion of the Aegean Sea.

Jenny found Seven exactly where she knew he would be: at the very front of the boat, as if he were its captain. As if the waters below him moved at his will. Like Neptune with his trident.

"Sora-appa," she said.

He turned, his eyes widening. "Why are you still awake?" he asked in Korean.

"I can't sleep with the boat swaying like this."

Seven smiled to himself, as if he knew her so well. "You were always a bad sleeper."

"No," she replied. "I wasn't. When I was home in Korea, before we met, I slept well."

"Your stories always kept you awake."

"No. I chose not to sleep because I loved them more than I loved to sleep."

He laughed. "You haven't changed, you know. You still like to argue with me."

"You shouldn't talk to me like that. As if we are still familiar and close."

"You are the mother of my children. I will always value you, even if you don't believe that I do."

"Kuhjimal," Jenny murmured. She switched to English. "If you valued me, you wouldn't treat me like this. You wouldn't have done what you did."

He sighed as if he were the one exercising extreme patience. "I tried to be there for you, Jeeyun-ah. You didn't want my help."

"I was dying. I needed you. Every day I wanted you to be there."

"I tried my best." He shook his head. "But with you, my best was never good enough."

"No. Even when I became sick, it was never about what I needed. It was you who always wanted more. I gave and gave. Then, when I needed you to be there for me—to help me—you complained about the burden."

"It isn't easy watching someone you loved die."

Jenny gripped the metal railing beneath her fingers. "I know you, Park Chilsoo. Watching me die made you feel sad and old, and you hated to feel sad almost as much as you hated to feel old, so you found someone who made you feel young and strong and powerful again."

For the first time, anger creased his brow. "No one asked you to sacrifice everything for your family. I'm entitled to be happy, Jeeyun-ah. I've earned it."

"If your happiness is at the expense of your responsibilities, is it truly happiness?"

"That sounds like the exact thing you would say." He switched back to Korean. "I am not sacrificing myself for anyone anymore. Our children are grown. It's time you found another purpose."

Jenny started to laugh. It racked her tiny body until coughs began flying from her lips. Still, she continued laughing. "Keegah makyuh," she mumbled. *How ridiculous.* "Life lessons from the man who has stolen everything from his children."

"They will be fine." He spoke in a measured tone. "Minsoo is smart and successful. Sora is a doctor who has married into a wealthy, influential family. And now maybe Suzy will finally accomplish something with all her wasted talent."

Anger sparked, and Jenny doused it before it could catch flame. She didn't have the willpower to control the heat of her emotions. She needed to be cold. Steady. Calculating. The exact sort of person her husband had always wanted her to be. "They told me to fight back. For a long time, I didn't want to. But I will fight back now. Until the day I die, I will fight."

"For the money?" He laughed. "What a hypocrite. You always said the money ruined us."

"No." Jenny shook her head. "It's not for the money. It was never for the money. I will fight to tear down this idea you have built of yourself. I will fight until everyone you know—everyone whose opinion you value more than that of your own family—sees through all the lies and the storytelling. Until they see the small, worthless man you are. The kind of man who would steal from his kids. The kind of man who would abandon his dying wife. When I am done, no one on the Upper East Side will invite you to anything. No charity balls. No philanthropic societies. You will just be Seven Park, the man who was once someone who mattered. Forgotten."

She watched the words land on him, selfish satisfaction warming her veins. That was the thing about sharing a life with someone for decades. When you were there to share in all the highs and lows of life, you knew exactly what to say or do to provoke a certain reaction. With Seven, Jenny had spent most of their marriage knowing what *not* to do.

She'd avoided making him angry because it was the way of things. Her aunt had turned an unseeing eye on her husband's extramarital affairs. Everyone had known. No one had said anything, even while he bought and maintained a home for his mistress and their two children. In Jenny's generation of women, saying something made it real. Shattered the illusion these women had labored all their lives to construct.

It was about loyalty. Loyalty meant keeping silent and staying true. Jenny believed in loyalty. But why did it only seem to matter to the women?

Park Chilsoo was a small-minded and weak man who needed the praise and acknowledgment of other small-minded and weak men. The kind of men who cared about the legacy they left behind for their families more than the type of human beings they'd shaped them to be.

His nostrils flared. His eyes narrowed dangerously. He took a step toward her.

Jenny wanted to back away. Instead, she held fast. Defiant.

Seven scoffed. Then he relaxed, his features softening. "You won't fight. I know you won't. You've never had the stomach for it. Fifty million to walk away, right now. Fifteen million cash for each of the kids. You keep Park Avenue and the apartment in Kangnam. Everything else stays with me." He paused. "Soljigi, you wouldn't know what to do with all of it anyway."

*Soljigi*. Truthfully.

Jenny laughed, the sound tight with pain. "*Soljigi?* You shouldn't even be thinking of such a word." She advanced a step farther. Lifted her chin, though her knees shook. Not with fear. But with emotion. Like a dam shuddering under the weight of everything it has held back for far too long. "Fifty million is not half. I want half of everything."

"Where is your proof it isn't half?" he asked.

"We found it. We had it. We will find it again."

"No, you won't. There's nothing to find. You don't have enough time to look anyway." Again his expression turned sympathetic. "Take the deal. Be done with this so we can both move on. Spend the days left to you with your grandchildren, not with your lawyers."

Jenny lunged for him. He sidestepped and took hold of her wrist.

"Let go of me," she said.

He pushed her back, more forcefully than necessary. Jenny stumbled. Then she stood again, her legs still shaking. "You are not a man. What kind of man pushes his wife?"

"You are sick and weak. I didn't push you. You tripped."

"You wanted me to fall," she said. "That would make your life much easier. But I won't make it easier for you. This new family you want to build, the one you think will be better than the first? It won't be. Because you will still be that poor boy's father. Because of that, he will never learn what it means to be a man."

Jenny had always known how to make him angry. He stepped toward her again, his stance menacing.

Jenny remained defiant. "I won't stop, Park Chilsoo. I will never stop."

# DEATH ON THE AEGEAN

## *T Minus 8 Days*

A bloodcurdling scream sliced through the night air. Jia Song leaped up, the papers in her lap falling to the polished wood floor of her stateroom. She raced to the door and threw it open.

Jia heard the shouts before her foot even touched the bottom step leading to the deck.

She ran up the stairs into the wind, rain streaking sideways toward her face.

Seven Park's hands were in his hair, his face a mask of horror. "She fell," he cried. "She fell. Jeeyun fell into the water!"

Jia sprinted toward the railing and looked over the edge of the yacht into the dark waters of the Aegean far below. The waves tossed about, cresting against the bow, sending sprays toward her face. For an instant, she toyed with idea of diving in after Jenny.

But that would be suicide. Anyone with eyes could see that.

Footsteps pounded behind her.

"What happened?" Suzy demanded.

Seven's shaking hand pointed over the railing, his eyes black with fear. "Your umma fell off the boat."

"What the fuck?" Suzy wailed.

A beat passed in stunned silence.

"What did you do?" Minsoo glowered at his father. His hands turned to fists.

"I-I did nothing. Nothing!" Seven stammered. "We were arguing. But I would never—"

"Liar," Minsoo seethed. "You pushed her before. That time we went to Aspen for Christmas." For an instant, it looked like he was about to attack his father. Then he spun around and rang the bell hanging from the bow pulpit. *Clang, clang, clang.*

An instant later, the captain and two members of the crew burst onto the deck. Cries of "Man overboard!" resounded from the wings. All the lights on the yacht came on, and the two sailors began donning gear to dive beneath the water in search of Jenny Park.

Minsoo moved to join them without hesitation.

The captain stopped him. "No, sir. It's far too dangerous during a storm."

Another scream resounded through the night. "Did you kill my mother?" Sora's bare feet battered across the deck, the rain soaking through her silk dressing gown. She threw herself at her father, her fists beating into his back. "Did you kill my mother?" Her cries ripped from her chest. "I'll kill you. I'll kill you, you motherfucker."

Jia started to shake, the wind and rain continuing to buffet the boat. Darius snagged her by the elbow, and they both reached for each other, under the guise of offering a steadying hand. Darius's eyes swam with unshed tears.

Had Seven Park shoved his dying wife into the sea?

A *family of murdering thieves.*

Suzy grabbed her screaming sister by the waist and tried to pull her away. The next instant, a crewmember ushered them past the cockpit into the main cabin.

Jia watched through a haze as blankets were placed around their shoulders. As calls for the Greek Coast Guard were made.

As the divers resurfaced, grim and empty-handed.

---

The yacht's sprawling main cabin reminded Jia of a Las Vegas hotel suite, with its varnished wood and gleaming stone and gold accents, its warm, ambient light mixed with the occasional flash of neon. Like an updated version of a sixties mod pad, complete with weird glass art and a random grand piano.

She hadn't spent much time in this room. Whenever Jia touched something here, it felt like she was leaving greasy fingerprints. As if the yacht knew she was nothing but a freeloader and wished to remind her of that fact. Jia found herself constantly trying to wipe away the evidence of her existence. So, unless it was necessary, she'd stopped coming into the main cabin about two days after they'd arrived.

Now Jia sat on a leather divan beside a silent Darius Rohani, trying her best not to let her thoughts run away from her.

The crewmembers who had braved the sea in search of Jenny Park had found no trace of her, save for a smudge of what appeared to be blood on the hull below the railing. The Coast Guard and the Greek police were on their way, but it could take up to an hour for them to arrive, given the choppy waters. Sora and Suzy sat together on one side of the L-shaped couch. Minsoo sat on the floor between their feet, his ankles crossed as if he were still a small boy. Seven Park huddled in the far-right corner, his expression haggard. As if he'd aged ten years in the space of a day.

Jia thought she should give them privacy. But Sora had asked her to remain in the room.

As their attorney. As their witness.

"I didn't kill your mother," Seven said in a hoarse voice. "I know you will never believe me, but it was an accident. She fell when—"

"No," Minsoo interrupted. "We won't believe you. And neither will the authorities." He sat up, his features resolute as he challenged his father, face-to-face. "You're finished, Dad. This entire scheme is done. I will make sure you go to prison for the rest of your life for this."

Anger rippled across Seven Park's features. He barged from the corner toward his three children. "There is no proof that I—"

"I saw you arguing from my stateroom window," Sora interrupted, her gaze unflinching.

"And I ran from my room when I realized it was becoming physical," Suzy continued without hesitation. "I could hear you yelling at her. Calling her names."

"And I will tell the police about that time at Christmas when you shoved her backward, and she fell over the ottoman in Aspen," Minsoo finished.

Jia bit her lip. She could be bearing witness to collusion. Or she could simply be witnessing the inevitable. The unseen hand of justice, served all too late.

Seven's fingers clenched and unclenched. "My lawyers—"

Minsoo stood up. "You will hire the best. And so will we." He nodded toward Jia. "When the news of your affair and your pregnant fiancée becomes public, everyone will understand your motive."

"I can't even imagine what people will say when they find out what you did to your dying wife." Suzy's voice trembled. Tears spilled over, trailing down her cheeks.

To Jia's lasting surprise, Sora put a comforting hand on her sister's back. "You have one chance," she said from where she sat, refusing to look at her father. "One chance to leave this situation, free and clear."

Minsoo strode toward the long lacquered dining table to remove a computer from his briefcase. "You'll log in to every offshore account you possess. I will move the funds to the accounts I've created. And then you will send an email to the board announcing your retirement as CEO of Mirae, effective immediately."

"Do it now, and we will agree that Umma's fall was an accident. If you don't, we will make sure you end up behind bars for the remainder of your pathetic life," Sora said.

Seven paled. "You can't do this. You will never get away with it."

"We can, and we will," Suzy said, taking to her feet. "But we are not totally heartless. We don't want our half brother to grow up with nothing. We will offer you a shitty deal like the one you offered Umma. Twenty-five million to walk away, the Caymans house, and a trust fund of fifteen million dollars for Ani's baby." She glowered at him, tears collecting on her chin. "But we get to keep Park Avenue."

"Take the deal," Minsoo said. He flipped the screen around to face his father. "Before the authorities arrive. And if it totals a penny less than eight hundred million dollars, we will know you are lying."

Jia knew she should speak up. What she was watching amounted to extortion. Her cold, wet clothes clung to her body. She was a degree away from freezing. As a lawyer, she had an obligation to object to this situation.

Seven deserved his day in court. And Suzy, Sora, and Minsoo had no right to forgo the necessary investigation that should take place regarding their mother's fall into the Aegean.

Still, she hesitated. "I don't think I should—"

"No," Sora said. "I asked you to stay for a specific reason. You represent my mother. Everything transpiring here is privileged."

Jia steeled herself. They needed to win the right way. This wasn't the right way.

Was it?

"It isn't privileged if I am bearing witness to a crime," she said.

Sora stood from her seat, her face deathly calm. "What crime have you witnessed?"

"Coercion."

"No," Minsoo replied. "We are simply telling our father what we may have seen. We are giving him the choice as to what happens next."

Suzy sniffed. Swiped the tears off her chin. "And who knows, Jia Song. Once we get rid of all the cronies at Mirae who are loyal to Seven, we are going to need a new law firm to represent the company." She looked Jia straight in the eye. "I'll bet we're talking about millions of dollars flowing into Whitman Volker every year for the conceivable future. More money than you could ever dream of making."

Jia swallowed. Coercion. And bribery.

"I understand this is not an easy choice." Sora's expression hardened. She faced Jia from across the black marble coffee table. For a second, it was like looking in the mirror. "Nevertheless, the choice is yours to make." She glanced over her shoulder at Seven. "Just as it is our father's. Go with your gut, Jia Song. Trust your instincts."

Jia looked at Darius, who had remained silent throughout this exchange. Watching her.

"You're running out of time, Park Chilsoo," Minsoo said softly. "If you don't take this deal, you'll lose everything anyway. Once you go to prison, it will simply be a matter of time before we decipher the code and find the money ourselves."

Darius stared into Jia's eyes, searching. Waiting.

"If he killed her, he deserves to go to prison for it," Jia said to Darius. "That's justice." She swallowed and dropped her voice until it was barely a sound. "Remember Orlagh?"

"I remember," Darius said. "If he was responsible for what happened to her, he already escaped justice once. Are you prepared to risk that happening again?"

"You and I . . . we know better."

"I told you I have never been neutral in this. I chose a side a long time ago."

Jia swallowed. "It isn't right."

"But is it justice?"

Jia couldn't answer. Seven looked at her, his eyes pleading. "Song Jihae, I will—"

"The choice," Sora interrupted, "is yours, Jia Song. Now make it."

# A FUTURE FILLED WITH GREEN

When Jia walked into Whitman Volker the following Monday, it was to cheers and imaginary raised glasses. She responded in kind, her cheerful demeanor masking the deeply unsettled feelings within.

Less than a day after giving her version of the story to the Greek police, Jia returned home to New York on a commercial flight, with a promise that someone in the Park family's entourage would be in touch.

Technically, Jia had not lied to the authorities. She had not witnessed the argument between Seven and Jenny. Nor had she seen Jenny fall into the water. No one had, save for the two individuals in question.

Jia hadn't lied. But she also hadn't stopped anyone from coloring the truth.

Half an hour after Seven Park yelled for help from the boat deck, Jia watched him grant his son access to a total of twelve offshore bank accounts, containing just short of $815 million. She stood silent while Minsoo drained them all in a matter of minutes.

Jia doubted she would ever see anything like that happen again in her entire life.

When Sora, Minsoo, and Suzy chose to lie to the police to corroborate their father's claim of innocence, Jia was not present to witness that either. Sora said she saw her father retire to his stateroom alone, earlier in the evening, a lie she apparently told without so much as a second of hesitation. And when Minsoo said he ran into his mother just as she was beginning her nightly stroll alone on the deck of the yacht, he'd allegedly suggested to her that it might not be a good idea, given the approaching storm.

Did Jia truly believe Seven had murdered the mother of his children?

She wanted to think he couldn't have done such a horrific thing. But she'd wanted to think that about Orlagh as well. In truth, Jia didn't know who Seven Park really was. Her time practicing law had taught her that anyone was capable of anything when pushed to the brink.

In the end, Seven Park had surrendered to his children much faster than Jia would have thought. She'd expected him to put up more of a fight. But maybe, just maybe, the realization that Jenny was truly gone had done something to him. Maybe a part of him had, at long last, felt some semblance of guilt.

Though the divers had been unsuccessful, Jia had held out hope that Jenny might have survived. Perhaps clinging on to driftwood or rescued by a nearby fishing boat. That hope had been dashed when she learned that the smear of dried blood found on the hull of the yacht had been tested and most certainly belonged to Jenny Park.

The authorities surmised that she must have struck her head after falling overboard.

Almost one week later, no trace of her body had been found, but this didn't seem to surprise anyone familiar with the area. The waters around Greece are notoriously temperamental.

The whispers abounded, especially when the news of Jenny's long-term battle with cancer was revealed. Perhaps if she was suffering a great deal of pain, her accident hadn't been entirely accidental. Still, Jia couldn't fully believe that Jenny might have died by suicide.

Their last conversation replayed through her mind.

There were definite signs that Jenny Park had made peace with her fate. But she'd also said she wished to fight. That she wanted her children to remember her as strong.

Maybe Jia was simply remembering the version of Jenny Park she wished to see.

When Jia closed the door to her office and sat down in her swivel chair, she allowed silence to fill the space for a moment.

It felt wrong to be here. It was the first time since Jia had begun working at Whitman Volker seven years ago that she felt this way. As if her job were a pair of shoes she'd once loved, only to realize they never suited her.

She wiped away the thin film of dust clinging to her computer screen. A strange weight settled on her shoulders.

Suddenly, the idea of just going back to work felt . . . wrong. As if she were missing something vital about herself. Something she'd only just begun to realize.

Jia cracked her neck, trying to fight this unsettling feeling.

She'd worked and worked and worked for most of her life, all for a specific purpose. For a dream she could see on her horizon, almost within reach. That chance to be the firm's next Emily Bhatia—a self-made woman with the highest billables five years running. The kind of lawyer who inspired fear and awe in the same breath.

The kind of person who could make sense of this mess.

She'd been counting down the days until she could make her promises—the ones she'd made to others and the ones she'd made to herself—a reality. By winning this account, Jia had put that goal within reach.

Yet she felt . . . unsettled. And wrong.

Not at all the way she should be feeling after such a triumph.

Jia remembered her last conversation with Jenny. The one that had caused her to flee into the rain on Park Avenue. How Jenny had said that everyone needed the space to dream.

Jia had thought she was making her dreams come true by reaching her goals. But when was the last time she'd granted herself space to truly dream? To be wild and ridiculous and ask herself—absent the weight of expectation—what she truly wanted?

Her time with Zain wasn't a dream, even if she'd desperately wanted it to be. The hope she'd had for a future with him had proven to be painfully false. In the end, it had been the opposite of a dream. The kind of thing that had haunted her sleep for months.

If Jia really thought about it, the last time she'd given herself the space to dream freely was that morning in her parents' bodega, with Lexi Niarchos's Birkin.

Jia eased back into her chair and stared up at the ceiling.

The last time she'd really dreamed about something for herself—

something outrageous and absurd and wonderful—she'd been a teenager. Almost twenty years ago.

Someone knocked on her door. Jia sat up and plastered a fake smile on her face. "Yes?"

A beaming Candace appeared in her doorway. "Mr. Volker would like to see you."

Still wearing her fake smile, Jia followed Candace to the upper floors of the building, where all the firm's bigwigs and senior partners maintained their offices, surrounded by walls of glass and lush wood paneling.

When Jia started working in the bullpen as a first-year associate, she would often imagine a time when she would be granted a place here, in the firm's highest echelon. An office on this floor, where even the air smelled different.

"Jia." Ben Volker stood the second Jia crossed the double-door threshold to his immense corner office. Sitting on the leather Chesterfield sofa beside him were Emily Bhatia and Andrew Whitman himself.

Jia almost gasped. Andrew Whitman was eighty-two years old. A legend in Manhattan's legal circles. He still kept an office in the building, but he usually came in once a week, never before noon. Watercooler gossip said he had a drop-down movie screen that covered one entire wall of his office. He used it to play virtual golf.

Not once in the seven years that Jia had worked at Whitman Volker had she ever been invited to speak with Andrew Whitman, much less in such an intimate setting.

Andrew stood slowly, but his movements were steady. "Jia," he began, his voice both soft and booming. It reminded her of the gong in her aunt's temple on the outskirts of Seoul. "Congratulations are in order. This is a tremendous achievement." He put out his hand.

Jia took it, grasping it firmly. "Thank you so much, Mr. Whitman."

"Andy," he corrected. "When you win us a billion-dollar account, you get to call me Andy."

"Andy," she murmured.

"Have a seat." Ben indicated the chair beside him.

"Thank you." Jia smoothed the front of her pleated pants and pushed up the sleeves of her cashmere sweater.

"We have been chatting about everything you managed to accomplish with the Park family's account in such a short time," Ben began. "Part of me wants to ask how you did it." He grinned. "But I probably shouldn't."

Andy's chuckle bordered on a rasp. "No man gives up that much money without a damn good reason."

"But I was sorry to hear about Jenny Park's accident," Emily said in her lilting British accent.

Jia pursed her lips. She'd chosen a path. Now she had to walk it. "Jenny was a wonderful person. I'm glad her husband finally chose to do right by their family."

"Of course." Emily nodded. Then she tilted her head and gave Jia an admiring glance. The kind of glance that Jia would have fallen over herself to get a month ago. "I wanted to speak with you specifically about *your* accomplishments. I've been watching you recently. It's no secret that I plan on retiring within the next five years, and it's been my goal to mentor the person I wish to take on my accounts once I leave." She smiled at Jia. "I believe that person is you."

Jia's head swam. Emily Bhatia worked with some of the largest, most powerful conglomerates in London and most of Asia. Companies that had worked with Whitman Volker for over a decade. Her billing hours—and the size of her accounts—were the stuff of legend at the firm.

If Jia took over for Emily Bhatia, she would be rich and admired beyond her wildest dreams. She would have everything she'd ever wanted. Be able to provide her family and her loved ones with everything they deserved and more.

Jia would become one of the most powerful attorneys in Manhattan.

She thought back to the last few weeks. Then considered her work over the past several years. All the stress and all the long hours and all the time away from her friends and family. The last vacation she'd taken without having to do any work was the few months she'd spent between graduating law school and starting her job at Whitman Volker.

Jia looked at Emily. She knew from office gossip that Emily was divorced and shared custody of a son and a daughter with her banker ex-husband. Their children were likely in their late teens or early twenties by now. Unlike many of the other senior partners, Emily rarely brought her family to anything work-related, even if it was a party or celebration.

Emily's reason for this—whispered among many of the other female attorneys at the firm—was that she didn't like reminding anyone at work that she had children. She thought it gave her less of an edge. As if she would be less likely to be considered for important roles if anyone remembered that she was also a mother.

It had made sense to Jia when she first heard it. She'd thought to herself at the time that this would be what she would do if she ever decided to have a family. And who knew? Maybe she wouldn't have kids. Maybe she would never get married. Maybe her work and her friends and her parents would be more than enough.

Success. And every accolade that came with it.

They were offering her the chance to become the firm's next Emily Bhatia.

So why was she hesitating?

The silence in the room stretched on far longer than it should have. From the corner of her eye, Jia watched Andy frown at Ben. Emily cast her a searching glance, clearly waiting for her to react.

Only a complete fool would waste this opportunity. Jia was no fool.

She brightened the next second. "I'm . . . overwhelmed." Jia shook her head as if she were trying to wake from a trance. "I can honestly say this is one of the first times in my life I am at a loss for words. Of course, I would be absolutely honored to have this opportunity."

The words tasted sour on her tongue.

Emily relaxed. "I'm beyond thrilled. It has been my wish to pass along this torch to another woman from an immigrant background, and I am so glad we all agree it's meant to be you."

Andy nodded with satisfaction. "Let's celebrate. And then you should take the rest of the week off, Jia. You've more than earned it."

Jia chewed at the inside of her cheek before smiling back at Emily. The three senior partners made a toast with a chilled bottle of Cristal to Jia's future at the firm. She laughed and cheered and carried on with them. When she returned to her office, her head was still swimming. She said nothing in response to the inquisitive looks sent her way. By now, word would have gotten out about her meeting on the top floor with the managing director. She wondered how many of her fellow junior partners knew that Andrew Whitman had also been in attendance.

She surmised that everyone would know what had transpired within the hour.

People like Never Late Nate would be at her beck and call, tripping over themselves to gain her favor.

Jia sat down at her desk in front of a pile of papers, her mind continuing to whirl.

Why wasn't she calling her family or texting Nidhi and Elisa?

What the hell was wrong with her?

There was a knock at the door.

"Yes?" Jia said.

Candace walked in, her face luminous. In her arms were two things. A large white envelope. And an immense Hermès gift bag, its orange color and dark brown border all too familiar.

Jia stood at once.

Candace handed her the Hermès gift bag first. "It's from Emily. She apparently made a few calls after she found out how much you loved Hermès." She spoke fast and excitedly. "One of her clients knows the family."

Jia's heart thudded. She unwrapped the Hermès parcel in silence and removed the bag within it.

There was no question that it was stunning. A green Birkin 25 with palladium hardware. Epsom leather, which Jia had always liked, though it wasn't Barenia Faubourg.

The note attached simply read:

*To a future filled with green.*

*~ Em*

Wrong. All wrong. Everything about this was so wrong.

Jia turned to Candace, who was waiting beside the door, a puzzled look on her brow.

"It's beautiful. I'm just so . . . overwhelmed."

Candace relaxed just like Emily Bhatia had. Chalked up Jia's silence and lukewarm reaction to a case of nerves.

Because who wouldn't be thrilled with such a gift?

"What is that?" Jia asked, gesturing to the white envelope still in Candace's hand.

Candace startled. "Oh!" She handed it to Jia. "It arrived not long ago for you, via messenger."

It was a simple envelope of thick card stock, Jia's name handwritten on the outside.

She tore it open.

*The new CEO of Mirae has requested your presence.*

*A car will be sent to your residence this evening at 9 p.m. EST.*

*Please bring your passport and garments for a summer holiday.*

"Candace?" Jia said. "I'll be taking the rest of the week off. Feel free to forward my calls."

# A GREEK TRAGEDY

The first time Jia had arrived with Darius at the Park family's olive tree estate on Crete less than a week ago, their stolen boxes of paper in tow, she hadn't spent much time at the actual house. They'd been too focused on getting to the *Marado* and hunkering down with their ill-gotten goods, which had largely proved useless beyond serving as a lure for Seven.

This was the reason for her surprise now when she entered the estate in the broad light of day: the home wasn't at all what she'd expected.

Most of the Park family's residences around the world were elegant and modern, with touches of the traditional. Here and there were signs of their Korean heritage, but for the most part, the properties were decorated to suit a specific aesthetic. One of tasteful wealth. Generically expensive and inoffensive, but perhaps lacking in character.

This home was completely different.

The Park family had constructed a hanok on the coast of Crete. A hanok with Greek touches, of course. Dramatic eaves and a tiled roof and decorative wooden screens, all in the color palette Jia had come to associate with the Greek Isles. White walls and blue finishes, with the occasional splash of bright pink.

It was a home designed by a romantic.

As she looked around, Jia felt the tension in her body easing. She could understand why this had been Jenny Park's favorite place to vacation. The residence itself wasn't large, despite the sprawling landscape around it. While it was obviously the vacation home of someone with means, it managed to appear homey and intimate.

Darius was waiting for her by the front door. At first, Jia avoided meeting his gaze. They had not spoken since that night on the yacht.

"Hey." Darius put his hands in his pockets and looked away. He was dressed in a gray linen suit with a cream-colored button-down shirt. Dark circles and lines had gathered under his eyes.

"I'm sorry again . . . about Jenny," she said.

Darius trained his attention on the stone walkway at her feet, as if he wanted to hide. It gave her pause. She wasn't used to him acting so cagey. He nodded. Then he gestured for her to follow him.

Jia gasped as they entered the home. All kinds of Korean art hung along the walls. Antique scrolls and traditional folding screens, along with celadon pottery and mother-of-pearl-inlaid serving dishes. Every so often, Jia noticed an eclectic modern piece placed in a thoughtful location. As if they had been collected not for their beauty but for the sentiment they conveyed. The smell inside reminded Jia of cedarwood and incense. A water feature—with a centerpiece fashioned from jade—burbled just past the sliding screens inside the foyer.

"This is beautiful," Jia said softly.

"It's the only one of the family's residences that Seven had nothing to do with." Darius glanced around. "This is entirely Jenny."

As they moved through the hallways of the stunning home, she considered Darius once again. She'd never seen him act so formal. He carried himself differently, too.

As if an invisible weight rested on his shoulders.

Jia stopped in her tracks. "Darius . . . are you the new CEO?"

He halted. Careful. Always so careful. Then he turned toward her and truly looked into her eyes for the first time since her arrival. "No."

"You're lying."

"I'm not."

"Then why are you so uncomfortable right now?" Her features hardened. "Is it some kind of lingering guilt for pressuring me into the whole blackmailing thing?"

"No. I don't feel guilty at all about that. Do you?"

"No," Jia replied, startled by the truth of it. "I thought I would. But I don't. It . . . isn't comforting to know that."

"Because you're still not sure if it was right?"

"Because I shouldn't be okay with blackmail, and neither should you." She shifted from one foot to the other. "So forgive me if I'm wondering what happened. The loss of one's moral compass can do that."

He started to say something, then stopped. "I'm sorry, Jia. These last few days have been . . . difficult."

"I can only imagine." She bit her lip. "Darius, I just need to know that I'm not stepping into something else like that."

He said nothing.

"Great." Jia groaned. "Am I going to be party to more ethics violations?"

"Minsoo wanted you to sign an NDA. It's probably a good idea."

Jia crossed her arms. So Minsoo was the new CEO. Not too surprising.

"It's definitely a good idea for you to sign it, at least from our perspective," Darius continued. "But I still think it's not necessary. Just . . . please, just listen."

He slid open the large silk-screen panels in front of him, and a cascade of warm light descended on Jia from a wall of windows running along the back of the home. In the distance on the horizon, the Aegean Sea sparkled beneath a setting sun, a rainbow of colors bleeding across a bright blue sky.

Jia felt lulled by the sight of it. As if peace—and the forgiveness she needed to achieve it—could be found here beside the sea. She turned when something moved in the corner of her eye.

She stumbled backward. Caught herself on the arm of a fluffy white sofa.

"Hello, Song Jihae," Jenny Park said. "I'm so pleased you came."

# DONATIO MORTIS CAUSA

Perhaps for some, this was not at all a shock. People who love stories are often speculative by nature. But for the readers surprised by this turn of events, I must take a second to say how delighted I am to finally share my identity with you.

Perhaps small clues were noticed earlier in the tale. The hint of a past filled with ancestors who dove deep beneath the surface of the sea on a single breath. Strong women who were taught to be strong swimmers. To never flinch in the darkness. To remain quiet, stoic, and calm, even amid a storm.

Or perhaps it was just the simple longing of one who wished to see true justice serve those most in need of it.

I, for one, have always been both. I have loved stories since I was a child. For a time, I even dreamed of becoming a person who performed stories on a stage. But life quelled that desire. I was not raised to perform. I was raised instead to be a person of service, first to my parents and then to my family. A stepping stone on the way toward achieving their goals.

For over sixty-five years, that was who I was.

Now this is who I am.

I am a woman who is tired of taking up so little space. Of sitting small and quiet and proper while the ones I love walk all over me.

I am not just a mother or a wife. I am not defined by what other people call me. I am a human being, with hopes and dreams and desires abounding. Perhaps the years have not been as kind to me as I would have hoped. Thankfully, I have no intention of being kind in return.

I am not a stepping stone. I am a destination.

And I will be the one in control of my destiny now.

I will not sit back and fade into the distance, relegated to regret and passing fancies, as I did with the man who truly did love me. The one whose love I refused to see until it was too late, out of some ridiculous notion of loyalty to a husband who had long since discarded any vows he made to me.

That was the day I began this journey of self-realization. A journey without regrets. When I lost Nasir Rohani before I even gave myself a chance to find him, I decided I would not let anyone—not the cancer or the philandering husband or the unmoored children—steal from me again.

I decided to stop searching for the love of my life. And I finally realized that it was me, all along. Because once I began to love myself, I found the forgiveness I desperately sought and the peace I greatly needed.

Nasir's son, Darius, whom I have come to regard as my own, often enjoys asking people he has just met who they are. Like Darius, I enjoy watching how they answer this question. Their discomfort or their surprise or their immediate willingness to offer up small pieces of themselves is telling. Just as it is telling how Darius seeks to understand, even from the very beginning.

Who am I?

My name is Park Jeeyun. The Jenny Park you knew before is dead.

For the first time in my life, I am in control of my story.

I will live and die and love for no one but myself.

# A DEAL WITH THE DEVIL

Jia didn't speak for a full two minutes.

Jenny sat on a low white couch with a serene smile and allowed her to take it all in.

Though Jenny Park still wore the same style of fabrics in the same hues she'd enjoyed before, there was something completely different about the way she moved in them. Her hair, which had been grayish white and usually tied into a neat bun, was now shorn short. Almost spiky. Modern and alive, while her old style had hearkened to an elegant past and a fading future.

This was not at all the same person who, only last week, had supposedly been at death's door.

"You're not dying, are you?" Jia asked.

Jenny inhaled slowly, taking a moment to let the air fill her lungs before exhaling. "I think we are all dying, no?" A flame lit in her eyes.

"Please." Jia squared her shoulders. "I deserve the truth."

"You do. And I wish to give it to you. You have more than earned it." She gestured toward the end of the pillowy white sofa.

Again, Jia was struck by the change in her. Life abounded from every look and motion. The afternoon Jia had met Jenny at her Park Avenue penthouse, she recalled how pensive Jenny had appeared. How ribbons of sunlight streaming through the windows had captured her attention and caused her to sigh.

Jenny gazed at Jia, her features expectant.

"I'll be more specific," Jia said. "Since it's clear words—and details—matter to you a great deal."

"Words are one of life's great pleasures," Jenny said. "I think about how humans are among the only creatures who can articulate our thoughts and feelings with such specificity. Like an artist with a paintbrush, we can illustrate the world inside us. Make it so we might, if we are very lucky, find someone who understands. We can write poetry and send love letters. It is truly a gift."

Jia considered Jenny's response before speaking. "Humans are also among the only creatures who inflict pain with intention. Who kill for sport. I think these emotions we struggle to articulate are often to blame."

Jenny inclined her head with a thoughtful smile. "You are not wrong, Jia." She set down the cup of tea in her hand. The sound of the bone china clinking into its matching saucer echoed through the space.

"You're not dying of cancer, are you?" Jia asked.

"No," Jenny said.

"But you were."

Jenny nodded. "At one point last year, my cancer was deemed terminal."

"After the mastectomy."

"Yes. I was told I had less than a year to live. Eighteen months was generous."

"What happened?"

Jenny met Jia's stare with one of her own. "Some would call it a miracle. And perhaps it was. Perhaps it was a miracle that my doctor knew of another group of researchers conducting experimental trials on the very type of cancer trying to kill me. Another miracle that they could find a place for me in those trials. A month later and I would not have been eligible. And of course the greatest miracle is that it worked. I am in remission now and have been since I embarked down this path."

"Why didn't you tell your children?"

"I always intended to tell my children. When the time was right."

"Okay. Why was the time wrong before?"

Jenny reached for her tea and took another sip. "Jia, I am still unsure of many things, even though wisdom is supposed to come with age. But after my cancer diagnosis, I became sure of one thing: myself. The goals and dreams I came to this country to fulfill. And it was never a goal of mine to be immensely wealthy. I wanted enough so that I would never have to worry. So that my children would never have to worry. But more than that,

I wanted a strong, united family. I dreamed of a time when my grandchildren would be in my home, eating the food I made or making a mess of everything, filling it with all the love and light we lost when I was a child, after my parents died.

"I did not dream of all this wealth and all this distance. I did not dream of my children calling each other horrible names and doing terrible things just to cause their brother or sister pain. I never once dreamed of the fractured family I now have." A shadow crossed her features. "I share in the blame. I did not see what was happening until it was too late. Perhaps I did not try hard enough. But I do not believe that to be an excuse for my husband's philandering."

"It isn't," Jia said. "There's always a more graceful way to leave a marriage than to cheat."

Jenny sighed. "Sora-appa gave up on us long before he began cheating. His attitude and behavior are to blame. It is not just that he was a philanderer. He taught our children that contentment was for the weak. That wanting and desiring were for the strong. By his example, he made it so that my children did not truly understand gratitude. They only understood how important it was to be hungry for more."

Realization dawned on Jia. "This wasn't about the money for you. But it *was* about making him pay."

"I had to get my family's attention. To do that, I had to speak to my husband in a language he would understand. For too long, that language has been money."

"You did this to get your children to work together. To try and repair what you had lost." Jia considered this. "Does it trouble you at all that you resorted to duplicity in order to achieve your goal?"

Jenny canted her head.

"You did lie to your children about dying of cancer," Jia said. "Just like you lied to me, point-blank."

"I have struggled with this. Believe me. It is true I did not correct them when I knew otherwise. Just as it is true I lied to your face." Again Jenny paused to think. "I do regret that. Perhaps I was trying to speak to my children in a language I thought they would understand, as well. I am not perfect. I do not wish to be." She studied Jia again. "But I think you might understand now that sometimes the best paths are not always the most righteous."

It was Jia's turn to fall silent.

"Now I have a question for you," Jenny said, her expression one of open curiosity. "Why did you not say anything to the authorities?"

"I thought my duty was to you. And I don't know many lawyers who turn on their clients in such a spectacular way and then go on to have succcssful careers."

"You never believed that what you were doing was right?"

"I'm still not sure." Jia looked at Jenny. She had many questions about the logistics. How this small yet formidable woman had managed to pull off such an astonishing feat. But now, facing the real Jenny Park for possibly the first time, it wasn't such a stretch to see her methodically planning how to frame her philandering husband for her murder. How her family's history of free diving as haenyeo had made her a much stronger swimmer than anyone assumed. How Jenny might have hidden a small vial of her own blood in her pocket, which she smeared on the hull of the yacht herself. Or maybe she'd even gone so far as to stash diving equipment on the back of the boat. How she'd swum under cover of night the entire mile it took to reach the shore and hidden there, waiting for her family to take care of the rest.

Everyone had underestimated Jenny Park, including Jia. The realization was humbling.

"Darius knew," Jia murmured. "Didn't he?"

"He did. But as my attorney, he could not have revealed anything. So please do not be angry with him." She pressed her lips together. "Everything he did to thwart your efforts, I asked him to do."

Understanding dawned on Jia. "Darius was the mole?"

"No," Jenny said. "*I* was the mole." She took a careful breath. "And I would like to offer you two apologies."

Jia braced herself. When this family caught her off guard, it usually wasn't for an inconsequential reason.

"First," Jenny began, "I'm deeply sorry for causing you so much stress. But you were too good at your job. To make my plan work, I needed my husband to come to Greece of his own volition. So I made sure his spies always knew what you were doing. I left notes and information scattered everywhere. Allowed people to listen in on conversations they should not have heard." A half smile pulled at the edge of her mouth. "It really wasn't that difficult. Chilsoo's paranoia did the rest."

Jia swallowed. "I appreciate you saying this."

"The second apology is because I wasn't truthful with you the last time we spoke at my home on Park Avenue."

"How so?"

"I intentionally neglected to mention the most important part of finding my peace. I worried that, if I said it, you might figure out what I was doing."

Jia waited.

Jenny continued, "I learned that I needed to stop seeking purpose beyond myself, whether it be to my work or to my family. I needed to look within so that I could become the love of my own life. In learning that, I was finally able to forgive myself for all the times I lied to myself and hurt myself and caused myself so much unnecessary pain." She reached for Jia's hand and placed it between both of hers. "I'm telling you this because you need to hear it. I know you do."

Jia looked at the floor, her thoughts roiling. "Thank you for telling me all these things. I suppose, as your attorney, I also can't really speak out about what I've learned, but I appreciate you trusting me with the truth. And I"—she hesitated—"I'm not sure what you mean about being the love of my own life, but I'll keep it in mind."

"Of course." Jenny nodded. "But I did not ask you here merely to explain myself and ask for your forgiveness. Next week, the authorities will reveal my safe return. We have requested that they not say anything in the interim, as I am given time to heal."

Jia assumed it was not quite that simple. Someone important was likely being asked to look the other way for a considerable financial incentive.

"Jia, I have asked you here because I intend to become the CEO of Mirae," Jenny said. "Minsoo will be the new CFO. Suzy does not have any desire to work for the company at present, and Sora says she would rather wait until her children are older before joining in any official capacity.

Darius will serve as Mirae's COO." She locked eyes with Jia. "And I would like to formally offer you the position of Mirae's corporate counsel."

Jia's eyes went wide. "What?"

"I liked you the day we first met. It wasn't merely because you were Korean, but rather because I saw how comfortable you tried to be in an uncomfortable situation. How quickly you thought on your feet." A smile touched her lips. "I also saw how you enjoyed art and had respect for your family's culture. Most importantly, I appreciated how you tried to offer solutions even at the expense of losing money. That quality is rare these days. Your loyalty over this past month has been admirable. Would you consider working as Mirae's corporate counsel?"

Jia's thoughts spiraled. This was not at all what she had planned for herself. Her dream was to be Whitman Volker's next Emily Bhatia. A power player in New York's law circles, whose name echoed into the rafters even before her arrival.

A corporate counsel was not that.

"As you can imagine, our compensation package will be highly competitive," Jenny continued. "Preferred shares and excellent company benefits are to be expected. But more importantly, working for me will mean that your life will not be solely about work. I aim to change the conversation at our company. Profits will always matter, but even more than that, I expect those like us in positions of power to do better for everyone who works at Mirae, shareholders and employees alike. You will also be fully in charge of our nonprofit efforts, which is not an insubstantial sum even at our current standards. My goal is to triple our outreach in the next five years. I want you to spearhead that effort."

Jia remained at a loss for words. But a strange feeling was beginning to take root in her stomach. A warmth. A tingling that was slowly spreading into her limbs.

That feeling she'd been waiting to feel when Emily revealed that she wanted to make Jia her successor.

Excitement. Purpose. Perhaps it wasn't what she thought it would look like. Perhaps it didn't match the goals she'd set for herself. But maybe it could be something bigger and better than she could have ever imagined.

Maybe she could be a new kind of fire-breather.

"Take the job, Song Jihae," a voice said from behind her.

She turned to see Sora Park-Vandeveld waiting in the wings beside a bouquet of purple hyacinths. Her face was free of makeup. Her hair was long and loose. Wilder than she'd ever worn it around Jia. Her linen dress was wrinkled, but not in a way that seemed unkempt. Rather in a manner that indicated relaxation. A sense of ease Jia had never associated with the eldest Park sibling.

"Why?" Jia asked, emboldened. "Why do you think I should take it?"

"Because I'd wager it isn't what you planned or expected. And because it might mean you actually get to have a life outside of work."

"I have a life outside of work," Jia countered. "A pretty nice one, actually."

"I meant a real one. Where you can take time off to care for your family, or ditch your phone on vacation and not fear for your future."

"I worked hard to get where I am. Giving it up now—when I'm so close to achieving everything I wanted—seems foolish."

"An even better reason to do it," Suzy Park chimed in as she breezed into the room, her paint-stained hands stretched over her head. "You don't do enough foolish things." She yawned. "I told you we should have gotten that stupid Barenia Faubourg Birkin for her. That would have sealed the deal."

"No," Sora said, her attention steady on Jia. "She doesn't want someone to give it to her. She wants to earn it herself."

Jia swallowed. Strange to be seen so clearly by someone she thought she disliked.

"Trust yourself, Song Jihae," Jenny said. "And the answer will come to you."

*It's up to you to make sense of this mess.*

Jia heard her harabugi's voice in her head.

*You will be the one. Not your brothers. Not your cousins. You.*

Jia stared back at Sora. She started to grin. Slowly but surely, Sora grinned back.

"Gijibae," Sora whispered.

Jia bowed her head.

Sora bowed back.

# THE BIGGEST MOON IN THE WORLD

"Jesus," Jia whispered the moment she stepped onto the immense balcony of the Park family's Grecian vacation home. She marveled at the view of the glittering Aegean. "I've never seen a moon that big in my entire life."

"It's because we're so close to the equator," Darius replied from where he stood by the railing.

"Did you make that up or do you know that for a fact?"

"For a fact." He didn't turn around.

Jia walked up to the railing to stand beside him. "You lied to—"

"Tell me something true, Jia Song."

"Not this again."

"Okay. Tell me a story, and I'll tell you one in return."

"Fine." They both stared out at the dark water, the moon casting silver shadows on everything in sight. "On the night my grandfather died, I saw his ghost."

"Interesting."

"He came to me to tell me he was leaving me in charge of the family."

"How old were you?"

"Thirteen."

"Sounds reasonable to put all that on a child."

Jia smiled. "He wasn't reasonable. He was irascible. Irreverent. He didn't do things the way he was told to do them."

"And he chose you." Jia could feel Darius smiling without looking at him. Despite all the lies and the mistrust, Jia's traitor heart missed a beat. "Are you going to take the job?"

"Do you want me to take the job?"

"I thought you didn't do things the way you were told to do them."

"In that case, I guess you don't want me to take the job."

"In that case, definitely not." He grinned. Then he took a deep breath. And reached for her hand.

But this time, Jia didn't thread her fingers through his.

He pulled back. "I understand. And please know, the way I feel will never affect how we work together. I respect you too much for that."

"Thank you." Jia faced him. She rested her palm on his cheek. "I like you too much, Darius Rohani."

"I like you too much, too."

"I need some time to decide what I want." She inhaled. "To figure out what the love of my life should be."

Darius nodded. Together, they gazed into the white light of the immense moon.

# SINGIN' IN THE RAIN

A month after Jia started working as Mirae's corporate counsel, she decided it was time to have a potluck dinner at her place. It had been ages since she'd last hosted one. More than a year ago, when she and Zain were still together.

Jia smiled to herself. Letting go was getting easier and easier. Now, when she thought of Zain, there were no more pangs of regret or twinges of memory. Soon he would be just another footnote in her past, where he belonged.

She didn't hate that idea. For better or for worse, he'd left an indelible mark. And she was on her way to being better for it.

Jia invited her parents to the potluck, of course. James said he would come later, and Jason asked her to save him a plate, as usual. Nidhi brought a huge pot of her famous chicken biryani. Layers of rice and fried onions and spices and potatoes that fell apart in Jia's mouth. And Elisa made her Frangelico-flavored flan with the burnt caramel crust. Umma made japchae with the mushrooms Jia liked, and Jia went all out and made beef kalbi *and* bulgogi, along with some of her mother's favorite jjigae.

Soon, Jia's small apartment was filled to the brim with the scent of delicious food, the hustle and bustle of people running into one another, sidestepping, and laughing before exchanging hugs.

After she grabbed the cake and doughnuts she'd ordered for delivery, Jia paused by the front door. The sight of all the shoes strewn across her floor in haphazard fashion made her smile.

These were the things to be thankful for. The sights and sounds of chaos that strangely brought Jia peace.

The meal was just beginning to wind down when it started to rain. Fat droplets that kissed the pavement and filled the early June air with a bright mineral tang.

Jia went to the window to crack it open.

Her phone rang.

Another smile toyed with her lips. "Yes?" she answered.

Darius's warm voice emanated in her ear. "I'm outside the door to your place. Do you want to go for a walk with me?"

She peered through the crack in the window until she saw him standing on the sidewalk. "It's raining."

"So?" He gazed up at her, his black umbrella held out to the side.

"I have guests."

He paused. "Do they want to go for a walk with us?"

Jia looked over her shoulder. Nidhi and Elisa were watching her, their faces filled with eager encouragement. "Maybe."

"I'll be outside waiting. However long it takes." Then Darius hung up.

She shrugged and turned to her friends and family. "Does anyone want to go for a walk?"

Umma frowned. "It's raining. You'll get sick."

"I want to go for a walk in the rain." Elisa raised her hand. "Especially if it means you'll introduce me to Darius." She nudged Nidhi. "Come on."

Nidhi scowled. "In the rain?"

"Yup." Elisa linked arms with her. "Lead the way, Song Jihae."

Appa sent her a secret smile as the three friends put on their shoes.

When Jia exited her building, Darius was still waiting on the sidewalk, holding his umbrella. Without pausing, he passed it to Nidhi and Elisa. In a matter of moments, the rain had soaked through his hair and his navy polo shirt.

Jia walked through the rain toward him without blinking, letting it drip into her hair and down her neck.

He held out his hand. "Are we doing this?"

"I think so." She laced her fingers through his.

"Then let's go."

# ACKNOWLEDGMENTS

I knew I wanted to write this book for years, and that it would be the most Korean thing I'd ever written. I just didn't know if I was ready. That's the thing about straddling two worlds all your life—you're never certain if you're ever enough of one thing.

Thank you to everyone who made sure I believed I was enough while writing this book. To my editor, Caroline Bleeke, who believed even when I sent her messy, half-formed drafts. Who patiently coaxed us toward the end, with her eagle-sharp eyes and thought-provoking questions. To my agent, Barbara Poelle, who has believed for more than a decade and continues to be the best advocate and wisest friend. She probably cackled at the wise part, but it's true.

To the incredible team at Macmillan Flatiron: thank you so much for hitting the ground running on day one. Special shout-out to my publicist, Bria Strothers, and to Devan Norman for the incredible design. Endless appreciation to Maris Tasaka, Emily Walters, and Morgan Mitchell, and to Megan Lynch, Nancy Trypuc, Marlena Bittner, Malati Chavali, and Keith Hayes for your unflinching support. Also to Mary Retta for being an organizational badass.

To Mary Pender-Coplan and Celia Albers: you weren't kidding about the roller skates. Thank you for being the dream makers that you are. To the team at UTA: so much appreciation for everything.

To Roshani Chokshi for the endless enthusiasm and for all her keen insights when it comes to story. I'm the luckiest writer alive to have a book-fiend sister like her.

To Sabaa Tahir, who texted me from a hotel lobby to tell me a scene I wrote had punched her in the face, but in the best way. Everything that gets to the heart of this book is because she pushed me to go there. Some of my favorite scenes were planted by our conversations. Because of her, I never have to wonder what it feels like to see and be seen in any story. Thank you is not enough.

To Elaine Mejia for embodying what it means to be a girl's girl from the beginning. There is no greater hype woman in the world, and I'm grateful to every star in the sky for pointing me in your direction twenty-five years ago. Fuck, we're old.

To Erica, Chris, Tahlia, and Maia for all the love, all the laughter, and all the memories. I can't wait to see what the next ten years bring us.

To Umma: your bravery when you emigrated from South Korea to the US with almost nothing is the reason I am here with this book. Thank you for every sacrifice and every lecture.

To Mama Joon and Baba Joon for all your love and support. For being a source of healing and trust, always.

To Dad for giving me one of life's greatest gifts: a deep and abiding love of books.

To Ian, Izzy, Maddie, and Lilly: so much love to you all. To Omid, Julie, Evelyn, Isabelle (go, Heels!), and Andrew, thank you for always cheering me on and never failing to brighten my day. To Navid, Jinda, Ella, and Lily for unfailingly holding an umbrella over our heads in every storm. I am beyond lucky to have family like you.

To my favorite little thieves, Cyrus and Noura: it is a strange thing to realize my heart no longer resides in my body. That it has been stolen away, never to be returned. Keep it. It's yours until the end of time.

And to Victor, who believed before I even knew how to believe. I love you.

# ABOUT THE AUTHOR

**Renée Ahdieh** is a graduate of the University of North Carolina at Chapel Hill. When she's not reading, she enjoys cooking, skincare, and fashion. The first few years of her life were spent in a high-rise in South Korea; consequently, Renée enjoys having her head in the clouds. She and her family live in Charlotte, North Carolina. She is the #1 *New York Times* and internationally bestselling author of the Wrath and the Dawn series, the Flame in the Mist series, and the Beautiful quartet. *Park Avenue* is her debut adult novel.

**Recommend PARK AVENUE**

**for your next book club!**

**Reading Group Guide available at**

**www.flatironbooks.com/reading-group-guides**